LAKE OF FIRE

VOLUME ONE

Mark Sant

ISBN: 978-0-9948257-1-1

Cover Art designed by Matthew Burton.
Interior Art designed by Tommaso Tagliabue.

For Frank, Rob, Lina, Debbie and Mike

MARK SANT

SMOKELANDS

(November, Temperatures Slide As Daylight Shortens, It's Windy, Cellphone Reception Optimal, Seasonal Marketing Underway, Migratory Birds Depart, Most Watched YouTube Vid Is Of A Macaw Riding A Pygmy Hippo, In Ireland An Oddity Precedes Judgement, There Is The First Fire Which Spreads, Elsewhere Is Quiet, What Will Happen Will Happen)

MARK SANT

ONE.

One of the lambs stares down at the end.

Their pasture on the highland is backed by a bluff to the east that overlooks a lake. The field where they graze has plenty space. The sheep are never crowded. None have never been dim enough to fall. There's never been an issue but tonight there's concern.

Inside the decades-old farmhouse, worry has Seamus gazing in on his son as he hears another siren beyond the walls of his home. His boy's asleep in bed in the same position he's maintained for hours. Already, just at seven, he resembles his father quite a bit. The persimmon hair, prominent forehead, the unmistakably placed trio of freckles on the right cheek below the eye. They named him James after his grandfather on mum's side, and Seamus tilts back his stout watching James sleep, hearing sirens and wildly bleating sheep. Tommie's suddenly hollering to him from the front of the house and he frowns and shuts the door so James doesn't wake.

Miraculously, the boy sleeps despite the emergency-sirens.

"*Seamus*! Cominere, Seamus!"

"I'm standin right here, Tommie." Seamus has arrived in the living-room to his find his wife at the window. "...That another?"

"Ambulance this time." The siren peaks and flashing hazard lights whip across the white drapes and ceiling before diminishing and then it dies away. Tommie turns to her husband. "Gotta be fifty a'the shades so far... I heard helicopters an hour go."

"All up to Darrows Glen, aye?"

"Lord knows what's going on up there."

"Sheep can't be liking this. Any more of this'll sour the wool."

"Y'can't sour wool, love."

"Can too. It isn't as soft. It's... you know, squirrelly."

"You're so fulla shite... How's our prince?"

"Could sleep through a buzzsaw witta radio blarin."

"Still? Jaysis." Tommie blinks. Staring out the window at a fog creeping across the land. "…Cripes, it's rolling in heavy now."

Seamus nods weakly and Tommie cuddles him when he nears. She keeps one arm around his back and steals his beer with the other hand. Sips. They stare at the night outside their home. The unclear sky has an orange glow that's emitted from the northeast, but its origin and meaning are a mystery. Seamus shakes his head.

"What's happening in then Glen, y'think?"

"God's up to sometin, love."

Here the bleating loudens and alarms the wool-farmer and his wife. Then there's shattering glass and a *thud* and the scrambling of hooves and the couple look to the kitchen, where they spot a lamb shuffling and reclaiming its stance atop window shards and bits of the pine frame. There are other sheep of the flock crowded around the windows and doors bleating, wanting inside. The intruder lamb charges at Tommie, who recoils in terror. But the animal hasn't come to attack. It merely stays close to her, bleating and defecating onto the laminate floorboards. It stinks.

Riot still. The flock that wants in and the dogs who're barking at them. Sirens that come and go. I hear something, Tommie says. Grabbing her husband's sleeve, looking up at the ceiling over their heads. Under the sheep and the dogs and the firetrucks, she says, I can hear it. There's something up on the roof.

Abrupt unaccountable footsteps confirm her.

Seamus, standing still, tilts his head to frown at the ceiling.

"…James." Seamus whispers the name of their son. Grabbing his coat and a flashlight. "Tommie, go get James. Call the guards."

The farmer's opened the backdoor in the laundry-room and screaming sheep barge past him, hurrying into the house. No. No, *get out!* Stop it! But they break in and are chased by the fog. Seamus is heading for the field behind the house, meandering through sheep that want inside, passing the old birch trough overgrown by grass and millet. He squints to see what's up on the roof of the house but there's this fog hiding so much. Breathing, he realizes the it's dry as sand. It stinks like an ashtray. It isn't fog, it's smoke.

Whatever was on the roof, he's pretty sure it's gone now.

Seamus treads out across the grass looking for the rest of his livestock in the smoke, and he listens to them bleating as orange transcends in the northern skies. Shining his flashlight, he finds the rest of his flock. They march to the cliff and fall.

"No! *No*, ye gimp beasts! Ah fuck ye, *no!*"

The wool-farmer calls out but his flock marches in a hurry. Amid the bleating there're curt rushes of wind. Thuds. They're all around but he can't regard them. Stumbling in a huff to the kennel beside the barn, he looks to the dogs who bark insane. Hurriedly lifting the latch, he frees them and the dogs stay put. Barking.

"Go! Get up the yard, will ye? Geddem! Herd!"

The dogs won't leave the kennel. They bark at him and jump onto one another and lie down and whine. Seamus kicks at the dogs and they bare their fangs and retreat from him. They bark.

Inside the house, Tommie kicks at the sheep who stay near her, bleating and shitting often. She's got her mobile to her ear, waiting for the cops to come back to her and she pleas. Hurry! We're at Dartmouth Lane, just outside Darrows Glen. *Hurry* please! She holds her iPhone to her ear so fiercely she might well be trying to shove it into her skull. She retrieves the iron fire-poker from the rack and she sets on her way down the hallway to the bedrooms.

The 112 respondent tries to keep Tommie talking. The mother attempts to talk or she thinks she does but she trails off in the end, gasping and silenced when she hears another window break. Not speaking, she's barely listening. Tommie is tiptoeing or floating just above the carpet, heading into the hallway to find her son.

The sheep stay behind in the den. Bleating and looking around, rectangular pupils dilating when the lights go out. They knock over a side-table and smash the lamp on top of it. They urinate on the fireplace and huddle beneath the coffee-table and the smoke ekes in through window gaps and the open laundry-room door.

Footsteps, heard again on the roof. And Tommie's cowering. In the dark she uses her mobile as a light. Calling to Seamus. Looking up at a black ceiling and calling Seamus, get back in here dammit.

Outside the house, the last lamb looks to the lake. Seamus leaps onto it before it can jump and it thrashes and screams. The farmer pulls it to the grass and they both pant, looking around, losing the world in a billowing grey. Orange in the north skies, now hidden. Seamus can't see more than ten feet in front of him.

It sounds as if a cavalry of horses is trotting by en route to war. He can't see the dogs but they sound harassed, yelping, barking, and then they aren't heard at all. There's thunder. Far off, there's the blowing of a shofar.

Tommie finds the door to her son's room and clutches the knob and turns it. Her foot lands on something brittle. Its pieces break apart. Warmth soaks into her sock. Glancing down, she can't see. So she crouches low. She shines the screen of her mobile. And she sees it's a lower-jaw and its molars and incisor are crushed out of it and strewn around her foot. The window is shattered and the wind takes the drapes. Grey billows into the room.

The commotion outside is rising. The cavalry sounds now like a stampede. Seamus is howling and the lamb is screaming. Tommie can't see anything anymore. The house is filled. Cinders clog her windpipe but she's too broken too dead to cough it out and she can't breathe, huddling over a flattened piece of cheek and a trio of freckles just below the eye. Suffocating. There's the thunder and the shofar and police sirens going silent. Smoke pours across the county coming from the town of Darrows Glen.

Sixteen years young, the Buick has seen five owners in its time. The AC is a bust and the brakes are spongy. Six months overdue for an oil-change. It hasn't been taken for a lengthy run like this since July but thank god it's pushing along now at eighty K. It's reliable enough to take them far away from Darrows Glen.

The radio is on. Newscasters report events from around the country – none of which involve the attack on the Glen – but here it's suddenly plagued with static as the signal is left behind. A tattooed hand save for a middle-finger reaches over and switches to a different channel, soon finding some EDM station playing an Avicii remix. Mike Schrader lowers the volume but keeps it high enough to hear because he can't currently abide silence. Returning his incomplete hand to the steering-wheel, he keeps a couple raw sleepless eyes on the road.

Reagan Brodie, in the backseat, can be called neither asleep nor awake. She wears a fifteen-euro merino cardigan and a wristwatch she inherited when her mother passed. Shabby clogs on tired feet and a head of plain meagre hair. The wheels thump over a pothole in the M3 near Boyerstown and Reagan blinks, jostled conscious. She brushes a golden-red bang from her eye as she glances around the car. The elderly Lora Malik is asleep in the seat next to her. On her lap is her oversized needlepoint handbag and on the floor at her feet is her walking-stick. A gold cross on her necklace.

Behind the wheel up front is the nine-fingered tattooist Mike Schrader and in the passenger seat is his fiancée Abigail holding their two-year-old as she searches for answers on her Samsung.

Mike's asking her: "Something yet?"

"There's nothing. Maybe they're not releasing it to the media."

"To hell with the media, Abby! Our town's just been run with arsonists! Someone has to have tweeted about it!"

"There's nothing, Mike. I looked."

With a tightened throat Reagan speaks up. She asks where are we. Mike examines her in the rearview and notes how he thought she was asleep. He returns his gaze to the road and tells her they're still on the motorway. Should reach Dublin within the hour. The infant's fussing, but Abigail bounces him on her knee to hush him.

Then Mike asks Reagan: What's going on, Miss Brodie?

"Why are you askin me?"

"Shouldn't I be askin ye? *Ye* got us into this."

"I like to think I saved us, Mike."

"Aye and lucky that was. Ye *know* something. The old bid too."

"Her name is Lora."

"I wanna know why yous knocked on our door in the middle of the night and told us to get d'hell outta Darrows Glen. Why we spent today in a backwoods motel worth a shit. How the feck could ye have known anything?" He sniffles a bit, then: "Or is it the old bid? What's *she* know?"

"Lora doesn't know anything."

"Who's she to ye?"

"…I rent her basement. I knocked her up same as we did ye."

"So why did yous?"

"We knew you had an infant. And a car."

"Ye *needed* me damn car, yeah?"

Abigail's prompting her husband for amity's sake: "*Mike.*"

"No-no-no, Abby – she's gonna tell us!" Again, his eyes in the rearview. "Ye needed me damn *car*, yeah?"

"I wanted us all to get in the car, Mike."

"Just in time too, aye? I mean, you-*you know something*, y'bitch!"

"Mike!"

"Honest to God, Mike."

Reagan presses but she can't maintain composure with his stare reflecting in the mirror. She's not strong. So she glances out the window at darkness passing by. Countryside. Harvested cabbage fields in the night. Seeing an orange glow that isn't there, trapped in her eyes. Fingering the large brown buttons of her cardigan.

Saying: I just… I saw fire, Mike. I saw the fires start.

I heard something was comin.

TWO.

Uwe Marrs, looking like he does, enters the terminal along with the other passengers of Flight 105 from Vienna, his carryon in one hand and an issue of Time rolled up in the other. His appearance attracts the odd glance but he isn't bothered. He's accustomed to discomfort by now. Stopping at the luggage claim, Uwe turns on his mobile and he's typing a text, addressing it to Clara Towns.

(Touched down now)

following with

(Can't wait to see you)

and then he waits. Eventually he sees his suitcase coming out from behind the rubber curtain and sliding onto the conveyor-belt.

When no reply returns, Uwe is disappointed though not entirely surprised. He's extracted the telescopic handle from his suitcase and he rolls it in the direction of the terminal lounge. If he has to wait he might as well do so here than on the steps of her building. He sits down at the bar and sets his carryon and magazine on the stool-seat beside him. The bartender eyes the medallion hanging off his neck when he asks him for a drink order. Uwe asks for a Coke with ice. The bartender asks him if he wants rum in that and Uwe smirks weakly and declines.

Sitting back, glancing at the television monitor embedded in the wall behind the bar. On it is a broadcast of highlights from today's rugby match which he watches with little interest. On commercial break there plays a spot for a new remake of *The Fugitive* starring Casey Affleck and James Spader and young heartthrob Dustin Tomson. Uwe drinks his Coke and glances down at his issue of *Time* on which there's a candid of United States President Duncan Clark sunbathing at his ranch in Daytona. Below it is a photo depicting battlegrounds in Syria.

Just a pint. Whatever's on the tap closest to you, mate.

Uwe looks over at the man who's just sat down on the barstool next to his carryon. The man's younger and worn and he's set an empty baby-basket down next to him. He appears tired to the point of it being terribly unsightly and Uwe has to take notice.

"It's pretty dull, isn't it?"

"…Pardon?"

"Just life, I mean. Like a roller coaster than never drops… The uphill climb gets dull, doesn't it?"

"…Right. Sure it does. Quite dull."

"You got a tot."

"Man, do I ever."

"Given the pink blankie, I'm guessin girl? Or unfortunate boy?"

"Girl." The man reciprocates mostly to not be unkind, mostly against his will, noting offhanded: "My wife's just changing her in the lavatory. Little shit-machine sullied herself on the plane."

The bartender brings over a pint of Stella and sets it down in front of the disheveled young father. Before he returns to wiping highball glasses the bartender again observes Uwe Marrs, this man with oddly styled facial-hair and a single braided ponytail rooted in an otherwise shaved head and a silver medallion hanging from his neck. Uwe ignores the bartender's scrutiny, asking the young father where they're coming from.

"Uh… the in-laws in France. Celebrated my girl's birthday."

"She turned one year?"

"In October. We wanted to go for her birthday last month but couldn't get the tickets cheap enough." Sipping beer, eventually asking to return the decency: "How about you, mate? Where you coming from? You got a bit of an accent. What's that – German?"

"It's Austrian if it's anything." Smiling, shaking his head. "Born in Britain, but I've… spent maybe one too many years in Vienna."

"Oh yeah? Brilliant, mate. Never been but I heard it's nice."

"It has its loveliness."

"What are you up to over this way?"

"I'm coming to visit my own little, uh…" Uwe smirks sadly, rotating the tilt of his tumbler and watching the Coca-Cola swirl. "I'm not going to call her a shit-machine, though… maybe." He stares into the fizzing cyclone and clinking ice-cubes, telling the stranger for no real reason: "She's gotten herself pregnant. Five months along now."

"And she needed her daddy?"

"It seemed that way."

"It's *always* that way, from what I've been warned. They don't want nothing to do with you until they need something, right?"

Uwe smiles weakly. He doesn't speak.

The exhausted young father takes another closer inspection of his conversationalist and he notices the black suit and blood-red shirt opened at the top. That thin goatee and irregular ponytail and the pentagram medallion in the revealed rug of chest hair. He asks Uwe if he's a magician back in Vienna and Uwe tells him that, up until recently, I was a FedEx courier… And on Thursday nights I led a modest congregation of like-minded theorists… A church. And I was better off once upon a time. I was still drunk then.

Life made a lot more sense in a daze. And far far less dull.

Uwe blinks and eventually realizes the father's gone, having left his Stella virtually untouched. The glass of beer sits there, and Uwe stares at it. Drinking his coke and thinking of his daughter.

Clara Towns has slipped out of her FCUK shirt and sweatpants and they've adjusted the SLR camera and the builder's floodlight that's matted with dead mosquitos. A fatter woman with patchy hair is rubbing down the girl's protruding stomach with baby-oil. Clara tries not to look at her as she's greased and doesn't look at the director beyond the sweltering lights or her co-star who's jacking a limp prick in the gloom off in the basement studio, trying to keep hard despite the fetid stench of mould that lingers in the rafters around the water-pipes.

"Can we do something about the eyes, mommy?"

Clara realizes there are tears clouding her vision again. So she wipes them with the back of her hand. Her co-star is called over and they're yelling action and they're rolling and Clara's sucking on the half-flaccid Russian immigrant who doesn't say more than "slow" every so often. The crew makes comments and the director will direct now and then but they'll remove the voices in editing. Clara hears her mobile in her sweatpants on the floor by the bed and she figures they'll remove that in editing too. Wonders who's texting, then she remembers oh yeah. Oh shit.

Her father.

When the dude is hard Clara's positioned on her stomach. And there's pleasure maybe but it's exhausting. With all the bucking into the mattress she believes it could be harming the baby. The director doesn't like the angle, so they flip her on her back. The camera zooms in for the cumshot that jets out onto the mother's bump.

The *eyes*, mommy – come on! You wanna get paid or not?

So Clara wipes them dry again. They yell cut. Nobody's happy about any of this.

After the shoot she gets her pants on. Texts her father, telling him she's leaving now. I'll be at my place in thirty minutes

(meet me there)

and she pulls her FCUK shirt over herself and she stops by the fat woman with patchy hair to collect her pay before she leaves to meet up with the former priest. Uwe Marrs, the man who ruined her life and the man who had better save it.

THREE.

Motion-sickness, maybe. Tired of being cooped in the rustbucket Buick riding all the way down from Darrows Glen. Whatever the cause, little Brent woke up and hasn't stopped crying even when Mike presented him his cherished stuffed snowman from *Frozen*. Abigail's been trying to console her toddler, lulling the boy softly – singing *Daydream Believer* sorely but with optimism. Cheer up sleepy Brent. Oh what can it... lent. Mike tells her that's rubbish, stick with the original words. Abby tells him just drive so he does and he takes them in past the Dublin city limits.

Reagan Brodie sits up in the backseat. Straightening her glasses, she gazes around at lights and cars and humanity, all of which leave her gravely taken aback. Looking over, she's gently jostling Lora Malik's knee. The old woman stirs and, as she wakes, frail crinkled fingers clutch the needlepoint handbag on her lap. She clears her throat and greets her companions before asking where the jumpin fuck are we. Reagan is the one to answer.

"Just comin up the city now, Lora."

Lora leans over and raises her eyebrows. *Hm?*

"Dublin. Just comin up to her."

Lora nods and leans back and she's casually touching a hand to her hearing-aid to test it. In Reagan's mind, the thing's been busted since day one. Since she moved into the old woman's basement she's hailed her for her uncanny ability to hear just about nothing the first time around. Reagan privately refers to old Lora as Missus Say-Again since that's usually how conversations with her play out. Despite a test of patience, Lora Malik's a decent person. A friend.

Mike's asking his fiancée: "Abby babe? Y'remember where your sister lives do ye?"

"I'm trying to find it. Signal's buggered or somethin." Abigail's

13

staring at her mobile over her son's shoulder. "Look for their pub. Fiddler's Sty, it's called. They own that – they live above it."

"Will ye just Google it, babe?"

"I canny get a signal, Mike. S'buggered, I said."

"Ah ye dried up nun's tits-."

"*Mike!*"

"Not ye, baby, sorry – I'm talkin to the fuel-gauge."

Mike's frowning at the gauge in his dashboard flashing empty and he proceeds to glimpse either side of the street in search of a station. They've driven another eight minutes before they find one in the suburb of Castleknock.

As the tattooist fills up at the pump, Abigail hops out for a stretch and to get her son some air. Reagan helps old Lora climb out and hands her the walking-stick as she hangs her handbag off her shoulder. The old woman says she could use an iced-tea or a water after a stop in the bogs and so she heads toward the shop.

Reagan, in the meanwhile, gazes around at the sleepy suburbs in the night. Crows on a lamppost peering down at her. Shivering in a cool wind, she holds onto her upper arms to keep warm and she glances down the street. There's a church seen over the rooftops. St. Brigid's poking steeples into the sky.

Reagan stares at the holy cross on its peak. Frowning.

The store's so whitely bright and after hours of black motorway it kind of stings and Lora loudly makes note, shuffling at a pace toward the restroom in the back corner. Reagan squints and blinks and she's heading down the aisles, vaguely hungry, glimpsing with absent eyes various snacks on the shelves. There's been nothing in her stomach for nearly a day now but she still can't fathom food. Instead she wonders at common products in a boring store and it somehow helps to clear the recent past that's so lingered. Hearing the door slide open behind her, she turns to see Abigail and little Brent have come in out of the cold.

Abigail's plainly callow. Grown up a plumber's daughter outside Darrows, she eventually got work as a hairdresser in county's only salon. At current Abby's engaged to her high-school sweetheart, Mike Schrader, who she always thought was an artist. Mike opened up a parlour above a pet-shop and started inking people and they made just enough of a living to not slip into cardiac-arrest when Abby realized she was pregnant.

The first year of parenthood is fading from Abigail's posture. Only now, tonight, she's weighed down by something worse.

The young man behind the counter has a face riddled with acne. He's turned to the back wall on which there's a television tuned in to a muted news program and a closed-caption at the bottom is transcribing the diction of an anchor announcing that, since the robbery in a Kilkenny jewellery store, police have been on the hunt for the masked perpetrators.

Abigail sets Brent down and the boy is waddling in an infantile way toward the racks of brightly packaged candy-bars. His mother stays close but she keeps her eyes on the television broadcast. She hears the shuffling of tired feet dragging and she glances over her shoulder to see Reagan creeping up next to her.

"Anything?"

"Nothin about the Glen, no. Apparently nothin happened."

"...Is that what y'think, Abigail?"

"I... I'll wait and see."

"Y'were there though." Reagan is cold. "Were your eyes open?" Tensely agitated, afraid. Her nostrils flare. "Ye saw what I saw. Ye saw what one of em did to... that man... Were your eyes open?"

"So what could it be then, eh? Jailbreak? Score of psychopaths came down upon the town? ...Now why would they bury that up? People'd know."

"You're right. We would know."

"So who were they?"

"I know just as much as ye."

"That man... Er, that *person*, or... If it was a..."

This unwelcome rush runs through Reagan as she thinks. She's barely maintaining her stance though it feels like she's been struck in the face. Dismal, plainly weak, crowfeet of a hobbled middle-age stem to her temples hidden behind drab hair and green eyeglass-frames and sprouting from eyes that still replay the horrors they witnessed hours ago in their town. Chubby arms in a blue cardigan hold rigid at her sides. Reagan's tall, proportioned, but she's frail tonight and always. She hasn't been strong in years.

Finally Abby tells her: "…I couldn't get a look attim."

And Reagan nods, cold. "Neither did I."

Lora approaches the ladies, holding a bottle of Irn-Bru gotten out of the back refrigerator and mentioning that jax coulda froze a penguin's prick. Lay out some bog roll if use her to dump. You'll get wretched icicles. Her huge knitted handbag swaying as she toddles along, relying on the walking-stick to keep upright. When Lora passes, Abigail observes her. She asks the old woman if she saw that man back in Darrows Glen.

"Say again, dear?"

"That… *person* back in the Glen. We saw… flatten that man…" Old Lora's face slackens when Abby asks her: "Did y'see him?"

"…Nay, dear." Lora answers after a while, cagey. "Couldn't see nothing for that awful fuckin smoke. Could burn the eyes outta a stone angel." Blinking hectic. Looking to Abigail. "If your man's vision is us cocked as mine right now, God blessim."

Old Lora carries on, passing the younger women and shuffling up to the counter where the pimpled boy runs the Irn-Bru under the scanner and rings up the total. Lora's fishing her pocketbook from her handbag.

Mike's tapping on the window outside and signalling he's set to move out. Abby's first to leave, taking Brent with her. And Reagan looks to old Lora who's finished her transaction and packing up her comically massive handbag at the counter.

"…Lora? …I'd like to know your opinion."

"My opinion?" Lora frowns. "What do I know, dear?"

Reagan breathes out, looking now at the gold cross on Lora's necklace and saying you got a lot in you that I don't have in me.

"Say again?"

"You... You know the Bible."

"Not every fuckin line, dear."

"I thought of God when..." Reagan stops. She frets, wounded. She utters: "I mean, I haven't thought of the prick in six years. But... I just thought y'might have an opinion." Breathing out, she asks: "...What were they, Lora?"

"They..." Lora purses creased lips as she considers what she doesn't want in her head. "Y'got your brown with the Almighty, Reagan, I know ye do – what happened to ye... But God's the one to pursue if ye want to be answered. Not a child of His." She clears her throat and she tenders in place of an opinion: "What I mean is my levels were mad. I can't think proper if me sugars go off. And like I tell ye, it was that woeful fuckin smoke. Felt like I'd stuck my face in a bowl of hot soup to have a gander."

Lora's turned to leave, leaning into her walking-stick, telling Reagan I think they're itchin to step lively out there. We don't wanna piss em off anymore, dear. Reagan's inclined to agree.

They head out the store and walk back towards the Buick in which Mike and Abby and little Brent are waiting. Mike, clutching nine fingers on the steering-wheel and shaking, looks over to his fiancée and sees she's typing on her phone again and asks her what she's doing, and Abigail tells him she's tweeting. Asking

(WTF happened? #DarrowsGlen #WhatIsHappening)

Abby...? Cripes hi, y'culchie bitch! How in the name of Christ are ye? Give us a *hug*! Jaysis, howaya? And is this little fuckin *Brent*?

The barmaid made haste through the rowdy pub, shouting over the riot of the regulars, setting down a pair of pints before seizing her young nephew and hugging him. Alicia Pederson looks like her sister Abigail save for the curves. Ally's a petit woman who works serving drunks in the pub she co-owns with her husband Fred, who generally works by egging boys into drinking matches until some git order off the menu and forces him to fire up the stove.

Abigail hastily explained to Alicia what little she understood about the situation in which her family and neighbours found themselves. Their hometown was overrun with madmen. Breakout must've happened at that prison two counties over. Murderers and arsonists were razing homes. Alicia and Fred, reasonably aghast, had to help them out. The group was welcomed into their modest place above Fiddler's Sty.

All of them exhausted, most went to bed immediately.

The old girl assured them the La-Z-Boy was comfortable and all she needed – she insisted Abigail and Brent take the only spare bed the flat has to offer. Fred rolled out a sleeping-bag for Mike and Reagan assured them she's fine to sleep on the loveseat in the den. But although her body wants to crash, Reagan doesn't sleep and she probably won't.

Instead she sits by the window and she stares into a loose photo she keeps on her at all times. A picture of a little boy she used to have and love. Only made it to age eight before what happened happened. And that was that, as they say. So now, six years later, while everyone else sleeps, Reagan Brodie weeps over the face of the son she misses too much. Feeling so supremely weak.

She hasn't been strong in years.

FOUR.

There's this distinguished man sat in an antique bergère smoking a calabash at the window of the King George Suite in Ellamoore Palace on the shores of Cape Town, South Africa. The front of his dressing-gown is stained with the Earl Grey he spilt a few hours ago. He's got his slippered feet propped up on a decorative table on which there's a fruit-basket sent to his wife, for whom he waits. The view from here is of the water in the moonlight and sailboats coming back to the harbour. Clive Halton, his name. And Clive has had his nose buried in a copy of M. L. Greywood's *The Deepest Mountain* for the past hour, making mental critiques he'll share with someone some day when the conversation happens onto the topic. Every so often he looks up and looks out at the sea.

When Clive's wife returns she's in an irate frenzy. Clive looks over and watches her scramble toward the bedroom without any greeting and he sets down his book to observe the manic woman dressed in a one-shoulder cocktail dress of bamboo and chiffon.

Though she's cold he's warm in return.

"Patty? ...Everything alright?"

"Not really, Clive. Can't talk."

"You do a sensational job setting me on edge when you say things like that." Patty disappears beyond the bedroom door and Clive is setting his pipe back into his teeth as he lowers his feet. "*Dear?*"

"I forgot my mobile, Clive. I have to get right back."

"Back to what? What the bloody hell is going on?"

Patricia Halton doesn't have the time or mind to answer. She's collecting her iPhone after unplugging it from the charger on the nightstand. She's still dressed in the blouse and skirt she wore to dinner with the South African president and his wife. That was hours ago but now it feels like weeks. Rubbing sweat from her forehead as her husband enters their room, Patricia tries to seem unapproachable but Clive's never cared so little to oblige her.

"…Hot enough for you?"

"I don't know how people live in this heat. It's the middle of the night and I'm *stewing*." Patricia grabs the Chanel bottle on the dressing-table. Douses herself to compensate. "I have *got* to change but I don't even have the time. And for god's sake, Clive, I asked you not to smoke that in the suite."

"Can you not tell me what's going on?" Subtly removing the calabash from his teeth. "You've been running around all evening like a rabid deer – I thought this trip was supposed to be time for relaxing."

"Something is…, It's just some *trouble* at home. Something's happened in Ireland. It's only twenty kicks from our border so it… might well become a concern overnight."

"Can't you deal with it in the morning then?"

"I will *deal* with it right now."

And she's leaving with her phone. Her husband puffs on his pipe as he turns to see her leave. Unsatisfied, unfinished, he calls to her. To ensure he gets her attention, he does so strictly and by title.

"Madame Prime Minister." So Patricia stops in her rush – stops in the doorway to their suite – and she spins around to gaze back at Clive, who's setting down his book and pipe and demanding: "What is going on? …*Dear?* Please, won't you just tell me?"

Patricia Halton stares back at her husband.

It's not her intent to keep him in the dark.

"Clive… we have no friggin idea."

"That's… ominous."

"That's how I'd put it." A single nod. Patricia approaches Clive and props herself up on her toes and leans in to kiss his cheek. "So don't wait up for me."

"…I love you."

"I love you too."

It's here that Patricia leaves. Clive watches her go.

Outside, waiting in the hallway of frescoed walls are three men in the Secret Service – two of whom escort Prime Minister Halton and one who stays to guard the door of the King George Suite.

Coming up the stairwell at the end of the hall, Halton sees her PA Marlene Jacobs-Moore. Short black hair, vigilantly pressed pantsuit, always wears too many rings. Marlene's holding a tablet in one hand which she's swiping at with swift adorned fingers as she meets up with her ragged employer.

"Where in god's name is O'Reilly in all this? Can't he take care of his own Republic?"

"I'm told they called but the prime minister's predisposed."

"Typical... What do we know, Marlene? Is it ISIS?"

"Emergency units are treating it as a terrorist incursion at the moment but intelligence doesn't think it's so. There's no point in them raiding a random hamlet in Ireland. It's a useless target in the grand scheme of things."

"Or possibly that's their point. What's being done?"

"I have Brigadier Novaks on a video feed. He's been asking the same thing."

"Novaks? *Emmett* Novaks?"

"You know him?"

"By reputation. He commanded a counter-terrorism outfit of the Army Ranger Wing, of most note was his work on the Chad-Darfur border. But last I heard, Novaks was out of commission... Gallstones, I think."

"Apparently he's down but not out then. Brigadier Novaks is the one leading the forces in the occupied counties. I've got him online here. He wants to discuss our options."

"*Options?* It isn't my bloody republic. What's he want with *me?*"

"See for yourself."

As they reach the stairwell they stop. Marlene hands the Prime Minister the tablet, on the screen of which is a feed of Brigadier Novaks in a camp outside Darrows County in the northwestern reach of Ireland. Patricia looks upon the bearded and jaundiced commander that peers back at her.

Brigadier Emmett Novaks looks sturdy enough, but pained. In the background are infantrymen hurrying about through trucks and tents in the dark. The pops of distant gunfire are picked up by the mobile in the commander's hand. The sky's dense with smoke that glows orange and casts a hellish ambiance on the horizon.

"This is Emmett Novaks, Madame Prime Minister."

"Commander Novaks. I'd heard you'd quit this nasty business."

"Not me, miss. Never."

"Good show then. I want to know what's going on."

"I assure you the feeling's mutual, mum. As of right now, and excuse me, but we dinno our asses from our elbows."

"How in the hell is that possible? The Republic's paid up for resources, hasn't it, or has O'Reilly gotten behind on his payables? What about the bloody satellites?"

"Satellites can't see shite in town for all the *smoke*. The infernos are throwing off thermal-imaging. No phone reception inside. No communication with anyone in there, *if* there's anybody left."

"Then go in!"

"Beggun your pardon." Novaks shakes his head in the tablet. "Every time I send my men into those smokelands I lose contact wittem. Firefighters can't move in more than a hundred feet before the sirens go dead. No one ever comes *back*." Novaks is hard-faced still but with haggard confidence he has trouble keeping lit. "Now 112 tells us there was a break-in at a sheep farm just down the lane from this friggin Glen. Respondent listened to the whole family die, and I won't be the one to tell you how we found em."

Patricia breathes deep the sultry South African air. The Chanel just barely masks the musk of her sweat soaking into her bamboo-chiffon. Marlene stands between the two tall escorts, terrified of what the account they've just heard, and they wait for their fervid leader to respond to the brigadier in the tablet.

"…What's this about options then, commander?"

"Options, mum, are to help us now before anything reaches *your* soil. My men will retreat to the edge of the county and we'll quarantine the entire area. O'Reilly will bring us to red-alert and you send in the Royal Army quick as you can – and probably every damn fire-department in the empire."

"Done. Make your perimeter in the meanwhile, commander. Don't let anything come out of that town without a hundred rifles pointed at the front of it."

Brigadier Novaks salutes her and she tells him good evening. Communication cuts. Patricia gives the tablet back to her assistant and it *clinks* against excessive jewellery. Marlene observes the prime minister and sees the wrath in her eyes and she knows why the bloggers refer to her almost exclusively as the warhawk. The first knight of the kingdom. The real bitch.

This sleepless sweltered irate bitch is headed down the stairwell with her security grunts and PA in toe. She wipes the perspiration from her neck and descends the carpeted steps towards the lobby and she considers stakes and tolls. And she has to agree with Marlene who laments, winded, how none of this makes any sense. Asking who are they. Really, I mean… Who could it possibly be, Prime Minister?

"I don't know who, Marlene." Patricia scoffs in scorn. Glaring, her eyelids hang limp over wild eyes. "What I know is: I'll flay them if they touch our Kingdom. If they so much as look to our borders…" Marching onward through the hotel lobby, tilting her chin low to her neck. "I will burn each and every last one of them so help me god."

FIVE.

Forty-three minutes late, Clara Towns pulls up in a cab and meets her father outside her building in the east end. Uwe Marrs is seated on the steps of the run-down embarrassment, smoking a cigarette and thumbing lines on his face drawn by years of whiskey. When he notices his little girl, and he sees how big she's gotten, Uwe stands, welling up, the image of her blurring.

He tells her I've missed you. And she tells him the same.

Pregnant, it's a strain to make her way up to the flat she shares with her boyfriend, who they find seated in the hand-me-down recliner in the corner of the den. Kodi Becker, his name.

Kodi's in an Adidas tracksuit with a plaid cap on his head. He's the type of skinny that's impossible to fatten and his hair is greasy and cropped along the right side of his head. On the table next to him is a kitchen-scale topped with herbaceous green flakes and a bottle of cherry Coke. At current, at leisure, the chav's playing *Candy Crush* on the iPad he got off Gumtree last month.

Kodi is immediately put off by the man who follows Clara Towns into the flat. Just from the sight of him alone, that's all it takes. It's his goatee. Or the jacket with its pointed lapels and red pinstripes. It's his shaved scalp save for a thin braided ponytail. Right then and there, the chav wants to tell him to get the fuck out. But he bites his tongue. He looks to his woman instead.

"You're in late."

"Work went longer than I figured." Clara says. "At the *café*."

"Right. *The café*." Kodi's almost too bored to play along. Eyeing his pregnant girlfriend and her father in the villainous getup. The weathered judicious face. Get the fuck out. Kodi breathes. "...This must be your *dad*, yeah?"

"Yeah. Technically." Clara answers sardonic. She steps forward to make minimal introductions, informing her father: "Uwe, man, this is my boyfriend Kodi."

The ex-priest holds out his hand.

"Nice meeting you, Kodi."

"*Uwe.*" Kodi gazes incredulous at the silver pentagram hanging in the man's exposed chest hair, frowning and asking: "What's your business with my girl?"

"To know her."

"Alright... Fair."

Kodi watches the mother-to-be as she heads for the adjacent bedroom saying she's going to get changed. Kodi sees fit to stand up and shadow Clara, telling Uwe: Two seconds, mate. Just, uh, find a spot and sit in it, yeah?

The skinny chav follows his girlfriend into their bedroom. Uwe remains seated on the rank loveseat and in the back of his mind he decides it must've been carted from the curb outside someone's house. Much of the other furnishings in here are about the same for quality. Listening to a conversation begin in the next room, he can't quite make out the content. When the words become more distinguishable, heated, he does his best to avoid eavesdropping.

In their bedroom, Kodi watches Clara undress and notices her stomach is still glossy for the oil rubbed against it and the flecks of dried semen salting her breasts. He asks her how the shoot was and she gazes over her shoulder. She answers: Savage.

"How much?"

"Six hundred quid."

"*Six* fuckin hundred, Clara? He always gives you eight."

"I was crying during the cumshot."

"Oh for fucksake, baby-girl. It's shit, I know it's shit, but can't you hold it in? ...You're breaking our fucking bank, know that?"

"Kodi, I don't want to *do* that shit."

"Nobody wants you doing that shit, baby-girl. You think I want other guys in you? You think I'm happy?" He's close to her now and he's taking her hand in his, posing: "But how else we gonna pay for that kid of yours once he comes out – on a *barista's* salary? Tips are grand, are they?"

"Kodi-"

"How you gonna support you both?"

"I don't *know*, Kodi." Clara pulls her hand out of his grasp and she's turning to her closet to find some shirt to put on, broken in her eyes, admitting: "I don't have the first fuckin clue."

Kodi sighs. He watches Clara select an oversized shirt that can hang loosely over her distended stomach and she's slipping into it and taking a seat on the bed to yank her socks off. Kodi catches one when she tosses it at him and he holds it a moment before dropping it.

When Clara nears him, reaching for the dresser, Kodi grabs hold of her waist with gentle hands. He holds her. He tells her.

"You know I love you, right?"

"…I know, baby."

"We survive, don't we? Together?"

"So far."

Kissing her. And she kisses him.

Taking back his head to look at her face. I love you.

"What do you want, Clara?"

"…I just want a better life."

"We all want that." He says. "…Where's the quid, baby-girl?"

"I have it."

"Where?"

"I *have it*, Kodi. And it's going right to the landlord when I see him tomorrow."

"But… Not *all* of it though."

"We owe the miserable shark a K."

"So give em like five hundred."

"Baby, we owe him a K."

"You can't give him all our money, Clara! We gotta *eat*. Don't be thick now. Come on, babe."

"Where's *your* money then, you prat? Sell any green this week?"

"A couple hundred P and that covers groceries and the fuckin lights, and don't call me a *prat!* Come on, babe!"

"Groceries? I see you got a fresh bottle out there."

"One bottle, you uppity witch!"

"One bottle *left* probably! And can't you get a proper job, steada living off your pregnant girlfriend? The hell kinda man ye think you are?" She tells him: "Stoned and drunk, worthless prat."

Kodi's face is hardened. There's urge in his expression to lash out. Instead he tells Clara to stop projecting, reminding her he doesn't have to stand by to care for a bitch and a bastard. He's retreating back into the den. When he spots the ex-priest seated meekly he realizes how loud their conversation became. The mildest look of apology washes Kodi's unwashed face as he reclaims his seat in the secondhand armchair.

"...I can leave." Uwe offers. "If you need me to."

"Don't bother." Kodi jeers lowly. "She does that a lot – starts up shit. Think she's trying to win something but all she does is lose it. S'ridiculous really."

"There shouldn't be losers in what you two got. That's the thing about teammates, you both lose – *if* you want my opinion."

"I don't want it if it's just Hallmark bollacks."

"You could so label any truth that doesn't suit impudence."

"...The fuck's *that* supposed to mean, y'prick?"

"Sorry." Uwe shakes his head and holds up a recanting hand, saying: "I'm out of line. Never insult a man in his home."

Kodi blinks, gaping or glaring at Uwe who won't give him the time of day. And all in all it just pisses the prat off and he has to curl his lip and return the stab in kind.

"...So you worship Satan, yeah?"

"No."

"I thought you was archbishop of Satanists? Alcoholic and devil-loving. That's what Clara said anyway. Sloshed for her communion, she said, yelling at the holy water... *Ain't* you, mate?"

"...I'm not archbishop, Kodi. And we don't believe the devil exists. We believe in the potential of man with responsibility rather than dependence. Satan is merely a symbol of us on this Earth just as he is: alone and self-made."

"And horny."

"Carnal."

"…You guys have a lotta orgies at your black masses?"

"No."

"Slaughter goats then?"

"No, Kodi."

"So what do you worship?"

"…The internet, I guess."

"…I was raised Christian, myself. Like a lotta people – like your daughter, y'know?" Kodi drums his hands on a soft flat abdomen and smirks sort of, gazing up at the cracked particleboard ceiling-tiles. "Guess it's a good thing you wasn't the one to raise her."

"You believe that because I'm faithless I must be wicked."

"No. I think with that goatee, you must be wicked."

The priest's getting fed up but he remains seated. He doesn't show the young man any concern. He stays put and doesn't falter, because that's the best he can do to the little degenerate. He stays. Clearing his throat.

"So… Money's tight for you, is it Kodi?"

"Pity for me, yeah. For *pregs* too."

"Yes. Amazing. When even the pot-dealers are scrounging the dirt, you know the economy is crumbling. Scary, this world."

The prat's done. He's had enough and he's on his feet again. He's heading for the door, telling Uwe I'm out.

"Out?"

"Not sittin around here if you're up. She's pissed to hell and I don't need her daddy and her ganging up on me. The one bitch is crazy enough." He says. "You two suck and fate's waitin for me, y'Hallmark cunt."

No objections, and the skinny prat makes his leave in a huff. Takes his keys and a flask with him. Farts just before he's gone, and Uwe curls his lip. The ex-priest considers who he has to smell now and, seething, he looks to the bedroom door. He waits for his daughter to reappear but she isn't coming. Twelve minutes go by without a sound from her, so he gets up off the crappy loveseat.

Uwe knocks before he enters and Clara looks up at her father standing in the doorway. She sits at an IKEA desk that she uses to write and that Kodi uses to chop green. She expresses nothing and returns her gaze to the wire-bound Hilroy notebook and ballpoint pen and all-important words she's been writing. Uwe approaches slowly, trying not to judge the size or mess or stench of the room. He looks at her. Seeing damp red eyes, he asks her if she's alright and Clara insists she's fine. Stressing the word.

"I'm *fine*."

"You're fine." The priest waits. "…Whatcha writing, hon?"

"…Wedding vows."

"Of course. Fabulous. So my next question then…" And he's frowning. "You're getting *married*, Clara?"

"There's that disdain I remember. Although, to your credit, I remember it slurred." Clara sets her pen down. She's closing up the notebook and as she does Uwe notices the many proceeding pages are all filled. Dejected, she's telling him: "A friend of mine got married two years ago. She's dyslexic, doubted she could write her own vows. She asked me to write them for her."

"And…?"

"And when I was done writing out these thoughts – promises for perfect love, perfect family… perfect *life*. I kinda…" Hunching over, seeming as if she's dragging herself up from her desk, she wipes a wetted nose on her forearm. Hiding the journal away in the drawer of her nightstand, she tells Uwe: "Anyway, I write a new one every now and then, I guess."

"Why?"

"…Promises, or… Preparing myself for a life I'll live one day."

Uwe's struck. Broken to know her grief and proud of the poetry in her heart. He tells her you get both of that from me, honey, and he takes a seat on the foot of her unmade futon. After clearing his throat he asks if Kodi is the father. Clara quickly tells him no.

"Okay. Not that I don't like Kodi."

"You don't like Kodi."

"...But you do."

"But I do... Sure."

"...And, uh..." Uwe blinks. "Earlier, in your less than private chat with him... When you said 'crying during the cumshot'... That's a cheeky euphemism I'm not aware of, right?" He looks to his daughter, who's broken. "What's it mean? Spoiled an order at the coffee-shop?"

Clara observes her father.

"...You're an idiot, man."

"No, actually, if you think about it-" Uwe refutes as he's getting up, running a hand across his shaved scalp and grazing his braid, correcting her: "-I'm trying my best, honey." Uwe looks upon his daughter like it's the last time. She looks like she did the last time. "My belief thus far is... you have no intention of doing the same."

Clara doesn't argue. So Uwe nods.

"Maybe I'm not the person you shoulda called for help, Clara."

A dirty poor daughter tenses. Ruined eyes agape, staring at the baseboard and unblinking and drying out. A deep breath is taken but it doesn't do a thing for her. Clara quietly admits there was nobody else to call, man. Just you, you prick.

GLASGOW – 02:42 GMT

The air-traffic tower over Glasgow Airport. Controllers inside drink buckets of coffee to keep alert so early in the morning. They woke up and they got their asses to work and it's more of the same stress. Even the new fellow on the end of the control-line – he's jaded with the same hasty routine only three weeks into the job. But he's furrowing his brow this morning as an unusual reading comes through his screen. He checks satellite imagery but there're too many clouds tonight. So he's calling over his supervisor when he's sure he hasn't buggered anything himself.

"Sir, um… I got somthin here I don't fully understand."

"Is it an aircraft?"

"I've nae gotten a callback."

"So it's a UFO?"

"It's a… It's a wee bit more than *one*, sir."

His supervisor approaches and leans in and observes and he's immediately baffled. His tie is already loosened as it commonly is while on position in the tower, but he tugs at the half-Windsor anyway. Brings it down below the sagging chest.

"What are they?"

"*Dunno*, sir. Too big for birds. Way too small for copters."

"…Where're they headed?"

"East, sir. They're coming cross the sea from Ireland."

His supervisor gapes at the monitor. He mentions how it must be a computer glitch. But the screens of his other colleagues begin blinking as well as the swarm of unidentifiables ventures towards their assigned sectors of Scottish airspace. The readouts don't lie. There are 27,459 unidentifiable aircrafts detected.

27,463.

27,479.

Divert all flights! Clear a path! Turning to his controllers. Get word out and start relaying flightplans. Get everything away from those crafts! He's picking up the phone embedded in the control desk. Get me those coordinates. Don't take your eyes off the bastards. He's dialling and setting the phone to his ear, begging: Connect me with the airbase in Heathfield *immediately!*

SIX.

Florida.

This property here on Crystal River is one that few people in the world could hope to tour. Five buildings in total and over a thousand meters of concrete walls enclosing lush grounds featured often in top-ten-list publications. A putting range, a landing-pad, two tennis-courts, three interconnected pools and enough cars to open a luxury dealership.

This is the Merran Estate.

Also on the grounds is a small cabin segregated from both the mansion and guest houses toward the river. It's a bungalow hidden with purpose by ivy and surrounding trees – the living-quarters of two current full-time domestics, the senior of whom named Sasha Stokes. A slight and weary woman. The cabin's minimalist but it's more than hospitable and Big-Time even upgraded the kitchen last autumn and there are worse places to call home. That's something Sasha tells herself in order to stand her standing in this world.

Erin, the new blood, is sat in front of the television watching *Harvey Nest's Paranormal* so late, so loud. When Sasha Stokes exits her bedroom down the hall and comes out to the living-room, she startles her much younger housemate and co-worker, who didn't hear her slippered feet on the laminate floor.

"It's past midnight, Erin."

"I don't start tomorrow til ten." Erin blinks and reconsiders and asks: "*Oh* shit, m'dear, am I keepin you wake?" She reaches for the remote. "I'll lower it."

"S'fine. I don't sleep much no how. Family curse." Sasha runs a hand across her forehead and looks to the thirty-inch widescreen and the program presently airing. She sees the star of the show: a fellow with a spray-on tan rubbing off on a snakeskin blazer. Full

33

head of pomaded hair and a smile stolen from a realtor. His name's Harvey Nest and Sasha sees him and frowns. "...What in god's name are you watchin?"

"*Paranormal.* It's unbelievable."

"That'd be the word for it, oh yeah." Sasha rolls her eyes. "How can you possibly swallow that snake-oil rat's asshole?"

"You *know* Harvey Nest?"

"...You could say that."

"Well he ain't no rat's asshole, Sasha." Erin says. "He does this program here reading people's minds and talkin to ghosts and predicting the future. It's unbelievable."

"None a'this is *real*, Erin. Y'get that doncha?"

"Well let's hope so – Mr. Nest there has been goin on all night about a nasty vision he's been getting. Says something terrible is happening in the world."

"There's a stretch of the imagination."

"You never know, m'dear. Says it's happenin yet. Never know."

"I know because I know Harvey Nest is a hack. No need frettin for him. None." Sasha takes a seat on the sofa next to the younger maid that only just started last month. There's a pair of Calvin Klein jeans with a worn-out seam folded over the armrest and on the table is the sewing needle and thread with which Sasha's been repairing them. The senior maid resumes sewing as she blinks the dryness from her eyes, asking: "How you like your job so far?"

"Cleaning up after rich people? Who doesn't wanna do that?"

"It's always a steady job."

"How long have you been working for *Big-Time* Bob Merran?"

"How long?" Sasha runs her needle through denim. Pulls the stitch tight. "...Nine years now."

"Is it true he's... y'know... Is it true?"

"What?"

"Y'know." Erin's grave. "Did Merran... *kill* that guy they say? I mean... is it *true*?" Asking: "Are we cleaning up after... a *killer*?"

Sasha considers it. And she concludes.

"Don't ask those questions, Erin. Deniability, if it ever comes to it. C-Y-A." Here a meagre breath escapes her, sounding doleful in its extent. "I only mean, you know... Bob is hardly ever round, so... what does it matter really? Ignorance is bliss."

"So then... who do you tend to then, if Bob isn't around?"

"Mostly his wife and kids."

"They tolerable?"

"I'm happy to live separate from them."

The front door opens and again Erin is startled and Sasha rolls her eyes and reminds her it's just her son. He must've just snuck in through the back gate near the river. He's not a night-owl sneak by nature. Due to circumstance, he's always got to keep his comings-and-goings under cover of darkness.

Aiden Stokes retired from a career in the US Army last month and, home from his long-lived tour in Syria, he found himself needing a place to stay. For three weeks now he's been living with his mother in the maid's house on the Merran estate. He sleeps in the storage-room on sofa cushions. Big-Time Bob and his wife Estelle are as of yet unaware of Aiden's presence.

Tonight Aiden's coming in after a late class at the University of Florida, where he's been taking courses with the goal of becoming a paramedic. Aiden's leaning over as he reaches the couch and he's giving Sasha a peck on the cheek. Heya, ma.

"How was class, pumpkin?"

"Same as always. Lecture was boring, training was exhausting. Finally getting the hang of the defibrillators, I think."

"Well I'm proud of you, Aiden. Ain't no better fit for you than driving round and savin lives. I'm proud of you."

"That's the target achievement right there. I'll quit while I'm ahead." Aiden's heading into the kitchen, opening the brand new fridge, noting: "Think I seen Miss Merran as I was coming in the gate. Wandering out back by the pools. Don't think she seen me."

Aiden selects a plate of saran-wrapped meatloaf from the lower shelf. Sasha gets up from the living-room to meet her son, asking him if he's heard from his brother lately. Unwrapping the meatloaf, Aiden tells her that Jacob sent a text this morning.

"Said he's going to try and Skype tomorrow or the next day."

"Thank god. I'm gettin worried."

"Ma, let it be already. He'll be okay."

"That ain't certain. It's certain if he stayed here." Sasha's gotten a plate out and she's handing it to Aiden. "I finally get one son home from Syria and the other picks up and joins the army."

"It'll open doors for him like it did me. Lookit now, I'm going to school – gonna be a paramedic like I wanted. I had to pay my dues and so's *he* now." He uses a fork and knife to lift a slice of loaf onto the plate. Rewraps the leftovers, which he returns to the fridge. Tells her: "He'll come back and he'll be better for it."

"Y'aint bettered by witnessin missiles and bloodspill, Aiden."

"Jake's a tough fuckin kid, ma."

"That's what he wants you to think. That's what he wants everyone to think but you and I know better. Never mind what Jake wants, he's not fit to be in that over there. No. He's…"

"Ma-"

"He's not fit for it."

"Ma, dang; you stop bitchin over the kid night and day. Let it be already before you start rippin out your hair."

As Aiden nukes his loaf in the microwave, they hear the tanned medium on the TV in the next room. Erin watches Harvey Nest as he restates his prediction to a hushed studio. Something's going very wrong on our planet. There's something coming and its arrival will begin a new day. Brace yourself, because I really feel this one kicking. I know it. It's going to bring us to our knees.

There will be judgment.

SEVEN.

Mike Schrader awakes on the floor of the flat above Fiddler's Sty, atop an unrolled a sleeping-bag he didn't bother to get into. Didn't undress or brush his teeth or take out his contacts. He slept for five hours tops. Now he pulls himself up and glances over at the bed on which his fiancée and infant son are curled, dreaming, looking peaceful all things considered.

Picking up the cuddly stuffed snowman off the floor, Mike's setting it next to his sleeping toddler. Then, kissing his wife on the cheek, Abby stirs but doesn't wake. Brent sleepily takes hold of the snowman. Mike smiles at them.

A piss first, then he splashes water to his face in the flat's only bathroom. Dries himself with a towel he snatches off the rack. And he glimpses the tattooed hand that's missing its middle-finger as he does every morning. And he thinks of carpentry and art.

Lora Malik's still asleep in the La-Z-Boy that's reclined all the way back. Reagan Brodie said she would sleep on the loveseat but Mike finds it empty this morning. Reagan's not here. She must've already gotten up and crept out. Mike's not too concerned if the inky bitch ever comes back.

Opening the door this morning, Mike steps into the pub from the stairwell between the bar and kitchen, and he sees that three of the thirteen tables are occupied by regulars either eating or waiting. Fred works the griddle in the back and Alicia's out front bussing tables and taking orders and refilling cups of coffee and tea. When he catches her eye he smiles to her like a doubtful beggar.

Howaya, Ally. Can I take a snug?

"Anywhere you like." Overtired. A pot of coffee in her hand. A decade of thoroughly lived nights in lines beneath her eyes. Every night a blast. Every morning a killer. Today though she's a nervous waitress. Not herself. "You wanna caife or a tea?"

"Sooner the black."

"S'quarter of eight, Mike."

"Pity. Tea it is then."

With a nod Alicia leaves him so nervous. And the nine-fingered tattooist takes a seat at an empty booth by the window. He notices a discarded copy of today's Examiner on a nearby table and he gets up and grabs it and is peering through it in search of some answer, but there's nothing on Darrows Glen. When Alicia finally returns she brings him an empty cup and a pot to fill it with.

"Pretty shite for the breakfast rush here?"

"Uh, we get regulars most Saturdays." Ally fills his cup. "How's Abby and Brent? They good?"

"Still out like a pair of snuffed candles when I left."

"Yeah. How about the old girl? *Lora*, waddunit?"

"Lora, aye. And same. Thankye again for letting us stay here." Mike takes his tea and sips it, then asks stonily: "You didn't see the that shady gesha didja? That Reagan Brodie bitch?"

"Saw her." Alicia nods towards the corner of the pub. Mike looks to see Reagan Brodie sitting alone at a small table and drinking a coffee and picking at a scrambled-eggs that have been tepid for about an hour and a half now. As Ally leaves, she's telling Mike: "She was in here before Fred and me this mornin. I don't think she slept a wink last night."

The barmaid is moving onto a table of older women all grave as if they'd just attended a funeral. Ally mentions something to them quietly as she refills their teas. Every other patron in Fiddler's Sty seems to be fixed on the television behind the bar, Mike notices, but not Reagan Brodie. She isn't looking at anything. She's blankly engrossed in the steam that floats out of her coffee mug. Seeming sheepish. Done in. So Mike collects his paper and his tea and he gets up to join the dodgy bitch he cannot trust.

"…Supwicha there, Miss Brodie."

Reagan lifts her gaze and observes the tattooist that's taking the seat across from her. She returns a mordant greeting but it's done with a dry throat and little voice and it sounds like she's dying of thirst. Mike sets his paper down sideways so they both can read the headline "Man Run Down By Cyclist". He asks her how she slept.

"…I didn't."

"And bears shit in the woods hi. I didn't sleep much myself."

"…You still on about Darrows?"

"Y'mean my home? My feckin life? Crossed my mind once or twice, yeah. S'a fine thing."

"Spoke with your woman about it, but…" Reagan raises her cup and after glimpsing the room through her peripherals she asks the young tattooed father: "What'd ye see back there, Mike?"

"I just saw fire. Fire and… people running… What'd ye see?"

"Fire, oh aye. Pasty white men in the shadows."

"Oh aye? White men? None too many of those in Ireland."

Reagan barely smiles, and still her brow keeps creased. Her eyes still dead behind green frames and spotty lenses. Hopeless.

Alicia is coming by with a notepad to take Mike's order and he asks for toast and sausages. Ally glances over at the TV as she jots down his order. Nervous. She tells him Fred makes up some grand omelettes but Mike declines. Tells her he's allergic but thanks her. Ally leaves and Mike sips his tea and he returns his stare to Reagan.

"…Didn't see nothing in the paper here."

"I'm thinkin news didn't break in time to make the presses."

"Probably. Damn good you got us out in time."

"I agree."

There's a *bang* heard, muffled, coming from outside. Reagan looks up and gazes out the window. She sees a big dump-truck passing by the pub with flaking faded orange paint and there's a flash in her eyes. She remembers a truck just like it on summers day years ago and she doesn't want to remember. She averts her eyes from the truck and looks down at her coffee. Mike's frowning at the weak woman who's quieted.

"Something the matter?"

"...No." Reagan lies. "Just a headache."

"Ah. Pits." The fiancée and father frowns. "So...? Ye gonna tell me what's *going on*, Miss Brodie?"

"Y'haven't looked at the telly at all, have ye?"

"...What?"

Reagan lifts a tired chubby arm and points to the TV behind the bar and Mike follows her direction. He finally starts to listen to the reporter narrating a scene. Footage plays of a burning farmhouse and a line of bodies under tarps. People bludgeoned. Stabbed. Corpses burned. Helicopters. Armed Forces marching infantry across clover fields and smoke amassing on the horizon.

-in Donegal. Attacks have also been reported in Letterkenny, Milford, Strabane, Drumquin and Castlederg. Sightings of invaders have come from as far away as Dumfries and Glascow. Casualties are innumerable at the moment as army and air-force troops are still trying to secure sites of attack. Local police maintain the raiders as they appear. At the moment, these assaults are believed to be part of a terrorist incursion. Questioned this morning outside parliament, officials refused to comment on the attacks but said that Prime Minister Matt O'Reilly's overseeing the matter diligently along with British Prime Minister Patricia Halton, reportedly on holiday in South Africa. A time for a formal address has not yet been set... Once again, for those of you just joining us, there has been an attack on Ireland and the United Kingdom which is still occurring in our Republic, Northern Ireland and parts of Scotland. We don't know how many there are but the military has moved in and is beginning to hold off their position. Stay with us for further updates as we-

Mike looks to Reagan, his mouth ajar, grimacing as he looks upon the dodgy bitch. Reagan is calmly miserable, and something about her or maybe everything about her has always spoke with an unavoidable vibe. The quintessential image of something. Maybe the tatty cardigan sweater or the plain hair or the cheap green glasses or that sadly hardened face. Whatever it is, she's always looked like a victim but never as much as she does now. Calmly miserable, he thinks. Condemned but not broken up over it.

CAPE TOWNE – 10:12 SAST

Patricia Halton has arrived on the apron for the private flight that's waiting for her. She finds her husband already on board with a secret-serviceman standing nearby. Clive's on a Sony tablet reading a post on BBC.com and he looks up to Patty as she steps onto the plane along with Marlene Jacobs-Moore, who's got a phone against her ear but who doesn't seem to be speaking to anyone.

Clive immediately stands to embrace his wife.

"Patty, sweetheart. I've been following it since this morning."

"How bad does it look?"

"Well… the people will be shitless, I wager."

"I trust your judgement there."

"What's your plan then, love?"

"We have none so far. Just to fight whoever comes at us."

Marlene is taking the phone from her ear and telling the Prime Minister I still can't get a hold of Sir Arnold. Patricia tells her to try Will Kagan. Will never lets me down. Glancing at her wristwatch, presuming he'll be in his office now, saying: Try Will Kagan.

So Marlene ends her call to the CDS and rings the office of the Defense Secretary, William Kagan. Halton is taking the seat next to her husband and, when the flight-attendant peeks out from the front of the plane, the Prime Minister asks for tea and something decent to eat. She sits with both hands gripping the armrests like an aerophobic in a nosedive. Inside her is pressure like carbonation that builds and needs to burst out from under her skin. She has to force her eyelids shut and when she does her eyes sting. She feels Clive set his hand atop hers. It squeezes firmly with care.

"…You've never looked like this, Patty."

"How'd that be? Weak?"

"No, never weak… If anything, even stronger."

"I love you, but for god's sake don't blow smoke up my ass."

"Patricia, you're always strongest when you meet a challenge."

"This isn't a challenge, Clive. We are fighting for our lives."

Marlene exchanges greetings and is then stepping back toward the prime minister and holding the phone out to her, telling her she has Will Kagan. Patricia takes the phone from the ring-laden hand and sets it against her ear. Hearing the voice of the Secretary of State for Defence somehow makes all of this more concrete and more sickening and she regrets ever saying hello.

"You're heading home now, are you?"

"Just on the plane waiting to take off."

"You've been kept up to speed?"

"If not then I'm hesitant to hear what I've missed." Patricia says. "Tell me what we're dealing with, Will. Is it ISIS or isn't it?"

"At this time we have to doubt it's ISIS. There's no way they have the resources or the manpower to orchestrate this level of attack. This is something else."

"So *what* then? The Russians? The bloody Germans?"

"We don't know."

"Goddamn it, Will – then what *do* we know?"

"I can tell you the attacks are spreading. I'm getting reports all through Scotland. Authorities arrive to find widespread fires that swallow up anyone who goes near them."

"This is absolute insanity."

"I'm not disagreeing, mum."

The flight-attendant returns having fetched a cup of tea. Patricia removes her hand from under Clive's and she takes the mug and nods a thank you before she sips her tea. Her husband reclaims her hand and she looks to him and sees his face and soft hopeful smile and she sighs.

"I'm calling an conference to discuss our response to take place as soon as I'm back in Westminster, Will. I ask for your attendance along with Fowley and Sir Arnold. Chancellor Marks as well."

"We need word from the frontlines, mum."

"I've called Lieutenant Jeffrey Ipswitch to head to the origin point in Ireland. It's a little county called Darrows. He'll meet up with an old colleague – Brigadier Emmett Novaks with the Army Ranger Wing. Novaks is the one running the circus up there."

"Novaks? You mean the hero in Chad?"

"That'd be him."

"I thought he was out of duty with a stone in his gallbladder."

"Apparently not one big enough to slow him down."

"Have you *spoken* with this Novaks fellow?"

"I have."

"And?"

"And he's doing his best." Halton utters staring ahead, blue-veined hands grasping the armrests, asking Kagan: "Has our office been outlining scenarios?"

"Since dawn, mum."

"Email them. And I want the numbers and locations of every man we have from here to Syria. Every faction, active and reserve. I don't care if it's a bobby or a meter-maid as long as they can squeeze a trigger."

"I'll get a list made up and ready."

"Fine. I'll meet you in parliament. Until then, Mr. Kagan, you be sure to keep my country safe from whatever the hell this is."

EIGHT,

A can of pale ale is chucked at Kodi Becker's sunken stomach and the skinny chav chokes and sputters awake. He passed out here last night, though he didn't plan on doing so – he just didn't want to return to the Satanist priest and his knocked-up daughter. He's cursing out his mate and tells him to go to hell but Amin Nokhari is saying get your ass up. Shit's unreal.

What?

Look, mate.

Kodi sits up on the couch he slept on. Crusted red eyes find the television that's hooked up to a laptop and the clips on Reddit that his friend Amin is streaming. Amin is seated in the rocking-chair with the Vaio on the accompanying ottoman. He's got a bag of Brownies biscuits in between his thighs which he takes from every so often as they watch the clip play.

Apparently the vid was taken by a cellphone.

Four firefighters some distance from the cameraman enter a building in some village or town with axes drawn. Flames in the windows, charring them black before they crack and burst. Fire-engines idling outside. Police officers helpless. In the foreground, some half-naked woman runs past the camera in a panic. There's a great deal of commotion heard in a static roar and suddenly the building explodes with what appears like molten iron that gushes out the windows and doors before cooling in the November air. The firefighters can't have survived.

Kodi gapes.

"What the *fuck* is this?"

"You gotta lot to catch up with, my friend."

Amin clicks another post that's all text which has the headline "Terrorists DESTROY My House". He tells Kodi that it's been all over the web. He skims through the article and finds a link to an adjoining post. "Dog Cut in Half" and here's a few JPEGs of a Springer-spaniel. He returns to Google and his search "Ireland Attack". He selects another Thin Mint and finds a YouTube video with a title "BAF in Letterkenny" and he clicks it.

"Serious now – what's going on?"

"Fuckin invasion, mate."

The video is of infantry troops marching into a wall of smoke. Assault-trucks roll in and guns go off. From out of the black cloud a soldier is launched and he smashes into the windshield of a truck. The clip ends. Amin backs out, continuing the search, swallowing the cookie in his mouth. Kodi texts Clara, asking are you alright, but he forgets to hit send and the message remains as a draft. He looks to Amin and frowns.

"What is it? Izzit *your kind*, y'feck?"

"Knob off."

"Serious now, izzit Arabs?"

"They say so, I guess. I've been sifting through it all morning. You didn't hear this?"

"I was out."

"You drank a fuckton, my friend. You were pissed."

"Pissed or pissed off?"

"Y'just kept slagging off Clara and the devil-priest she brought home. Kept callin him a Hallmark Cunt for some reason."

Kodi sucks his teeth and Amin bites a hunk off another cookie and clicks on another article – this one released by the Telegraph. Kodi tries to read it but his head hurts and he's got to rub his eyes with firm fingers but it doesn't assuage the ache in his brain.

"So… What the hell? Are they fucking *coming* then?"

"Says the army's holdin em off in Ireland. Reserve troops being sent inta Scotland. A lot of cops too. They're saying Halton's gonna pull our blokes out of Syria." Amin looks to his mate and asks: "Want a cookie? They're quite scrumptious."

"I want a fucking cig. Got one?"

"Plum out."

"Right, well let's stock up. Get some food while we're at it."

"I got work in an hour. Martino called in sick again."

"On your lonesome?"

"Yeah... Maybe no one's coming in for pills given *this* shit."

"...Right. True." Kodi's face suddenly takes on a quality of deliberation. Tugging lightly on his lip ring, he remarks carefully: "Maybe... could be time to do what we talked about."

"What did we talk about?"

"The *pharmacy*, mate. This... this could be our go."

"How do you figure?"

"*Look*. If the old git is staying home tonight, you're the only one with access behind that tall stupid counter. You got the *keys*."

"We're not discussing this."

"We've discussed it, y'prick. This is the fucking moment."

"They'll know if I help you. They'll figure it out."

"No one's going to know a thing, Amin. You gotta trust me."

The clip ends and a grid of recommended vids takes its place. One is an interview with singer Kary Benz on her recent album release. Amin clicks it while the skinny chav ponders his crime.

A young superstar on Maui's beaches, wet and in a red bikini. A microphone is shoved in Kary Benz's face. A then-fresh tattoo on her hip was still covered in a little transparent bandage and the camera zooms in on it before Kary has a chance to grab a towel. Kary avers she got the tat in dedication of her amazing boyfriend. Amin lets the clip play but mutes the audio. Kodi makes mention of what he'd like to do to that chick. Kary Benz. Fuckin gorgeous. Amin nods and doesn't speak and keeps his eyes glued to the telly.

HEMSEDAL – 12:04 CET

Outside the sedan limousine are Norwegian mountains rising and falling, peaked with snow and loomed over by clouds that just graze the highest of them. Verdant valleys on either side of a shallow river that cuts through them. Kary Benz looks out at the vista and listens to the Bruno Mars track playing from her iPhone earbuds and she sucks on the hard-candy they handed out when the plane landed half an hour ago. They're approaching the famous Frossunslott Skisenter where her celebrity boyfriend is intent on conquering powdered slopes for his birthday.

Relinquishing her stare from the mountains, Kary turns and gazes over at Dustin Tomson, with whom she shares the title of America's Sweethearts. Their candid photoshoot of a stay in Maui crashed the web. The star of the hit show *Hoops* and a recent summer blockbuster – a remake of *The Fugitive* with Dr. Richard Kimble reimagined as a med-student – is hunched forward in his seat and mesmerized by the new *Family Guy* game he downloaded last week on his iPhone. And his girlfriend, the one with the voice, just listens to music.

"Babe... *Kary?*" Kary pulls an earbud from her ear. Dustin tells her: "I'm crushin this game, babe. You gotta see my Quahog."

And Kary blinks. She speaks with that voice she's known for.

"You showed me yesterday."

"I just unlocked Joe the cripple."

"I'm happy for you, baby."

Kary pulls out the other bud.

Wraps the cord around her bright pink phone.

"...You don't care."

"I'm happy you enjoy your game, Dustin."

"Don't talk at me like I'm stupid."

"Sorry. Let's see."

"Naw. Screw it."

"*Serious*, Dustin; let's see."

"Screw it. Why don't you gimme a foot massage."

"Right *now?*"

The actor's sitting sideways and he's putting his D&G boots on the singer's lap. He's collecting coins from the Griffin house and Quagmire's house and Kary is looking slack and appeasing as she pulls at his lace and undoes the knot. She removes the boot and finds an odour about his sock that pervades the back of the sedan. She begins to rub but he tells her barefoot and she's pulling the damp sock from his foot. Dustin removes his fur-lined coat and returns his attention to his game, enjoying the rub with fair but partial acuity – the only notice he'll afford it. When the game flips over and the phone vibrates he clicks to answer the incoming call and then sets it to speaker so he doesn't have to hold the phone against his head. The voice of his manager comes through, sounding excitable but less enthusiastic than the norm.

"Yo yo."

"Dustin?"

"Sup."

"It's Saul."

"I have caller-ID, Saul. Kary's here." He glances over at the pop-singer and says: "Say hi, babe."

Kary utters a hello and continues working her knuckle into the bridge of Dustin's foot. The actor runs his hand across his blondish-brown hair and, dragging his fingers across his scalp and down his ear – over the diamond earring Kary bought him for his birthday – he asks his manager how Beverly Hills is keeping. Saul's not answering, asking the stars for their whereabouts.

"Norway, bro."

"Norway?"

"My birfday yo. I let Kary take me skiing."

"What? How long have you been in Europe?"

"Just flew in half hour ago. Not even at the hotel yet. We're goin to that old fortress lodge, *Frozenslut* or whatever – you know it?"

"Frossunslott, yes."

"Yeah Frozenslut. Cool. How'd the screening go, by the way?"

"…Dustin, have you not heard what's going on?"

"We gonna do a sequel?"

"Dustin, turn on the goddamn TV once in a while."

"Nobody watches that anymore." Dustin's reaching forwards to flick his hand for Kary's attention, and once he has it he gestures for the remote-control that's Velcro-stuck to the top of the TV beneath the partition into the driver's cab. She fetches it for him and he presses for power as he asks Saul: "Why? Sup, bro?"

The TV's on and NRK is covering the invasion. The first image seen is a distant shot of the black smoke and towering fires that have overtaken half of Ireland, where the majority of the threat is localized. Reporters are saying that British Armed Forces have been deployed alongside the Irish and they are engaging the enemy. More reserve soldiers are on their way to other points of attack throughout Ireland and Scotland. Kary sees it and she's darkened, grasping a ripe foot. Dustin gapes and takes a moment to comprehend.

"...This ain't real. It's fuckin fake."

"That's in *Ireland*, guys. An hour's flight away. You two cannot be in Europe right now. *Think*. Celebrities will be target number one for Muslim extremists. You two are the devil to them."

Kary's set the actor's foot down to sit up at the edge of her seat. Beside her, Dustin remains reclined with his head propped against the tinted window. He watches with a hard frown of upheaval, his phone held but completely forgotten in the palm of an unmoving hand. When his manager speaks again it's like some omnipresent commentary coming from nowhere important and beyond its core message it's barely recognised.

"This is happening. You two get the driver to turn around right now and head back to the airport. I'm going to get my assistant to book you on the next flight back to the States."

But Dustin has none of this and he has to be heard.

"Naw-*naw*, bro – it's just a fuckin *scare*. It's not even nine-eleven and it's against micks and limeys for fuck's sake. We're gonna be just fine over here."

"You can't take that risk."

Kary voices: "I'm with Saul, Dustin. We should just go home."

"You're both pussies. Chicken-Lilies, or whatever it's called."

"Babe, I just think-"

"We came here for my birfday. I'm not gona leave just because the Arabs are bombin Ireland. Jesus fuck, we're a million miles away. We're not going." And resolutely he's holding up the remote and he's turning off the TV. Agitated, he asks Saul: "How'd the screening go?"

"Dustin, man-"

"The screening, bro – or I'm hanging up."

"It-it was an amazing screening."

"What'd the critics say?"

"Critics don't know a movie from a Hot Wheels commercial. Fuck the critics, man. Audiences loved you. You're an H-bomb on that screen. That scene with you running from the feds on the beach – goddamn magic, man. You killed it."

"I look hot?"

"You looked very hot."

"…Aight."

"But Dustin, please get out of there. Postpone the trip until this thing in Ireland clears up. Just call your cousin and postpone."

"I don't believe you two. I'm ten minutes from the slopes and you want me to ditch. I'm not scared of some Indians tearing up Ireland that are going to be mowed down by the army in twenty minutes. Y'all stupid clueless."

Kary wants to protest in some hope that Dustin will reconsider, but she doesn't. She's realized that he's pulled up his oversized t-shirt and is unbuckling the red Gucci belt threaded through his frayed jeans. She remains quiet, forcing her gaze out at mountains beyond the tinted windows.

"Dustin, just come back, man. I'll rent out a resort in California and you can be skiing here by nine tonight. That's just as good."

"Naw, Saul. I gotta go."

"Dustin, *wait* man – please-"

But the young star has ended the call and he's tossing the phone onto the floor of the sedan. Having undone his belt, he unzips his fly. The pop-singer is still fixed on the mountains outside the car and he snaps his fingers. Kary turns and sees the actor's got his cock out, laying atop his tattooed abdomen and the hem of his loose shirt. He's telling her look what you did to me. Look what you did. She leans over but decides the position will strain her so she slides off the seat. Kneels on the floor.

For a moment he closes his eyes and for a second he pets her blonde-punched cinnamon hair. He pushes her skull down into his crotch and feels his head poke into the back of her throat and it sends frissons through his body when he hears choking.

Good girl.

Good girl, whom all the tabloids rave about, saying that voice that voice. She speaks so meek, so vulnerable, pouty. Submissive but maybe even sly. Dangerous. And when she sings, a lot of that comes out of her in a transcendent way. When she sings she seems to silence everything else.

Dustin finds the control on the door and he lowers the partition to the driver's cab. He's asking how long until they arrive at the hotel. He watches the rearview and sees their driver look back and he hesitates a moment as he comes to terms and then he replies. It won't be long. Fifteen to twenty minutes. Dustin takes his time raising the partition again. There's a tear leaking out from behind the lashes of the singer whom all of the internet raves about.

NINE.

DARROWS GLEN

Here's a soldier that's finding his way in the smoke. He fires his weapon but the vaguely seen target has escaped him, like it leapt into the air and never came down again. The solider peers into the sick obscurity that swirls like a dustcloud in a desert cyclone. He can see nothing. He can hear everything but focus on so little. From behind him comes a rusted baselard that digs into his back and carves upwards until it's halted by his shoulder. Pushed into the grass, the soldier bleeds.

Another private by the name of Daltrey is not twenty feet away and he's listening to his comrade as he's left to die spliced upon the heath outside of Darrows Glen. In orange and black there're jets of red. There's the mounting reek of bodies that accumulate all around him in the bloody mud.

A loud and feral battle-cry. Daltrey spins, squeezing the trigger. The figure that's lunging out of the smoke immediately staggers for the rounds that embed into its white skin. The private can see it now – can see its impossible head – and he's holding up the SA80 and unloading the last of its magazine. He has to have shot it thirty times or more straight in the head and chest. There's a *thud* as the body falls and the mangled face plants firmly into the ground.

The camp set up by the Army Ranger Wing near a granary of old festering timber on the outskirts of Darrows County.

Brigadier Emmett Novaks sits in the back of a Land Rover and pops ursodiol pills. He's thinking back on his video-chat with British Prime Minister, and how even a warhawk like Patricia Halton is amazed that a man as sick as him is fighting a battle such as this. Sorry for himself, Novaks returns the orange medication bottle to the pocket of his decorated jacket. Jaundiced eyes sunken, he swallows the pills and his gut throbs and he sets his hand atop the door-handle and he sucks in a good breath before he throws open the door. Suddenly all the gunshots are even louder.

Novaks is shouting at the nearby sergeant firing over the roof of a local Ford Victoria, behind which she's taken cover. When the sergeant finally notices her commander she releases her trigger and yells back an affirmative. Novaks tells her they're moving forwards. She and the rest of her company are to take another sixty yards of what the special ops have been calling "smokelands".

Another private is running out from behind an assault-truck but is caught in the neck and shoulder by a crude hatchet hurled from the unseen battlefield. The private collapses instantly, pouring quarts of himself onto grass and clovers. Novaks tells the sergeant to *go* and she obliges in haste and the brigadier is calling out for medics as he crouches down to the shaking soldier.

"Hang with me now, brother. *Fight it.*"

"He's *done*, commander."

Novaks wheezes. He turns to see a thick-bodied and thickly-moustached Colonel Jeffrey Ipswitch arriving with a lieutenant he appointed merely for her endowments. Behind them is a three-man team of the Close Protection Unit armed with HK417s. Novaks holds the dying soldier and grimaces at the sight of the colonel.

"What are *you* doing in a mess like this, Jeffrey?"

"O'Reilly requested it. He wants the report and you need the assist. On that note-" Ipswitch bends over to get a better look. Saying: "What're *you* doin in mess like this? You're looking like hell, Emmett... Hasn't that stone in you gotten *any* smaller?"

Novaks doesn't hear him or doesn't care. He's trying to clutch the wound around the hatchet blade to stop the bleeding but the troop is slipping into his death throes and arterial blood washes out over the commander's hands and stains the sleeves of his uniform. Bullets fire within the smokelands and Novaks listens to it all as he grits his teeth. His stomach hurts so goddamn bad.

"…Did you bring any body-bags, colonel?"

"No."

"Then I fail to see what good you'll do here." Novaks lets go of the dead solider, telling Ipswitch: "You can scurry on back to yer office, Jeffrey."

"If you'd kept control here, Emmett, I would gladly. All you've done is failed to keep this isolated."

"If you've got some information as to what we're up against, Jeffrey, I urge you to share. If not, then you can just stay out of our way and let real men do their duty."

"'*Do your duty* – what the hell are you all *firing* at? You have no targets out here!'"

"We can *see em*, you gowl! In the *smoke*! Things coming at us! If we get in close enough to see the bastards, we're dead! Feel free to test that theory."

Incoming. They duck, and the fiery engine of a Subaru smashes against the truck the colonel arrived in, crumpling its roof like a candy-wrapper. Ipswitch is hunched over with his hands on his crown and telling them we need to find shelter, we're too out in the open here, we're gonna be killed.

A chopper passes overhead and is lost in the orange blackness.

That's when the mad shouting of Private Daltrey is heard.

Novaks, Ipswitch and the buxom lieutenant are immediately focused on the private that rushes from the smokelands. His SA80 drops from his grasp as he stumbles across the field toward them – soon tripping over his own feet and tumbling forwards into the bootprint-riddled grass. They run to him but he isn't getting up. Novaks lifts his head from the mud. Ipswitch is demanding to know what happened. When Daltrey finds his voice he tells them it's dead.

"*What's* dead?"

"Back there… It's…"

"What are they? Iraqis? Koreans?"

"…The body."

"You shot a *man*, soldier?"

"…*It can't be…*" Daltrey's eyes widen as he recalls what he saw, looking to his brigadier and uttering: "It *can't be… God save us.*"

"What the hell is he talking about?"

"I haven't the foggiest." Novaks, with the help of one of Ipswitch's escorts, is rolling the petrified Daltrey onto his back. The lieutenant radios for medics but Novaks tells her he doesn't have a scratch on him. He slaps the private's face hard enough to jolt him from the stupor and asks him: "Where, lad? Where is the body then?"

Daltrey lifts his arm with all his strength but it still shakes in the wind and cinders. He points a frail finger into the smokelands from which he came and he mouths words but doesn't produce any sound. He's succumbing to delirium again and fading away and Novaks rests him down. He tells the soldiers standing by to help Daltrey to cover. He then takes up the SA80 and reloads it with a magazine from his ammunition pouch.

"Lieutenant?"

Ipswitch's lieutenant looks to Novaks, answering him: "Janine Tulson, sir."

"You've seen much in the way of battle before, Miss Tulson?"

"I was part of the 98th Infantry Battalion deployed in Chad, sir. In the beast of it, alongside you sir."

"I don't remember you there. Any good?"

"I'm proficient with a gun in my hand, sir."

"Then you're with me, lieutenant." Ipswitch asks what about me and Novaks straightens the rifle in his arms and answers: "You can stay here, colonel. Knit something pretty."

"Like hell I'm staying *back*, Emmett!" Ipswitch holds his ground and inelegantly produces the 9mm semi-automatic from his hip-holster, insisting: "I'm here to *report*, remember?"

"Have you ever *fired* that thing, Jeffrey? The damn gun still has a price-tag on it."

"Mind your own arse, you fool." The colonel switches off the safety and points his pistol at the smoke that billows across the field – inching ever closer to swallowing them all. "I want to know what we're up against! I needta see a corpse!"

"Keep a keen eye on yourself then, Jeffrey. Try not to blink."

Ashes and char churn and blind them and hide away whatever's caused the riot. Novaks leads them into the raucous smokelands. Colonel Ipswitch and Lieutenant Tulson and three privates stay close behind him. Five steps into the swirling black and nothing can be seen more than ten feet in front of them. Sightless and coughing up soot from their lungs, the group carries onwards until they come to the scattered bodies of Irish soldiers left hideously frozen in their final instances of life. These looks of terror are adopted by Ipswitch and his lieutenant, who look down upon the fallen troops and assess what's happened. One is without a face. Another has a fencepost impaled through his head and he's been stripped from the waist down, turned on his stomach. Another is ripped and his intestinal tract lies in the mud. They hold here a moment and they listen to a stampede that shakes the ground.

"What the fuck *is this?*"

"It's a *battle*, colonel! You'd better have my *back*, y'useless piss!"

Two of the Close-Protection men are opening fire. HK417s blast in their eardrums and Ipswitch flinches. He asks them what they see and they tell him there's something in the smoke. They catch glimpses of pale white skin illuminated by flames that burn the grass in contained areas of the field. They fire again. Then a tremendous *crash* is heard followed by an explosion. A helicopter has been brought down somewhere to the east. Colonel Ipswitch is clutching his hefty gut as if he's readying himself to vomit. Breathless, he keeps repeating the name of God.

This way, y'buggers!

Ipswitch looks and sees Novaks and the others are venturing onwards. Continually disappearing into the smoke. He realizes he's alone and he's hopeless. It's a brief wait before he can move his legs to keep up with the team. He keeps himself hunched over with his head held low as he listens to the endless anarchy and warfare that rages unseen all around him.

"Commander Novaks! It's here!"

The call of a CP man catches his ears and Ipswitch is following it, soon coming across the brigadier and the rest of the group. They move toward an elm tree that's alight with embers. Standing ten feet away is the soldier standing motionless with his gun slackly in his grip. He's got his back to them. His stare is fixed on the body that's laid out in front of him.

It's got pasty white skin like it's never seen sunlight. Raw, smooth, lightly lightly red like new skin beneath an old scab. It's a fair-sized thing at six-foot-five. Its face, as it is, is just a repulsive unsolved jigsaw gunned away by Private Daltrey before it could strike. Its demolished skull sprouts a horn, and another's broken off and at arm's reach away in the cold mud. About five inches long. Curved. Pointed and blackish red and dripping dark marrow. From underneath its torso is a thin tail reminiscent of a donkey that sputters as if struck with rigor mortis. On either side of it lie the fetid and decomposing wings like those of an enormous crow that died in the midsummer sun. It sparks speculation that goes unuttered. It's beyond them. So the brigadier is shouting out to his soldiers. Ordering them fall back. Retreat, god almighty. He shouts to them through the smoke but he doubts anyone can hear him.

TEN.

The applause dies.

Just getting back from commercial, filming today's episode of The Tara Williams Show. Her first guest was David Duchovny but he's moved down the couch for her second guest, a doctor from Johns Hopkins University who's not used to having his expertise filmed for national broadcast. Tara's now turning to camera one.

"My final guest needs no introduction, though he does require an entourage of secret-service agents. You all know him as our commander-in-chief but, as you'll witness here, at heart he's a loving father raising a young son who has autism. He's here today to discuss how this condition has made such a major impact on his life, his family, and how he intends to aid the country and possibly the world at large. On that note I ask you, my fellow Americans, to please give patriotic welcome to the President of the United States – Duncan Clark."

The audience is heard. They remain seated but for better or worse they greet him. They've been infiltrated by subtle men standing almost casually at every corner and at the ends of the aisles. There'll be more of them backstage. A lot of them are dressed like tourists but the more blatant are in black suits listening to clearance checks through earpieces. It's a lot tenser than it is with other guests when the President walks on set. Nonetheless the people clap for the most part. A few even cheer. Despite the number of them booing, Clark is all smiles as he walks out from behind the beige curtain. He's waving at the audience. Tara Wilson shakes his hand when he outstretches it.

When he speaks it's in a lax Kentuckian drawl he's known for.

"We're honoured you could join us, Mr. President."

"It's my pleasure. It's for a cause very close to my heart."

Duncan Clark is an ordinary looking man in his early fifties. Portrait of a politician. Average but stout. Cleanly shaven every morning. Short peppery hair parted down the left side. His wardrobe and the makeup applied tonight was supervised by a PR team that manages his image on all television appearances and they did a fine job of not making him seem too wussy. He shakes the hand of Dr. Porrough and pleasantries are exchanged but too quietly to be picked up by the spot-mics.

The President sits down next to their radiant host.

"Now, President Clark, as most of the public is aware, you have an autistic son named Randy."

"Yes, yes I do, Tara. And I can't tell you how incredible he is."

"How old is he?"

"Randy is twenty-two."

"So you've known the challenge of your son living with autism for over two decades. You know as much as anyone how difficult it is nurturing a loved one afflicted with it. Does Randy live with you?"

"He does. He's in the House with my beautiful wife Faye and we have a live-in specialist who helps Randy and helps to teach him and keep him calm. But mostly to accommodate Randy on a minute-by-minute basis because, end of the day, with a case as severe as ours that's what it boils down to. Hour by hour, minute by minute."

Pan to Tara nodding. Shots of random clusters of the audience. Stern faces, many sympathetic. Then back to the couch shot, and everyone feels for Duncan Clark. But there is, as is always present, some sense of script about his answer.

"I can imagine you don't have a lot of free time."

"I find time when I can."

"But I suppose his caregiver is necessary most days."

"I wish that I myself could be there to give him my undivided attention, Tara, but now I have a nation that needs just as much or more. How do I balance my son and the free world? I thank God, at least, I can see my boy every day settin down at the dinner table with the wife and me. And I can sleep sound knowing he has a guide and tutor who loves him just as much as we do."

"Do you sometimes regret running for office? If that's not too personal, Mr. President."

"No it's not too personal, Tara, and you can call me Duncan if you like. They don't like me saying that but I'm a first-name kind of guy, especially when we're tapping the marrow as we are. And no, despite the powderkeg a'difficulties that come with the job, I can't ever say I regret running for office. Maybe-" Clark chuckles. "-maybe I never believed I'd *get it*, but God help me if I ever regretted the race. Y'come upon the life I've seen and you start recognizing things like that."

There's truth in him, it's just difficult to peel back the shell. He wears his handsome little smile just as often as he can. Remembers words of influence passed on by the great politicians he worked for as a younger man. Recites misdirection whenever a question stands to see him negatively. Side-steps with genius. Always charming and faultless, even when half of the country is calling him a useless coward. One of too many. But it is sad he's got that son.

Tara Williams looks out to her studio audience and through the cameras at future viewers at home. Camera-one is on her. Camera-two's holding on a shot of Clark they can cut to for reactions or variety. Tara tells everyone they're going to take a short break but to stay tuned for more with this interview with President Duncan Clark.

Someone yells cut. Cameras rest and monitors above the studio-audience turn off and general unenthused entertainers come out to keep the crowd busy but are harassed by the vacant stares of the secret-service at every turn. An assistant to Tara Williams brings the host her Fiji water. Duchovny's playing on his phone while the doctor makes chit-chat with the President. Tells him he'd love to meet young Randy.

Then someone in the audience shouts out. It's an angry voice.

Betrayed. It's demanding to know how Clark can sleep at night. How can he stand up straight when he hasn't got a spine. Secret-service then promptly show the woman and her husband out of the studio. Tara Williams apologizes.

"We did a screening before we let everyone in."

"You can't keep em all out, and probably you shouldn't." Clark eyes the audience before them. "It's *fine*, Tara. If I couldn't handle a low-blow now and again I never would've been a democrat."

"*Tara.*" A producer is stepping onto the set from backstage. "Tara, beautiful, I love you darling but I really think you need to reconsider talking about *Ireland*. It's all over the web now and every show has got coverage. This is a *world*-event-"

"Bernie, my show is not for sensationalism. I'm not some blood-fueled media vulture – I don't *do* international terrorism."

"Tara, you have the *President* himself right here. At least just get a *comment*."

"Actually-" Clark leans forward. "-my staff wouldn't want me to say one word on that subject, Tara. Not in this… venue. And not without a carefully written address."

Duchovny asks: "Off the record though, Mr. President, what *do* you think of it? …Just curious." He's got his phone up and he's glancing images, asking: "You think we might spare some troops to help out, or would that go against your new Peace Act?"

President Clark smiles in that practised way. He maintains that air of a laid-back and confident soul. He tells Tara and the doctor and Duchovny and the producer: We are absolutely monitoring the disturbance in Ireland and the UK at this time and we will proceed accordingly. In the meantime, our hearts go out to our allies.

HEMSEDAL – 20:19 CET

Dustin Tomson relaxed on the sofa. Tanned arms designed by sculptors held onto himself while their driver and bodyguard, a tall man in a cardigan by the name of Franklin Grier, brought in the last of the Louis Vuitton luggage and skiing-equipment. Dustin told their bodyguard to take the night off so Grier left, happy to excuse himself from the actor's presence but, before he left, he stopped and glanced down the hall toward the bathroom door.

Kary Benz insisted she take a shower the minute they got to the hotel. The singer has been there ever since. Hiding, maybe. Grier sighs for her before he leaves the hotel suite.

It's a chic enough bathroom. Steam fills the stall and her lungs and her head. She's got her phone playing music on the marble counter. Bruno Mars *Count on Me*. Listening to loving and lovable lyrics, she's looking down at her waist and hip on which she's got Cantonese characters permanently scarring her.

It was twelve months ago to the day that she got this tattooed on her body. The symbols now are red and her skin is scratched hideous. In her hand is the wire hairbrush she retrieved from her toiletry bag. Kary's been in here almost an hour now, losing tears to the drain. And blood now.

When the singer finally turns off the faucet and opens the frosted stall door she's pressing her hand to the savaged tattoo and she's shaking as she reaches for a towel. And Kary sees Dustin is sitting on the toilet in boxers and a Lakers jersey. On his phone, sending a text to no one special.

"…The door was locked."

"Credit-card. You been in here a *while*, girl." Looking up at her. Looking at her red eyes after he looks at her tits, then he notices the hand on her waist and the pink leaking out from beneath her fingers. "The fuck happened to you?"

"…I just wanted a moment alone, Dustin."

The actor's frowning and he sets his phone next to Kary's on the marble counter. He's gotten up and she's got her back turned. Trying to wrap the towel around her waist. Dustin grabs her wrist and turns her. The towel falls and she's naked and dripping and he sees the bleeding mess she's made of herself. The Chinese she tried to scratch out of her skin.

"…On my birthday?"

Tries to explain but can't. Doesn't want to.

Dustin is pressing Kary against the wall. Shedding shock, angry to see her and to know. Staring at the blood collecting and trickling away down a supple thigh. What've you done. He asks what've you done.

"…I just…"

"That was for *me*, Kary. The fuck are you *doing*?"

"I'm sorry."

"That's mine. You're *bleeding*, you crazy bitch."

Dustin sees her and knows, inspecting her and the blood.

"…You're fuckin psycho."

"I'm *sorry*."

And Dustin calms, handled.

"…You should be. You're gonna fuckin kill yourself one day."

"I'm sorry."

"I'm not pissed, Kary. *Jesus*… I forgive you."

So Kary's smiling. And Dustin moves in, pinning her. Pushing his torso into hers and mashing his pelvis against her wet bare groin. Kary whines I don't want to. He tells her it's my birthday. I forgive you. Taking off his jersey. Giving her his tongue. And she's trying to push him away. Kary tells him don't, I don't want to, but Dustin's hard in his boxers and presses against her scoured ink.

NEW YORK CITY – 15:58 EST

JFK Airport. Air Force One has been ready to take off for the past forty-five minutes. Crewmen and passengers have been waiting on the arrival of Duncan Clark from a TV-studio in Manhattan. The pilots now watch as a limousine pulls onto the tarmac escorted by police. Secret-service exit first and the President follows and he's saluted and led up the staircar and onto his plane. He's always been an avid fan of flying but never more so than in this style.

The head of the attendants offers him a copy of this month's

National Review and the lumbar-pillow he requests on every flight. The pilot and co-pilot greet him and Clark wishes them another grand romp through the clouds. They head upstairs to their seats behind the armoured doors of the cockpit as the President makes his way to the bow of the main deck – headed for the Presidential Suite. But he stops before he can reach it. A voice has called to him and he knows it in an instant. Clark turns around to see the Vice President is on board.

Offering him the smirk of a bad influence.

"Sam… Didn't realize you were catching this flight."

"Just getting a free tow back to DC." Samuel Seale extends a hand as the President approaches. They shake and Seale asks: "You're not retiring at this hour, Duncan?"

"Just thought I'd take a moment to myself." Clark weighs the circumstances. "But…" Looking to Seale, reconsidering, giving in to what's unescapable. "…now you're here."

"Now I'm here…" Seale says it swaggeringly, smiling at his old friend, holding his arm out to suggest: "Let's us set down in the boardroom, uhn? Just a minute, I swear."

"Business, Sam?"

"No business. I swear." The VP steps away and the President reluctantly follows, his fatigue already dispersing. Peer-pressured like a high-schooler. He's been this way his entire career, his entire life, but he wears it well. It's the go-with-the-flow of a man without worries. Nothing can tear him down. Nothing to lose. "I heard you were on Tara Williams today. How was that?"

"About regular. Have you ever done Tara Williams, Sam?"

"Twice. I think. At least once. If I remember correctly, she has the best snacks in the green-room. Mighty good little sandwiches." They pass the head-attendant and Seale asks her for a couple fingers of bourbon and she tells him right away. And Seale claps Clark on the shoulder as they approach the meeting-room of the senior staff. "We come *far* from Princeton, Duncan. Gotta lot to thank god for."

Seale opens the door and they head into the meeting-room and take seats on either side of the table. The attendant soon returns with their order. Smiling and setting the glasses down. They can hear the engines powering up. Soon they feel the motion as the plane rolls slowly toward the runway.

"So what was the show for? Still about you pulling forces outta the war on terror? The Peace Bill and all?"

"Actually no. We stipulated, a'course, that was off the table. Stuck entirely to the today's topic, which was actually quite near to my heart. Being *autism*, that is."

"*Oh*. Interesting choice. Play up the father role to win em back. Did you have Randy on the show? That would've cinched it."

"No." Clark rolls his glass to allow the bourbon to slosh around hypnotically. They're picking up speed. They'll take off soon. The President keeps his eyes on his drink and answers: "No, Randy is safe at home with Faye."

"Ah, that just woulda cinched it."

"All the same, Sam… Best not exploit the boy."

Lift off. Air Force One leaves the ground behind. It climbs into cleared airspace above JFK and Clark and Seale hold onto their glasses and enjoy the rush of defied gravity. The pilot is on the radio not long after they level out in the clouds. They'll be arriving in Washington in an hour. Seale swallows another mouthful and savours what's still coating his tongue as Clark grabs the remote Velcroed to the table. The President turns on the TV.

CNN is covering the terrorist incursion occurring in Ireland.

Smoke over cold grassy hills in the distance.

Sam's thinking aloud: …Something I was thinking about today.

"What's that, Sam?"

"The glory days of Princeton, Duncan. Before politics and all. Thinking of us. Us and… Well, *Big-Time* Merran, of course."

"Learn to put the past behind you, ol dog."

"Do you remember what you wanted to be back then?"

"A lawyer. Criminal attorney."

"Besides that. I mean what you really *wanted*. There was a good solid period there when you wanted nothin more than to be a radio host. Do a political debate program. Or a comic-book review." Seale grins at the President. "You remember, Duncan?"

"I remember." Clark holds his glass up. "The dog days."

"The dog days." Seale repeats. "Got to hand it to life."

"I do. Or I try to, I think."

CNN breaks from the UK, turning to domestic news.

Footage is of the federal district court in Chicago and media representatives swarming around lawyers and agents and the man accused, who's just been acquitted. A magnate, a billionaire. Clark and Seale both know him well and they now look to the TV and the image of Big-Time Bob Merran, who's proud to have won.

"So the bastard was acquitted."

"Was there ever any doubt, Sam?"

"Well he's free of the murder charge, sure, but the Feds got more on Bob, if you wanna know. They ain't done with him yet." Seale blinks and Clark turns off the television and Seale smiles. "It was Big-Time who got me thinkin of us. The glory days."

"...Learn to put the past behind you, old dog."

There's flat knocking on the reinforced door. Clark's weary voice manages to call out and grant entrance. The attendant is stepping in and alerting the President he has a call from his chief of staff and Clark thanks her and asks her to put it through. The base on the table begins to ring and the President employs the speakerphone.

"Mr. Falwell. What's weather like round the homestead?"

"Mr. President, Ireland and the United Kingdom are pressuring us for our response. I got Secretary Jackson waiting for clearance. He says he's got a few thousand infantrymen he can have unloaded outside Dublin by tomorrow morning. Another thousand or so by the afternoon, I would think. We need your go-ahead, sir."

Clark pokes his tongue into his cheek, glancing over at Seale.

"...You've heard a'this, of course?"

"Head ain't buried in the sand, Duncan." Seale nods with raised and arched eyebrows. "To tell the truth: I've been pretty curious as to how you'll respond, Duncan... Given the circumstances."

"Yeah... Really wasn't countin on this."

"...But?"

"But this ain't dang Iraq or Afghanistan, this is the UK and Ireland. If I turn my back on em they might never get over it."

"I'd have to doubt them forgetting that, yeah."

"...Hank?" Clark asks the phone. "The soldiers Jackson has to send... Who are they?"

"Active-duty, sir. Stationed outside London."

"...What sort of equipment they after?"

"Trucks. Bells. I can send you the order, sir."

"Quick as you can."

"Right. And..." Falwell's voice coming from the base of the phone pauses briefly. Something caught in his throat. He's asking: "...you've seen the videos? Online, sir, I mean?"

"...I haven't." Clark admits and breathes out to hide the tinge of ignominy. Looking at his bourbon again. Looking doleful. He's reaching for the base of the phone. "I'll see you in an hour, Hank." Then Clark ends the call, then he falls back into his chair and he appears exhausted and he's shutting his eyes. "Got to hand it to life, Sam... You run yourself ragged vying for peace that nobody seems to want."

Seale chuckles.

"Maybe that was your first mistake, my friend."

"Deep down... people don't actually believe in peace, Sam. It's so far outta the park. Yet, go on and hear em cry for it." Clark's gotten to his feet. Sleepily wandering toward the window. Looking out upon clouds and how white and heavenly they are. "What I think is that people believe in magic, Sam. And magically it'll all work out. Everything'll... They'll believe in magic before world peace – I betcha my left nut. S'at the heart of every red-blooded American... But I have faith in peace. I wasn't blowing goddamn smoke in my campaign. I want it but can we achieve it, Sam?"

"I've always figured maybe, but... we tried and failed to bring concord to other countries in peril."

"We ain't much of a saviour to em when we got our own shit so fucked up. If we were to focus on the homeland then maybe we can have peace here. We have the ability. We can." Clark stares at the clouds out there. "I had an agenda to *save* this country from ballooning unemployment and empty-handed healthcare. Poison foods made in Chinese shitholes. Put a dent in the debt. Resources are already sunk too dire in the military and my intent was to correct that. And we can." He says. "...I believe in America."

Seale nods because he respects his old friend.

But it isn't enough.

"But... doesn't this crap in Britain just prove the military's still necessary? It's our strength to be so damn strong. Peaceful are the ignorant, and ignorant are the peaceful."

"How long have you been planning to use that one on me?"

"Goddamn it all, Duncan, you can't be blind to what's going on... What happens when they turn to invade US soil?"

"They come for us, it'll be the worst mistake of their lives."

"You believe that?"

"I believe in America, Sam. Period. Our supremacy... I believe in it finding us a grand nation. Defended. Pampered. Hell, they elected me for it, or at least enough of them did. Might as well deliver and I wanna deliver the America we've always dreamed." Clark blinks. Seeming to find it all so clearly, remarking: "May the rest of the world go nutty, as far as I'm concerned. Stings in my ass to say so, but..." Sighing, continuing to gape tiredly at the clouds. "Sometimes I get the feeling the world is a lost cause."

ELEVEN.

Uwe Marrs, seated on the steps of his daughter's building, dislikes this neighbourhood. The ex-priest is smoking again and watching an irregular amount of traffic on the roads as the night gets late. He's halfway finished his second fag when he hears the door open behind him and he leans over into the railing to let whoever pass. But then he hears his daughter's voice and he relaxes. He smiles.

You know, you could smoke in the flat.

"...I like fresh air when I'm killing myself." Uwe turns to gaze back at his pregnant daughter. Telling Clara: "And I'll remind you that someone isn't supposed to be breathing secondhand smoke... That *scum* doesn't smoke since you've been pregnant, does he?"

"...He blows it out the window most times."

"As long as it's most times, well done." Uwe flicks away the cigarette. Watches some agitated family hurrying by and headed for the bus-stop. He clears phlegm from his throat and drinks in the late autumn damp. "You had an alright nap then?"

"Think so."

"Still under the weather?"

"No, I'm... fine."

"Fine is a fine word, isn't it? Conclusive at a tidy distance." Sirens are rolling as Uwe nods. An ambulance is speeding through an intersection a couple blocks down. The priest turns again to his daughter and tries to read her but he can't. That's one tome he's never been able to decipher. So Uwe gazes around at the shadows, broaching: "So at what point do we finally cave to the inevitable? ...And talk?"

"Is that what you came here to do?"

"Actually, I came because my daughter asked me to. After not speaking to me for five years."

71

"I don't believe I was looking for a stern lecturing."

"Then what do you need from me, Clara? Why call me at all?"

"I don't know."

"Is it money? Because I have astonishingly little to give."

Clara has exhausted her patience so she's getting up and she's retuning into the building. But Uwe follows. He catches up to her on the stairs heading to the second floor. She's not slowing down as he asks her again what she needs. I don't need anything. She turns at the landing and continues upward. All I want is faith from everyone who doubts I can be a mother.

"…I never said you couldn't."

"You don't have to say anything to doubt me."

They've entered the flat. Clara heads into the kitchen, slighted, and her father shuts the door and follows without chasing. As he does he's glancing around at the home he didn't want to judge too harshly but he can't hold intolerance back. There are beer bottles on the floor next to the couch that's encrusted with filth and stains and cigarette burns. The carpet needs to be vacuumed. In the kitchen there're plates and dishes stacked high in the sink. The old Hotpint fridge, he knows, is stocked with condiments and sliced cheese and moulded tangerines. At nights this place gets cold on account of a busted radiator. Potheads come and go to score off Clara's scuzzy pot-dealer boyfriend. It's not somewhere he can envision the raising of his grandchild.

Clara's taken a seat at the table that's topped with McDonald's bags and wrappers and a baggie of fries that weren't finished at lunchtime. They're cold and hardened now. Uwe stands in the doorway and looks in on his daughter and he doesn't know what to say to relieve either of them of their miseries.

"…Can I get you anything, Clara? Something to drink?"

"I'm fine."

That tidy word. Her father sighs a bit and he opens the fridge. He steals a bottle of Cherry Coke that Kodi buys for occasions when he's awake before noon and doesn't feel like vodka. It hisses carbon-dioxide when he twists off the cap. Uwe leans back against the unwashed countertop and watches his daughter as she lowers her neck and sets her head in the folds of crossed arms.

…You're scared, he says.

"I'm angry."

"Fear translates easily enough. People are too proud to be afraid so they hide away under wrath."

"I said I don't want to be preached at, Uwe."

"I'm not preaching and I'm not lecturing, Clara. I'm telling you that things will work out and that I'll be here for you. Whatever you need, I'll give it." Uwe smiles. It's a gesture dedicated to her, though she can't see it. "And if you need me to just… shut my gob, then I will."

Clara takes a deep breath as she lifts her head out of her arms, saying I don't know what I need. She looks over at her father. And the helplessness and the pain in his bags and posture pierce her. Pierce her resentment. …Come sit, man. Please.

Uwe does so. Unable to stand seeing his daughter like this, and knowing why for. Knowing who's responsible.

"…You never recovered."

"From what?"

"From… the life I left you to. With your mum." Infinitesimal bubbles surging though the bottle in his hand. "I never figured you'd have the greatest future, but still I never…" An afterthought before he sips his soda: "I guess I probably wouldn't have made much of a difference though."

"You might've tried."

"I probably should have tried. But then… I was wasted…"

"Too busy being you… Hating mum and cursing me."

"I never hated your mum."

"You probably don't remember. That'd be the whiskey, man."

"I never hated your mum. I hated that… she refused me. And I saw her as another puppet spreading subjugation. Telling you God is watching, God is watching all the time. I… disagreed. I vilified her for making you believe in Him and not believe in yourself."

"Ranting in a haze. Too busy being you."

"Yeah… Exactly, Clara, that's why I wasn't around… I was too busy trying to find myself."

Clara stares at him. She gets up and walks over to the counter to retrieve a box of Kleenex which she brings to her father. And she bends over, leaning against the backrest of her chair, watching as he dabs a tissue to his eyes. Uwe takes a deep breath. His throat clenching. His brow cramping. His eyes glimmer.

"…And I've always wished I was sorry."

Two boroughs over is Black Crest Pharmacy, halfway between Poplar and Greenwich. Since news of the invasion emerged the people have been on the move in hordes of panic sweeping like a plague. When the doors opened, Black Crest, like most stores that sell food and other essentials, was swamped with customers that cleaned the shelves of everything they could get their hands on. Madness went on before the cops started lining them up, patrolling the streets. Things at least have quieted down now but there's still time.

Amin Nokhari, twenty-four, has worked for Black Crest the last six years. Started out stocking shelves and moved up the ladder to assistant-manager. It isn't a big store and on the rare occasions that no pharmacist is available they close up the counter at the back and direct patients to another joint just down the street. Tonight is one such night. Amin is doing so now and the trembling old man finds his way out in a hurry appropriate to his age and arthritis.

Amin's turned the open sign off.

Amin, a full-fled manager tonight, currently carries a few boxes of chewing-gum. The store around him is in shambles and he has to navigate over toilet-paper packages and bags of crisps, making his way up to the counter to the only cashier that's come to work. She's older and she's been retired for three years but she just had to get out of the house more when her husband died. Amin sets the boxes down on the check-out counter and he's asking the wrinkled cashier to restock the empty ones. She's too focused on the radio she brought with her and the coverage of the invasion. She has to ask him to repeat the question.

"Margery, I need you to restock the gum."

"But… I've never done that. "

"You just throw out the empty boxes and open the new ones."

"We… We just been looted, Amin."

"Even still… Please restock the gum, Margery?"

"Have you been listening to this attack?"

"…I saw it online, yeah."

"*Ghastly*, isn't it? Can you believe it?"

"No. I can't, Margery. Not at all…"

"An terrorist *invasion*. Didn't think I'd see one in my lifetime."

"Some people say it's not terrorists." Amin offers. "Say it's, like… monsters."

"Well of course they're monsters." Margery's shaking her head. Listening to the radio. Breathing: "Bloody extremists. Just sick awful monsters." She says. "S'all they've ever been."

When the doors slide open and the electronic bell *dongs* they both gaze over to see their last customer of the night.

A thin degenerate in a werewolf mask and an Adidas tracksuit is holding a gat and telling them not to move or make a sound. Kodi Becker moves in quick. For good show he asks which one is the manager and Amin is appalled and furious and he's stammering I am. Kodi has no qualms about seizing his friend's shirt. Thrashes him briefly before throwing him forwards. It has to look good.

"Should I push for the silent alarm, Mr. Nokhari?"

"*No*, Margery. Please don't."

Kodi holds the gun on the old woman and tells her to put her fucking hands up and she does so. Tells her to move along and get beside the assistant-manager. Fucking move it. Go on then.

"*Where?*"

"To the drug counter, y'brown prick. Move your ass."

With the gun held on them they move down an aisle of looted condoms and tampons. Kodi asks if there's anyone else in the store and Amin tells him the cleaning crew will arrive any minute. They come every night at closing time. He doubts they'll actually show up tonight but he doesn't mention it; he'd rather this end quickly and without issue. As they approach the back they come upon the pharmacy counter that's been closed up with a locked retractable gate that doesn't deter the werewolf.

"Get your keys out! *Fast*, asshole!"

Amin hates that he obeys. Old Margery stares daggers at the gunman. She tells him the pills won't make you happy and Kodi promptly tells her to shut your fucking geggy. Amin finds the key among the ring of others clipped to his belt. He's unlocking the gate partition and Kodi tells his hostages to get inside and they oblige him with little resistance.

"Where's the mud?"

"*What?*"

"The fuck are the opiates?"

"I don't *know*, dude. I don't work back here."

"Figure it out!"

So Amin attempts to, but he doesn't do so fast enough and Kodi is getting pissed and he's rushing forwards at him. It's got to look good. It's got to be scary for the cameras. It's hard to see through the slits in the mask – he doesn't mean to get so close. But he can't back down now and he's pressing the gun into the back of the assistant-manager, who tries to ignore dread while he continues searching shelves and drawers for the drugs. Hoping they're out of Margery's earshot, Amin attempts to whisper to the wolf.

"Listen, I don't *know* where they keep the bleedin *dope*, Kodi."

"S'here *somewhere*, mate."

"The heavy stuff's locked up tight." Amin tugs at a drawer that doesn't budge. "I don't got the keys for this shit."

"Who the fuck does?"

"You should get out of here, mate. Serious."

"Where's the fuckin *keys?*"

"The *pharmacists* have em. I don't got access to-"

Interrupted. Cut short by the blare of sirens. Kodi turns to see red and blue lights coming to a stop beyond the front windows. Margery is fleeing through the narrow doorway at the end of the gated counter and Kodi is panicking and he chases after the old woman. Amin doesn't want to look at his friend, who's gaining on the cashier when the bobbies start shouting through a megaphone outside. He taps his teeth together and won't look back, listening to wrinkled Margery scream when Kodi seizes her and hooks his arm around her neck. Marge whines, gagging on fear as the skinny werewolf presses the gun to her head. Tells the bobbies I'll kill the bitch. I will kill this goddamn bitch. Then he turns and he snarls at the assistant-manager – his best friend.

"*Oye!* You fucking *rat!*"

Amin doesn't look back at Kodi.

"You snitched, *dinnyeh?*"

Doesn't answer his best friend.

"You can burn in fuckin Hell!"

Amin's stepping to the end of the counter. Closes the gate and relocks it. Kodi huffs and the old woman squeals and the police sirens outside blare and there's a ringtone playing from the phone in the werewolf's jacket. Kodi doesn't answer. It's not a good time.

The cops know Kodi's gat isn't loaded but still they don't advance. They stare down the werewolf and Kodi stares back and one side will eventually break. In the meantime they're readying snipers on the bookshop across the street.

Clara looks to her mobile when the call ends with the ungainly voicemail message mumbled by Kodi last summer, stoned off his ass. Clara leaves her boyfriend a message, where are you, you've been out all day. I'm... I'm sorry. Just come back. And she holds for a moment and considers things and then she ends the call.

It's a moment before the mother-to-be lies back on her bed. Staring up at water-stained ceiling tiles, her hand resting atop her baby bump which rises and falls as she breathes, waiting for time to stop. Clara shuts her eyes, calling out shortly, asking Uwe if he found Netflix on Kodi's laptop.

Uwe in the den is weeping, watching the video left paused on Kodi's Dell laptop, seeing his daughter before she got pregnant. There's sweat and strain showcased in features and flails, and the father's remembering her as a little girl when he left her. Unable to wipe his eyes.

Misery is when Uwe's gaze is finally pulled away and it's suffering this glimmering blur and it falls onto the half-finished bottle of vodka left behind by the thin chav, and in this light and through the glinting haze it sits there, and Uwe shuts the laptop and hears Clara call from the bedroom and ask if he found Netflix.

TWELVE.

Unrelenting in the mountains, winter pummels Frossunslott Hotell & Skisenter. It charges against the French-doors of the balcony that overlooks the snowy Norwegian range. Kary Benz has remained in the empty Jacuzzi centered against the bathroom wall for hours now since she showered, since Dustin had her against the wall. Her hair has long since dried and so has the scouring of the tattoo on her hip. Scrapes and scratches crisscross over the Cantonese characters she branded herself with one year ago. She'll never get rid of them. Her body will decompose with the foreign script forever marking her as what she is.

Her phone's on the counter and though it's bleeped a few times Kary doesn't want to see it. As far as she's concerned, she knows no one and no one will touch her. On her naked lap is a pad of paper and on the rim of the tub is a Bic ballpoint. The singer tried to write a song but she couldn't keep her eyes on the paper. Instead she's been staring blankly at the tile walls, muttering her broken lyrics, humming the incomplete tune she's been composing in her head for weeks now.

There's knocking at the bathroom door and Kary is jerked out of stuporous woe, turning her head and looking over and she's clearing her throat, frightened to ask who's there.

It's Grier's pressing voice she hears come back to her, asking if she's alright.

"…I thought Dustin gave you the night off, Mr. Grier?"

"He did. I stayed in the lobby. I'm not one for sight-seeing." Grier says. "Saw Mr. Tomson leave about fifteen minutes ago. He told me he wasn't goin nowhere tonight. I figured he was lying."

Kary wonders or perhaps she doesn't wonder at all. Her eyes wide and staring at the stainless-steel faucet and knobs extending from the porcelain, she's telling the bodyguard to come in and he does so, slowly and with respect. When he sees her he immediately averts his eyes.

"I'm *sorry*, Miss Benz."

"*Oh.*" The star is looking down at herself. And she's crossing her legs and folding her arms over her breasts. "*Don't...* I mean, it's fine. It's okay." Kary's looking down again at the faucet and telling him: "I trust you."

"I'll leave."

Grier turns away, but Kary frowns very mildly, enough.

"...Why did you come back, Mr. Grier?"

"...Just..." Weakly he shrugs. "Worried about you."

That's that so the bodyguard is leaving. And again Kary doesn't want him to go. Studying him and seeing a tall square-jaw in his forties. Or fifties maybe. Greying hair. Cheap wire eyeglass frames. Bit of a beer-gut under an olive-green sweater. Mostly though he just seems like he's always seemed to her: someone to keep watch. He's someone who watches out for her.

"Mr. Grier?"

The bodyguard stops in the doorway and looks back at the popstar in the dry Jacuzzi.

"...Would you stay?"

"Oh. *Here?* ...In the bathroom?"

"*No*, I mean: would you stay the night?"

"Yeah." Grier blinks. "Fine. I'd be happy to, Miss Benz."

"I would put clothes on."

"...Despite that, I will stick around."

Kary smiles. And she gestures to the hotel robes folded on a shelf in the ebony console and Grier collects one for her as she gathers up her notepad and pens and sets them on the floor beside the tub. He opens it and holds it out for her. As Kary stands, Grier can't help but notice the mutilated tattoo on her hip. Dried bloody scratches over Chinese characters. The bodyguard lifts his gaze to observe her eyes.

Angry.

"…Did he do that?"

"*No* no." Kary smiles cheerless, cinching up the belt of the cotton robe. "No, I… *I* did that." The singer cowers kind of. Her head sinks. "…I didn't mean to do it so hard."

"Why?"

"I was… itchy."

"That must've been some friggin itch."

Kary doesn't disagree. She's raising a toned leg and she's getting out of the tub and Grier watches her without ogling, telling her she's right to be on as many magazine covers as she is. She thanks him with cheeks and brow like soft eroded stone. Her eyes again remain fixed on the faucet of the tub. She leans back against the granite-tile wall and in her peripherals she sees her bodyguard take a seat on the toilet where Dustin had sat.

"You shouldn't be with him."

Kary blinks.

"…I'm sorry?"

"I said: you shouldn't *be* with him. Especially if it's just because he's a looker. Just because his face ain't shredded ugly doesn't mean it shouldn't be." Grier thinks he's soothing her but Kary isn't pacified by aggression so he calms down. Looking to her notepad, asking her: "So what was that there? You were writing?"

Kary finds weary eyes to the lyrics on the floor.

"Just a song I've been working on."

"What's it called?"

"I uh… I should have never loved at all."

"*Ah*. Nice… I love the creative types. I was never one."

"No? Never?"

"Oh, I *tried* when I was young. Tried to be an actor."

"…What did you want to act in? Hollywood?"

"Ideally, sure." Franklin Grier grins but it's with both pride and humility. "Figured I'd be a fine action star. Kick European baddies to death." The bodyguard shrugs and shakes his head a bit. "Never got a break before reality set in. I'm… nobody special."

"…I got my break on YouTube."

"Lotta people are doing that these days." Grier looks to beauty, who's finally getting up and out of the tub. "Good for you, I mean. *Really*. Good for you… Something to be said for a girl who made it to the tippy-top all on her own."

"If I'm tippy-top, Mr. Grier, why do I feel I'm on the bottom?"

"That's doubt, Miss Benz. You tend to doubt, I've noticed." The bodyguard offers to help the singer when she wavers off balance. But she straightens. So he smiles. "You made your life for yourself and that's dignity few people ever know. For that alone, they'll adore you." He says. "But it's your voice they'll remember forever."

"You know that for a fact?"

"I know that for a fact, yeah. You can't question hard fact."

Looking down at her lyrics, collecting them, hearing music in her head that's muted and unfinished but it's there. And Grier is following her as they finally leave the bathroom and the bodyguard eyes her body in the black robe. Following her but not stalking, stopping when she reaches the bedroom door and he offers his smile when she turns to him.

"…I will save you from that little bastard." The bodyguard says. "Whether you love him or not. I don't really care. Your future, Miss Benz: I'm seeing to it from now on. Swear on my life… I'm taking you out of the darkness."

Grier watches the star lower her gaze, shying. He's rigid though and he soon sees her almost brighten. Kary's closing the door this way, almost brightened, telling the bodyguard goodnight as she shuts the door and finds herself alone, and the singer sighs.

THIRTEEN.

Sasha Stokes sets a snifter of brandy down on the nightstand beside the king-size canopy bed in the master bedroom. Estelle Merran is under the covers in a Dolce & Gabbana nightie. Lazy dark eyes watch the flatscreen on the wall and CNN's coverage of the terrorist invasion on Ireland and the UK.

It's Estelle who initializes conversation. The domestic knows better than to speak out of turn.

"Have you been following this, Sasha?"

"Yes, Miss Merran." Sasha answers. "Of course."

"Unbelievable, isn't it?"

"Sure is, miss." The senior domestic clears her throat, glancing at the genteel woman of the house, mentioning with care: "Today, um… one of the birds escaped. Flew away."

"…What happened?"

"The new girl, Erin. She didn't close the door to the aviary properly when she went into mop the floors this morning."

"Well… that smelly cage is Bob's domain. Let him deal with it."

There's a brief and sudden *clatter* in the master bathroom, as if some shampoo bottle or something fell off the edge of the tub. Sasha glances over at the closed door and watches it for a second before pulling her gaze away. Estelle looks to the news and the mysterious attack. She has to say something to divert attention, and war is as good a topic as any.

"Of course-" Estelle speaks up. "-if it *is* war, this mess, then my husband will be all smiles."

"Why would that be, miss?"

"Oh, Bob's got his fingers in a lot of pies. It stands to be big business in a time of war… Just got himself majority shares in the military's chief weapons distributer and I suppose it amounts to profit if the US joins the ruckus."

"Then yes, war would be nice." Sasha agrees. "Except my son is in the US Army."

Estelle nearly chokes on her bandy, ashamed.

"I'm *sorry*. I forgot, Sasha. How is… um… *Aiden*, right? Is it?"

"Aiden's fine. He's air-force but he's reserves now – he's home, trainin to be a paramedic. It's my youngest, Jacob. He's just going into his first tour." Sasha gazes somberly at the Sony widescreen. "…I'm scared as hell if this becomes war." Looking over to the housewife in bed. Smiling because it's her job. Uttering: "Is what it is though… I'm actually supposed to talk to him tonight on Skype."

"When?"

"Whenever I finish up my shift."

"Then please go home, Sasha." Estelle sniffles a little as if she has a cold, which it often seems like she does. And she tries to subtly glimpse the bathroom door, soon insisting: "Go talk to your boy."

"…You're sure you won't need anything, Miss Merran?"

"If I do then I will get it myself. Or Erin's still on the clock isn't she? For another hour or so? So you go on and talk with your boy and send him your love. I'll be fine."

So, after straightening a painting of Florence on the wall, the maid makes her leave. And Estelle breathes out some odd breath she didn't realize she was holding and she turns a dispirited head and looks at the door to the bathroom.

"You can come out. She's gone."

The bathroom door opens and her paramour comes out of hiding. He's naked except for Estelle's kimono he slipped into while he waited for the domestic to leave. Now that she has, he can smirk at the woman in bed. Estelle Merran. Wife of a billionaire, a man who doesn't know she's been screwing a psychic behind his back for five months now.

Harvey Nest is handsome to the minimum requirements of late-night programming. His chest hairs are trimmed and his spray-on tan occasionally rubs off on the Egyptian cotton and there's something about the gap in his two front teeth that makes him immediately appear like a simpleton. But he's younger than Bob Merran and hasn't got as much of a gut. Despite vague physical attraction, though, Estelle's forgotten what made her first give in to his advances.

"...I knew she was gone, my lovely."

"You read my mind from the bathroom?"

"No. I heard the door close. But if I'd *wanted* to read your mind, rest assured I would've." Nest steps across the wool carpet toward the bed. Estelle sort of welcomes him but sort of not. When he gets in under the covers she turns away to glance at the forty-six inch TV on the east wall. Brianna Pereira is narrating the grisly shot taken on a cellphone and posted to YouTube – smokelands in the distance, glowing orange. Faint screaming. Nest isn't paying attention to the news. "And so?" Running his hand over the satin covering her thigh. "...All ready, beautiful?"

"I think I might be tired tonight."

"...*Oh*..." Nest's delighted face drops. "Alright." He rubs a stuffed nose a little and he's lying back. Gazing at the canopy. Some of his bronzed neck is coming off on the pillowcase. Jaded, inquiring: "So uh... when's old *Big-Time* coming home? Should I be climbing out the window?"

"I really couldn't begin to presume where he is or when he's coming back."

"You're not your husband's wife."

"Wow, you really *are* psychic, Harvey." Estelle sort of rolls her eyes. "I caught your show yesterday. Heard your little prediction." Still staring at the flatscreen. Newscasts of the invasion. She sips the brandy and then hands Nest the snifter. "Is *this* what you saw? What you meant by the 'end of days'?"

"You know damn well a groundhog can predict the future better than me."

"I know you can't see shit, Harvey. Just... You never made a prediction of that scale before, and to make such a deal about it." Footage of soldiers and helicopters. Rampant fires in the distance. "Now there's *this* happening. Helluva coincidence."

"I'm down in the ratings, my lovely. The producers were talking about cancelling me. Had to give em something that would sell." He tilts his head sideways on the pillow. Takes her in as he holds the snifter atop his tanned trimmed chest. "I love you in this nightie." A few seconds waiting for a response, but none is given. "...I love you, Estelle."

"Harvey... I'm really tired."

"...Should I leave?"

And Estelle considers it but never weighs in either way. The psychic stays beside her and kisses her neck, and they watch the TV and see fires burning a distant chapel in Northern Ireland.

In the house behind the mansion, a little after eight. The place is dark except in the kitchen because Sasha thinks it's dutiful not to waste the boss's hydro. Her son Aiden has two lamps on in the living-room and he's hunched over the HP laptop that's set on the coffee-table. Sasha, off early from work, changes into sweatpants and a t-shirt and she's asking him if he's logged in yet.

"It's logging in now..." Then: "It's *up*; we got it."

"Is Jacob online?"

Aiden tells her not yet and Sasha is bummed but she knows he'll sign in. He will. Probably he's busy. Maybe he can't get Wi-Fi. So she heads into the kitchen to grab a bottle of vitamin-water from the fridge and then returns and they sit beside each other. Mother and son, staring at the Skype account of Jacob Stokes.

Currently offline.

"...Madness, that shitstorm in Britain."

"Hear any updates?"

"Only what I could when I passed by a TV. Just... madness."

Sasha sips the orange vitamin-water. "…What's gonna happen if Duncan Clark decides to send our boys over there?"

"He'd choose special ops. They're not gonna send Jacob."

"…What about you?"

"Well… not me no more. I'm not on active." Aiden pulls the tab of his Budweiser and tosses it onto the coffee-table next to the laptop, easing back into the couch and glancing over at his mother. "We're safe, ma. The Stokes' will be fine."

He's sure of it.

Stare at the laptop, they see Jacob Stokes come online.

He IMs them soon after

(hey)

and follows with

(sorry long day)

Mother and son lean forward. Aiden sets the beercan down and types back. Says it's no worries and then prompts the video chat. It's accepted and when the cameras sync up they see the face of the younger Stokes brother fade in out of darkness. He's shaven and crew-cut, wearing his fatigues. He appears to be at the back end of some barracks at the base over in Mayport. And he looks healthy but strung out, so his mother worries.

"Hey guys."

"Jacob… you look *exhausted*, pumpkin."

"It's good exhausted, ma. Really now." Looking over in the Skype window to see his brother. "S'happenin, Aiden?"

"Sup, dipshit. You're lookin older."

"Feelin so, yeah, that fits. How you been, college boy?"

"Fightin."

"Seein anyone?"

"…Naw, bro." Aiden's slack-faced, pensive, shaking his head a bit and then asking: "D'ja stop bitin them fuckin fingernails?"

"Ain't easy, that's for dang sure." Jacob holds a hand up for the webcam, presenting marred nails bitten in past the tip of the finger so habitually that the flesh has calloused. "It helps whenever I keep my hands occupied."

"A rifle ain't your worst bet."

"Hush *up*, damn it Aiden." Sasha slaps his buzzed crown. "You sound like your dumbspit daddy."

Frowning, their worn-out mom glares a moment at her eldest then looks to her youngest in the laptop. Ask him how the ASVAB went last week. She hates that the question exists at all. Jacob is proud and glowing and telling them he got a ninety-eight in combat. He smirks, presuming: "Figure we know where that'll send me."

"Jacob, don't go in for infantry. Goddamn it, pumpkin, apply for something else. I don't like the thought of my boy enlisted while this nightmare's happening overseas."

"I'm gonna be fine. Don't worry so much."

"What if they send you? Or what if Clark changes his mind and goes full barrel against the Middle East? You think I want to see you die in the desert?"

"Ma, *please-*"

"You coulda done something."

"I weighed my options. I chose."

"But it didn't have to be like this, dammit!"

They hear *hi* and it startles the mother and she jumps and spills the vitamin water. Erin, just getting in, is standing in the doorway in her work attire. She's saying sorry and backing away, feeling like that's her best move. Aiden is setting his hand on his mom's leg to try and calm her down. Sasha's heartbeat slows as she looks back to her son in the laptop.

"This ain't you, Jacob."

"Have a lick a'faith maybe. Don't be so *scared*, ma. Whoever I gotta fight – I got this." Jacob smiles in the little window. Seeming like he's truthful, telling them: "We're all gonna be fine."

FOURTEEN.

Right up front is Colonel Jeffrey Ipswitch. He was the first to turn tail by a fair margin. They beheld the ruined thing in the mud and the colonel saw the enemy he faced and wasted no time. He ran. The others followed directly afterwards. For all the billowing black soot in the air and in their eyes they can't really see where they're going but no one cares. No one has the mind to consider it. They ran toward the darkness, away from the orange that's approaching, and were quickly lost in the smoke.

Brigadier Emmett Novaks is behind the rest of them, unloading bursts of his SA80 into smokelands behind him. His gut throbbing, weighed down by a stone. It's as he turns around that he trips over the body of a dead private and he collapses into the wet matted field. Wheezing. One of the CP men notices and he doubles back to help him up. The brigadier meanwhile keeps his jaundiced eyes on the shadow looming in the cinders overhead.

Don't! Don't bother – just *run!*

But the trooper doesn't flee. He grasps the brigadier's arm and hauls him to his feet, up and attem, and he's almost got Novaks on his knees when the shadow above lands and trembles the earth around them. Pallid hands seize him by the neck and snap his head and lob it at Novaks, nearly knocking the brigadier unconscious. In the grass and filthy clovers, he's willing reality back to his mind as he looks into the CP man's face lying in the grass. He holds tight the weapon and he's firing into the stomach of the beast. He runs out of ammunition after only a half-dozen rounds.

The thing is still standing, and it's angry.

Up ahead twenty yards are the rest of the group and some of the few soldiers left in Darrows County. Every dozen feet they come across another body or parts of one or scraps. Lieutenant

Janine Tulson and two of the CP men are trying to catch up with Colonel Ipswitch. They could hear his frantic stride and stumbling a moment ago but they can't hear him anymore. He's gone. Tulson stops and whispers for them to halt and they gaze around through the raging smoke. They listen. It sounds as if an imposing mass is charging towards them.

...Lieutenant... What do we do?

Fuck, brother. You think I got the first clue?

A black iron lance flies in from behind them and shaves the meat off a man's bicep before it sticks into a felled plum tree. A face is glimpsed in the cinders and it's pasty and has bugged pink eyes. They're firing and running. No one follows anyone save for the lead of blinding terror.

Tulson is separated from the others and she's alone in the grass and she's got her assault-rifle held in unconfident arms and her eyes are wide and they dart all around as she surveys the smoke that burns them so bad. She's backing away from nothing and turning suddenly. Panting. Something snarls not far from her and she spins but there's no target to aim at. Growling behind her and she turns again. And as she's staring into nothingness she realizes she's lost her way.

Lost and alone, and it sounds as if someone's playing a fiddle.

A flat slab of blade is flung and it sticks into her side and she's screaming as she falls to her knees. It's the blade of a lawnmower ripped out of its bearing without ceremony. She's seeing a tall thick figure approaching in the smoke and she's grunting and heaving up her gun. So heavy. It takes all of her will to squeeze the trigger and the recoil nearly floors her, the lawnmower blade singing curses in her side. The figure is flinching as it takes the bullets. She can hear the thing calling out in pain. Animalistic, it could almost be human. It's indistinct now as if it's withdrawing, but it isn't going away. The lieutenant clenches her molars and forces herself back onto her feet. She's running again. She doesn't know where she's running to. When she sees an abandoned ambulance that's crashed into a willow she considers it as good a sanctuary as any.

Dropping now, she's on her stomach atop wetted mud. It's a bit of a tight squeeze near the axels but she crawls her way underneath the ambulance. She listens to her panting and her pounding heart. She tries to settle down but she couldn't possibly. Waiting. Praying. She lies beneath the ambulance watching the world smolder.

The ground on which she lays is rumbling like stampeding cattle are coming for her. She hears the rush of air push against the ambulance and suddenly there's a pair of feet planted beside the front left tire. They aren't wearing boots or anything. They're pale and with dark nails sprouting from oddly bulbous toes. They could belong to a man but only one disfigured since birth.

When there's creaking of stressed steel and the ambulance is shoved and thrown on its side and Tulson is uncovered, she sees the thing that's come for her and she can't stop screaming.

What follows is hell.

.

FIFTEEN.

Mike Schrader, fiancée and father and nine-fingered tattoo-artist, hasn't slept and yet he's barely been awake for most of today, ever since he saw the telly downstairs and confirmed the hell he was fleeing from back in Darrows Glen – their home.

After speaking with his fiancée and Reagan Brodie and Old Lora, Mike's come to accept what he saw that night wasn't dreamt. There really were things and they were pale and possessed only the principal qualities of a human. They attacked. And they weren't of mankind. So he lies on a sleeping-bag in the flat above Fiddler's Sty, not sleeping and not moving, just thinking in spurts between mindlessness and they weren't human and he feels nausea and a migraine but he can't get up and he can't close his eyes.

His fiancée Abigail sits and stares at her mobile on which she's opened her Twitter page. Over the past twenty-four hours about three hundred people have started to follow her, all of tagging or directing messages to weigh in on #DarrowsGlen.

(@AbSchrader yu from #DarrowsGlen? my mum's there)

(I live in #Hennigale south of #DarrowsGlen.. armys making us evacuate)

(terrorists attacking #darrowsglen!! We barely got out alive!!!)

(wtf is going on up there #WhatIsHappening)

(Earth will burn @AbSchrader #TheFirstIsFirst)

(i swear to god it's monsters #WhatIsHappening)

Abby hasn't replied to any. She doesn't have a clue. She looks up at the TV on a stand in the corner and it's got shitty reception, tuned into BBC News. Ongoing updates about the invasion have been playing since yesterday. The young mother has her toddler on the floor and he's playing with a stuffed snowman from *Frozen* and the family is listening to a statement issued an hour ago by Britain's

Deputy Prime Minister, Stephen Fowley. And that fat bespectacled Fowley promises people of the UK and the Republic of Ireland that everything is perfectly under control.

Abigail hears her son speak. His vocabulary is limited but it grows weekly. He adds a new word when one soaks into his brain enough. He doesn't always exhibit perfect pronunciation but he's looking up at his mother now and saying something along the lines of pizza. Abigail glances down at him but can't bring herself to appreciate him. Not right now and not for a little while.

"...Mike? Y'awake?"

The tattooist doesn't turn over. Doesn't move. He remains on the sleeping-bag staring at the ventilation duct and appearing dead.

"...I, uh-" Mike clears his throat. "What *time* is it?"

"Just past midnight... Ye listenin to this?"

Mike lifts his head enough to look at the TV on the stand.

"To Foghorn Fowley? I'll wait until O'Reilly shows himself at last." Shouting languid at the telly: "Show yourself! Defend your *country*, ye gimp feck!" Mike finally stirs, getting up off the sleeping-bag, ruffling bed-head out of his blonde hair. "I'm goin down to the pub." And he's looking at his high-school dream and the son they have, suggesting: "Probably can bring him with ye, love."

"*I'm* not comin, Mike. I'm off the drink and so are *ye*."

"But Abby love, my home's been burned to the-"

"Mike, the bloody country's under attack and any minute those rotting savages might storm down this very street. Even the most perfectly dense tool isn't getting tit-faced tonight."

The door opens and the family looks up to see old Lora Malik coming up the stairwell from the pub, a pint in her bony hand. Leaning into her walking-stick when she settles a woozy stance, holding her oversized handbag at her side. She's ragged more than drunk, and it makes sense. She's been watching the same madness on the telly in the bar. She's been reliving the same memories of their hometown on fire.

Slurring: "...Any af ye seen Reagan?"

"She not with ye, Lora?"

"Ah say again, dear?"

Abigail repeats, louder: "I said I thought she was with ye."

"*Ah*, not for the past couple hours she hasn't been."

Lora squints clouded eyes at the news playing and cutting out every so often. Solemn, hiccupping as she vaguely watches footage taken by a cellphone that presents a smoke-filled town outside of Edinburgh. Uploaded to YouTube just four hours ago. Some kid and his mates come into town and find it drowning. A speeding Ford Escape takes a hill too fast and loses control and it's swerving and smashing into a fleeing woman before pinning her against the asphalt. The phone is dropped and the footage goes black.

Mike looks over at his son in his mother's arm, and the toddler looks up at his dad in need, uttering barely a something. It kind of sounds like he says ossified.

Mike sighs. Tell that to your mom, boyo.

Instead Mike asks the old girl: "How about you then, Lora?"

"Say again?"

"Y'alright?"

"Bloody grand, dear. Most fun I've had since I could shag."

The old widow take an unsteady seat in the rocking-chair next to the sofa, letting out a sigh as she relaxes, sipping her pint. Mike's scratching the pillow-itch from his cheek as his fiancée retrieves her Samsung once again. Lora notices and clears her throat.

"I never did catch up with tech… Watcha searchin there?"

"Lookin for updates on D'Glen."

"…Anything?"

"Twitter's been alive since I tweeted yesterday. One guy says its orcs that attacked. Replies actually *agree* with the tool." Biting her lip, gaping miserably at the phone, desperate, cold. "One in Lucan says them things are hellspawn or gargoyles… *Monsters*, swear to God. I really wish someone could tell me. Just… just tell me."

The young mother keeps on her phone – keeps on the hunt for answers – and the tattooist is scrutinizing the old biddy with whom they escaped their town of fire. Wondering ireful, and it leads him to ask drunk deaf old Lora how she knows that Reagan Brodie.

"…Reagan's me tenant. Rents the basement of me gaff."

"She a sound housemate?"

"Never bothered me. She's… a quiet girl."

"How come she knew t'leave Darrows?" Mike leans against the wall next to a print of some mountain in the Rockies. Crossing his arms. Spitting: "She hasn't smelt right since we started drivin."

"Say again, dear?"

"Oh feckin hell, woman… I said what's Reagan *know*, Lora?"

"Ye don't really think Reagan *knows* somethin, do ye?"

"All I know is with everything happenin, Reagan's the one bitch who dunnit seem surprised bout any of it. Looks like she can tell me right-out what's gonna happen next." Frowning. Angry, but not at the old widow. "Fuck me, I wanna know."

"Aye." Lora breathes out doleful, thinking things over in a drunken brain, fingering a gold cross on her necklace. Her eyes shut as she sees the recent past and she has to avert her gaze to snap out of revulsion. Looking to a blurry Mike and his tattooed impatient crossed arms. His left hand with only four fingers has her sort of fixed. "…Mind if I ask… how ye lost your bird?"

"Why d'you care?"

Wrinkles multiply as Lora smirks, holding out her walking stick over her leg and she gives her right shin a single cruel whack that elicits only the sound of wood on hard plastic. Mike, raising his eyebrows, nods as if to apologize.

"…When uh… When'd that happen?"

"Say again?"

"When'd that *happen?*"

"Seven, was… Seven years ago."

"How?"

"Diabetes. Beware of sugar, dear. It'll fuck ye sick."

Mike smirks, holding his hand up and observing the nub where a finger used to be. Regaling her: "Me dad's a carpenter… The kind to see no use in a man who draws bollocks. Art's a fuckin joke, so he showed me how to work like him, the cunt... So there was me when I stumbled and got this pretty bit in the table-saw."

"Fuck off. Really? ...Oh word, Mike, that's brown."

"Ah. I was fine in the end. Maybe gotta bit wiser that day."

"Say again?"

"I said I wassun born to be me daddy... I gotta do me."

Lora smiles. We all do.

Little Brent's gazing big eyes up at his mom. He utters ossified or something like it and she runs numb fingers through the tot's blonde hair. She reminds Mike we really got to eat.

"So whaddaya want then?"

"I don't gotta clue... Lora, have you eaten? ...*Lora!*"

"Say again, dear?"

"Have you eaten?"

"One more time?"

"Oh for chrissake, y'deaf feckin biddy – have you *eaten?*"

"Oh aye, *have.* Thankye." Lora tells Abigail: "Your brother-in-law fries a brilliant bloody haddock. If you're hungry, I mean. If, uh... If Fred's not too twisted to cook just yet."

No one bounds at the suggestion so old Lora doesn't further it. Everyone's somber, staring at the telly. Mike and Abigail quake to see footage now of a collapsing high-school eaten by flames.

And here, staring at the wreckage onscreen, Lora asks no one specific: "...How long til they reach Dublin, ye think?"

The TV goes dead when the power cuts out. The lights darken. The furnace is silenced. The floor rumbles as if horses stampede. Through unwashed windows they hear sirens speed through streets where stoplights start flickering. Smoke's rolling in like a fog.

SIXTEEN.

White claws drop Brigadier Emmett Novaks five feet onto cold hard ground. Iron shackles bind his hands and feet and he writhes on the dirt and clovers and red Maple leaves dropped from the tree looming over them. Seeing with jaundiced eyes a fire set to a pile of nude bodies stacked atop the clouded hill and it's giving off cinders that surround them.

Gaiety in the fiddle music he hears. Faces in the smoke, and a lot of them have horns growing out of their skulls.

When a bloody hand reaches for him Novaks gasps and throws himself backward. But then he notices the hand is similarly chained and is owned by Colonel Jeffrey Ipswitch, who's very recently and very messily been relieved of his sight.

"...*Jeffrey?*"

"*Who's that?*"

"Jeffrey..."

"...*That you, Emmett? ...Y'prick?*"

"...Wha..." Novaks is ill to look upon the colonel. "What the hell did they *do to you?*"

Emptied sockets leak blood that trickles down the pockmarked cheeks of Colonel Ipswitch, who harrows the grass and dirt around him and squirms upon it like an earthworm in the rain. He's been stripped of his uniform and undershirt and pants and socks and everything. They let him keep the Casio wristwatch. Shock numbs him enough and he's wriggling and he's reaching for nothing with hooked seized fingers. Jeering: "You sure have this under control, commander."

"...Jeffrey..."

"Of course..." Smiling demented. Leaking sockets staring right at him to quip: "Of course they'd make me die with an asshat like you... beside me... God bless life."

Shrieking. They both know the voice but only Novaks can look up to see the brawny Lieutenant Janine Tulson dragged by her ankles through the grass. Bleeding out from a gash across her side, she's dropped next to the firepile. Her arm is white from the loss of blood. Her uniform's soaked red. Seeing her and her defeat and her horror, Novaks hears Ipswitch ask what's happening. I can't see. But Novaks just gapes at the bucktoothed grinning thing that brought Tulson in and it's like all of reality has gone sour. Atom by atom, it's bursting before his jaundiced eyes.

It's definitely male, the thing, because it's naked and it's swelling as it observes Tulson and her deconstruction of sanity. It's six feet tall but from the ground looking up it seems bigger. It has a lanky body but vascular arms and legs. No nipples or naval. Two pointed charcoal-hued bones protrude from its skull on either side of its forehead. Salmon veins spiderweb its skin.

Around the sick brigadier, coming out of the smoke, are a few dozen others. Some small, some much bigger. Some with festering raven wings that span eight feet or so. Some with convulsive goat tails seeming to emote like a sentient malicious dog. Some with bulging eyes and others with dark lips and others with torsos fitted atop hairy hinds and cloven hooves that trot upon the mud and clovers and leaves around the firepile. One who's thin plays the fiddle giddily. The brigadier gawks at nasties, pacified knowing this has to be the end.

...What's *happening*, Novaks? Tell me!

The brigadier can hear Ipswich and he'd like to speak to him. Certainly he hates his guts. He'd like to speak to him just the same. They could both use a friend in this. But Novaks can't talk and he just gawps at the implausible. It's impossible panic for impossible things that enjoy the fires. A midget thing masturbates and snaps an ophidian tongue. The bucktoothed one giggles in a deep voice, sounding vacant and dull. The thin one plays the fiddle.

Tell me what's happening, y'prick!

Their hands are unwilling to wait and Tulson is screaming again as they begin to rip the bloody uniform from her fit body. She attempts to fight them off. She flails and kicks at freaks. A big one with mammoth wings and wearing chainmail chaps bounds and he grabs her wrists and pins them above her head. Two littler ones hold onto either bucking firm ankle and spread her legs.

Novaks pulls at his chains but monsters heave them back and yank him down into the mud. He shouts at them. Fuck off. What are you freaks. Leave her alone. One who's without a nose is grabbing rocks and is stuffing them into brigadier's mouth. Novaks notices the cluster of entry-wounds in its abdomen. It's bleeding but only a little and it's red but dilute and translucent. It packs in the stones. A fat one meanwhile hops around with its hands on its jiggling waist, dancing to the fiddle music.

No sooner do pallid claws rip Tulson's bra from her tits does another set begin to knead them. Don't. Pinkish fingers close over her eyes. A grey arm reaches in to join. Don't. The one without a nose and a stomach full of ammunition has filled Novaks's mouth with stones. Novaks has put up a fight but they hold him. They hold his head so they can pack the rocks in enough to abolish his front teeth. He's emptying his lungs and they turn him so he can see Tulson and what they do to her.

Bucktooth is first. Dumbly giggling and his smile is affable and Tulson cries. Novaks protests through rocks and teeth. If he can just get free. If he can just slip the shackles over the bones of his thumb. But the one without a nose has been handed an iron mallet passed along by the horns, raising it high before smashing the sick brigadier's skull.

Ipswitch can't see any of it, quaking as he listens in blackness but he hasn't got much of a thought in his head. There's only the tune of the fiddler, who plays.

SEVENTEEN.

Just past midnight. Despite the lateness, the Palace of Westminster is alive with panicked voices and frantic feet that hustle though lavish halls and corridors. Some sweating into suits and others into robes passing portraits and courts. Security personnel has been doubled since this morning. Tellies in offices broadcast twenty-four hour coverage of the invasion.

When the doors of the Peers Entrance open, guards stare cross at the entrants but loosen with due respect when they recognize Prime Minister Patricia Halton is coming in from Old Palace Yard. Halton's followed by her own protection and by Marlene Jacobs-Moore who's carrying an attaché and an iPad. Halton slows to pass through the metal-detector, for which the guards apologize. Her bodyguards register their weapons and she and Marlene carry on up the Peers' Staircase to the antechamber.

Modelling a nice tan from her holiday in Cape Town.

"Madam, I've just gotten word from William Kagan. I told him we'd arrived." Marlene taps away the text on the tablet as they ascend the steps, telling Halton: "He asks you to meet him in the Peers' Lobby."

"What the bloody hell is he doing in there?"

"I've asked. No response and his line's engaged now."

"Typical. Have we heard from Sir Arnold yet?"

"Not yet. We'll keep trying him."

Halton's bodyguards have caught up and they keep pace as they reach the principle floor and head northbound up the Chancellor's Corridor. Passersby dawdle and look to the Prime Minister. Some try to smile to convey confidence. She looks at none of them, even when one whistles loudly and derisively. Due to pride, Patricia presumes the whistle wasn't meant for her.

This certain whistler watches Halton and her entourage march onward in a urgency. Standing next to the lobby of the Lord Chancellor's Room, he wears a judge's robe. A powdered wig and thick-framed eyeglasses over black irises that gleam and watch the Prime Minister hurry away from him and disappear down the western Lobby Corridor. After that the whistler is gone. Everyone else here is too busy and tired and panicked to notice he's suddenly vanished into nothingness.

White stone walls enclose the square Peers' Lobby outside the Lords Chamber. Surrounding them are six arms of royal dynasties that shaped this empire. Tilework draws heraldic patterns around a Tudor rose under daylight peering through stained-glass windows. Seated on a leather davenport near the House of Lords is the Secretary of State for Defence, Will Kagan. Kagan's currently with his phone against his ear – talking to his wife who's yet to board a plane with the rest of his family.

"Sienna, I'm telling you to *go*. Get my children on that plane. Please go." Kagan notices Halton approaching. Swallowing, telling his wife: "Sienna, I'll meet you in Bruges… Be safe." And he ends the call and tucks the phone in his jacket pocket and stands up to recognize his Prime Minister.

"What are we doing here, Will?"

"It's Sir Arnold, Prime Minister." Kagan gestures to the Lords Chamber and begins leading them towards it. "We finally found him. In here."

"Is there a division I'm not aware of?"

"See for yourself, mum."

The doorkeeper opens the gilded doors for the Prime Minister. Kagan leads the way into the House of Lords. It's empty. It's been years since Halton's seen these red benches so unoccupied. It's humbling, except she's not in the mood for humility. Wondering why the hell they've come here. Kagan directs her eye further up the hall. Drooped upon the bright red woolsack is the Chief of the Defence Staff. A bald and weathered man with broad shoulders and a strong build. The magnificent gold throne and canopy loom over Sir Arnold Booth.

Booth is presently joined by a younger female clerk whom Halton doesn't recognize. The woman stands up to sadly greet the Prime Minister, who doesn't accept it under the circumstances. Too fixed on the CDS, who's moping. Halton laments it.

"What in god's name are you doing in here, Arnold?"

"…I'm not young anymore, Prime Minister."

"Maybe you could pull yourself up and look at me."

"Apologies." Booth peels himself off the woolsack and Halton can see his eyes – can see the agony in them. "Nonetheless I'm at a loss, Madam."

"The *empire* is at a loss. If you man up and hide the bloody laundry we might try to combat it. For god's sake, Arnold, you're supposed to be chief of defence. We're being *invaded*, you poofter."

The young woman is stepping forward, saying: "Prime Minister, good morning. I'm Leigh Booth, I work in the Palace. I'm a clerk."

"I haven't the foggiest as to why the doorkeeper let you in."

"I let her in." Sir Arnold's now upright on the red woolsack and he nods to Leigh. "Leigh is my granddaughter… Her father lives in Edinburgh. We haven't been able to get a hold of him… nor my grandson."

Patricia immediately lowers her back. She's quiet for a moment and ashamed and she glances to Will Kagan, who grimly turns away. The Prime Minister takes a deep breath before she speaks.

"…I'm very sorry, Arnold… but right now we have *so* many more people we need to worry about." She's rigid, though hurting. Almost gulping. "Their lives depend on us and what we do." She looks to Kagan, asking: "Where's the most recent sighting?"

"Kilkenny. Reports started coming in about half an hour ago."

"Kilkenny?" Her mouth hangs open, taut and crooked. "Do you mean to tell me that in the span of twenty-four hours they've gotten across all of Ireland?"

"They weren't *prepared*. *We* were no better prepared. Dumfries,

Glasgow and Edinburgh have been hit. They're heading south now, crossing Leeds. They came with masses and we couldn't call to arms fast enough to keep up…" Kagan tells her this solemn. "At this rate, they'll be in London in twelve hours."

Halton gapes. Her eyes glimmer.

"…It's been two days. After two days I think we should know something. *Something*. What has Colonel Ipswitch told us?" She doesn't get a response from Kagan so she looks to Booth. "*Well?*"

Booth's telling her: "We lost contact with the colonel and all companies serving under Brigadier Emmett Novaks. We have also lost contact with Prime Minister Matthew O'Reilly and his staff… Around midnight, it all went dead."

Halton gapes and her eyes glimmer.

"…I beg your pardon?"

"At the present, mum… everything north of Dublin is just a black hole."

Halton registers this information with a vacancy. In this daze she doesn't hear the gold doors when the keeper opens them but, despite this daze, something inside her senses Stephen Fowley when his presence is upon her. Halton turns around to face the stout and goateed Deputy Prime Minister and she glares at the bag of crisps he's holding in greasy salted fingers.

"Where the bloody hell have you *been?*"

"I'll have you know, Patricia, I was out giving a formal address to the *people* while you skipped on in from your African holiday." Fowley eyes his prime minister, goading: "Lovely tan by the way."

"Yes I caught your statement, Stephen. Everything is perfectly under control, isn't it? Brilliant. Well crafted. Who'd you get to write that one for you?"

"I actually don't remember his name. It's the funny fellow in the wheelchair."

Fowley selects a crisp to eat and Halton just curls her lips.

"For god's *sake*; eating is not *allowed* in the House of Lords, Stephen."

"I can't ever hope to appease you, can I?"

"What's pathetic, Stephen, is it really wouldn't take much."

"I'm sorry to *interrupt.*" Kagan has to step forwards – step between them. He looks to the Prime Minister, reminding her: "We've got a war on our hands. Let's try not to miss it."

Halton turns her back to Stephen Fowley. She wanders toward the steps of the Throne. Kagan tells her they've collected the numbers regarding available servicemen. The numbers are low, he says. No more than six-thousand men.

"Pull all of our forces out of Syria."

"That's including them, mum. It's not the Cold War anymore. The reserves and guards are one thing but we aren't prepared for conflict of this magnitude."

"Ireland's already called its reserves to arms, but that's to fight for themselves." Booth is finally getting up off the woolsack, fixing his jacket as he does, noting: "We have Poland. France. I've spoken with both and they got soldiers on the way..."

"How many soldiers?"

"I'd consider it a lovely gesture... We have to realize they'll want to protect themselves from this." Booth clears his throat and purses his spotted brow. "...We've got what we've got and we have to make the most of it."

Patricia, defeated, is leaning back against the railing guarding off the throne. Running her hand over her forehead and staring at the carpet, she listens to Fowley as his molars crunch apart another crisp and she has to shut her eyes.

"...Have we heard at all from the bloody *States?*"

"I've spoken with Henry Falwell. He's waiting to hear back from the Secretary of Defense... but supposedly *he's* waiting on a call from Duncan Clark. From what I hear though, mum, under Clark's recent bill, we'll be lucky to see a couple thousand men."

Shaking her head. Grumbling: The one term they're stuck with a mouseketeer. She looks up at the group that looks to her. ...You know, I really wish that someone could tell me who the fuck is attacking us. It seems like that's the first thing we'd know. She looks to Kagan to question him. Is it the *Russians*, damn it?

"Russia's denied. So has China. Course, who's to really say?"

"Alright, but-" The young clerk is butting in, holding up a hand to keep polite. "Beg your pardon, but we're not seriously going to look past all the first-account *rumours*, are we? Surely everyone has heard it by now."

"What are you on about, Miss Booth?"

"I'm talking about over hundreds of different posts online from people *within* Ireland and Scotland at the sites of attack… It's all over the net."

"What is? What are people saying?"

"…They vary, but the…" Leigh looks to her grandfather, who's looking away because he can't stand it. "…the general consensus is fairly agreed upon." Sir Arnold holds his arm out and Leigh is leaning into him lightly, saying: "It's all over the net. It's all over everything…" Trembling in her grandfather's arms. Eyes staring blankly at the gold throne and canopy, she hardly even whispers: "It's Judgement."

EIGHTEEN.

DUBLIN

Armed with a flashlight, Alicia checks the breakers at the back of her husband's kitchen. Fred turns off the oven and dishwasher but she tells him never mind – never blew a fuse before. Power musta cut. Out there in the pub they can hear the door open and shut and Fred's picking up the meat-cleaver but Alicia tells him to pull his head out his arse. The barmaid heads through the out-door and shines her beam on the woman that's just come out of the setting sun into Fiddler's Sty.

Reagan Brodie is horrorstruck.

"We gotta go! *Now! Right now!*"

"Stop the *lights* hi. S'just a powercut." Alicia points the flashlight at the floor to stop blinding the woman, and she's gesturing to one of the empty tables and urging: "You like a sit-down, y'think?"

"Alicia, pack and scatter or you're gonna die here."

Reagan's storming through the pub and heading for the bar and the door and stairwell behind it. As she passes Alicia she looks at her and expresses nothing beyond her dread and she opens the door to head up to the flat, but Ally is shouting to her.

"Ye mean to say them feckers are… Jaysis woman. I mean it's Dublin. I mean… they can't invade fuckin *Dublin*, can they?"

Reagan's up the stairs and not looking back. Fred comes out of the kitchen with the cleaver at his waist and Alicia tells him to put the fucking thing down but he tells her I ain't takin chances, love. He then heads for the pub door and gazes through the wired little window. Applies the deadbolt. Immediately after he turns around, Fred notices the elderly couple sitting in a booth in the corner. They look back at him and Fred points a fat finger.

"Ye can *stay* or ye can *leave!* Choose now – I ain't unboltin that yoke again!"

In the flat above the pub, Abigail found a number of tealights in her sister's bedroom and lit them. The group's washed in orange in the den. There's a vanilla-scented candle on the floor between them and it keeps the family and the old deaf drunk woman lit as the sun goes down and the city gets dark and very loud. Mike's got Brent on his lap and illustrated arms and nine fingers clasp the boy. Abigail's next to her fiancée and son, leaning forward unnerved. Old Lora's in the rocking-chair trying to sober up.

When Reagan bursts in, it scares them all.

"We have to leave. *All of us. Now.*"

"I heard this shite before."

"Weren't watchin the news, Mike?" Reagan heads to her bag of clothes she threw together back in Darrows. Grabbing the faux-leather strap, she tells them: "They're comin for us. *Right now.*"

The door opens again. Alicia hurries into her flat and notices the family sat in shuddering yellow. Her nephew in particular looks scared. The barmaid looks to Reagan. Bags packed to go.

"It's Reagan, yeah?" Ally doesn't wait for confirmation. "I can't seriously believe this cake, Reagan. If it were a *proper* invasion happening, cripes, we'd be hearin-"

Gunfire. It's muffled by the closed windows. Reagan turns to part the blinds. Abigail bounds off the sofa to join her, and when she looks outside she sees people. Not many people, but everyone who's down there is legging it. A few blocks down, there's a torrent of black smoke draining up into the sunset sky. So Abby spins around to face her sister and husband and son. Yeah, she's not kidding – we gotta hang a scheet right feckin now.

A collision shakes the building. Abigail notifies the group that a BMW just slammed into the chippers next-door. Mike has gotten up and he's holding Brent, who whines. Reagan helps Lora up and Abigail grabs the walking-stick for her.

"Getcher stuff, Abby." Abigail does and Mike looks to Alicia. "Ye as well, Ally. Ye and Fred – pack up."

"Where the holy hell do we go?"

"Me father's down Cardiff. We can head there."

"...You're a Welshman, Mike?"

"For fuck's sake, Alicia! Seriously? *Pack*, y'eejit!"

They hear: Oh no.

Fires across the street. Mike hurries to investigate and Reagan holds open the blinds for him. Horrified to see. Shielding his son's eyes but Brent still cries. The tattooist turns to Reagan.

What the fuck do ye *know*, woman?

And Reagan's dolorous in return.

...I know we need to run, Mike.

Tumult downstairs. They can Fred hollering. The floorboards shudder as if something bashed against the ceiling. Footsteps and yelling. Hoarse voices and screams of the patrons. Alicia is flying out of the bedroom with only half her bag packed. Her other hand tightly grasps a whiskey bottle she had under the bed. Heading for the stairwell but her sister calls to her. Ally, *wait!*

"*Don't*, Alicia." Mike's handing his son off to his fiancée and stepping forward. "Y'got another way out of here?"

"The fire-ladder into the alley out back."

"Take it then. Get to our Buick and start drivin."

"I'm not leaving me husband!"

"I'm gettin fuckin Fred! We're gonna be right behind ye."

Glass shatters downstairs, a lot of it. Outside, gunfire again but closer. Helicopters overhead. Dublin is a battleground. Mike tells the group to *go* and Alicia leads them into the bedroom, where her window doubles as a fire-escape. Alicia first and Abigail follows with the boy clenched in one arm. Lora's pulling the strap of her crocheted handbag up onto her shoulder. The tattooist meanwhile is looking around in haste and he's grabbing the bike-lock and chain from the rack in the closet. Opening the door. He's staring down the darkened stairwell that leads to Fiddler's Sty.

The alley behind the pub is empty but Alicia keeps watch as her sister jumps off the bottom rung of the ladder with Brent crying in her cramping arm. Lora, sobering slowly and even with her plastic leg, manages to keep from losing her balance until she's only five feet off the ground, whereupon Alicia breaks her fall.

"Ah fuck me. *Sorry*, dear."

"Just get *off*, Lora!"

"Say again?

Reagan remains at the window above, listening to the barmaid curse the drunk old woman, and listening to the tattooist hurry down the stairs behind her. Fretting for Mike, considering helping him find Fred, Reagan decides it's useless. She isn't strong enough. So she climbs down the ladder to join her friends and flee.

Kicking open the door downstairs, Mike peers into the pub.

...*Fred?*

Broken pint glasses. Bottles shattered. The TV is smashed and a spiderweb of fractures spiral from where something round made contact. There's a guttural *huff* and Mike turns to see the door is battered open. In front of it is an old man and woman who were moments ago patrons. Mike isn't sure which one of them is still wheezing so hideously but he doubts it'll last much longer.

Jaysis feckin Christ... Peering around. Trembling. Holding the bike-lock tight. Whispering. *Fred?* The hell are ye? There's a clatter of pots tumbling off the counter in the kitchen. Mike spins to face the in- and out-doors. He can see through the crack between them, and he sees someone move back there. ...Fred?

No response, but here's a light sound that's unmistakable: the striking of a match. Orange flashes and subdues to grace and Mike's wide-eyed and stiffly pivoting to look into the light.

There's a nude child sat on the bar and he's got a book of matches. Except, not a child. Four feet and very gaunt. The face is long and inane, yellow in the light of the match. Bald save for two protrusions sticking out just above its forehead. It glances stupidly at Mike without contemplation before losing interest, looking back to the flame it holds in filthy fingers and haggard nails. Clopping thuds come from under him and Mike notices its feet are cloven hooves like those of a fawn and they alternately kick back into the cupboard door like a jaded teen on a family vacation.

Mike gapes, his brow crinkling slackly, waiting for his brain to process reality. The little guy, bored with the flame, is tossing away the match and it lands on the floor and dies out and Mike finally lets go of his breath. His knees suddenly give away and he's falling and grabbing onto the support-beam at the end of the bar and he's holding himself up. Watching the pyro strike another match when the in-door opens and something much larger exits the kitchen.

And Mike really wishes he was tit-faced about now.

Outside, Reagan Brodie jumps from the fire-ladder to join the rest of the group. Alicia asks her sister where the car's parked. Abigail tells her they'd found a free spot just a couple streets over. Reagan notes deadfaced they'll never make it that far.

"Where's Fred's car?"

"In the garage." Alicia points down the alleyway at a detached motor-house in which they've rented a space to store the Dacia. It's an old little building, its bricks overrun with creeping ivy. So Reagan marches without fear and Lora follows and so then do the sisters. Brent still freaking in Abby's arms and Alicia's frowning abruptly, asking: But what about the *boys*...?

Mike has got a dagger in his abdomen. The brute atop him is pasty bulbous and ugly as sin. Nude save for an almond-coloured sash made of something like burlap. A tail like a coyote with mange hanging limp over sagging buttocks. Pulling the blade out, studying what it's sown. Mike seethes. The little gaunt pyro on the counter keeps lighting matches and tossing them away.

There's a rush and a flare from in the kitchen and then wailing. Then a man is stumbling through the out-door engulfed in flames. Peering through the orange licks, Mike determines the inferno is Fred. Relieved of his right arm and the rest of him is fire. It stinks.

His face before, it's black, is tightly pulled in pain that overloads his mind. Fred collapses against the bar and slumps to the floor as he sears and the gaunt pyro tosses a match at him and Mike can't believe anything. A dream, and in it he sees the bulbous bastard giggling and leaning in. The knife outstretched. Something in the tattooist forces him to lash out. Hold the chain tight with three fingers and a thumb. The bike-lock meets that ugly face.

Mike tries to crawl away while the freak grasps its jaw, howling.

They slam their doors of the SUV. Alicia finds the key into the ignition while Lora fastens her seatbelt and Brent wails in fear. Abigail holds her son against her chest and Reagan grasps the tire-iron she grabbed off the wall. They listen to the world outside. Sirens and gunfire. Crashes and screams. Stampeding oxen rushing through town. Abigail looks to her sister beside her, whose hands remain atop the steering-wheel as she stares directly ahead.

"…Ally?"

"…Where the hell is Fred?"

"We… We autta bolt, Ally."

A *smash* and the garage door in front of them bows inwards. Something strong wants in, wants to see them. Again a smash. The infant is bawling and old Lora hyperventilates. Reagan is wide-eyed and Abby is telling her sister to move move move. Alicia puts the car in drive and she hammers the pedal down. The SUV is blasting forwards and it breaks through the dented garage door and runs over something pallid on its way into the alley.

What was that?

Just *drive!*

The Dacia careens into the alley. Alicia straightens her wheels and they turn onto the street half a block away from the pub and they've stopped. There are fires. They blaze in a building over here and another over there. Smoke gathers in the sky.

There's a Pakistani fellow running and leading a blood trail and there's a toppled pram unaccompanied by parents in the middle of the street and there's a crashed Volkswagen enveloping a lamp-post and there's an immense horned thing molesting a girl that's catatonic and young children are ushered by a guardian from a burning tenement and there are short winged men landing on a length of power-lines like finches and there's an older man limping and with the end of his catheter lodged into a hole in the back of his skull and an empty bag dragging behind him and a Vauxhall cruiser flies through an intersection and its siren's ingested by a city that's yelping like a booted mutt.

All of them gape at the nasties. Even Brent has stopped wailing and gazes with wide juvenile eyes that somehow understand more than the adults. Terror generates howls and fear holds them in.

"…Alicia?" Lora clears her throat, fidgeting with her handbag, asking with dry lips: "Could, um… Would ye please start driving? Boot to the board, dear… Please?"

So the barmaid tightens her hands on the wheel. Pushing her foot back down on the pedal, ramping up to thirty, taking the turn onto Frendal Lane. Abby looks out through the window and sees a man fleeing on a moped. A little freak with hooves whips a hatchet and the man veers before crashing. In the rearview she watches and she sees the little goat-foot pick up the moped and pretend to ride it. A taller paler one jumps down from a rooftop and surveys the man's quivering body and it begins to remove his trousers. Reagan can't see them anymore in the amassing smoke.

There's been a great deal of hallucination. Mike holds nine fingers against the wound in his stomach and he's been watching twinkling pictures in a mindfuck. The fat one dragged him to the kitchen and the pyro has followed, floating by molting wings, and the tattooist and the wonders are all washed in the orange that rages on the stove with Fred's fat sizzling on its elements. In front of the stove is a three-armed obscenity. A naked back and a loincloth made of something oddly rigid like organic plastic. Its superfluous limb swats the smoke away while one of its others is turning up the heat. The remaining hand roots through the utensils drawer. Fred's arm sticks out of the garbage-disposal in the sink.

...Wha... What are...

Gawking with little in him. Hearing police and ambulances and fire-trucks but he knows they're not for him. He can hear Fred's body still effervesce in the bar beyond the in- and out-doors. He knows he'll never look at Alicia the same again, if at all. His wife or son either, he figures. The slit muscles in his stomach sing and he realizes this is it. He won't see his family again until they join him.

The one with three arms has found a knife with a thick plastic handle. A trio of hands behold the blade to study it and the black protrusion on its side. The fat one's grabbing Mike. Holding him steady. Pallid fingers of the third arm push the black nub and it slides upwards and the carver begins to saw at the air with a *whir*. Its voice, when it speaks, is throaty with the same quality of an old audio cassette. Its language is indecipherable.

The pyro is seated on the dishwasher and strikes another match. The fat one with the broken jaw holds Mike's left arm and forces it onto the counter. Lays it against the cutting-board. Enjoyment as the three-armed one brings the electric-carver towards this hand. But the freak stops very quickly. Suddenly. It notices the finger missing on the hand. It's mangled already. So he's pushing Mike's left away and grabbing the better right.

The carver does well for the tissue and cartilage but it's useless at the wrist-bone so the demon tosses it and finds the cleaver Fred dropped. All the while there's the shrieking. Mike's never known white noise like this. About to pop. Sure to pop. After they remove Mike's hand they show it to him.

The wrist is driven against the stove burner to cauterize.

They shove the tattooist to the floor and he shrieks. The three-armed one is yanking the cork out of some brandy Fred keeps back here for special customers and he chugs. Shaking his hips while the fat one claps rhythmically.

When the front of the pub detonates, the monsters all look to the entryway. Sounds as if the front door and windows and load-bearing beams were taken and the whole building shakes unsteady. The fat one seems almost bored to check it out.

When it's through the out-door and stands in the pub it sees the Dacia SUV that's just bashed itself inside. Its doors are opened and the vehicle's only occupants are a deaf old woman and a toddler.

Then the band appears all around the demon. The mad women. The sisters Alicia and Abigail have taken up a chair and a barstool. Reagan wields the tire-iron. Fear drives them and anger makes them mad. Screaming, they attack together.

Alicia breaks the chair against the monster. Reagan cracks her weapon against its hand when it reaches out. Abby knocks a stool-leg hard into its kneecap. It tumbles over and they beat its head and eventually it bleeds enough and bellows but they keep up. Alicia is the first to cease the barrage and look behind the bar at the gaunt and winged imp hovering outside the kitchen.

...This is right horseshit.

The pyro sits himself down on the bar and watches them with an idiot's face. Ready to strike another match. The girls are so fixed on the little creep they don't notice the battered one coming to its senses. It's got a broken jaw and a gashed head and its eye is gouged and its horn is cracked. A couple ribs and fingers broken. Trying to stand up, it reaches for Abigail, lurching forwards and piercing claws into her calve and shin. And Abby screams.

Reagan hurries to help her friend. Stabbing her tire-iron into its skull, she exposes a red red brain. And it surprises her. Strength surprises her.

The gaunt one strikes a match. They pant as exhaustion catches up and, soon after, reason follows. Alicia is first to announce it. Asking what is it. When no one can give her an explanation or even a theory, Ally looks back at the pyro. She asks what the fuck to do about him and Reagan tells her don't go near it.

Abigail is calling out for Mike but Reagan tells her to hush. We don't know if any others are in here. So they're quiet and they watch the pyro toss the match. Someplace beyond it, Mike cries.

Alicia meanwhile is squinting and examining the charred corpse in the dark. She recognizes Fred's shoes and she gasps with a hand cupped over her mouth. Her eyes well. His name escapes unfeeling lips before she drops next to him. Weeping, oh no. Oh Fred.

Inside the Dacia, Lora witnesses. Her throat is raw and seizing. Sniffling as she lets go of the toddler on the seat beside her. She wipes a tear from his cheek with the sleeve of her jacket. Tells him be still, boyo. Then she reaches for her needlepoint handbag and sets it down on her sore lap before peeking inside.

Abigail's in front of the kitchen doors – about to reach forward and push them open. And her fiancée is thrown at her. The doors bash forward, cracking her chin and knocking her down. Mike lands atop her flailing a severed wrist like a defective sprinkler. Life spurts and it's warm and it soaks into Abby, who seizes screaming and pushes the tattooist off of her. Reagan has undone the belt around her jeans and she's rushing over and crouching down next to Mike and she's fastening the strap around the burnt nub. The gaunt creep is kicking its hooves against the cupboards again and he's watching and looking stupid. He lights another match.

The doors to the kitchen crash open once more and the women look up to see three pasty arms and a set of livid eyes. Yellow teeth and rosy veins overtly crossing its body. Its redundant hand is the one brandishing the cleaver. Mike gapes at the obscenity, gasping

no no no

and there's an arresting gunshot and the three-armed freak is caught in the cheek and right eye. The bullet plants into its head before colliding with the back of its skull. The thing goes slack, about to drop the cleaver, but then its white arm tightens again. Its lips, beneath dilute blood, are curling back. Its wail is of vengeance.

Reagan has turned to see Lora leaning out the backseat of the SUV. She's hunched over and her left arm cradles her right, which holds an older-model Beretta semi-automatic that's smoking from the barrel. Reagan hurries to her. Abby meanwhile is crawling away from the one-eyed and three-armed demon who stumbles left and right, slicing at the air with its cleaver. It advances on the young mother but Alicia steps to her sister's rescue. Whipping liquor bottles and telling it to die. Die ye septic old flea.

Reagan reaches the Dacia and the groaning old biddy. Lora says the recoil nearly broke me arm. Could bruise concrete, the prick. Reagan watches those wrinkled eyes shut and she turns to see the beast's now after the barmaid who's picking up a chair to fend him off like a lion. Reagan takes the gun from Lora's shaking hand.

Old Lora instructs her. Line up your shot. Plant your wankin feet. Squeeze the trigger, don't pull. Reagan isn't prepared for the recoil and she falters back and lands against the door of the SUV. Her arms are dead for a moment. Nothing can be heard.

The shot just shaved the prick's arm. Reagan regains her stance. Aims. Fires. Again she stumbles back. The shoulder. Fires. The stomach. It's charging at her. Again. The chest. It crashes against the Dacia and collapses onto the hood, looking woozy. Hateful. Its fingers curl into a white fist. Reagan presses the gun between its horns and supplies a final shot and it dies, she's sure.

Abigail shakes Mike, attempts to pull him up. Reagan helps and they're dragging him. Begging him wake up. Mike's eyes flutter and he gurgles. He grimaces as different agonies strike from all fronts. Reagan's using the sole of her boot to shove the destroyed freak off the car. She helps lift Mike into the backseat next to Lora and his crying son. Reagan then looks to Alicia. The barmaid's on the floor next to her smoking husband. And it stinks.

"Alicia?"

Ally isn't sure she hears her name.

"Alicia, we gotta *go*! Look around ye, y'twit!"

Alicia looks around at the pub in ruin. At the two dead demons and the gaunt one who's tossing another match, which lights the spilled whiskey and burns the bar. She looks at Fred. Outside in the streets she hears another siren. She doesn't speak.

Reagan behind the wheel. Abigail takes her child and watches over her fiancée. They shut their doors. Reagan puts it in reverse and they see Alicia through the windshield. Abigail says they can't go and Reagan keeps her foot on the brake and keeps her eyes in the rearview, looking at the street that fills with smoke. Abigail opens her door and calls desperately for her sister.

Alicia stands looks to them. The fire behind her getting hot.

The barmaid, in a trance before grief, takes the passenger seat. Reagan reverses and they're on the street where the grey amasses like lethal smog and buildings burn down and people are running in horror and Reagan keeps her eyes on the road. She's driving away, hitting the fog-lights, narrowly avoiding an oncoming Camry.

Alicia utters directions now and then. Reagan doesn't know where she's leading them and she doesn't see her surroundings. Smoke. Can barely see a couple schoolkids lying in the gutter and gushing into the sewers. Barely see the black horses ridden by buxom females with heads and faces like asses. Barely sees the man chained to a lamppost wailing as a winged one plays with his toes. Out there in it all, someone blows a shofar.

Lora clutches a numb arm. I forgot the kick that fucker's got. Reagan remembers the handgun and she looks down and realizes she's still holding it. Resting it in her lap. She breathes and removes her finger from the trigger.

Alicia tells Reagan to take a left and she does and then the thin barmaid mentions, hypnotized, hospital ain't much farther. After that she turns and looks back at Mike, asking her sister: Mike. How's Mike, Abby?

"He's…" Abigail chokes out the words and holds onto her boy and watches her fiancée slip in and out of consciousness. Mike tries to lift his hand to her, to reassure her, and Abby's taking it, crying. "…I have faith in him."

NINETEEN.

Rumbling in the black clouds. Lights up there.

Kodi Becker has been incarcerated in West End Central Police Station, arrested following his attempted robbery at Black Crest Pharmacy last night. They took his werewolf mask. His mobile. The prop-gun he bought off Gumtree. His belt and shoes. Now he bleeds from a split lip – an introductory gift bestowed by the fellow with dried blood across large knuckles. Scars drawn up his face. He's Kodi's cellmate until his arraignment. At current, the skinny chav just gawks with red-drawn peepers at the shadows behind the toilet-bowl. Hoping the bruiser stays asleep.

All the while, he wonders where Clara Towns is this morning.

Someone in a cell down the hall calls out, demanding to know what's happening. Where is everybody. Kodi hears voices but can't register words and only vaguely hopes they aren't loud enough to wake the bruiser. Staring at shadows behind the shitter between the beds, and when one begins to bulge he knows he needs rest.

Time's rolling on. He's at the point of exhaustion when one begins to hallucinate, and now as his legs give away and he slumps down the walls of the cage, Kodi just watches the shadow spread out across the brick. Like a bubble forming in sauce, it grows and fans outward. As the lights flick off and on, the illusory apparition crawls along. For a second it appears as the silhouette of a man's head. A profile. But it's formless again, extending out like black paint trickling up the wall. Shifting. Changing its shape into glimpses of a man and then reverting back to nothingness.

It's almost six. Cops have got to come around soon.

Clara Towns finds herself in the bed she usually shares with Kodi Becker. Under her arm she notices the Hilroy notebook she's filled with hope. Some ruckus has stirred her from dreams, she's sure. Dreams of white lights, she thinks, and the sounds of trumpets.

Blinking and rubbing her nose, reaching for her Samsung that's charging on the nightstand, the young mother-to-be unplugs the cord and glances at the screen for the time and realizes she slept through an eventful night. There are a number of texts she never heard and Clara checks them out at last.

One came from her director

(We're gonna try again Fri – think you can keep from crying this time?)

and one's from her friend Haley

(this is fuckin insane)

and another few are from her co-worker at the coffee-shop

(hey so I'm gtfo wif Cam n some ppl. You in?)

(sorry girl couldn't wait)

(good luck n fuckin text me wen yu can)

But that's it.

No texts from Kodi Becker, wherever he is.

Clara's frowning and swiping at the screen and opening her browser just as Uwe Marrs calls to his daughter from the next room. The voice of the Satanist priest sounds sharp in the morning silence but it's stunted by alarm. So Clara's suddenly got a wound heart that beats in her ears and she gets out of bed just as an earth-jarring *boom* knocks her off her feet and onto the unvacuumed carpet floor.

It's like the moon's fallen and crushed London. The ground still shakes for moments afterwards. Amidst it all is distant crumbling and shattering and collapse. Destruction. Reaction in the streets and apartments around them.

Clara feels the baby is roused inside her and she's in pain and she's grasping her stomach. About to keel over, sick. Listening to trumpets in her head, she can barely hear Uwe shouting for her and hurrying to her door.

"Are you *alright?*"

"I'm *fine*, Uwe. The baby... *hurts* though."

"Let's get you up, honey. Come on now." Uwe helps Clara back onto her malodorous bed. He holds onto her shoulder and studies her. Seeing the notebook in her hands, he's wounded. He tells her: "It's okay. You're okay, honey."

"W-what was that crash? What was that?"

"That, Clara, if I'm not mistaken, was a 737, honey." Uwe looks to the window and the city of screams outside, noting: "From what I could see, most of it came down in Hyde Park."

Two floors down from flat rented by Clara Towns and Kodi Becker is the residence of a heavyweight known as Pieman. It's widely considered an odd nickname for a man like him. By now the moniker's lost its origin and meaning but it's endured long enough to keep going for at least a while longer.

The Pieman keeps a virtually empty home, unfurnished save for a mattress in the bedroom and a couple mismatched folding chairs that face the dumbbells and stacked weights and the bench-press and the kettlebell that's rolled against the cracked mirror hanging slanted on the wall in the living-room. A gigantic man with acne dotting his back. With a shaved dome of curled black hairs atop serious eyes. Purple veins jut from his neck as he turns and looks to the shorter and lesser-chiselled Curtis Merchant, who's seated in one of the tatty second-hand folding chairs surrounded by sixteen cans of Red Bull.

"*Damn...*" Curtis is checking the text that caused his phone to bleep, and he's impressed as he declares: "Bates already got back to me, eh?"

"At this hour?"

"No shit."

Another rep and he holds the bar and weights above him.

"What's he sayin'?"

"Got the juice in from his source… Said come by whenev. I knowed you got shit wiffim but that bloke is mad fast supplyin." Curtis pockets his mobile. Scratches his ear and looks over at Pieman who lowers the bar and then forces it up again. "…Still haven't forgiven him then?"

Pieman grimaces as the weight starts to thwart him. And he's just about to respond and explain what he thinks of an asshole like Gareth Bates when he hears and feels the disastrous *boom*. He's lying back on the bench with gargantuan arms tightly clutching two hundred and fifty kilos above an inhumanly thick chest and he freezes up like he's posing for a photograph.

"…You hear that?"

"I ain't fuckin *deaf*, bruv – I heard it. I *felt* it."

Pieman drops the barbell as he stands and lets his arms stop screaming. Hoisting his hulking body off the bench, the giant heavyweight steps towards the window to peer outside. He can see a bunch of people here and there and they're agitated or freaked but he can't see what they're pointing at from this angle.

"So? The fuck was it? *Bus* crash?"

"…Can't see shit."

Curtis keeps at the itch behind his ear and stands and slips his phone into the pocket of his sweatpants. He asks Pieman what he's feeling for breakfast, rubbing a solid gut as he glances towards the empty kitchen. But the giant at the window just turns and shakes his head and utters somethin's not right.

"Whatchu mean?"

"I mean somethin's fucked." Pieman is grabbing his pullover off the unoccupied folding chair and he's pulling it on. Heading for the door of his flat. "I'm gonna go see."

"You goin out like that?"

"Why not?"

"You's knackered, bruv."

"Bad?"

"Like you stayed up all night poundin Red Bull doin reps, stickin your arse wiff oil... Your eye's *twitchin*, bruv."

Pieman considers this evaluation. Then he nods a small round head over a barely present neck. He's unlocking his door and leaving his apartment and Curtis Merchant is rolling his eyes and reaching for his pack of cigarettes on the floor by his ankle and he's fishing out a fresh white cylinder.

Pieman is heading for the stairwell, finding other neighbours are either leading or joining him on his way. People like him rushing out to the streets. Ahead is an oddly goateed man in his late fifties and with him is a pregnant brunette who can't be much older than twenty or so. Pieman thinks he's seen the girl around the building before, heard talk she does some nasty videos to pay the rent, but the man she's with – the one with the pentagram medallion around his neck – is unknown.

Outside in the streets before dawn. They look westward where the remnants of a commercial flight from Dublin Airport breathe smoke out of fires raging in Hyde Park. Pieman stares with his thick hands twitching at his sides.

Clara Towns, not far away, is frowning at her father, who removes his hands from her shoulders. Uwe Marrs tries to listen to the chatter in the crowds. A few different voices utter the word monsters. Uwe glances around and soon spots the giant Pieman, who scowls at him. His eye's twitchin.

"The fuck you lookin at, ponytail?"

"Nothing." Uwe says, backing away. "Apologies."

So the Satanist priest looks away. Still curious in the crowd. Still frowning and looking around, he here spots someone standing at the back of them all. And this one's particularly out of place.

Dressed in a thick poncho that hangs down almost to his knees. Odd, like it's from Canadian natives. There's a white powdered wig on his head like he's some lord from Westminster. His eyes hidden behind wayfarers that are spotted with red. He's rigid and glaring at the crash-site in the distance and appears as if lost in consideration of it, somehow enraged. When he turns away he finally notices Uwe staring at him and he offers only a curt whistle of awe before he starts to stroll away. The priest isn't sure but it looks like there's something wagging under the whistler's poncho just below his spine.

Uwe is too unnerved.

Judgement Day, says someone in the crowd.

Uwe is again setting his hands on Clara's shoulders, telling her we have to go, honey. We've got to get out of here.

The Pieman overhears and immediately agrees. He's got to get out of London, he thinks, but he's got one thing left to do here before he can go. There's one person he's not leaving behind.

The Satanist priest ushers his daughter back toward her dilapidated building, and he and Clara snake through the crowds that still awe at the smoke, afraid. And Clara, as they reach the door to her building, holds onto her throbbing baby-bump and she whines, hearing trumpets that deafen her, seeing white light that blinds her.

TWENTY.

It's a town on the eastern coast of Scotland and this morning the harbour rests lit by a crescent moon that hangs low over the North Sea. The crane's been worked cold all night to load the freighter and now it's set to sail and they're heading home to let the day-shift take the reins. The crew aboard is preparing for the voyage and most are tucking in for a rest. On the docks still is the ship's captain overseeing the last of the provisions and formalities. Signed the last of the red tape. Bored and sleepy and apparently a bit under the weather, breathing delicate clouds into cold littoral air. He slept since midnight and woke just an hour ago to be here on time, despite the fact he doesn't want to be here at all.

A bushy-faced harbourmaster meets up with the captain on the wetted boards as the captain makes his way toward the rusted gangplank – the last one still fitted to the side of the ship.

"Captain."

"Mr. Fenwick. We right to shove off?"

"Shove away, far as I'm concerned. Get her outta this mess. Kinda, I envy ye." The harbourmaster's taken his brief stroll around the freighter. All's ship-shape, it looks like. And anyway, at this point he just wants to get home and crawl into bed and hide from what's coming. "Klitmøller agae this week?"

The captain coughs briefly, holding his fist to his mouth. The harbourmaster's gazing at the ship, asking how's that trip take you.

"Just under twenty hours, if the skies stay clear."

"Well waywiya. Hope the country's still inna piece when you get back." The captain coughs as he heads up the gangplank. Fenwick narrows his eyes. "Fightin a *cold*, captain?"

"Fightin. Not sure who's winnin."

"Get some rest then. Try and stay outta the damp."

The captain smirks and climbs up the ramp onto his freighter. On deck, he looks over the three lonely crewmen around to see about undocking. Then he heads to the wheelhouse to supervise his helmsman. The ship will depart in the next fifteen minutes.

There's this female about a mile and a half down the coastline. A beautiful monster standing in the dark before dawn.

Coffee-brown straight hair. Thin frame but with powerful arms and childrearing hips. A silk overshirt hangs unbuttoned from her shoulders barely covering moulded breasts. A sundress tied around her waist. Skin pink. Irises a purplish-brown. Her fingernails are without any polish but they're naturally oval and smooth. Clasped within her hand and hanging beside a muscled thigh is a ragged and thick-bladed sword that appears as if used by boors of the Bronze Age. Extending from her backbone and perfect ass is a golden tail like a lioness.

The beautiful monster is staring at the moon above the North Sea that's fading with the coming sunlight and she's waiting. Just passing the time, waiting patient, enjoying the pleasance of that moon.

The beauty's been alone now for almost thirty minutes and she hasn't minded it. And she doesn't even notice when she's joined by someone who appears from out of pure nothingness. Dressed in a poncho that hangs down to his knees. A powdered wig on his head and blood-speckled wayfarers over his eyes. He watches her as she watches the crescent white light in the sky and he whistles to get her attention. And he gets it, but he shares it with the moon.

The beautiful monster tells the whistler I knew it was beautiful.

Nothing's ever as beautiful as you, Lilith.

I know, she says.

The whistler smiles. He asks her if she's been waiting here long.

Not long. I am here... The prince is here... The beautiful monster looks high into the dark clouds that hide the stars. Saying:

We just have to wait for the others. She blinks and her smile fades and she's glancing over at the whistler who's removing his wig, revealing a modest coupling of black horns poking out of the corners of his forehead in front of cropped blonde hair. She attempts to read him though she knows she never can. Eventually stooping to ask: …You are sure about this, Rosier? This is… necessary for the Fourth?

The whistler just looks back at the beauty. Solemn, he doesn't need to speak. And this female – Lilith, her name – just smiles and snaps the lion's tail behind her.

Above them there's an immense stud crossing the moon and blotting it out for only an instant before disappearing back into the clouds. Lilith lifts her head to see him up there, and all she sees is the moon, and she grins like a bride in love.

.

In his quarters, the freighter's captain stands hunched over his desk with his brow and collar soaked with sweat. He's poured a glass of water and he's set it down to retrieve a Tylenol Cold & Flu from its package. He's taken off his coat and draped it over the armrest of the small sofa against the starboard wall. Through the blinds of the porthole at his back are the whitecaps of the North Sea.

It's as he reaches for his water that a shaking *thud* is heard on the deck above his head and he lurches and the glass falls, spilling before it shatters. The captain looks at the ceiling. The lightbulbs in their sockets are quivering. More can be heard, as if cannonballs were bashing the freighter or paratroopers landing from a carrier plane or huge fat albatross, and from the collective force the ship is rocking side to side. There are muffled shouts and hollers heard up there. Hectic running feet. Shouting. He drops the pill in his limp fingers and looks out the window. He can see shadows on the water of things flying with elegance in the light of the rising sun.

There's a whistle then. To get his attention.

Spinning around, finding there's this whistler that's gotten into his quarters somehow. Like he appeared purely from nothingness. And he's smiling, this blonde demon, and setting a pallid hand atop the captain's shoulder in a way that suggests he offers his condolences. After driving an iron stiletto into the captain's eye, the whistler vanishes away like he turns to air.

TWENTY-ONE.

Blackness billows from the crash in Hyde Park behind me.

Police are attempting to keep onlookers at bay. People are cut off from entering. There's talk. This was caused by the invaders in Ireland and Scotland. Terrorists or Russians or gargoyles. This is September Eleventh or Pearl Harbour. The Invasion of Poland. This is impossible. This is Wendy Malstrom at the entrance of Hyde Park, reporting live for BBC News.

Clive Halton stands in a Tesco supermarket and he's watching the television mounted above the check-out counter on which he's set a box of tortellini and a jar of rosé sauce and a head of romaine. He had big plans for tonight when Patricia got home, whenever she finally got home. The cashier too is turned and transfixed on the screen. They listen to Malstrom. They see aerial footage of the wreckage and the burning trees that were cut down by the crashing plane. Neither Clive nor the cashier seem at all aware of the mob that's looting food off the shelves behind them. Clive just tucks his wallet back into his trousers and then reaches for his mobile. He dials for his wife. He holds it to his ear and keeps watching the news as they show different angles of the 737 blaze.

"Hello, Mr. Halton."

"...Yes, evening. S'at Marlene?"

"Evening, Mr. Halton."

"Can I talk to my wife please?"

"I'm sorry, sir, but the prime minister is preoccupied at the moment. I'm sure you've seen the smoke."

"Is she safe? I need to know she's *safe*, Marlene."

"We're just leaving Westminster now. We're *fine*, Mr. Halton." A brief pause, then: "How are you?"

"Oh lovely, thank you. Just out for a stroll." Clive is shoved against the counter as an obese couple ram past him with a cart full of buns and sausage and milk. He nearly drops his phone but he composes himself and leaves his groceries and begins hurrying for the exit. Asking Marlene Jacobs-Moore: "Where should I meet her?"

"She says to proceed to the house. You're to pack up and leave immediately."

"Where are we headed?"

"Undetermined, Mr. Halton. Right now we just need to get the Prime Minister out of the United Kingdom. She hopes you'd be good enough to tag along."

"She always wants so much of me."

"We'll have a chopper sent to pick you up outside the house."

Clive is waving his free hand into the streets and watching the taxi approach and fly right by. Fire-engines are blasting their horns as they speed through the city toward the wreck. Ambulances and cruisers sail along beside them. Pedestrians are chasing buses, fleeing with suitcases or armfuls of pilfered goods. Kids with knapsacks overflowing with clothes. Cars speeding directionless, escaping what's coming. Everyone's on their phones but some of them seem to be having trouble maintaining a signal.

"…Marlene? You still there?"

But there's no voice coming back to him. Clive is looking down at the Samsung and he realizes the call has ended. He lost the connection. He's lost her.

Chrissake.

Home. That's his mission. He's got to get home and he's got to wait for the helicopter and he's got to go meet his wife god knows where. So he's dialing the number for a car service he uses when on dates with the Prime Minister or luncheons with colleagues. But he can't get a signal and here there's a thin hard fist that knocks his face sideways. Clive's collapsing to the ground – more from the surprise than the force. He's grasping his chin and waiting for his senses to return. A couple kids steal his phone and the wallet from his pocket before they take off down the street.

Clive gets up, cursing with a throbbing jaw. Seeing his assailants but blurrily. He's trying to chase after them except he can't keep a straight line. When he trips up, he's staggering in front of the oncoming Honda Accord. He crashes up and over and he lands on the asphalt and everyone around him screams but the driver doesn't stop because there's no time like the present.

People call 999 but the lines are all engaged and it's just *beep beep beep*. They huddle around a mess of a body, and Clive Halton breathes terrible breaths. Listening to them, somebody says that looks like the Prime Minister's husband.

Clive thinks of Patricia before he thinks of nothing.

TWENTY-TWO.

Six hours in this. The Dacia has inched through the burning capital to Saint James Hospital. Alicia led them without thought. Reagan drove in the same manner, keeping slow to find their way in the smoke and navigate pedestrians and the flaming car and the felled streetlight and the collapsing cathedral wall.

In the backseat, Lora and Abigail look around and see people fleeing on foot or in vehicles. Some are armed with blunt objects. Some with hunting rifles or kitchen knives. Police are occasionally spotted, but dead or succumbing. Time and again they spot unnatural black horses with burning citrine eyes. Some are mounted by monsters. Some are outfitted with chains that drag people through the streets by their arms or necks or genitals. Brent has cried for a good while. Mike struggles to breathe, holding a stab-wound with the four fingers he has left.

Hold y'self, Mike. Don't give in yet. Almost there.

The mother holds her son and weeps over her fiancée. Lora prays for them but she can't shut her eyes or fold her hands. Reagan takes a left when she sees the sign for Saint James and Abigail realizes they're at the hospital. She has hope.

Then they notice the parking-lots and the long path toward the emergency-room alcove is packed with others like them. Gored victims stagger through the sea of cars and trucks and ambulances headed for the light of the hospital. Five-hundred yards from the building, the Dacia meets the wall of vehicles blocking the road and Reagan has to stop.

"We'll… have to carry him the rest a'the way."

"S'gotta be half a kilometer to the ER hi."

"And what better choice do we have then?"

Mindless voices. Heads sticking out of car windows to holler.

135

We need a doctor. We need a doctor here. Others hurry on foot. A policeman with a megaphone instructs everyone to remain in their vehicles. The hospital is beyond capacity. Doctors will be coming out to meet patients in their vehicles. Nurses roam the haze and knock on windows and grade the injured by their severity, looking for that medium between non-fatal and untreatable, but there's got to be thousands of cars here. Millions seeking help. Someone's got their door open and an iPod hooked into the auxiliary is playing loud enough so the dying can hear *Take Me to Church*.

Abigail's getting out of the SUV. Alicia demands to know where she's going. The mother says I'm going to find a doctor to save my fiancée and she leaves her son with Lora, who holds the boy close. Reagan unbuckles her seatbelt and throws open the Dacia door. She hops out to join Abigail. She's got Lora's Beretta and she's tucking it into the pocket of her cardigan.

The two women venture into the sea of trapped cars and head for the light of Saint James. Alicia sits in the passenger seat, watching them as she shivers. Wide eyes, and she sees her husband all around her like he's still alive and she's very still.

Mike stirs and Lora gazes over at him. She sees the pain in his face and she worries a little more. The tattooist is settling down, breathing deep. The belt cinched around his severed wrist has helped stopped the blood-loss but his abdomen still throbs and leaks and sings.

Try and talk, Mike. Keep talkin. Don't fall asleep.

Alicia`s forcing her eyes away from the smokelands outside. She`s turning around in her seat and gazing back at them. At her nephew and the old biddy and the guy she never thought was right for her sister. She asks Lora will he make it.

"…I'm not the one to answer that, dear." Lora bounces Brent on her knee twice to try and relax the boy. She reaches out and tries to jostle Mike's arm and the tattooist lifts heavy eyelids. "Say something, Mike. Ye bloody shit carpenter. Talk to your boy here. Come on. Please."

The father hears the old woman. He looks to his son.

Lora says: "Tell him you're gonna be fine, y'bastard."

And Mike's drifting off. Lora continues to joggle his arm at the elbow but it doesn't do much for him. Alicia watches and remains blank. A thought comes to her and she swallows to wet her throat. She asks Lora where she got the gun. Lora just rests back in her seat and continues to jounce the little boy.

"Was my husband's… before he died."

"You kept her?"

"Never used it, but I knew how. I never cared for em though."

"So why didn't ye throw her away?"

"…Because I hate to see things go to waste."

Abigail and Reagan come upon the horde of panicking Irish that are packing into and overflowing out of the ER. Most of them maimed or broken or finished. Holding detached arms or hands. Carrying dead children. Succumbing to injuries and fainting, but held up by the rest of an unmovable herd. No space enough to topple over and die. Loved ones scream out help but no one comes to them. The girls can't get through the horde and more are arriving behind them, blocking their escape.

A gunshot. Everyone ducks and screams. There's a burly older fellow with a revolver aimed at the sky and adding another little wisp of smoke to the suffocating city. Holding the man's hand and coming up behind him is a little girl. There's a bloody stripe of red running from her armpit to her naval. Now she's losing colour, dead-faced, and her father is telling everyone to move aside. Get outta the way. He points the gun at the crowd and questions who's first and people retreat. Reagan and Abby step back to clear the way. The gunman pulls his daughter along.

Above them there's a rush of wind like a plane flying too close to the ground. Shadows appear in the smoke to the north. People begin to flee. They know what's coming because they've seen it.

They've suffered. In the sky are biblical obscenities that drop corpses that slam onto people in the crowd. Some swoop down and land atop the hospital. One of them bashes through a fourth-floor window. A voulge spins as it plummets and then sticks into the gunman as he's bolting for the entrance. He falls over and his daughter tumbles. She's trampled as people rush for the gun.

Reagan grabs Abigail by her sleeve.

"We canny stay here!"

"We need a doctor for *Mike!*"

"We ain't gonna *get one*, Abigail! *We gotta bolt!*"

Abigail doesn't want to leave but she sees Reagan is off. And she's alone with the wild and scared and she knows there's nothing ahead except ruin. They'll find no rescue here. So she's hurrying and trying to catch up with Reagan and they hustle through the crowd and the gathering smoke. They barely see the Dacia in the distance and they realize a van has smashed into the back fender. It looks like Alicia is getting out and Abby can see she's rushing over to claim the driver's seat. She thinks she can hear her baby crying so she's teary and finding the strength to push everyone out of her way.

Reagan stops. She's gazing into the front window of a BMW that's trapped in the sea. The man in the front seat has succumbed. In the backseat, she notices the plastic bags he packed. A loaf of bread and bananas are sticking out the top, so she's opening the door and she's gathering up the groceries before she hears Abby.

There's a monster that's landed atop the hood of the Dacia and it's shocked the young hairdresser into stumbling and falling backwards against the taillight of a Jag. The little fuck is ravening, snapping a frothing mouth. It has no arms but two feathered wings flap crooked from disjointed sockets in its shoulder-blades. Reagan drops the goodie-bags. Retrieving the Beretta from her cardigan as she rushes in, but she can't aim well enough. She's too far and the bastard is moving too quick. It leaps forwards in an instant.

Claws hook onto Abby's chest. Its teeth snap as its wings spasm like separate-minded lunatic entities. Alicia lays on the horn to try and scare the beast. Lora hyperventilates in the backseat, clutching Brent tightly but the kid just whines high-pitched and disturbing.

Reagan arrives at last. Unknowing what to do, unthinking, she beats the handle of the gun into the beast's skull. It screeches and lets go of Abigail and topples to the ground. Its hectic wings lift it up but it falls again and it spins over and snarls and shrieks at Reagan, who points the handgun. In this. With all this going on around her. So tense as she is, it's effortless to squeeze the trigger and she barely realizes she's put a round into its neck. And here, shaking, watching the monster fall down, she thinks she's strong. She hasn't been strong in years.

Abigail falls to her knees. Blood drips from teethmarks. Reagan seizes her under the arm with her hand still wielding the hot pistol that adds smoke to the smokelands. She helps Abby up and leads her to the SUV. She puts her in the front seat next to her sister and then climbs into the back just as Alicia shoves the gearshift in reverse and hammers down the pedal, bashing into the van behind them.

The vehicles here take part in a round of bumpercars as they flee from swarming monsters. A Sprinter slams into the passenger side of the Dacia. Reagan and Abigail both yelp as the doors crumple inward. Abby's window is cracked. The sideview mirror hangs by wires when the van pulls away. Alicia is finding a path of cars finally moving in a reasonable line through the hospital gates onto James Street. Scraping and scratching as she cuts through the corner of a hedge, shaving leaves and branches off before retaking the narrow street between townhouses of brown brick.

They head south but are caught in traffic. More people flocking to the highways or ferries. A lot of them struggling with mobiles. Reception is spotty. Texts won't send. Calls last no longer than twenty seconds before dropping. The lights of streetlamps and homes and buildings shudder as their power-supply is met with some crisis they can barely imagine.

The motorways are packed. The on-ramps are stopped dead with cars. Fires burn and creatures of abomination appear and they can't wait. Can't stay still. People are ripped out of windshields when they're sitting still. Alicia keeps moving. Brent keeps crying. Abigail clutches a bloody face and watches as the world passes by through the smoke. There's someone ahead, she sees. A male. Standing in the middle of the road. It's pale and it's turning to face them. Ally floors the pedal and rams through the monster and Abigail watches through her fingers. Alicia hits the wipers to clean the running mess from the windshield, which smears.

Mike's long been taken by shock and again he's fallen asleep. Lora reaches over and checks his pulse every so often. They don't know how much longer he'll hold on. When they pass another hospital they look in and see another packed parking-lot and the building is on fire. Burning bodies lie atop the roofs of cars. Shadows fly overhead through the raining ashes.

They head north. It's the only direction of traffic that's moving at a safe click. Once out of Dublin they'll head east and try to escape to Scotland. Upon finally reaching the borders of the city they gaze out the windows of the SUV at the sound of the earth rumbling. Out there in the smoke is a field left empty for the winter. There are tanks appearing. Combat vehicles. CT tactical forces with the Army Ranger Wing and they're trekking onwards into Dublin ready to take on the enemy.

All the while, Reagan Brodie drives. And mostly she keeps her eyes on the road, but now and then she looks in the rearview. She looks back at the wounded father and, in particular, she stares at the mother holding onto her son.

TWENTY-THREE.

The shocks of a cherry-red Fiesta are relieved and the frame rises a solid few inches when the gigantic Simon the Pieman exits the passenger's side. Curtis Merchant kills the engine and gets out and looks up at the rundown building at which they've arrived. A place they come to often enough – once every couple months at least. Curtis lights the Carlton he had tucked behind his ear and he leans back against the fender of his car. He and the hulking giant stare up at the window on the south corner of the fifth floor. Lights are on up there. Shadows on the ceiling. The Pieman asks if Bates answered yet and Curtis tells him yeah. Says to text him when we're here.

"And didja?"

"Yeah."

"...*So?*"

"So it's only been ten seconds, Pie. Give us a minute."

Behind them in the streets are cars speeding off in the early dawn. Sirens fading in and out. People running. Curtis glances back at the hubbub and comments: "This is pretty fucked, mate."

"Yeah."

"Should we like... bail? Get ahead of the rush?"

"Can't do a fuckin thing till I see Bates."

"You need juice that bad, bruv?"

"I'm not here for the roids, y'twat."

Curtis blinks, confused, and Pieman's still glaring up at the window, in which he sees a face appear that's big and round and ugly. Smug. And the giant hears the text finally ring and he tells Curtis: I'm here to get my sister.

Above, it looks like Gareth Bates is happy to see them.

The Pieman is immediately in motion and advancing on the door to the crappy building. Curtis is exhaling his drag and jogging to catch up, telling Pieman he'll buzz Bates but the Pieman isn't listening. Isn't waiting. He's grabbing the knob to turn it. Curtis reminds him it's locked. It's deadbolted, bruv. Yet the furious giant breaks the unbreakable and yanks open the metal door. Curtis follows him inside and nods, impressed, and he presses the call button for the elevator. But the Pieman's not waiting for a lift. He's suddenly halfway up the stairwell. Curtis just sighs and keeps up.

The fifth floor.

A fifteen-pound fist is banging on the door of Bates' flat. There's music playing inside. Sounds like Kanye West and *Power* and it doesn't need to be so loud, but probably no one complains in a shithole like this. Curtis stands behind Pieman and finishes the Carlton and openly ashes it onto the carpet, thinking to himself.

"...What'd you mean – 'came for your sister'? Charlene ain't seein *Bates* again, is she?" It's not an easy topic to broach, given history. Curtis rubs his nose before asking like a timid little boy: "...Is she?"

"...Mum told me a week ago."

"Oh. Then... Maybe we should bounce, Pie."

"So bounce then, Curtis. I can take the prick, just me."

Again Pieman pounds on the door. They hear the barking of a dog in the apartment. Scratching little paws on the other side of the door. Eventually there're footsteps and then a chain-lock is unfastened and a bolt is released. A five-month old Rottweiler pup is excitedly trying to wedge itself past a leg that keeps it at bay. The door opens but only a hair.

"S'at *you*, Pieman?"

"Let me the fuck in, Gareth."

"You came fast yo." Bates is shoving the dog back with his foot and he's grinning and snickering like he's stoned, opening the door wide enough to let in his visitors. His customers. Bates isn't as tall as the Pieman but he's got just about every pound of mass obtained through a strict regimen of lifts and dosing. Vein-embossed arms, neck. Hair tightly braided in vertical rows that pinstripe his skull. He welcomes his customers into his flat, asserting with apology: "Check it though, the lot's gone. M'*out*."

"Fuck does that mean?"

"Means the juice I promised is now unavailable." Bates waves his beefy hand, ushering them into his living-room while his Rotty sniffs their heels. Curtis takes a seat in the dusty IKEA loveseat and Pieman leans against a warped windowsill. Bates relaxes nicely into a Papasan directly in front of which are the TV remote and an opened bag of pretzels and a few orange pill-bottles and a bong and a Nokia phone. Saying: "Spoken for, bruv. M'out."

"The whole lot?"

"*Straight* yo. Cleaned."

"Who wants the lot?"

So Bates eyes the Pieman. Doesn't answer his question and it isn't minded all that much. Curtis is holding up his butt and asking where to crush it, so Bates hands him an empty can of Pepsi he finds behind his chair. Then he claps thick and heavy hands.

Almost, he seems excited.

"*So...* whaddaya think of this *plane crash?*"

Curtis doesn't answer. Pieman frowns.

"...Just a crash. Mad, but... not unheard of."

"Could be terrorists."

"Figure they's already dead then."

"Could be... demons."

"...I knew you was fuckin *on* something."

"What?" Bates blinks. "Haven't you seen the vids?" He nods at the window, through which another set of sirens can be heard. Rioting in the streets. "Why ye think everyone's gone *mental?*"

"T'aint fuckin demons."

"Sure about that, Curtis?" The dealer looks to the giant. "What about *you*, Pieman?"

"What about me?"

"Do *you* believe in Hell?"

"...I wanna know where the fuck my sister's at."

"Charlene?" Bates sucks his teeth. For a moment he considers denying everything, deny deny deny, but he soon rules against it unbothered. Still smirking a little. Stoned. "…Who told ye?"

"Where's she at?"

"It was yo *mum*, wadunnit? They gab, those two. Never leave a stone-"

"Where's she at?"

"…She's sleepin, Pie."

"…You fuckin *prick*."

"Hold up yo-"

"Got her wigged out again, *doncha*? On mud, you ruthless *prick*!"

"*Eh, fuck you!*" Bates has gotten to his feet. Incensed. Skin clenched tightly around his face and neck. "You can't come in here throwin that shit on me, y'cocksuck! I ain't put her on any cotton and I ain't letting her near any a'that yo! It's not like it was – I crawled back to her for one fuckin purpose!" Walking over to the front-hall closet near the apartment door, Bates turns back to look at them as he twists the little knob in an oversized hand. Telling the Pieman: "I love her."

Bates has to bend over to reach into the closet and lift the barbell off the floor. It looks like he sawed it off at three feet. Threaded five fifteen-pound cast-iron weights onto one end and screwed in stoppers for reinforcement. Duct-taped up a padded handle at the other end, onto which he grasps with a mighty paw.

"No one's gonna come near her. No one's gonna touch her. *Straight* yo." And here Bates is smiling again, looking to his visitors. Customers. Friends. Holding the weapon tight and easing them: "…So relax."

The Pieman is unmoved but Curtis frowns at the weapon, asking Bates: When the fuck'd you make that, Gareth?

"Few months ago." Bates answers. "Heard about Ireland and monsters so I gotter outta the storage-locker." Rubbing his nose, blinking too often, saying: "And eh, check – my cousin Richie? Works the chop-shop in Liverpool? He's the one got me the juice guy. S'got *mad* connections, bruv."

"What about him?"

"Said if I drive up…" Bates tilts his head, raises his eyebrows, seeming like an older cousin revealing the best porn sites he knows. "…if I wanted a real weapon, he'll straight supply." He looks to Pieman, then to Curtis, then to Pieman. "You wanna come wiffus?"

"Us…?"

"Charlene's goin where I go. How else is I gonna protect her?"

Pieman stiffens.

"…She's not goin with you, Gareth."

"You gonna try and stop her, big guy?"

"All it takes is stoppin you."

"So…" Bates clutches his weapon. Curls his upper lip. Holds out his arms to invite the giant, smirking: "Let's give that a go, mate."

Pieman's about to, but the door to the only bedroom opens and swiftly ends the fight. There's she – Charlene Pupsy, standing in one of Bates' hoodies and looking like she's found gum stuck to her favourite jeans. She stops in the doorway and leans against the scuffed white frame. About two feet shorter than her brother, quarter of his weight, rounded cheeks in a heart-shaped face and bushy brown curls. But she has his eyes, their dad's eyes.

"…Heya."

"…Hey yourself, stringbean."

"Why're you here?"

"Why're you?" Pieman steps away from the window, putting himself between her and Gareth Bates. Unable to stop himself from spitting: "You need him? Need your pills again, princess?"

"And you, Simon? Muscles not shootin out your back enough? Need to get back in the underground, beat men fuckin purple?" Charlene's marching sleepily or dejectedly and passing her gigantic brother, and she cozies up to Bates who takes her with a daunting arm. He holds his crippler in his other paw and lets it hang down by his leg. Charlene is looking back at Pieman. "Stop obsessing over me. I'm fine."

"Don't look fine. Look zonked, bitch."

"I was asleep, thickit. It's eight o'clock in the mornin."

"Why you here then?"

"Because you don't get a say in the matter, Simon."

Charlene has this way with Simon. She's the only one who can shut him up when he's got something to get out. He's silenced now, and in Bates' obscenely muscled arm Charlene stares down her big brother and makes the giant seem about six feet shorter. Leaving her boyfriend, Charlene saunters into the kitchen that's separated from the living-room by a shift from frieze to linoleum. Pieman has to follow her and Bates just shakes his head. Charlene heads for the T45 on the countertop and retrieves a Maxwell disc of coffee from the box beside the machine.

"...You wanna know why I came back here?"

"Ain't the time, Leen. Shit's fucked up."

"Yeah, seems like it." Charlene's set a God Save the Fucking Queen mug under the T45's spout and she's gazing over at her boyfriend, who's ambling away and headed for the bedroom. She sees his homespun bashing-stick and asks him: "What'd you got your crippler out for, babe?"

"Monsters, love."

"...Good thing then."

Bates has disappeared into his bedroom, and in the apartment upstairs it sounds as if a mirror just smashed. Curtis glances at the ceiling and frowns. Charlene and her big big brother both study the other. Sticking to the task at hand, which neither of them really wants to approach.

"You know what's funny, Simon?"

"...I'm not gonna guess, Leen. Just say what's fuckin funny."

"What's funny is I'm fully aware I'm going to destroy myself."

"...That's not that funny. I don't get the joke."

"No matter what I want and no matter what I do... I really

can't live life without buggering it." The girl with the heart-shaped face just stares at the T45 steaming before pissing coffee into her mug. She listens as Bates slams shut the antique chest in the adjacent bedroom. She looks to her brother. "I never toldja that, I guess."

"Didn't really have to."

"You think I need someone to hold my hand, Simon? Protect me from myself?"

"...Right now, yeah. I think you need protection."

"She gonna *have* protection, yo." Brother and sister turn and look to Gareth Bates who's exiting the bedroom and still clutching the crippler. In his other hand is something in a loosened fist but no one can tell what it is. Bates is still smirking. Stoned. "We're headin up to Liverpool right now."

Charlene frowns a little lax.

"What're we goin to Liverpool for, baby?"

"*Chrome*, love. My cousin Richie's gonna hook us up."

"Brilliant. Just what our relationship's been lacking." Charlene's added hazelnut creamer to her coffee and she's stirring it as Bates looms, supposing: "You just want an excuse to ride that stupid bike."

"S'not a *bike*, woman. It's a Ducati. Learn yourself." Bates stops in front of the Pieman and he holds out his arm and opens his hand saying *here*. In his thick palm are three glass amps with indecipherable Arabic labels. Medical-looking cautions, directions. Both the Pieman and Charlene recognize them immediately as anabolic-androgenic steroids. A CC each. "Check it, mate. S'good fuckin oil yo. I'm swole."

"Thought you said the lot was sold?"

"*Spoken for*, I said. But there's plenty there."

"How much?"

"Free of charge yo." Bates plants his hand across the Pieman's wide concrete back, saying: "We're fuckin bruvs now, geddit? I'm gonna look after yo sis, Pie, and I'm gonna look after ye." And

Bates asks: "You comin with us or not?"

"The Ducati sits four, yeah?"

"…I don't think it sits two really."

"Right. Fuck ye then."

Pieman takes the amps and turns away, glancing one last time at his sister. And, because he has to, he's looking over at the slimy jacked Gareth Bates. And he's laying down the order.

"You can't take her, Gareth…" Charlene averts her eyes so Pieman does too. Promising: "…Try it, and you'll know why they don't let me in the ring no more."

"Fighting won't make a difference, thickit." Charlene holds her boyfriend. Holds her coffee. And she banishes her brother. "You can't protect me."

The Pieman stiffens.

"…No one ever could."

"Dad never could. Mum never could. You never could. Figures I'm beyond saving." Pieman seizes, his fingernails clenching into his palm, and once more looks upon the girl with the heart-shaped face who's telling him: "I'm going with Gareth, Simon. You isn't fit to save anyone… So why donchu try saving yourself?"

TWENTY-FOUR.

Father and daughter stood in the street with everyone in London's east end and they stared at the wreckage in Hyde Park left by the 737. Returning in a rush to the flat she shares with the degenerate Kodi Becker, suffering for nausea and the inexplicable sounds of trumpets and a throbbing foetus, Clara Towns headed straight for the bathroom and locked herself in. Morning sickness, her father assumed, standing outside the door and listening to her retch.

Uwe Marrs worries for his little girl, telling her through the smoke-stained door: I'm here for you.

Seventeen years too late, is the queasy reply he receives.

So Uwe is headed into the kitchen, a rejected father listening to unbridled anarchy in the city outside. Knowing what has to be done. Knowing they have to leave. So now in a panic or dream he's retrieved the mobile from the pocket of his trousers. Dialling information, waiting to speak to the kindly voice, a recording soon comes to his ear and asks if he would like business or residential.

"Business."

For what name?

"Airport. London Heathrow Airport."

One moment please.

Uwe glances over at the closed bathroom door. He can hear his daughter spew sick for a pregnancy she doesn't like to talk about. Uwe's swallowing lumps in his throat that keep recurring. Tapping his foot against the floor. In his head replays the shockwave he felt course through the walls and floors of the building and the sight of that 737 on fire in the distant park and the poncho-clad whistler who vanished into nothingness.

None of it could ever be called real.

"*Yes*, good morning. I'd like to book a flight for three please." Fishing his wallet from the back pocket of his jeans. "Uh, *anywhere* in Europe. If there's a flight to Vienna leaving in the next three

149

hours then *sold*. Yes it's fine if they're not together." Thumbing his credit-card out of the faux-leather. "Marrs. Uwe Marrs." Spelling it out. He always has to spell it out. "My credit-card number?" He's reading it off for them and while doing so he hears the faucet of the sink come on in the washroom. "Eleven forty-five? Perfectly fine. *Thank you.*"

After Uwe ends the call he sets the phone down on the table next to last night's McDonald's ketchup packets. He's pushing back his chair and he's getting up on his feet just as his daughter groggily exits the washroom, clutching the baby-bump beneath her loose sweater.

"Who's that you rung?"

"Airport." Uwe joins Clara in the living-room and he's heading for his suitcase and carryon and the few belongings he unpacked here, telling his little girl: "I've booked us on a flight to Austria."

"We're leaving?"

"You expect to stay?"

"I have a *job*, man." Clara's stiffened her already knitted brow. "I got a shift at the coffee-bar in two hours. I can't lose that job."

"Clara honey, no one's buyin a goddamn macchiato *today*."

Another rolling siren passes by their building, heard through the windows, and after curt reflection Clara's inclined to concede. Her phone *whistles* as another text comes in and she checks it. It's not who she hoped it'd be, and it makes her wonder. Makes her scared.

"…What about Kodi?"

"The one who's never around to look after you?"

"I can't leave Kodi, man."

"Why? Is he the *father*?"

"I already told you *no*."

"I know. I just love hearing it. Nonetheless, I got the skinny shitstain a seat." Uwe waves frantic, ushering his daughter, saying: "We gotta be at the airport for quarter to twelve if we're to make this flight, so grab anything you want to bring but do it *fast*. You said you went to Paris last summer – where's your passport?"

"I have it."

"Get it. Get your boyfriend's while you're at it. Pack up for him." He's looking at his daughter. He's glancing around the flat for a second. Asking: "Clara... where *is* your boyfriend?"

Clara hangs her head, looking ill and desolate.

Uwe asks her.

"Honey...? Where's Kodi?"

Holding her bump. Five months down. Four months to go.

Admitting: "...I have no friggin idea, man."

West End Central, where Kodi Becker is locked in a drunk tank in the basement. Courthouses won't be open until Monday morning and until his arraignment the skinny werewolf thief will sit tight. He hasn't slept and this morning, lying on the stiff cot, he came to notice mayhem. The station has been a live wire, cops and felons alike. When officers pass it's with speedy strides. Brawlers pound on the doors of their cells and shout at the guards. For the most part they're ignored, but Kodi kind of wishes someone could give them an answer. Just a hint. Do us all a favour.

Throughout it all the skinny chav's been zombified, his split lip dried but throbbing. Right now his bruiser cellmate is sleeping but Kodi's learned that can change pretty quickly. Immediately upon waking, the bruiser's usually irritable. He insults and threatens. Ten to twenty minutes afterwards he has to shit. After that he hums for a while and beats his foot into the wall before passing out. It's all become just a question of when something wakes him. So as the outer door opens and shuts and a man comes walking down the hall, Kodi begs he won't be coming to talk.

"...Are you Kodi Becker?"

"*Lower*, mate. I'm two feet in fronna you."

"I'm... *sorry*." The man is young but not a kid. He's got a conservative haircut and Perry Ellis eyeglass frames and a decent suit, though Kodi can't tell. "Uh, Mr. Becker, I'm from Maclay &

Silkins. The, uh, *firm* you hired to represent you... Are you *alright*, Mr. Becker?"

"Just... very *tired*, mate."

"*Ah*, right. Can't imagine. The whole world's been crazy this mornin though, hasn't it?" The man pushes his glasses up his nose, anxiously fidgety. "You know a plane just crashed in Hyde Park?"

"...I heard something loud."

"That's probably what it was. Just a stone's throw away right? Could probably see it if you had windows." The young man, biting one side of his lower lip, eventually goes on: "Reason I'm here: it's about your arraignment, uh... regarding the pharmacy robbery."

"Yeah, *that*." Reason yields in Kodi's eyes. Frowning a freckled forehead and glancing back at the bigun in bed, at shadows on the wall, he whispers: "So when you go in, you tell em they got the *wrong fuckin guy*. You tell em that. You go in and you tell em it was this brown fuck, *Amin Nokhari*, who-"

Watch your lip, sugar

"...What'd you say?"

"I'm sorry?"

"What'd you say to me?"

"I didn't say anything, Mr. Becker."

"...Oh."

"And *actually*, Mr. Becker, in regards to your... uh, innocence... I'm not a solicitor. I'm a paralegal. I work for Don Maclay – I'm here on his behalf." The well-groomed young man is apologetic or at least holds that air. He's clearing his throat, rubbing the back of his neck, explaining: "I'm uh, I'm sorry to be the bearer of bad news but unfortunately Mr. Maclay will be unavailable to act as your attorney tomorrow."

"...You wanna repeat that, mate? *Quietly*."

"We have to drop you as a client."

Kodi takes a step forward so his nose pokes through the bars.

"...*Why's that?*"

"Well, see, the thing of it is: Mr. Maclay is... *leaving*. In light of the invading forces and now… this *plane-crash*, I think he, uh… Well, needless to say, we thank you for choosing us."

"…I found your business card next to the phone here."

"Right. And we thank you for calling, but uh… Unfortunately we will be unable to represent you in the coming indictment. So, you know, with that said… Best of luck, Mr. Becker."

Inside his little cell, Kodi listens, cogitates and understands, feeling the heat that singes his face from beneath his cheeks. Feels the anger rising in his chest, which fills him until it meets a ceiling that surges upon hearing the portending snore that bores out the throat of the bruiser. Kodi keeps his jaw clenched until he finally whispers Imma kill you, mate.

"I should be going."

"Imma *find you* when I'm outta here and Imma kill your *stupid fuckin face.*"

"Get some sleep, Mr. Becker."

So the well-groomed man is leaving. Kodi wants to bellow but he's soundless, clutching the bars and listening to the snoring thug on the cot behind him. He watches the paralegal leave through the outer door and he's powerless to kick and scream, hiding out in a lion's pit and there's no escaping what happens when the beast wakes up. He needs sleep but in order to do so he's got to let his guard down, so he fights his eyelids when they start to fail him.

Kodi's turned around now. He watches his cellmate and listens to him fart between snores. His eyelids droop and he snaps them open again, keeping his watchful gaze on the bastard. He's heard a ringing in his ears fade on and off again like a faulty set of earbuds implanted in his brain. Since about an hour ago – since the crash was heard and felt – the lights in here have been screwy and they falter every so often. Plane must have nicked some powerlines or something. Kodi isn't bothered when it suddenly starts to flicker again. The young degenerate just gawks with weary peepers at the shadows that appear and are lost on the wall. Their origin isn't clear, but at least they aren't moving.

It frightens him when the shadows are moving.

Tiredness is getting to the skinny chav. Kodi wants sleep so badly and his body concurs as a yawn pries open his mouth. And in doing so he cracks open the fresh scab cutting his lower lip.

Rude

Kodi spins. Electrified eyes search his cell. Someone spoke. Absolutely certain, someone just spoke. Someone sounding like a woman accented by the American south. But there's nobody here except the bruiser, who stirs in his sleep. Then, of course, there's the shadow on the wall.

Rude, what he done

Kodi stares at the brute, who doesn't wake. Then he glances to the shadow. A second one is slides across the ceiling, crossing over any surface and reforming all the while. Shapeless, for the most part but only for the most part.

You gotta fight your battles, sugar

"Who the hell's talking?"

But the woman's voice doesn't answer. There's a man's now.

Gonna be a boy your whole life

"…Who the fuck's there?"

The two roaming blots converge near the northeast corner, melding into one another before slipping away. Shapeless for the most part. Occasionally they look like silhouettes.

Gonna be a boy or a man, son

The degenerate shuts his eyes. He needs sleep. He regrets the pharmacy. He thinks of Clara. He needs to get some sleep because he's going insane. So he thinks of Clara.

You listen to daddy now, sugar

Shadows move along the wall. They speak to him.

So Kodi is afraid.

Watch your back or you're dead, son.

TWENTY-FIVE.

Some students were out for a round of football on the western end of Hyde Park when the 737 came down. Boys from King's College were just dropping the ball onto the grass for a match before sunup when the park was still serene and spectral and stirring. Some saw the plane approaching out of the morning clouds and fled before turning and seeing the disaster. Feeling the earth shake, wounded. They stood staring and occasionally approaching with caution for a good forty minutes before police began evacuating the area, ushering them into the streets.

The crowd of onlookers grows, and beyond them is the mad horde of panicking Londoners like squirrels in a lightning storm. Glancing around, the goalie is fascinated with the elms above him. Some leaves already have fallen but there'r thick bunches of goldenrod still lurking on shaking branches. He can't be sure, but it looks like someone might've thrown a coat or something into it. Or it's a big bird. Some sort of snowy hawk lost in the leaves. The bird or maybe the wind is causing the tree to move and sacrifice more dead golden spades to the ground and onto a jogger who's watching, listening to her iPod through earbuds. Only a few people notice when the white thing lunges down and scoops up the jogger, instantly returning back into the elm. They gasp and scream out. More people are turning to investigate. Seeing for themselves. The goalie stammers to the player beside him.

"M-*mate*...?" His friend's too preoccupied with his phone to respond. So the goalie tries again: "*Mate?* Jesus *fuck. Look!*"

The player finally looks and there's a lot more yellow leaves falling onto the grass. He tilts his head to survey the branches. The jogger's up there, obscured by gold. Much of her midsection and lower-body are hidden in the folds of something pale and bloated and seizing. People are screaming. Police-officers are unholstering their weapons and charging forwards through the crowd. They aim and shout: Drop her. It doesn't drop her. The jogger is here going limp and showering red onto the goldenrod. It rains from the tree when her torso disconnects from her pelvis and crashes through branches on its way to the ground. Dying eyes look to the crowd and lips try to speak to them. Most people can't look at her because they have to look at the thing in the tree.

Shuddering flaps open to reveal a sharply-cut face with a set of eyeteeth like a jungle cat, spattered with gore. It's bounding from the elm, thin with a lean upper body. It has no arms but pasty wings of mammalian flesh which it spreads as it takes to the sky above the park. Officers fire at it and a couple bullets cut its wings. They'd put more rounds in it but the freak sails fast, evasive, and it's lost in the smoke of the downed 737.

Off it flies into London.

Every station. Every channel. Coverage of the insanity is spreading across Ireland and the United Kingdom. It's every network and it's around the clock and everything else is running reruns of trite on a loop or they've gone off the air. Clips uploaded to YouTube and Reddit are showcased and tell of brutal aftermaths of places that were safe and unsuspecting until so recently. Personal finds of bodies and sightings of figures and voices coming from within walls of smoke. London is itself featured, showing the madness that's stuck once the population started hearing the word *Judgement* enough times. Roads are jammed with traffic. Mutinous hordes overwhelm police and storm through shops, looting everything. Massive turnouts in churches. Families flee with their valuables and are mugged. On BBC News, Lloyd Patricks is reading an excerpt from the King James Bible.

But the cowardly, the unbelieving, the vile, the murderers, the sexually immoral, those who practise magic arts, the idolators and all liars – their place will be in the fiery lake of burning sulfur. …Just how much of this is prophetic is still yet to be seen…

Turning back to word from parliament, it looks as though our government is deserting us. Only moments ago, an EH101 Merlin landed on the grounds of Westminster in front of the Burghers of Calais monument. Air-force officers jumped from the helicopter with readied rifles. Secret-servicemen cleared a route through the crowd of journalists for Prime Minister Patricia Halton to escape, surrounded by her security team as well as Marlene Jacobs-Moore and Defense Secretary William Kagan and Deputy Prime Minister Stephen Fowley. The passengers were loaded and the soldiers waved to the pilot and the Merlin thrust itself off the ground and rose into the air. You can see a couple kilometers behind the helicopter is the wreckage in Hyde Park, which continues to cloud the sky with fires that won't die down despite the firefighters on scene.

Of course, Prime Minister Halton is not the only one looking to flee Britain. Eurostar is booked solid and the stand-by lists climb by the second. Airports and ferries have crowds of people lining up outside the gates. Cars with virtually nowhere to go are honking irate symphonies down endless stretches of motorway. Those of us who remain, please take caution. Stay in your homes and lock your doors. Keep families close. If you *must* go out, then authorities urge that you don't go alone and that you exercise extreme care.

We're suffering an invasion that's unlike any we've ever known. Estimates right now put their numbers in the tens of thousands. If... what we have seen in these pictures and videos... if what witnesses are saying is true then what we are up against is... *mythological.* Where they're coming from, we have no idea.

This is BBC News remaining live. Stay with us.

TWENTY-SIX.

Alicia drove hours before she was done and at least it stalled her mind. Her final stretch endured heavy eyelids but also unwelcomed dreams – a wife's remembrances, six years' worth. Six years with her husband Fred. The thoughts are a trickle at first but they're soon a flood. Ally can't stay focused on the road. All too often her foot dawdles as it switches from gas to brake. At least twice she's narrowly avoided a fender-bender. When the widowed barmaid realized she was going to vomit she woke Reagan. They pulled over to the side of the road while cars passed. Surrounded by blackening grass and a towering range of soot like a tidal wave.

The morning sun comes through the smokeclouds but barely. The dawn's unforgiving grey offers no hopeful path except this procession down an unending road. Ally's choked out her stomach contents and Reagan has gotten behind the wheel and they've set off again while the barmaid promptly falls asleep. Mike stirs and groans in delirium and Abigail, with drying scabs across her face and neck, is asking Reagan where are we.

"Still the E01. Your sign back there said Drogheda. Somewhere north of her, I figure." Rubbing her eye, then thinking to assure them: "Haven't seen... Haven't seen them *beasts* in a while. Maybe we're outta the wood then."

"Any hospitals?"

"Haven't seen one. What's your mobile tellin ye?"

"I meant... I meant to charge it at Ally's, I just..." Abigail looks at Mike. Crying. "He's... gonna die. Godsake, he's gonna die."

The others listen. Reagan tells her no he isn't gonna die.

Ahead of them is the bumper of a Chevy Tahoe. Behind them is the grill of a BMW 6-Series and a thousand other Irish trying to find sanctuary among the smokelands. But they're moving too slowly and Reagan fears the reason why and Abigail just wants to find her husband some chance to live. When they approach an off-ramp Abby reads the sign. Ferris Village. Population 8,450. She tells Reagan let's take it. Beside her, the sore aged Lora Malik keeps awake and, since she has no better suggestion, she doesn't object when Reagan takes the exit and finds their way onto backroads into a ghostly hamlet. Somewhere here they'll find hope.

Brent has finally cried himself to sleep. His head rests against the incomplete arm of his father and he dozes, dreaming of other worlds. Places he used to know. This new world inside a Dacia SUV in the middle of nowhere is far from home.

The tot whines ignorant and unsettled as his mother tightens her arms around him, close enough to feel his hurried heart. She gazes out the window to see the first building they come across – an old house apparently renovated to be used as a notary office. The front door is wide open but the lights are off and it doesn't look like anyone's home. There are deep gouges clawed into the siding. Reagan presses on with Lora and Abby gawping and spying for trouble like grazing gazelle.

The further they move into Ferris the more it becomes clear the town was not spared by the invaders. There's smoke but maybe it's lessened. It rises from smoldering embers still glowing in buildings that managed to survive the onslaught. It lurks about the ground like mist after a rainstorm and makes everything reek of dry cinder. There's a felled streetlamp smashed through the second-floor window of a townhouse. There's a sofa in the middle of the street and bleeds white stuffing. There's a small beagle wandering across lawns and sidewalks with its leash dragging behind it.

No people.

Passing the residential area they come upon this retail district. There's a corner-shop with a shattered front window. There are police cruisers left abandoned and some have bullet-holes poked in the doors and fenders and there's a Dodge Caravan that's burning from under its hood. There's a fire-engine that's toppled over on its side. Two firemen on the pavement nearby. One of them has got a cavern cut through his chest.

"…Where the feck's town then? Not one man in sight."

Reagan peers and supposes: "They ran. Or they're hiding."

"Think there're any a'those… *things?*"

"…Maybe they moved on, Abby."

"We ain't that *lucky*… Probably they're right on our arses."

"I should chop a ripe oniony one then." Lora smirks. "Lettim keel, the putrid snots. Never known *my* ancient stank, have they?"

Abigail would laugh but that's right out. There'll be no laughing for a long long time. Out there, she sees, it's all one nightmarish dreamscape and she can't reboot her mind – can't remember what real life was like before true survival.

Old Lora thinks the same, and the smirk she wore fades quickly. The blood and the bodies and smoke don't disturb her like they did at first. She's still afraid but not of dying. She looks at the young family beside her. The young widow in the passenger seat up front. And Reagan behind the wheel, bereaved but there's still time for her in this world. Lora's afraid for them.

Abby holds Mike, cold and colourless. He hasn't got much left in him, she knows. With that severed wrist. The knife-would in his gut. The love of her life will be dead soon, she knows.

We have to do *something*, she pleads to them.

It's Lora who points out a Lloyd's Pharmacy that's barely seen through the smoke. Saying it'll serve. Saying I can help your man, I think. Saying I used to be assistant to a veterinarian.

No one has the mind to doubt her. They have faith.

Reagan speeds into the parking-lot. The occupants lurch slightly and Alicia's waking and looking around. As the Dacia pulls into a spot out front they all gaze through the windshield at the deserted Lloyd's and deem it good enough. They have faith.

The windows and doors are intact. That's a good start. The hardware shop beside it, however, has a demolished front window. Glass and a box of woodscrews strewn about the sidewalk outside.

Ominous, they think, but this is the best they've got.

Reagan puts the vehicle in park but keeps the engine running.

Abigail breathes deep, finding the courage for Mike's sake.

I'll go first. To… check her.

Reagan tells her she'll come too. She claims Lora's handgun and she and Abby get out of the SUV and listen to the engine and the quiet beyond it. Lora holds the boy. Ally remembers Fred. Reagan and Abigail scrutinize the store ahead and they figure it's empty. They pray, their shoes softly taking the sidewalk as they approach the entrance. Abigail pulls the knob to find it locked.

"Left in a fuss." Abby breathes deep. "Yet they still *lock up*."

"Let's smash the windows."

"We ain't gettin through the wires. *Fuck!*"

Abby frets in peril. Looking to the hardware shop and hurrying towards it, telling Reagan come on, insisting: we'll get a wrecking-bar. So they hurry to the shattered front window, their shoes crunching atop glass. After helping Reagan step over the jagged remnants sticking up at the bottom of the window-frame, Abigail follows. Reagan keeps the Beretta at her side.

Together, they turn to face the ghostly hardware shop.

"*See* anything?"

"Give us some *light*. Can't see shite for the smoke."

Reagan steps past a fallen shelf avoiding bolts and wrenches scattered about the floor, but it's hard to see with so little light. Time and again she's repositioning her fingers and tightening her grip on Lora's old Beretta, fearful.

Abigail finds nothing better. And she breaks apart. Now that she's here and so close hope is receding out of reach. She creeps down the aisles of garden-hoses and trowels and rakes. Mike is going to die. Where are they? Where d'fuck are the wrecking-bars?

There's the squeaking of a door-hinge and the women stop breathing. Stop thinking. There's a moment of unbearable hush before *thrashing* begins. The low twang tells of something heavy and metal. The cracking is of wood being beaten. It's startling and it's meant to be. It's followed by caution.

"Gowan outta here! Ever y'are, *gowan way from me*!"

The women remain silent, remain hidden behind walls of tools. But Abby hears the voice as it resonates in her skull. It's human, she's sure. It's Irish and he sounds equally scared as menacing. So she swallows and she calls out because she has to.

"*Please*! Please wouldja *help us*?"

"Gowan now! I mean it, ever y'are!"

"*Please*, mate! Give us a *break*, mother a'jaysis!"

"S'no break here!" Another bout of thrashing. Abby flinches, sobbing. Reagan tenses. The man begs: "Take a run and *jump*!"

"Please!" Abigail lets her eyes well. Lets herself shake. It doesn't matter because there's no being brave anymore. No impression to uphold. So she breathes another broken breath and she manages to step forward – down the aisle toward the back of the store. "Me... Me name's *Abigail*!"

"I don't give a dancing shite who y'are!"

"Me fiancée – he's *hurt*! He's out in the fuckin car – he's *dying*!"

"...S'not... S'not my hole to fill, miss. Gowan now!"

Abby reaches the end of the aisle. Gazing left towards the door into the back storeroom. There's a fellow there. Mid-fifties. Bald, moustached, holding a yellow crowbar. Hand wrapped in medical tape and missing one shoe. When he sees Abby he's nervous. The wrecking-bar shakes with his arm, but he squints to see through the cinders and he observes the dried red bite-marks across the young woman's face and neck. The blood of her husband soaking her clothes. Faced with the tears glinting in a doomed face, his scowl and body loosen.

Please, Abby begs him. ...I love him and he's dying.

TWENTY-SEVEN.

There was nothing to do in the suite and they were keen to let Dustin rest. They were hungry and considered ordering in but decided against it and crept out quietly and headed to the dining-room downstairs. Kary Benz visited the omelette bar and asked for Spanish. Her bodyguard Franklin Grier loaded up hashbrowns and sausages and a tall glass of orange-juice. By now they're halfway through their breakfast. Other guests at other tables often stare and snap pics and though the singer minds she's used to it.

An attempt at distraction, Grier asks how she got into music.

"YouTube." Kary answers. "Just… a few vids on YouTube…"

"That's all it took?"

"My agent found me on there and liked my views. He thought I was pretty and had enough talent to mark above backing singer."

"You're sellin yourself short, I think."

"I don't."

"You damn well master that piano."

"I know." Laughing at herself. "I really master, don't I?"

"How long have you played?"

"…I was young. My aunt told me that piano is played by gay white men or blind black men or weirdo little girls. Lo and behold, I really took to it… It was my comfort, living with that family."

Kary carves a wedge from the omelette. Her Ray-Banz on. Her back arched. She tries to keep low but she's still recognized simply from the rumours that began when her boyfriend was spotted last night at the local nightclubs. She hides but they always find her and her bodyguard, who notices her shying away, is trying to take her mind off them. He's telling her she's a queen.

"I *am*, huh?" Kary swallows the eggs and onion in her mouth. "Is that what Us Weekly says?"

"You're sublime, Miss Benz." The bodyguard nods, hoping it helps confirm. "Bigger than that douchebag upstairs; I can tell you that." With half a sausage stuck onto the prongs, he waves his fork at the singer, lecturing. "That piece of shit is a heartthrob. That's all the heck he is. He's like one of these dirtbags on the Disney Channel – and what do they amount to? But *you*, miss-" He stuffs the sausage into his teeth and is mashing it and he's saying: "-you have *talent* and that's what sticks." He swallows. Says: "I been in this biz long enough to know."

"...I have a couple hits, and nothing else to sing."

"Well that's your problem. I'm sorry to tell you, you *have one*... You don't think enough of yourself." Grier wipes juices running out the corner of his mouth. Sets the napkin down. Reclaims his fork and buries it into hashbrowns. All the while his gaze shifts often to a doorway across the room. Always interested. Saying: "Betcha I know someone here who can back me up."

"Who?"

Grier nods brisk to the doorway. Kary turns and peers between the heads of other guests eating breakfast and she sees the doorway into the central hall and the tall teenage bellhop who's been staring. Startled enough to leave when Kary spots him.

"How'd you notice him?"

"It's my job to notice. He's harmless, but a fan."

"He been staring long?"

"Long enough. He sent champagne to the suite last night, I think. Someone did. They always send champagne or red wine. Germans sent schnapps during your last tour."

"How come I never see any champagne or schnapps?"

"Could be poison."

"So what happens to them all?"

"What's left of them gets packed in my suitcase."

Kary listens. Keeping her head down, poking at her food with either a diminished appetite or a depleted heart, having everything and a son of a bitch on her back. She breathes hearty lungfuls and lifts her eyebrows, meekly still. She looks at Grier across the table, implementing a happy face in courtesy.

They continue to dine without speaking for a while, listening to an American-sounding group seated not far away. They're dressed for the slopes and they talk about mysterious invaders striking Ireland and the Brits. A lot of witnesses are saying it's hellspawn. Discussion on both sides. One of them asks how they got here and another says the gates of Hell must've opened. Grier glances at their table and wishes they'd shut the heck up.

Kary however is curious. She looks to Grier.

"...You buy into that crap, Mr. Grier?"

"While I don't deny they're being invaded..." The bodyguard takes up his glass of juice and is about to sip it, continuing: "...I know darn well it's not *monsters*."

"You don't believe in the apocalypse, Mr. Grier?"

"I'm *open*, if that's what you're asking. Could happen. But I don't think Judgement is happening there. Not in our lifetime."

"Why not our lifetime? What makes us so special?"

"Well that's just it, Miss Benz. Why now?" Sticking his fork into his last sausage. Raising it to his mouth, contemplating, asking: "Are you calling quits on that omelette? I'm... interested, is what I'm getting at. Services for goods type barter." It starts to chisel her wall. He tells her: "I will kill for that omelette, Miss Benz."

She laughs a little, holding onto the final stage of a grin for a moment longer. Grier can't believe what her face can accomplish.

Telling her: "You actually shine like an angel."

"Oh go on."

"...You do."

Sublime, she glances away. Her grin shrinking but still a smirk. Still remarkable. After a while she tells him to take the rest of her omelette and the bodyguard sanctions it, he says, concluding she's a godsend.

TWENTY-SEVEN.

It took forever and a lot of pressing phonecalls for Uwe Marrs to finally get a cab. Shoulda been at the airport ten minutes ago. The window is closing, he gripes. Their chance to escape slimming.

Clara Towns sits next to her father in the backseat of the cab and, ever since they pulled away from the curb in front of her building, she's been on her Samsung in search of Kodi Becker. She texted him but no reply. She's checked his Facebook but there's no status update. She texted his friend Amin, who's an alright guy considering the chav's mates, but Amin hasn't responded. Maybe Kodi's out there on the street being mugged. Or probably he's stoned and trying to count the freckles on his forearm.

Uwe's asking his daughter: Did you pack all you'd need?

"Oh." Clara has to think. Can't remember. "Uh, jumper. Socks. Shirts. My notebook… My curiosity as to why you're still around."

Uwe takes it and swallows it coolly.

"…Any food, hon?"

"I didn't think of food."

"…What did you pack for Kodi?"

"Just… clothes."

"Has he gotten back to you?"

"No." Again Clara looks at her Samsung. "…If you call ahead you might get a refund on his ticket…" She looks to the knapsack beside her suitcase. "…I feel bad we stole his shit."

"He'll survive." Uwe's retrieving his phone and he's selecting redial and setting it to his ear. But as it's ringing he notices they've stopped again. They've barely moved for five minutes. So he's craning his neck to look ahead between the seats, asking: "What the hell? We're never gonna make the flight in – *Yes, hello?* Yes, I'm calling about a ticket. I was wondering if it'd be too late to return it? It's for two-thirty this aft-… I have the ticket-number. Or, it's in my email." He glances to his daughter. "Clara, would you access my email on your mobile please?"

"Fine." Unenthused. Clara again stirs from a train of thoughts akin to that of a meth-addict, asking: "What is it? Gmail?"

"I'll have to spell it for you."

Uwe does. Clara reads what she's typed.

"U-Marrs of Brinnon?"

"Brinnon. It was the street our church was on."

"The password?"

"Uh… Clara07."

"Ah. Sure it is." Clara nods once as she plugs it in, not repelled but far from honoured. "…What's the zero-seven for?"

"…That was for July. The big month." Uwe frowns slightly and presses the phone closer to his ear again, saying: "*Yes* I'm here. Just looking for it. Give us a minute." And again the taxi comes to stop and Uwe is vexed. Halted again. Their window closing second by second. "What the hell? *Really* now!"

"Why don't you just conjure Satan magic, man? Teleport us?"

"That's not exactly how Satanism works."

"How does it work?"

"Same way therapy does, I suppose." Uwe holds out his free arm, begging. "Did you find the email from the airport?"

"Yeah." Clara hands him the phone. "S'in *attachments*."

"Thanks." So Uwe taps on the screen and opens the tickets and he's speaking to the airline servicewoman, saying: "Yes, ma'am – hello? Yes, I have the ticket-number…"

The cab slams to another stop and the driver curses out some Pontiac that cut into their lane. Uwe feels his blood-pressure rising. Brow knitted. If this traffic doesn't let up they're not going to make their flight. They're not getting out of London. Clara looks over at him as he frets or meltdowns. And thinks.

"…How come that's your password?"

"Pardon?"

"Clara07."

"*Oh*, it's... what I thought of when I made it."

"You can't be serious."

"Wasn't all at once. Sat there a moment."

Clara stares at the phone. "...Why's July so important?"

"You were born in July." Uwe says. "I lost you in another July, when your mum and you had had enough. I moved to Vienna, city of my parents, a place I always adored. I bought the bookstore on Brinnon and opened my church... something I'd always wanted."

"...Why?"

"Because I was born a preacher." Uwe blinks. "As time went on though, and the tabs added up, it dawned on me where I stood on this rock. Step one was hiding from anyone who gave a damn."

Outside the cab are demented Londoners scared out of their mind. And Clara watches, holding onto the bump of her stomach.

Ambulances rushed the patient through a frantic city after the accident. The problem is he has no identification. He had no wallet on him, no mobile or any sort of license or club-card in his pockets. Maybe he was mugged just before he was run over. Maybe he's a real unlucky bastard. One of the older nurses is saying he looks kind of like Prime Minister Halton's husband. Clarence or Clive or Chet or whatever. But her memory's fuzzy and, besides, his face is too swollen for anyone to be sure.

Clive Halton peers through one barely open eye. He can't move or his body won't. He sees lights. Hears shouting. Pressing voices call for this and that. Hydromorphone. Gauze. Neck brace. There's agony but its white noise. All the blurry people move beyond perception. Everything's chaos but he knows he doesn't have to worry. It's like walking into the stock exchange and knowing he's too poor to matter. He can lie back and unwind in the madhouse.

That is until he sees, or thinks he sees, a tiny person standing on his bed by his shoulder. A tiny pale man, just five inches tall, in tiny cumbersome robes made of black wool. Tiny hazel wings spout from its tiny back.

Drugged and dying, Clive is sure he hears it speak.

"Do you want to live, Clive Halton?"

Clive doesn't have the mind to speak to the imp or fairy.

"You can live. I can let you live, despite your injuries."

Nurses in the room, Clive realizes. But the imp doesn't mind.

"They cannot see me. No one ever sees me." The tiny monster says, aggrieved it seems. "I can help you, Clive Halton-" Removing its tiny hat to bow. "-for I am Lord of Trade."

Clive can't believe. He doesn't. Not like this.

The imp tells him regardless.

"I trade for souls in the name of the First." Strolling around Clive's pillow, around his aching head, this tiny winged horned imp of imps is whispering in his ear: "You can live, Clive Halton. You do not have to die if it is not your wish."

Clive cannot speak his horror. He can't speak anything.

"Trade with me, Clive Halton, and you will not die today."

Thinking on his trip to Cape Town. On the invasion. On his wife. On a speeding Honda Accord. Clive feels nothing. You feel nothing when you die, he knows. That's the brain doing its job.

"You will never die... say, in this *hospital*, Clive Halton."

The Imp of Imps makes a trade. Clive listens. He decides.

"Set foot outside this place, and the trade is complete."

Thinking on his wife. Their children. Their lives.

"You do not ever have to die, Clive Halton."

Heart-monitor spiking. The nurses shout for doctors. Clive is losing his vision to a murky abyss, but the blur of the tiny imp on his shoulder holds for as long as it takes. He's got a customer.

Asking him: ...Do we have a deal?

TWENTY-NINE.

In the east end, Charlene Pupsy keeps up behind Gareth Bates, who's decided their mission and is seeing to its completion. The jacked dealer's loaded up a gym bag and he's got it cinched around his girlfriend's shoulders like a knapsack that crushes her. He clutches the crippler in one paw and with the other he fishes the keys to his Ducati from the pocket of his puffy down coat. He and Charlene cross the parking-garage under their building and they head for the wall of storage lockers at the other end.

"Hurry up yo! No time like fuckin *now*, love."

"What all you *pack* in this friggin thing?"

"Whaddaya *think* I packed? I ain't leavin those fuckers behind."

Bates unlocks the door to his locker and he's revealing the few water-damaged shoeboxes and a set of old golf clubs and a Ducati Multistrada 1200 under a holey bedsheet. Charlene stands and suffers the load on her back and she watches her lover reveal the bike and throw away the cover. Bates leans it off the kickstand and rolls it backwards out of the locker and he's blinking a lot and clearing his throat. He looks over at his woman.

"…All set?"

"What about Beau?"

"Who's Beau?"

"Your Rottweiler."

"His name's fuckin *Blitzkrieg*, love. We *decided*."

"You just leavin him, baby?"

"I'll come back for him! But I can't fiddim in right now, yeah?"

"…How you gonna steer with *that thing* in your hand, Gareth?"

Bates holds up his homespun crippler. Observes it a moment. Tapping the heavy lead weights against the brick wall and listens to the rough scraping clang, he tells her he'll be super. It'll be fun yo.

He mounts the bike and gestures for her to join him. She gathers his helmet from the floor of the locker and climbs on behind the thug, wrapping her arms around his thick midsection after she tugs the helmet over her curls.

They're off to Liverpool in search of essentials.

Thinking of her brother as they ride.

Outside Bates' crappy building stand Curtis Merchant and the big big Pieman, loitering beside the Fiesta across the street. They hear the muffled *rip* of a high-performance engine and then notice Bates and Charlene booking out of the underground lot heading down the street of bustling cars and frantic people. It looked as if Bates was holding the crippler up like Don Quixote as he tore between cars about a block away, but now they're out of sight and Curtis breathes out in shameful awe and then he looks to the giant.

Pieman's got his arms at his sides, seeming torpid like a runner waiting for his mark or a gladiator waiting for tigers.

Three glass amps are still clasped in his fist.

Curtis just shakes his head.

"What a fuckin prick."

"Yeah."

"And *wow*, your dumb friggin *sis*, mate. No offence."

"Right."

"I knew Charlene had problems, but *Christ*."

"Yeah."

"Runs in the family, I guess… No offence."

"Right… Good chat, Curt."

The Pieman watches panicking London and ponders to the extent of his humble capacity. Something conclusive finally clicks and he's suddenly in action – on the move – heading over for the passenger's side of the car, telling Curtis: *geddin* mate.

"Where we goin?"

"You're droppin me at the metro."

"We going to Pancras? We getting out, Pie?"

Pieman's flung the door open and he's sunk the car when he takes a seat in it and Curtis is tossing away his fag and shaking his head and climbing in. Starting up the engine. They watch an Audi cut too close between a truck and van and it scrapes off its mirror in a flurry of sparks. The Audi slows but then speeds and merges into a roundabout. They listen to a freakshow outside and soft rhythmic panting in the backseat. So Pieman looks over at Curtis.

"Curt?"

"Yeah, bruv?"

"Gotta ask you something."

"What's up?"

"Has me wondering."

"Just on with it, mate."

"Yeah." Pieman frowns. "...Why the fuck'd you steal his *dog*?"

Curtis pivots to look at the Rottweiler puppy in the backseat. It's panting with a happy grin extended up its snout, looking back and forth from Pieman to Curtis, who shrugs and returns his eyes to the crowded street ahead.

"That prick was just leavin him in the flat there. No tellin when those two is ever gettin back – the dog might starve in there."

"The fuck you gonna do with a *dog*?"

"Hey, I always wanted a dog, Pie, and that's a nice dog right there. You know how much purebred Rotty puppies is worth? I mean that's a *nice* dog, bruv. Just lookit him."

They're moving a bit better now, though stuck staring at the ass of an LTC bus. Curtis drums his thumbs nervously against the steering-wheel as he observes pockets of anarchy striking this way and that. Cars honk with inspired aggression. Pedestrians throw caution into the wind as they dash into the jam. Curtis looks over at Pieman and sees he's observing the juice that Bates gave him.

"...Three hits."

"Big deal."

"Nice he gave you something though, yeah?"

"Bastard prick."

"You isn't even a *fighter* no more, mate. What you need oil for?"

"Cause…" The Pieman sits back. Wags his fingers around the amps in his palm. Closes his eyes, saying: "I'm not good enough."

"We don't need the shit. Neither of us."

"…I'm not enough without em."

"Yeah but, Pieman, you's a fuckin-*Whoa Christ!*"

The LTC bus is slamming on its brakes out of nowhere, so Curtis follows in turn. Just about slams into it. They've stopped and they watch through the windows as a scuffle occurs aboard the bus. They can't really figure out what's happening. Passengers are engaged in a fight or a lively discussion. Other cars are honking. Drivers call out. Curtis's door suddenly opens and there's a man with a pocketknife there.

"*Geddow a'the fuckin car!*"

"The *fuck-?*"

"*Geddout, nigger!*"

The Pieman in the passenger seat has already gotten out. He's made his way around the hood of the Fiesta. The carjacker backs away from the driver's door, holding up his weapon at which the giant scowls. Pieman swipes it away with a backhand. His knuckles are slit but the blade is flung and the man cowers, saying I have a family. He shouts but it isn't heard too well for all the honking.

When the Pieman beats the man down it's like maces clubbing a potato-sack. The man begs but then he's quiet and his face is different and the giant continues sculpting. The Rottweiler pup in the backseat is barking. A troublemaker is forced off the LTC bus by other passengers. The bus is moving and the path clears. Curtis calls to Pieman and tells him to stop already. We gotta go. Y'gonna break the amps, mate. Careful.

THIRTY.

SMOKELANDS

The man they came upon in the hardware shop introduced himself as Cillian Durst, and Durst helped them as he said he would. With the use of the wrecking-bar and a rubber-mallet they busted into Lloyd's Pharmacy. Durst and Abby carried Mike amid his delirious groaning. White as a sheet and couldn't open his eyes to discover his whereabouts. Reagan remained by the Dacia with the pistol and stood staring down the empty streets at a man who was wandering alone and who appeared to have ragged bleeding holes in place of his ears. He disappeared behind a laundromat and hasn't been seen since. Some distance away, far out of town, armies are still heard bombing an enemy horde.

It was old Lora who took charge of treating Mike. Peeling off the bloodsoaked tea-towel was a slow and assiduous two and a half minutes. Abigail held his wrist upright. Most of the smaller arteries had clotted and curled in on themselves but still blood leaked from others jaggedly slit and left lost in the flesh of his wrist. Durst held Mike up as the old widow rinsed his severed arm in the sink in the employee washroom. Mike barely noticed this but he woke when she poured alcohol into the wrist and into the stab-wound in his abdomen. Lora asked the shopkeeper to lay him down on the countertop. Durst did so and ripped open Mike's shirt to reveal the stomach wound. Upon seeing this, Abigail yelped, cupping a hand over her mouth while holding her fiancée's arm.

Lora searched the prescription medicines, asking Reagan to find her needles and thread.

Reagan was off on the hunt as they listened to the tattooist's tired whimpering. Lora found what she was after. Four hundred milligrams of Actiq fentanyl which she immediately began to tear from its kit. She hurried to Mike, barely needing the walking-stick, and told Abigail to open his mouth. The white lozenge, fastened to the end of a stick like a lollipop, was inserted into his mouth to dissolve. She says this is the stuff I was given for cancer treatment three years ago. Was the only thing that came close to numbing pure agony. They went to work.

It's all kind of a blur now but Abigail remembers what she can as she stands near the front of Lloyd's Pharmacy and stares at smoky streets. She remembers what they did. What they had to do to save the man she's loved since high school. The wrist was too damaged and rot had begun to set in. Lora was the one who asked Durst to bring his smallest powersaw and a blade for soft woods. They held Mike down as the shopkeeper cut below his elbow. Shrieks turned to notes impossible to sing.

Working under the pharmacist's lamp, old Lora sliced into the detached forearm with a box-cutter sterilized with rubbing alcohol. Extracted small lengths of vein with tweezers found on the prescription counter. A tourniquet was tied but it didn't stop the bleeding. Mike looked to Abigail, smiling weak but with a fretful brow. He told her, shaking, that it's sunny here. She held his hand and Lora felt for his pulse, and Mike looked to Reagan on the sidelines as his eyes closed.

And he almost frowned before he was gone.

Brent, sitting against the wall behind them, watched his mother as she pounded onto his dad's chest, telling him no you don't. When she gave up she fell on top of him, wailing and grappling him, giving up. The boy cried.

Now, it's later.

Reagan works with Lora and Durst to tidy up. They bandaged up the tattooist's arm before they wrapped his body in a painter's dropcloth. Alicia holds onto Brent and keeps him away from his father. Skittish, glancing owlish, she sees her sister and sees a need to join her. She does so without a sound, but Abby hears her.

"...Do I gotta be strong for my son? S'at what you're gonna say, Ally?"

"I wasn't set to." Alicia sniffles. "Probably s'not a bad bet."

"...Just... go on. Leave me a minute, Ally... I'm done..."

Alicia remains, right on edge. Disbelieving. They wait around for the grief to subside but it doesn't. They watch a Lexus drive by outside the store and it slows but it doesn't stop. The boy in his aunt's arms is shyly asking for his daddy. Alicia looks at him and says nothing. Abigail whimpers, staring away, saying I think I have a headache before she drops to the floor and cries.

Reagan, watching from across the room, is hurt.

Lora gazes over at Durst, who's leaning back against the wall and trying not to consider the broken sisters and everything he's witnessed. The old woman's shuffling toward him, leaning in on her walking-stick, observing the shopkeeper who aptly has the build and clothes and shabbiness of a handyman, and as the panic subsides into latent doom Lora's asking him where everybody is in this town. Whispering.

"...Dead." Durst answers eventually. "Some fled quick enough sure. Suspect more of em are here someplace but they're not gettin seen... I'm sorry about this man here. Another name to add to me prayers." Tongue poking his lower lip, looking to Lora, asking: "He your son there?"

"Say again?"

"S'he your *son*?"

"Oh. No, a neighbour. I didn't know much of him. Was a right proper legend though, that sweet fuckin git. He... got us out of the fray when it fired up." Lora looks to the body of Mike Schrader. Asking the shopkeeper: "...How's ye then, Durst? Where're your loved ones?"

"...M'divorced. My ones are both married with tots."

"They alright?"

The handyman makes a *clicking* sound with his tongue.

Saying: "...Names in my prayers, Miss Malik."

Reagan is standing up, having been listening. She looks to Durst who looks back sadly. Helpless but willing to help. He's a good man but he's scared and it shows. Reagan asks him what happened in Ferris before we got here. Durst recalls unwilling.

"Them things ran amok… Started yesterday. *Early*… No clue what was happenin but you just hear sirens. You go outside and you hear… poppin and cracklin. Bang ups. You hear screamin. Smoke poured in from outta town like mist… I'd been watchin the telly till the cable wennout and the minute I saw that smoke comin I closed up shop. Barricaded myself in the jacks."

"They didn't find you?"

"I *heard* em. Heard em out in the shop. Heard em bash the front window. Turn shelves over…" Durst looks to his yellow wrecking-bar he left atop the counter and he suddenly reaches out for and reclaims it without forethought. He's just better to hold it. Telling Reagan and the old widow: "Stayed in that feckin li'l bog eighteen hours."

"Where'd the beasts go?"

Reagan asks this but Durst doesn't respond right away. He's looking at Reagan and deciding on her face, thinking on that word. Wondering how much she's seen and how much she believes in or knows for sure. He's lucid enchantment but he barely masks his terror and soon he blinks. He tells her: "Fuck me if I know. But I get the feelin they'll be back."

Old Lora speaks up, sayin they need antibiotics for Abigail. Her wounds came from the teeth of one of them and there's no telling what infection those cuntmonsters carry. She mentions how we should grab food here but no one seems keen on the idea, though Brent is quietly uttering a word that sounds a lot like pizza.

THIRTY-ONE.

Duncan Clark would like to be sleeping, still in a cozy bed with a cozy wife, but instead he`s up at quarter to six and he's showered and dressed and he's headed out to tend to a nation. But Faye's sitting up with the sheets and duvet sliding down from her breasts. Noticing him in mid-sleep. Asking him if he's heard any news.

"I have not, darlin. I've been asleep next to you." Clark steps to the bed and leans in to kiss her forehead. "Dreamin."

"Nice things I hope."

"Dreamin of you, darlin. Always you." Clark withdraws and stands upright and steps away from the bed that so beckons him. Straightening his necktie as he heads for the door. "I got to find myself downstairs, Faye. Got to deal with this…"

"Need'jer… lucky tie?"

Clark smiles.

"I hope I don't, darlin."

So the First Lady finds her head to the pillow again. She's shut her eyes and it's like she never opened them in the first place. Sleep reclaims her, but in her daze she tells him he'd better be sending an army or two to fight alongside the Brits. I like Halton and her husband. We should have them over for dinner soon. And then suddenly Faye has relinquished the last wisp of consciousness and she's off again, softly snoring, and President Duncan Clark smiles as he leaves the White House master-bedroom.

Secret-service wait outside the door. A dutiful pair escort Clark through the wide corridors towards the elevator and then down to the west wing.

Standing outside her office is Haley Pfeiffer – White House Communications Director. She's on her BlackBerry and typing a text or email, and when she notices Clark she pockets the phone in haste. Mr. President, good morning.

"You been here long, Haley?"

"Since yesterday, sir." Pfeiffer takes to Clark's side as he winds through the wide corridors. "Was up all night penning this morning's press release. Douglas met the Corps half an hour ago."

"And how'd that go?"

"From what I remember it was enough without specifics. The US will not ignore the plight of our allies. What we *cannot* do is enter a war when an enemy is unidentified. There was a little more to it… Douglas Poole always makes it sound better than I do."

"Mr. *President?*" Chief of Staff Henry Falwell is catching up with Clark and Pfeiffer and the suited grunts. Saying: "I'm getting calls from overseas left and right. Everyone's looking to the mother teat."

"S'that what they think of America, Henry? A tit?"

"A tit full of gunpowder anyway, sir."

"There's a soundbite I can dabble with." Pfeiffer's smirking, then turning to ask Clark: "*Are* we sending troops, sir?"

"Well it sure as shoot seems right, Ms. Pfeiffer. But, then again, as you gone pointed out we don't know our enemy thus far… save for the odd chirping of supernatural." They're here approaching the northwest entrance of the Oval Office and two secret-servicemen stand aside and open the fine door for Clark and his entourage. "Decisions this weighty autta be suffered over… I wouldn't think we've suffered just yet."

Seen through the large windows behind the Resolute desk are the skies of the capitol which currently unload an icy November downpour. No stars or moon and no sun yet peering over the horizon. One of his accompanying secret-service is hitting the lights and illuminating the muted blue walls and the quartersawn oak-and-walnut floor on which the President has laid out his marine-blue rug embroidered with a pattern that disguises the predominant peace-sign at its center. Clark asked for Kennedy's white sofas and drapery. He originally intended for the same circular coffee-table on which a conference-phone could be set, but instead was presented a custom smart-table by Kitari Labs – a gift from supporter "Big-Time" Bob Merran. It's round. Stands a foot and a half off the rug. Mahogany frame and legs, with quotes from Lincoln, Ghandi, Einstein and Shakespeare engraved around the trim. Clark's spent many late nights in this office playing Angry Birds on the damn thing.

"Fetch Hellerman in here. And Jacoby and Dahl. Everybody. They in yet, Henry?"

"Uh, sir, you're…" Falwell frowns slightly and tilts his head like a dog – something he does often enough to be called a habit. "…you're booked – you're… set to receive a call from the British Prime Minister in thirteen minutes."

"That's right." Clark takes a seat on one of the white sofas in front of his desk, gazing at the digital surface of his coffee-table, telling Falwell: "And if I'm to speak to an ornery warhawk like Patricia Halton, I best come with a rally of militant advisors. They in yet?"

"Yes, sir."

"Fetch em in here for me please."

The chief of staff is nodding and turning to leave. There's a knock heard on the door just east of this exit. It's the door to the office of the President's secretary, who's here peeking her head in enough to address Clark. She tells him Marlene Jacobs-Moore is calling to confirm. What should I tell her.

"Tell her we're ready to launch." His secretary leaves and shuts the door and Clark gazes at Haley Pfeiffer, who's looking to the *George Washington* hung over the fireplace. Standing rigid. She's got a thumb pressed between her front teeth and she's biting down. Putting pressure in her temples. "…Ms. Pfeiffer?" She doesn't respond. "…*Haley?*"

"*Sorry.*" Pfeiffer shakes her head. She withdraws the thumb, turning from the Peale painting, uttering: "Just… just thinking."

"…What about?"

But she can't really formulate an answer.

There's a knock once again and Clark's secretary returns. She's pressing now and she's saying the British Prime Minister is calling. Clark frowns.

"She's *early*."

"She can't wait, Mr. President. That's what she said."

"…Just fine, Catherine." Clark sits up and leans forward on his couch, looking to the smart table set atop the rug. Rubbing his hands, trying to ready himself. "Put her into here for me please."

The secretary again leaves.

Clark glances over at Pfeiffer.

"…Guess I'm flyin solo this mornin."

The black screen in the coffee-table lights up with the incoming call. The display is of a blank figure in a grey square and underneath it is the name P Halton and a blocked phone number. Clark swipes his fingertips across green arrows to answer it. The blinking green light signals the connection.

"Madam Prime Minister."

"President Clark." Halton's voice comes through the speakers in the smart-table and she sounds restive and hoarse like she's been shouting all through the night. "…At *last*."

"I hear tell you got yourselves in a helluva fix, Patty."

"Yes, that's a hillbilly's way of putting it, Duncan. Hope you've been alright and splendid? My cuh-" She stops. A pause for a moment. Then: "…Am I on speakerphone, Duncan?"

"Actually you're on a coffee-table."

"…I'm sorry?"

"*I'm* sorry. I shoulda mentioned."

"…I liked your predecessor a lot more."

"That often goes without saying."

"*Look*, Duncan, you know damn well what's going on. Surely you know what the bloody hell is *happening* to us over here! We are being annihilated! My country is being destroyed – now where the hell is all-powerful *America*?"

"Patricia, first of all where are you? Are you safe?"

"I'm perfectly jolly."

"Where are you?"

"We fled London. I'm in Paris meeting with President Lemieux. You see, the French have come to our aid. Nice of them. Lemieux had troops shipping in before I even called for him."

"Tryin to make me jealous of a Frenchman?"

"But should I ever bother, Duncan?"

Clark furrows his brow and he's sitting back and he's glancing over at Pfeiffer who's standing by the bust of Lincoln, listening on, looking dour. The northwest door opens again and they both glance over to see Henry Falwell returning with the National Security Advisor and the Secretary of Defense. Vice President Samuel Seale is behind them, arriving last and remaining silent in the background. Clark taps his molars together and returns his eyes to the coffee-table.

"…Look now, I've already sent six hundred men and I promise you, you have my *word* now, you'll see another four thousand over there before tomorrow mornin."

"*Four thousand?*"

"Four thousand is a lot of my men, Patricia."

"We've already sent eight thousand men! Ireland has been *overthrown*, for God's sake! These freaks have torn through Scotland and now they've just brought down a 737 in London! Send your *horde*, you bastard!"

"I don't think you rude, Patty. You're scared." Clark considers. Ponders. Absent, without aim, he's breathing: "I'm scared too." Clark is patting his knee before standing up from Kennedy's sofa. He eyes his staff who stand around the office and listen without making a sound. Seale is leaning his shoulder against the bookcase and watching the President closely. Clark meets his old friend's gaze and he has to stop. He scoffs after a moment and he asks Halton: "…Why do you suppose America elected me, Patty?"

"Why the hell are you asking?"

"I'd like an outsider's perspective."

"Not *now*."

"Humor me. Please."

"...Off the record, if I'm being generous, then maybe just maybe it was the faith you have in your country. People pick up on that, your faith and love of country. I feel the same for mine." A pause, them Halton says: "But if I'm putting good fair money on it, why America elected you, then I say it's the accent, Duncan, and how you can make ballooning taxes sound like no big deal as long as you have a front porch and a fishing-pole."

"Is that it? That the best you got?"

"I'm not about to waste pot-shots on you. For God's sake, my country is being razed by the bloody unnatural! These *things* are obliterating us! Have you not wrapped your head around that yet?"

"...So you've confirmed it."

"I think a million eye-witnesses have confirmed it. Victims have confirmed it. That and the fact that every trooper I send in to fight is never heard from again. It seems pretty damn likely we're not dealing with a human enemy."

"Don't that just make me like to send ten thousand Americans to join the fit."

"If you don't fight it here, Clark, you're going to be fighting it at home. And you won't have any allies left to help you."

Clark is looking to his Secretary of Defense, who obviously agrees but in a solemn manner. His National Security Advisor isn't speaking or expressing her reaction either way – merely it appears as if she's having difficulty coming to terms with a corroboration she feared. Falwell looks vigilantly professional, fighting himself to remain so cold. Pfeiffer looks afraid, plainly, no longer present – miles away. Seale is looking still at the President and judging the seconds that pass.

"...I can get more men, Patricia... How many, I can't say at this time. But they'll be there ASAP, you got my word." Having paced back to the smart-table, the President takes a seat on the armrest of the sofa. "And Patricia? I should like to meet with you. In *person* I mean, a'course. You and Lemieux, and O'Reilly. We really gotta meet and figure this out face-to-face... if what you're saying is true."

"Troops *first*, Duncan. Before all of the kingdom is rubble."

"You have our support. UK and Ireland will see the US on its way."

"Thank you." The words sound bitter. "We'll be in touch."

"I'll bet on it... Good luck, Patty."

"Good day, Mr. Clark."

The display in his coffee-table notifies him that the call has ended and it reverts back to a selection menu of icons on his homescreen. Clark has to scan the faces of his staff. They're speechless as the account takes its toll. Screws with their heads. Vice President Seale is stepping away from the bookcase and is headed for the northwest door to make his leave. The President clears his throat and observes his rug.

"Ms. Pfeiffer... start writing up my address to the people. I want to be broadcasting live from this office for noon today." Clark frowns mildly, nodding to confirm, telling no one specific: "...And I shall need my lucky necktie."

OSØYRO – 11:13 CET

In the fjord just outside the Norwegian city they found a freighter departed from Scotland. Was travelling twenty clicks faster than it should've been in these waters and about forty minutes ago it collided with the rock walls of the inlet in view of the shores of Osøyro. Locals stood gawking at the ship, the bow of which is clearly engulfed in flames. With its hull evidently gouged, it's slowly sinking into the greyish black waters. So emergency teams are acting fast. It's considered odd that none of the lifeboats on the freighter have been deployed in all this time.

The choppers hover low to the deck. Men jump down and land

shakily and spread out aboard the ship. It seems abandoned. They call out in English so the crew can understand them, but no replies return. It's like the seafarers were all thrown overboard into the North Sea. The emergency-teams keep steady and press onwards as they feel the ship capsizing beneath their feet. Their orders are to keep to the stern – avoid the unpredictable blaze raging at the sinking bow. They continue shouting. They search.

Upon venturing into the bridge they find bodies. Only a couple. The rest must be someplace else. These here are just the helmsman and a second-mate. They're both with mutilated mouths broken and agape. Most of their teeth have been scattered about the floor around them. The helmsman's arm is snapped backward. His ears are missing. Their flesh is somewhat warm. Killed only an hour ago or less, but their assailants are nowhere to be found.

It's presumed the killers are now at large in the mountains of Norway.

THIRTY-TWO.

Sunlight pries open the actor's eyes. Someone left the drapes open. Dustin Tomson grimaces as he rubs his temples, yawning. He feels the brim of his Lakers cap and realizes he fell asleep wearing it. Must've been lit last night. Removing the hat, tossing it across the bed, he sits up, combing his fingers through greasy hair. He hears his ringtone and glances around for his iPhone but it isn't on the nightstand as he expected. He groans and throws the sheets off of himself. Finds the phone in the front pocket of his jeans that he just barely slipped out of before crashing early this morning. From what he remembers, he figures it was a good enough night.

It was Kary but he missed the call. There's no alert so she hasn't left a voicemail. Dustin isn't surprised. He's stretching firm muscles feebly like he hasn't earned them and he's yawning and scratching the itch in his ballsack as he wanders. The suite's empty. Kary's gone. That bodyguard ain't here yet. But then again there are two used coffee mugs on the counter. Two discarded K-Cups in the trashcan. The actor sort of smirks as he heads back for the bedroom, considering a shower.

In his phone is a text from last night he doesn't remember reading. Scrolling through messages, he finds an unsaved number sent him a pic. He opens it and sees it's a tit pic. A blonde in some familiar men's room. The club, he figures. Upon closer inspection he realizes it's the chick at the coat-check. One he liked. Sliding open the shower's glass partition and turning on the faucet, he lets the water warm up and leans against the towel-rack looking at the pic and finding his hand into his Calvins. He realizes he doesn't remember her name. He takes to Twitter just to mention

(good ol fashon #tomsonstupidnite)

and then sets the phone on the edge of the sink. Figures the

189

water's warm by now. Notifications *bleep*. Retweets already.

As the star showers he looks at the water dripping off of him and the steam filling the stall. Shampoos sandy brown hair. Soaps up and rinses. Gets out. He's got a towel draped over his shoulders and he's mostly hard. Jacking as he air-dries. More retweets *bleep*. There he is in the foggy mirror. With his free hand he wipes it clear so he can see better, listening to *bleeps*, freely coming onto the tiles and bathmat. When he dresses he puts on basketball shorts and a Hollister shirt with cut-off sleeves.

The replies are vapid but he doesn't give a shit about a gormless cult to spread his name. Briefly he scrolls through Twitter before losing interest. Prompts from his Family Guy game goad him to return to Quahog. Ten minutes ago his agent asked

(can you please get out of Europe?)

Dustin doesn't figure he'll reply. He's finding himself in front of the minibar and he's helping himself to some orange-juice. Chugs back a few mouthfuls as he parks his ass on the sectional facing the fireplace. Continuing on Twitter and Instagram while he lets the day come find him.

On TMZ's website is an exposé on the tattoo of pop-sensation Kary Benz. The facts are in and millions of impressionable girls are horrified to learn the truth behind Benz's Cantonese ink decorating her right hip and side. Since receiving it about this time last year, the young singer has told media that the saying means *virtue*. The literal translation, as it's now come to light, is something closer to *property*. Eyes shift to boyfriend, Hollywood heartthrob Dustin Tomson, as the likely candidate for Benz's "owner", since rumors persist that the singer got the tattoo as a gift for her ink-obsessed boyfriend on his birthday last year.

There's an inserted keycard and a deadbolt unlatching. Dustin looks up from his phone and sees Kary returning to the suite. Their bodyguard Franklin Grier is carrying bags. Apparently the beauty went shopping. Good. That always cheers her right up.

"Went shopping, baby?"

"Yeah we did. Just a few places."

"We?"

"Just… Grier and I."

Dustin glugs orange-juice. Grier asks Kary where she'd like her purchases and she asks him if he could please put them in the bedroom for her. And he's happy to oblige. Kary smiles weakly and sighs and looks up at her boyfriend.

"Sleep well?"

"…Sit down. There's something you got to see." Dustin takes a seat on the sofa, on the cushion that backs against the window. The mountains peek through the slitted blinds behind him. He's holding up his phone and he's patting the empty seat beside him, driving: "Com'ere, baby."

Kary doesn't move to him. She stays still.

"…What do I got to see?"

"Something terrible's happened." Dustin is almost concerned. He plays it well. Grier returns from the bedroom and walks in on the revelation and immediately picks up on the undertones present. "S'all over everything. Everybody's following it. Right now it's just Kary Benz and demons all over the place."

Kary glimpses their bodyguard, who wears a strict grimace and observes this exhibition like a scat joke at a baby shower. Watches as the pop-singer approaches reticent and with her back bent. Fingers held up and shyly grazing her chin. Eyes widely cheerless, she sits next to Dustin who hands her his iPhone.

The headline and the first sentence are read and it becomes clear to Kary where it leads. She already knows the translation. A friend looked it up six weeks after she got it. She's always known what it meant and her body begins to shake quietly.

"Not sure who first posted it. I read it on TMZ."

"…I knew I shouldn't have done that photoshoot."

"I've been texting our publicist all morning."

"…Really?"

"What you think I been doin? Gotta *PR* shit, right?" His arm around her, and she knows it makes her feel better. Grier is loath to see it. Dustin tells her: "I'm fightin for you, baby." It's not true and she knows it isn't true but it's enough to draw a story in her head. A story she can believe. It's less exhausting to just believe. "You were duped by some shit-kicker tattooer. We been trying to keep this quiet until we decided on a cover-up design."

"...But that's a lie."

"You and me know that. But that's it, babe." He fingers a bang out of her eye. "Just you and me."

Kary hears, and she's welling up but she shuts her eyelids upon the tears. She nods. When he kisses her, she keeps her eyes closed. Grier watches but can't speak so he remains silent by the bedroom door. Standing ready to protect. He watches as the singer gets up off the sectional and she's wandering dreamlike across the suite.

Dustin asks her where she's going but she doesn't answer. She just opens the doors to the balcony. Cold wind blows into the suite and Dustin shivers, but Kary enjoys the chill.

Out there are mountains topped with snow of the oncoming winter. Kary's on the stone balcony looking out at them, and she's lost. It isn't until she drops her head and looks down at the rock slopes that she seems to find clarity. Grier follows, asking if she's alright. The singer answers I want to be clean as the mountains.

But I'm marked. I know what I am.

"Don't say that. You're not."

"I am what I am."

You're not, Grier tells her. If you'd tell yourself that. Stand up for yourself just once, you'll see. But the star isn't sure she believes him. Instead she watches the mountains, quiet and clean, and she spits over the concrete railing to boulders at rest far below her.

THIRTY-THREE.

Sasha Stokes, petit domestic, is smoking a Camel and staring at a kind Floridian sunrise. She's on the bench on the front porch of the maid's house. She's been living in this cabin or cottage now for eight years and she's come to think of it as her own. Like it or not, she earned it. Sucking back another drag, looking up across the grass and gardens at the Merran mansion. It's quiet and there's the wind-chime in the morning breeze that ruffles the palms around her. Sasha's got the pack and her lighter and her cellphone on a weathered cast-iron tea-table set out front here and used mainly as decoration. All she hears is the jingling chime in the shape of a flamingo and then there's the door opening behind her.

Sasha turns and her sunken eyes settle on her eldest son.

"…You said you'd quit smokin."

"We both believed me. Shame on us, pumpkin."

"Shame on us." Aiden steps onto the porch and lets the screen door ease back into its frame. He joins his mother in gazing up at the sprawling Florida estate which she's cleaned now for too many years. He watches her take another drag and asks: "When'd you pick that up again?"

"Wasn't long after you flew off into Afghanistan. Bought a pack just for one. Then I'd just have a couple every blue moon but… then your brother decided his path in life." She crushes the smoke against the wall. "Maybe twelve a day now. A pack, sometimes."

"You know what you're doin to yourself."

"Every morning I wake up, hon. I hack wisdom out all the over the sink."

Sasha still holds onto the crushed dead butt. She'll toss it in the toilet as per her daily ritual – flush away the evidence, then shower and dress and get on up to the big house and see to breakfast for

Estelle and the kids. But for now she enjoys a moment alone with her son and she asks him, sighing, whaddaya doing up at this hour.

Aiden tells her I can't sleep.

"Didn't sleep much all night... Can't shut this brain off."

"Welcome to the family, pumpkin. Only gets worse, older you get... They say to try melatonin, but..." Sasha again glances over at her eldest, pivoting and leaning back against the porch railing. Observing the young man. Twenty-seven. Handsome. It dawns on her and she mentions: "...You look a lot like your daddy."

"You told me that before."

"I know... You do though. Really, Aiden."

"Fine."

"...It's his chin. The hair and eyes... You got *my* complexion. My cheekbones. Jacob got my nose... but you both got way too much of *him* in you." Aiden sort of gazes off in striking lament. He's looking to the pond and the fountain and he's breathing in the morning mist and listening to the wind-chimes tinkle. "...So what's that you been thinkin about all night, hon?"

"...Just thinking about Jake."

"...Aren't we all." Sasha straightens her back away from the railing, seeming like she's dragged by invisible pulleys. "But what can you do, hon? Diddly-effing-squat."

Aiden thinks. Weakly he nods.

Yeah. He clears his throat, soon saying ...He'll survive, ma.

In the distance and muffled by odd obstructions, there's the sound of a humming engine. Tires crunch grit over cobblestones. Headlights of a limousine are seen passing behind the hedges of the far-off front yard. Aiden notices but doesn't see his mother reaching for her cellphone on the cast-iron tea-table.

"Who'd that be at this hour? S'at Mister *Big-Time* Bob Merran?"

"That's the fella. Returning from his murder trial."

"Do you think he did it? Think he... killed people?"

"Doubtful. He doesn't like to do anything himself."

"Wonder why he woulda booked a red-eye... Figured he can

afford his own plane."

"Yeah he owns two. A Gulfstream and a warbird that fought in Korea…" Sasha dials a number she knows like her birthday. She sets the phone to her ear, telling Aiden: "That's the rich for you, pumpkin. Syrup of goddamn ipecac."

The phone on the nightstand starts ringing. Estelle awakes and finds herself in the overly-tanned arms of a psychic named Harvey Nest. The room is made out by the light of the screen displaying the incoming call from Sasha Maid. Upon crawling out from under Nest and reading this, Estelle wakes right up, tensing entirely like cold water just split down her back.

"…Hello?"

"Just saw his limo coming up the laneway."

"…*Thanks*, Sasha."

"I'll unlock the back gate."

"…Thank you."

The line goes dead. Estelle hangs up and sets the phone down. Harvey is stirring but he's still out with his mouth agape and wetting the pillow. He's not allowed to remain peaceful. Estelle has got her hands on his side and shoulder and she's shaking the hell out of him, telling him wake your ass up. He's trying to oblige while she gets out of bed and turns on the lights.

"*Wha*… what's *up*, Estelle?"

"Bob's home. Geddup."

"He's home?"

"Didn't predict that one, *didja*?"

"Divination is… selective of the mind, my lovely."

"So what are you saying? What am *I* saying? I don't give a shit." Estelle's hurrying about the room hunched over and picking up Harvey's clothes, saying: "Get the hell outta bed, Harv!"

The psychic sits up sleepily and Estelle throws him his clothes. Rushing him. Telling him get dressed. *Quick*. She's grabbing the remote off the long chest of drawers and she's turning on the Sony flatscreen. Switching inputs to view the surveillance feed of the mansion's exterior. She sees there's a familiar silver limo pulling up just outside the grand front entry. Motion-sensors activate the security lights. Estelle again urges her lover to hustle as she steals her nightgown off the hook in the door of her black walnut chifforobe and slips its sleeves down her arms and cinches its belt around her naked waist. She watches a chauffeur exit the driver's seat and come around to the back to open the door. Let out his employer. Her husband. Big-Time.

"We gotta *go*, Harv!"

"I only got my briefs on, Estelle."

"It's *fine*! It's *fine*! Come on!"

Estelle grabs his bronzed wrist and she's leading him to the door. Down the short hallway to the eastern stairwell – away from the front of the house – through a passage used solely by the maids to keep discrete. Nest has got his clothes bunched up under his arm and he's prodded by Estelle behind him, who nearly pushes him down onto the landing and then onto the main floor. She's leading now, heading for the kitchen while Harvey attempts to pull his shirt on. Threads his arm through one sleeve at least. Estelle hits the switch and lights up the kitchen she rarely sees and she's making straight for the backdoor through which Sasha brings in the groceries on Tuesdays. She unlocks it just as she faintly hears the front door opening on the other side of the mansion.

"Head straight across the garden along the path. You'll pass the maid's house and eventually you'll get to a gate in the back fence."

"Where's it lead?"

"The river, I think."

Estelle's opened the door and she's ushering out the psychic, who's patting down the pants lumped under his arm. He's turning and telling her he doesn't have his phone. Left it upstairs. Estelle assures him he'll live before she closes and locks the door.

Nest is left staring at the window and watching as the lights are killed inside. He presumes Estelle is running back upstairs now to complete the illusion. She'll collect his phone and hide it and then crawl beneath the covers so her husband can walk in and find blasé innocence as long as she's not too out of breath.

So Nest sets about his escape, sneaking across the gardens. His tanned chest almost hidden in the orange dawn. He's fled across the concrete path across the yard and he's passed the maid's house. Approaching the gate, he slows down. He sees a young man is standing at the small gated doorway that's built into the tall walls at the edge of the property. He's wearing plaid pajama-bottoms and a freshly-ironed t-shirt provided by the United States Air Force.

"Howdy."

"Uh, *hey*... You work for the Merrans?"

"Not me, brother."

"...Estelle said I was meeting the maid out here."

"Ma had to get ready for work."

"Oh. Okay, well... Good she didn't have to see me like this."

"I agree." Aiden raises his brow and nods, advising: "Maybe put them trousers on fore you reach the street." Nest thanks the boy and he's heading through the gate toward the river. Aiden locks up afterwards, telling the psychic: "Oh and mind the bloodsuckers down there. They'll be wakin up right about now."

THIRTY-FOUR.

Appearing out of nothingness, standing in snow on the mountain. Winds blowing his judge's robe. Blowing the powdered wig off his head to reveal blonde hair and modest black horns. The whistler stands the snowsqualls that have struck the area so suddenly, and he looks over to the beautiful monster beside him who flicks a lion's tail. Lilith.

Lilith holds onto the braided handle of the bronze sword in the scabbard on her firm hip, she watches a band of mountaineers hastily set up camp to wait out the storm.

Beneath googles, the mountaineers have eyes like caged fowl moving by conveyor, frantic and cold, fighting against the hard Norwegian wind. They can hear their guide shouting to them. Remain calm and get inside your tents. But they can't see anything for the whiteout. They can't see the legion of demons watching them from the mountains above.

Whistling here, the whistler calls for Lilith's attention.

...How many, Rosier?

About twenty of them. Unarmed.

Lilith nods, then she shivers for the cold.

I hate that we came to this frozen land.

I think it is a nice change of pace.

This is not a proper place to fuck.

We had to leave, Lilith. Humans will not stand for what is done on those islands. If the Fourth is to survive, we had to get out before it's too late... I did not control where the ship crashed.

Lilith shivers and scowls.

Above, in all the swirling white, a massive figure flies and the beat of its wings keeps the snow racing insane. The legion cheer for the great stud above. A dragon beast. Demons cheer for Prince of the Fourth, and they suck on one another and they masturbate, and Lilith knows they cannot wait any longer.

Drawing the leaf-shaped bronze sword, the succubus hollers into the storm and calls forth the legion that spreads diseased oily wings to take to the sky and descend upon the campsite below them. One with the arms and torso of a Kodiak bear bends low next to the wingless Lilith and she climbs upon his back before he spreads sickly feathered wings and he flies.

Rosier stands alone in the snow, looking up at the indistinct figure of a great prince above, and upon hearing distinct screams in the white chaos below, he shakes his head, smirking then, and then vanishes.

LONDON – 11:13 GMT

They're leaving on the northern line. Curtis Merchant parked his Fiesta and has brought the Rottweiler pup, which he carries in his arms. He sits down with the dog, but the Pieman remains standing and clutching a bar with slit fingers of dried blood where the carjacker slashed him. He's gazing down the length of the snaking carriages that speed through the underground. The train is barely occupied and the giant has to make mention of it, though he doesn't even realize he's done so until his mate responds.

"Well…" Curtis pets the grinning pup, supposing: "Not many wanna head *north* about now. Figure everyone's herding south – get outta the whole fuckin country."

"…So how come you're comin?"

"What? Wiffyu?"

"You dinnit have to come with me. Just my gym mate."

"Fuck else am I gonna do?"

"…What about your… parents?"

"Vay-kay in Greece. My shag left last month. My roommate's a cunt – you've met him. No shithole to hold up in… Nawp, figure I'm with you, bruv." The dog nuzzles his hand with its nose so

Curtis resumes petting it. The giant watches this and doesn't look charmed. Curtis, judging his listless ire, tells him: "You're sound protection, Pie. Dunno how I'd fare on my lonesome."

"You're big enough."

"So's the world." Curtis sets the pup on the seat beside him. Swiping a few of the hairs from his sweater, he breathes out. He wonders: "...How bad you think it'll be up there?"

"We're about to see for ourselves."

Other passengers are on their mobiles. Some with signals but most without and fuming. When pages finally load they read updates. There's been a fifteen-car pileup on the M25 just outside Basildon. Looting and riots continue to plague southern Britain while everything north of Leeds fails to report more than patchy pleas for help or harrowing pictures and videos of bodies. Twelve fatal hit-and-runs have been reported in and around London. Westminster, Buckingham and a lot of churches are all surrounded by Britons who demand some resolution. Sightings of impossible creatures go viral following the crash of a 737 plane in Hyde Park. A young woman out for a jog was left in pieces in full view of over a thousand witnesses. Footage of the winged thing was taken by phones held by shaky hands. It flies away into smoke and is gone.

A woman not far away is yelling into a Nexus that's apparently lost signal mid-conversation, and she's batting at the phone and calling out hello are you there and she's hysterical, slumping against the window. Passengers look. The dog looks. They've come out of the ground and are washed in grey daylight for a time. Far off behind them are London and Victoria Tower and the smoke still rising from Hyde Park.

"Whadda ye suppose made Charlene fall in love with that slick prick?"

Pieman shakes his head.

"She likes what she shouldn't... Always has."

"Yeah." Curtis chuckles. Then, carefully, while it's on his mind: "I never told you before, mate, but... I always had a thing for yo sis."

"…I didn't hear you say that, Curt."

"I'm bein true. For real, bruv."

"I'm real. And I'm right in fronna ye."

"Not just for *looks*. She's gorgeous, I mean, I'm just sayin-"

"Don't say nothing though. Let's both survive this, Curtis."

There's a *crash* and the train shakes and the occupants lurch to the left side of their carriages. People are hysterical after the initial shock. Some cower silently. Some have shut their eyes and some keep gaping in terror. Behind them a ways is something that's flying through the wisps of snow or cinder – defeated, as if it can't keep up with the speeding train. It's hard to make it out but it has wings. It's flapping away drunkenly like a dying housefly. People gasp upon spotting it. They point it out to others. The frenzied woman has got her Nexus out again and she's trying to call but there's still no service and she's shrieking and throwing the phone. Curtis again looks up to the giant and sees he's fixed on the thing out there climbing the sky. Curtis pats the stolen dog. Pieman just glowers and grips the aluminum bar enough to dent it.

NORDENBYEN – 21:48 CET

Fucking, for that is there pleasure of choice.

A group of the Fourth Legion, having escaped from the British Isles, now enjoys the orgy of a camp of mountaineers in a snowstorm. Things of the otherworld loving the flesh of the chosen kind.

Rosier wears a parka and a toque and gloves he took from one of the men who's already finished. The tail of an ass flicks absently behind him. Whistling a few bars of *Oh Susanna*. Blinking white flakes from his eyelashes as he watches Lilith ride a stripped man held down in the snow by a creature like a Kodiak bear.

The succubus is purely splendour. Alien but exquisite, desirable to even the middle-aged stockbroker she now murders after they both come together. Panting, her pink back hunched over the man gasping to breathe, her soft coffee-brown hair hanging over her face and down to moulded breasts that quiver as she huffs the bitter mountain freeze. Snow instantly melting when it falls upon her burning hot skin, trickling down her back to a buttocks and the flicking tail of a lioness.

Lilith withdraws her bronze sword. Then she rises up off the cock that's still pointing firm and straight. Dying slowly.

Then, suddenly, there are howls and roars of such displeasure. Lilith and Rosier and the Kodiak monster turn and peer through the whiteout, and just barely they can make out the naked little body of a young woman fleeing from the festivities. Holding onto herself, freezing and bleeding, used, getting away from the demons who can't find her in the storm.

A daughter of a wealthy Norwegian plumber. Blonde. Fetching. Whimpering and with teeth chattering as she hurries through the mountain snow and she reaches the precipitous cliff over. And the blonde is set to climb down it. But that's when the ground shakes. Something has landed from out of the sky. Something very big.

When a massive and salmon-coloured arm pierces through the whiteout, the young woman screams and leaps from the cliff. But a burning-hot hand has seized the pretty bleeding blonde and she shrieks no but the great stud pulls her in, holding her thrashing legs and spreading them.

Rosier merely enjoys the circus as a voyeur. It's enough for him. He is the only one out of a hundred here who do not enjoy the mountaineers. But the legion enjoys every drop. Their prince enjoys the blonde runaway, destroying her.

Beautiful pink Lilith shivers still, hating the cold, smiling though as she falls back and lies in the snow on the mountain.

THIRTY-FIVE.

Clark goes live in three hours. At his desk in the Oval Office he'll address his nation and world. There's little time left to decide what to do and what to tell about it. Haley Pfeiffer has been working on the sidelines, writing alterations and developments as the executive staff deliberates loudly and in chaos in the Situation Room, aided by advisors from Homeland Security and the NSC.

Duncan Clark has exited the meeting on the pretense of a pee-break. After flushing, however, he snuck past his secret-servicemen and he's come up from the basement. He has no destination in mind and he realizes this when he's in the waiting area outside his office, so he's slumping against the wall of the Roosevelt Room.

Clark feels like a knotted yoyo. Breathing too fast and he has to shut his eyes. His heartbeat overtakes the ringing in his ears. He's got his lucky necktie on but he doesn't feel blessed.

Duncan?

And this familiar word echoes in his head. So Clark opens his eyes. He turns without pulling himself off the wall and looks back at the First Lady. Duncan has always prized the sight of Faye. Hers is a round face accentuated by a layered bob of Titian. It's those fair cheeks and the way she's held onto youth where it matters. It's the way he knows that face and remembers it always being there when he's needed it. She's woken up since he saw her last. Dressed in a scarlet skirt, slate jacket, pearl earrings, and she's done her eyes up in those dramatic striking shades. Stepping toward her husband, Faye asks if he'd like to go somewhere quiet and read this month's *Amazing Spider-Man*.

"…Not the time to mock me, darlin."

"I'm not mocking you, Duncan."

The President finally leaves the support of the corridor wall and stumbles or trots away before he reclaims his balance. Faye is setting her hand on his shoulder but he assures her I'm alright. Just got some stomach issues going on. Head hurts. It's nothing.

"It's something."

"What's it then?" Clark looks at her. "Tell me."

"It's terror, Duncan. Duty… and terror. And you've never been master of either one." Faye walks around to his front to face him. Let's him see her. "…It's true, isn't it? About the invaders?" Clark doesn't speak but blankly he concedes. "Real monsters…?"

"…From Hell, is what they say. Or some galaxy or… I dunno."

"…*How?*"

"Unknown." Clark shakes his head. Rubs his neck. "But it's *not*, right? It's gotta be a hoax. Some diversion… Enemy just wants us to go on and *think* they're immortal. Dressing up to look inhuman – that's just what the Indians did with the feathers and paint."

"Aboriginals, Duncan."

"It's not monsters. It… It's *not.*"

"In any case-" Faye pivots with one hand holding her elbow and her other rubbing her chin. Wondering, pressing: "-Britain and Ireland are being annexed by enemies, mortal or not. However insane it is, you're still a leader above anything else. Our allies are in peril… What's Uncle Sam got to say about that, Duncan?"

Very suddenly and very smoothly Clark is an ashamed hound that's gone and shit on the rug. He suits it or it doesn't paint him reproachfully as it might a lesser man. But he's less the blithe Kentuckian charmer Faye fell in love with that afternoon in Lexington twenty-three years ago. Clark's losing himself. It starts to sink in what he carries on his shoulders and he's realizing that too much of this work is filthy.

"How many men are you sending?"

"…Eight thousand will be deployed by tomorrow afternoon. Five thousand army to unload in the south to help push enemy lines north. A thousand navy to meet up with French forces blocking off the channel and the North Sea." He pulls at the

Windsor knot below his Adam's apple. "Two thousand in air-force to maintain a perimeter around the islands."

"Will that be enough?"

"You're asking me, Faye." Clark slumps down into an armchair, sighing a fraction of the bubbling pressure that seeks to explode him. He tells his wife: "This is not why I became President."

"…We elected you, Duncan, because you were the fresh view this country needed… But unfortunately what America needs right now is the same thing the world needs."

"And that'd be?"

"A saviour… Damn it, hon, you gotta go be a fighter." Faye sits herself down on the armrest of his chair. Darkly drawn eyes look him up and down and then catch his gaze. "What happens in comic-books when evil attacks the innocent?"

"Don't do this. I don't need this."

"America is a superpower, Duncan."

"But I'm not a fighter, Faye."

"Then step down."

"Step down." Clark scoffs, biting his lip. "Faye, I can't step down and step up again when this is over. I resign and that's it for me." He grimaces. He loathes. "I will not step down. I have too much planned. I've got so much good to do for my country yet."

"Well you're a fighter then. Like it or lump it… But you got your lucky necktie on." Faye's reached soft hands to his collar. Tightened his burgundy Windsor knot. Before kissing his head, she offers: "That's got to count for something."

Here there's a ringtone that the President knows well. It's the signature tune he's set for his chief of staff. He glances at his sleek black phone specially-provided by the kindly folks at the Pentagon. He tells Faye he'll just be a second and he answers the call and assures Falwell I'll be right down. Tucking his phone in his jacket pocket, he looks over at his wife on the armrest.

There's another voice here. It's their son. Randy's laughing, which is what most catches their attention. Faye and Duncan both head down the corridor and upon turning the corner they see Randy and his caregiver Dr. Audra Heard. And they see Vice President Samuel Seale, who's apparently showing the young man how he can make his thumb appear detached by magic.

"Sam."

Seale looks up and looks to the President and the First Lady, answering her: "Good morning, Mrs. Clark." He smiles to her warmly. "It seems Randy was looking for his mom."

"Well he found me, as always."

Faye steps forward, observing their son. Randy is twenty-one and looks a lot like his mother. Spirited and inquisitive eyes are withheld from the faces of people. He doesn't look his mom in the eye. In wriggling hands he holds a plastic airplane. The President observes his son, smiling as he did on The Tara Wilson Show. Faye looks to Audra and asks her how Randy's been this morning.

"Oh had a *teeny* fuss at breakfast, but he settled well enough."

"I think the bustle of this place makes him uncomfortable." Faye tries to brush an unruly bang from the young man's face but Randy cowers from the sudden gesture. She breathes and glances over at the caregiver, saying: "Let's take him back upstairs, Audra. His father's busy right now."

After the First Lady and her son and the caregiver have started eastbound down the hall, the Vice President glances over at his old college dorm-mate, his commander-in-chief who's got his back to him as he continues to agonize over the revelations that have struck him increasingly and godlike. Fretting over the weight collapsing his shoulders. Seale scratches his eyebrow as he thinks of something worth saying. There's nothing.

THIRTY-SIX.

Big-Time Bob Merran loves his wife. Kissing her neck in bed, pumping into Estelle. CNN is on, reporting the invasion overseas, but the Merrans aren't really paying attention to the anchor or the footage. Background noise. Estelle kind of watches, scared. Bob on the other hand is more into the love.

Infamous Big-Time is in his early-fifties. Kept a good head of hair but grew out his gut sitting in Bentleys. Wire-framed glasses are knocked crooked over wild eyes. Fingers with hairy knuckles grip Estelle's flesh as he bucks. There are clips presented onscreen of a winged freak in London that halved a woman this morning. This he ignores. But then they move on. They discuss an Ellis Communications cell-tower that was destroyed this morning by a downed army chopper north of Leeds. The most recent tower to fall. Ellis, along with parent company Merran International, are taking a heavy loss. And Bob hears. And he can't ignore it any longer. He hates it because he was really close to popping.

Sonuva *bitch*. Not another one, *dammit*.

Clenching his teeth, Bob's straightened his glasses and gotten out of the classic-chic canopy bed. Pulling his jockies up from his ankles, he reaches for the remote on the gold-trimmed nightstand and raises the volume. Estelle pants and watches her husband storm off toward the master bathroom.

"...You been following this, bunny?"

Estelle lifts her brow, insulted but accustomed. Disregarding presumption and she's lying back on the pillow and answering: "Believe it or not, Bob." She sees him disappear into the bathroom for a moment before returning in a brown mink dressing-gown. Uttering: "Actually I thought you'd be thrilled about war."

"Why the hell would you think that?"

"Just... figured it was good business."

"Good business for *invaders*, bunny. That's *why* they invade. Two-thirds of Ellis Communications is in Ireland and the UK. They keep knocking out my towers and killing my subscribers, how do you suppose that affects business?" Bob glares loathsome at the flatscreen that replays the footage outside Hyde Park. A bat in the tree and blurred-out human halves. "Course, it's hard to tell... in this situation..." His disgusted mug hangs upon the screen, watching the bat fly away. "...What in the fuck is going on over there?"

"Why does it matter, Bob?"

"*What?*"

"What does it matter? So Ellis takes a hit. Big whoop. You still own dozens – literally fuckin *dozens* of million-dollar ventures."

"Ellis-Com, bunny, is my *baby*. My *first*. It's goddamn sentiment. You know better than anyone the big softy you married. That goddamn company is my child." Bob turns and glares back at the flatscreen. Telling his wife: "They're fuckin with my *baby*, Ester... You don't do that to a big softy."

There's a conservative and practised knock at the door and Estelle pulls the covers up over her chest when Bob tells the visitor to come in. Sasha Stokes enters and her eyes never wander to the bed for an instant. She's good that way. Professional and knowing. She looks only at Big-Time in the mink dressing-gown.

"...Morning, Sasha."

"Good morning, Mr. Merran. I didn't realize you were back." Sasha lies without blinking. "I woulda made you a breakfast."

"No-no, that's alright." Bob's mind is back on the TV. Footage from a local news-station in Glasgow shows fire erupting in a soundstage. Anchors and weathermen fleeing. Something smashes downward through the ceiling. It attacks the cameraman and the camera spins and topples over. "...Uh... Make it for the kids though. And Ester Bunny."

"Sir, there is one thing... I'm sorry but it's not good news."

Bob just gawks at the TV without hearing the tired maid in his bedroom doorway. Blinking, he hopes to remember what she said to give it a second listen. And he clears his throat when it registers and he finally responds. What is it, Sasha?"

"Your bird flew away."

"…My… *Oh*, bird. Right… Which bird?"

"Your favourite one, sir. The yellow and red one… I think you called him William."

"Will Halloway. It's from… a book I read in school." Again the magnate blinks to get a hold on reality. Then he peels his focus from the flatscreen and looks over at his maid. Sleepily disturbed, he frowns. "…Did you just say Will flew away?"

"I'm sorry, Mr. Merran."

"…*How?*"

"The new girl – Erin… She didn't fully close the door to the aviary… Will found a window after he got out… None of the others escaped though, sir. I counted them – they're all there."

Estelle's lifted her head off the pillow to observe this exchange. She watches her husband and wonders how he's taking this news, particularly in light of his other grievances. But Bob isn't ranting. Rather, it seems like he's maimed.

"…So… Will's gone?"

"I'm sorry, sir."

"He's… So what *now*, Sasha?" Bob blinks. "What do I do?"

"I don't really…"

"Do I fire the new girl?" Quiet for a moment and rigid, but then he slackens and he's stepping forward and pressing: "That ain't rhetorical – I'm *asking*, Sasha. Do I fire the dolt who lost my dang conure or don't I?"

"…She's a good kid. Better than some we've gotten in here."

Bob breathes, and he nods.

"…Chew her out for me at least."

"Can and done, sir."

"Good nuff." Bob's still gritting his teeth. "That's, uh… That'll be all, Sasha. That'll be all."

So Sasha leaves. Estelle lets go of the sheets covering her tits. Her husband is turning away from the television and heading for the nightstand on his side of the bed. Finds his Kitari Executive Slim and removes the charger cable. He taps away at it as he paces at an irritated measure.

"...*Bob?*"

"I'm textin, bunny. One second."

And he does. He sends

(call me)

(now)

and his wife asks him: "Who are you texting?"

"Vice President Seale. I don't have *Clark's* number anymore."

"Isn't he probably busy right now?"

"If Duncan Clark has even one minute, bunny, he can give it to the man who got him where he is... and I wanna *know*, damn it." Bob's scowling, but not at the flatscreen. He's fixed on the window and the morning sun shining on the gardens in the back of the estate. "It... It really pisses me off." Birds soaring on the horizon. "I mean... shut the door *right*, y'lousy bitch. How hard is that?"

THIRTY-SEVEN.

Where's the bloody world. Halton asks but no one answers. Six governing figures presently discuss matters within the Salon dole of Élysée Palace. More have promised to join and to aid them in the war but right this moment they need to assess themselves and their lands. Fortify their borders. Reintroduce conscription maybe.

Président Yves Lemieux drinks from a glass of ice-water that's gone tepid in his clammy clenching hand. His secretary has been coming in often to refill the drink as Lemieux supposedly has some sort of hydration disorder. He sweats profusely in times of stress. Needs to keep up those electrolytes.

Patricia Halton stands not far away with her back against a bookshelf. She's finally met a moment of rest or, more probably, she's exhausted her mouth and lungs. Stephen Fowley is seated in one of the rococo fauteuil chairs in front of the président's desk and he's chewing on a wad of gum he got from the co-pilot on the ride down from Lille. Every so often it seems like he's about to blow a bubble but then he remembers who he is and what's going on. William Kagan is near the door and on his phone with Sir Arnold Booth in London, but Booth is cutting out every so often. French Minister of Defence Édouard Allander is dressed in his best suit of aggressive plaids and he's staring out the window at the city of lights.

Further off in the golden room is Prime Minister Matthew O'Reilly of the Republic of Ireland who's curled up on a chaise and hasn't spoken a word in hours. Little to no communication can be had with anyone on his island. His phone hasn't rung since noon. It's becoming more apparent as the seconds tick off the clock that there's no longer a nation for him to champion. By now he appears as if he was released from futile psychiatric care.

Upon fleeing Westminster, Prime Minister Halton and select members of her staff were fled to Lille, whereupon they found O'Reilly had abandoned Ireland and was meeting with the French in search of sanctuary. Leaving Lille, they came here to meet with the heads of France's army, but Lemieux has had only one idea in mind despite Halton's persuasions, pleas and bargaining.

"What about the bloody *Spaniards?*

"A thousand men shipped in with some forces from Portugal."

"Italy?"

"It is another thousand at best." Lemieux is shaking his head. "This is not enough. Not for the entirety of the English Isles – not with these *things.*" He's poking a slick finger into his red desk, insisting: "Our only option, Patricia, is to establish a *wall.* We draw a line at the channel and we stop them from advancing into the rest of Europe." Lemieux looks to Fowley, hoping he'll listen to reason. "…We *have* to isolate the islands."

But the warhawk isn't convinced. Won't back down. She's left the baroque bookcase and steps once toward the French leader. Her sharp cheeks and stony eyes exude her repudiation and she accepts none of him. She cannot.

"If you think for one bloody instant that I'm about to sit back and allow my country and my *people* to be abandoned-"

"*Not* abandon! Never abandon!" Lemieux's gotten up off his chair. Sweating still. "We will fight for them, Patricia, we will not abandon! We will save all of them if we can!"

"But you propose to retract my forces to the channel and send no one else across!"

"Then don't retract them, Patricia! Leave them there to *die!*"

"I don't want to *leave them*, you dumb piss – I want to *aid them!*"

"With *what*, Patricia? I mean, with the eight thousand troops the Americans promised we're up to eleven thousand infantrymen." Lemieux looks to Allander. "What is the numbers, Édouard?"

"Oui. Eleven thousand infantry. We are looking at… less than three hundred aircrafts, monsieur." He runs a hand across a shaved scalp and lifts his brow, offering: "We are in excellent shape in regards to sea patrol. L'Atlantic, North Sea, Le Channel."

"For God's sake, Yves – it's eleven thousand able men! Let's send them in to save our people!" Halton holds a thin hand out to the Irish basket-case behind her, saying: "O'Reilly's *begging you*!"

"How many thousands of able men have already been thrown at these things? *Your* men. *O'Reilly's* men. The issue is that we do not know this we are dealing with! Be reasonable. Please!" Lemieux steps around his desk to better face the warhawk, begging her: "They have torn through every wave you have sent. Our only option is to amass the numbers we have and hold our ground before they advance farther. Once we maintain them we can then push back."

"I'm afraid to say he's right, mum." Will Kagan has ended his call. He's approaching, looking dead inside, looking to the prime minister. "I've just been on with Sir Arnold, still in Westminster. Reveals, uh… He says it's sixty-eight percent now."

"Sixty-eight of *what*?"

"We've lost contact with sixty-eight percent of our military, Prime Minister."

Halton gapes. There's trauma in fixed eyes. Lemieux shakes his head, wiping his brow with his shirtsleeve and reaching for his glass of water. Telling Patricia he prays to her. Please. We can't let them cross the channel. If they get to France or Belgium or Norway, who knows how far this will spread.

"What *difference* does it make?" Fowley finally speaks but doesn't bother getting up. He holds out his arms like he's asking for spare change. "They came from *somewhere*, dinnit they? They'll get to us the same way. How'd they get to North Ireland?"

"Satellite imagery…" Kagan tilts his head over, grinding his teeth, always chewing hard on a tough oddity that, upon prodding, only worsens. "…Satellites show no boats. Certainly nothing big enough to carry their numbers. No planes. The first report of the invaders came from a county called Darrows Glen… Landlocked by five other towns and districts."

"We have noted-" Allander interjects. "-that after appearing in Northern Ireland, their forces swept southward down the island but then stopped. The Irish Sea *stopped* them. They did not appear next in Wales or Liverpool. They took to Scotland first, in the north."

The prime minister looks to Kagan.

"Where were the first reports in Scotland, Will?"

"Just under Cambelltown. Our closest tip."

"How far would you say that is?"

"...About twenty kilometers, probably less."

"...So they can fly... but they can't fly *indefinitely*."

"This is just one of a hundred things we need to understand, Patricia." Lemieux has finished off his water and he's had to loosen his tie. His armpits are yellow. His jowls ache. "We need to be smart. They are *demons*. For all we know they are *immortal*."

"Immortal is a word we made up and used in fairy tales, Yves. We have no possible grasp on just what these beings *are* in respect to mortality. I may not be an authority on the laws of science but I'll tell you one thing: even hellspawn die when a grenade blows them to pieces."

"This is what you *want*, yes?" Allander's gotten his back up but his face wears a look of patronizing tutelage or mockery. "*Trench warfare?* You want to push the frontlines north? Send all the king's horses and all the king's men? Madam, and you will lose that game; I swear this to you."

Here again the deputy prime minister has a rat's ass enough to open his mouth, suggesting brusquely that we bomb Ireland. Just torch the entire island. It's where most of the scourges are right now, right? It's where they're coming from? I mean, I don't want to sound like Swift. It's not a racist thing.

"Oh for God's *sake*, Stephen, you useless muppet."

"What? Am I wrong, Patty? Only like a handful in Scotland, last time I checked."

"Check again, Stephen. There are *thousands* in Scotland and at least one flying savage in London that can bring down airplanes!"

Halton is holding onto herself suddenly. Trying to get a grip. But she's not too far from the breaking-point that O'Reilly has reached. She's looking over at him now and sees he's staring blankly at the white ceiling. Gone fishin, as they say.

Will Kagan is reading messages on his mobile and Allander is looking off at Paris again. The président's secretary is making a subtle entrance and she has a fresh pitcher of ice-water to refill his glass. The prime minister takes the chance to cool and let her raw throat recuperate. Letting her eyes fall again on the dehydrated Frenchman.

"I can't... I can't leave my country to die." After a breath, she looks Lemieux in the eye. She warns him: "I cannot allow your wall if it means damning my people to Hell."

"...You will fight me, Patricia?"

"...I'll fight you, Yves."

The président stands still, looking back at the prime minister. Meeting her. Matching her. Exchanging refusal to yield, neither one speaking nor breathing at all – merely waiting.

As the secretary is making her exit of the golden room, the door is nudged open and Marlene Jacobs-Moore is returning. She's holding her tablet in one overly-bejeweled hand and her phone in the other and she's looking to her prime minister gravely. When Halton notices her assistant she doesn't want to believe the face she bears. She tries to deny it. She can't take anymore.

"Marlene, good you're here. Did you manage to track down a reputable... *expert*, if that's what we're calling it? Someone who can explain what we're dealing with here."

"Prime Minister..." Marlene holds the phone out to Halton and steps towards her. "...it's the Royal London Hospital. You should take it."

But Patricia doesn't take it. She doesn't move.

"...What do they want?"

"Maybe out in the hallway, ma'am."

"What do they *want*, Marlene?" Halton begs. *"Please!"*

"…It's Clive. Your husband. It's…" Marlene's lost whatever words she thought she'd gathered. She's without further details she's comfortable divulging in front of present company. Again she presses the phone upon the warhawk. Insisting with her eyes that she take it. "…I'm so sorry."

LONDON

In her office on the third floor sits Dr. Yasmin Padamjeet who's holding a phone receiver to her ear. Presently speaking with the warhawk herself. It was not easy to reach her, but she had to be notified. Patricia is listed as Clive's emergency-contact. So now at last Padamjeet tells her what happened early this morning, shortly after the plane crash, not far from Westminster.

"We would have notified you sooner, Prime Minister. The body was without any ID but dental-records were a perfect match. It was one of our nurses who recognized him actually."

"What happened?"

"A hit and run."

"*Who*? *Who* was the driver?"

"I honestly have no idea… It's not my business." On the other end, Patricia Halton is quiet. "He can't be moved with a spinal fracture, I'm afraid." Halton says nothing. "…Prime Minister?"

"What's his condition?"

"There's a deal of internal bleeding. Broken ribs. Fractured sk-"

"Will he *live*?"

"…Are you still in London, ma'am?"

Silence replies. Padamjeet waits and wonders if she should repeat herself. When Halton finally speaks up again she tells the doctor I'm coming back. Padamjeet neither argues or affirms the decision. Upon ending the call, she sits for a moment at her desk, looking to the framed photo of her husband and kids. The door's closed but the unrest in a room down the hall still comes through.

When she opens the door the cries hit her with full force. It's a Thai woman who was bicycling outside Hyde Park at the time of the crash. Projected scrap from the wing of the Boeing 737 struck her down. They've tried to numb her pain but it doesn't let up.

It's here, stepping out of her office, that Dr. Padamjeet notices a speeding streak of white and black. Something small. Tiny. Had to have only been five inches tall – if it was anything at all besides a trick of the light. Flying or zipping down the hallway of the Royal London Hospital like a little shooting star.

The good doctor can't pay it much attention.

There are too many people screaming today.

Due to limited space, they've wheeled the shrill mindless Thai woman into Clive Halton's room. Clive barely notices because he's mostly unconscious now. The pain and the drugs taking him away to a point where he no longer remembers the Imp of Imps and the trade. It's nice here. In his curt dreams of reality he sees a doctor standing over him and he hears the screaming of a dying Thai lady and he recognizes this as life, more or less.

And he has all the life in the world.

Eternity, more or less.

And just before the painkillers put him to sleep, Clive hears Dr. Yasmin Padamjeet ask some Scottish nurse to ready the patient for a barb coma. All he can do now is rest.

THIRTY-EIGHT.

BIRMINGHAM

The Rottweiler pup lays down on the seat next to Curtis Merchant. The Pieman has sat down in the empty bench across from them and he's glancing out the windows at blackness when they rush into the tube beneath Birmingham. They would swear the train's running slower today. Their chase up to Liverpool was intended to head off Bates and Charlene, but now it seems that they on the dumb Ducati might beat them there. So the giant, ever restless, is fidgeting. He looks to Curtis and sees him with his head bowed and his eyes shut, so he asks if he's passed out.

"...M'wake."

"Whaddaya doin then?"

"I'm *prayin*, Pie."

"For what?" But Pieman's not really looking for a response. He's already shifted his focus to the speed of the train that seems to be getting even slower, demanding: "What's with the fuckin metro? We should be there by now."

"Maybe she's not gettin nuff power." Curtis glances around and so the dog does too. He realizes he's gotten the Rotty worked up so he's patting him again, settling him, settling Pieman: "Relax, bruv. Almost there."

"Don't tell me to relax."

"*Aight*, mate. Fuck. Just... trying to help."

"Nothin to help until I get to Charlene. I ain't leavin my sister alone in this nightmare with Gareth fuckin Bates. No bloody way."

"...You know, you probably don't hafta look after her so much. From what I overheard this mornin between yous. Just, y'know... seems she can find her own way."

"That's what I'm afraid of."

"And you think you's better choosin for her then?"

The Pieman has no intention to explain himself, so he turns his back to Curtis. He looks up the run of the snaking train that's turning around another bend. Toddling wearily as if it's a shattered horse giving one last brave gallop before its heart bursts. Other passengers have noticed the lag. They glance around, murmuring.

When the train comes to an abrupt halt in the middle of the tube there's cursory contemplation before immediate panic. The lights cut. Must be a citywide blackout. Something's happening aboveground and it's halted their train and left them stranded. People are screaming and using their phones as lights, what to do what to do. Far down at the front of the cars is the conductor who's calling out remain calm but he can barely be heard. Curtis has got his phone on and the dog has gotten up and stands on the seat and sniffs around in the blackness.

"What should we do, Pie? We's stayin put?"

"Yeah. Watch me stay put."

By the light of Curtis's phone, the giant gets to his feet. He's moving towards the back of the train. Curtis sighs and picks up the Rotty and follows. They're soon joined by a Filipino woman who seems to think they've got the right idea. People shine their phones on them when they pass, checking to see they're human.

"We just gonna stroll on through the tube, bruv?"

"Only came underground a few minutes ago."

"Think the line's still electric?"

"Touch it, let me know."

They reach the last car and find they've been joined by sixteen other passengers in addition to the little Filipino. Someone in here has a baby and it's crying out but no one can see it. No one knows where it is. Pieman approaches the rear door and he's grabbing a hold of its stiff lever, trying to pull it up and open.

"You think there's… those sodding *creeps* out there?"

"…Yeah I do. But it'll be better than dyin in here."

Pieman's pulled the lever and kicked open the traincar door. They wait for a moment, staring into the blackness and listening to the baby. They decide the coast is clear before Pieman jumps down onto the tracks. The rest watch him, looking for some sign that he might be hosting six-hundred volts melting godly muscles. But the giant stands fine in the dark and stares at small glowing rectangles held up to him, telling them we's all good.

Curtis jumps down and they're about to crack on when the little Filipino woman calls to them, impatiently slighted. They turn and see her and the drop she faces so Pieman returns and picks her up and sets her down. Does so for the old man that follows and then carries onward. Curtis drops the Rotty and it keeps up with them and so do the other passengers who've evacuated the train.

Through the tube the group wanders the only route. A lot of them keep using their phones as lanterns but Curtis figures that's a good way to drain the battery. He and his gym-mate lead without light to guide them, following the subway rail beneath their feet. Curtis is shouting warnings whenever they feel the track change direction. Bend to the right here. Slight off to the left. Occasionally they feel the Rotty pup brush up against their legs or they hear the stumble of somebody falling behind them. One woman asks what will happen if the power comes back on. With them all on the rails. Somebody replies goodnight madam.

"...Eh, *psst – you boys.*"

"*Whossat?*"

"You look like warriors, doncha? Especially the *big* fellow."

"*Whossat* then?"

"I'm nobody." The voice is a woman's. Age undetermined but seemingly not young. She sounds proper. Upper-class maybe, and she confirms: "But I'm *worth* a pound or two. You boys look like you might be worth something to a woman like me."

The bodybuilders listen. Curtis is the one doing the talking and Pieman merely listens. As they walk along through blackness they hear this woman's heels as they clack beside them. Curtis asks her what she wants and she pleads her proposal.

"Protection. Safe passage home. My *children* are there – *alone.*"

"Of course they're alone. That's what well-off do with well-offspring. Just *board* em."

"Gonna slag me off for having ambitions that get me outta the house?"

"For makin money off it anyway." Curtis tries to look over at Pieman – tries to read him but he can't see him at all. So instead he asks the woman in the dark: "Where's home?"

"Here. Just north of Brum."

"We can't." The giant's voice finally joins their exchange, telling the unseen woman: "We already got someone to look after and we's headin to her right now. Can't help ye."

"I have five thousand pounds to change your mind."

Curtis is interested. "...Five big?"

"Yes."

"S'pose that's not ready?"

"Not unless you think I'm daft, for chrissake. But I can *get* you it. S'in a safe at home. Five thousand at the house... another five if you can escort me and my children to the airport." A pause then: "I'll... I'll even pay for tickets for you both. Fair?"

"You'd think so." Again Curtis tries to see the giant beside him but he can't and only tells the woman in the dark: "Let's see how buggered it is out there. Then we'll talk..."

Another gentle turn to the left and Curtis calls back to alert the followers. The ground seems to slant upwards here. The Rotty pup is heard taking off suddenly. Bolting. Its claws are scratch against the gravel and Curtis calls to it but doesn't know its name so he calls it Dog but the pup is running onward – heading forwards. It isn't long before they can't hear it any longer.

Quiet again, listening to water drips echo through the tube like some anchialine cave. The woman in the dark asks them for their names. Curtis offers his. Tells her this one here they call Simon the Pieman. When she asks how he got the title he tells her he doesn't remember. She tells them I'm Tess Breighton. I own a franchise of women's boutiques. Nothing extravagant. The hours are torture, but money's comfy enough. Seemingly, she stresses this.

Light in the distance that's grey and subdued. Followers sigh relief or cheer and quicken their pace. At the end of the tube is pale weak daylight and the group is stepping into it. Curtis spots the Rottweiler pup and sees it's pissing on a lamppost just out of the tunnel. The dog turns and sort of smiles when it sees them.

"So... have we got a deal, boys?"

Curtis and the Pieman turn and see the woman there. Pieman says she must be Tess Breighton and she answers you must be Simon the Pieman. She's older but not old. Hair looks dyed but it's maintained. No roots. Fine colour like almond butter. She wears a little indigo number that probably sells for pretty brass in one of her three boutique locations. Her handbag is a Prada Saffiano that she holds closely as she looks to the humongous boys.

Curtis pats the dog jogging up beside him. Other passengers are marching exhausted from the tunnel and into the damp overcast afternoon. It's a hill of loose rocks and they descend it to the street below. Cars down there moving quick, ignoring signs. Sounding horns. Erratic outcries. Crazies made mad and Pieman scowls.

"...How far is you?"

"If we can get a cab, not far." Tess glances over at the giant. "You can *fit* in cars, can't you?"

"Careful. Be real careful, woman."

"Oh I'm not takin the piss, I'm just trying to keep this engaging. The more fun we have, the longer we'll keep from losing our minds." Tess bucks her shoulder to reset her Saffiano strap firmly against her neck. Asking: "Well? Ten thousand quid, boys, and a ticket *out*. Wassit gonna be?"

"Why do you have to get home so bad for?"

"For my *children*, Mr. Merchant." Tess looks to the shorter of the two, insisting stern but shakily: "I... have to get them. Have to save them... And I need *you* to save *me*." She begs. "Please."

"The bigun, miss. *He's* the one you gotta convince."

So again Tess looks to the giant. And in some way it seems as if he's swayed, but still he's single-minded. When he turns to the posh woman he's still got his treasure in his eyes.

There's a scream and Pieman doesn't get a chance to respond. One of the metro passengers down the gravel hill is pointing to the sky above Birmingham. Off in the distance is a birdlike thing too big to be a bird. It's something else. So people are running now and some trip and tumble down the hill of rocks. There's a Jetta that's crashing into the back of a Ram. A lamppost is knocked down by something with waxy yellow wings.

One with grey feathers and a snout of rodent teeth seizes a little girl in a pink frock, taking her up high as she screams. There's another with one nipple and one eye that's landed, retracting its wings. Six-two. Sturdy. Nude. Clutching a rusted cinquedea and it abhors, targeting the giant among the loud shambolic others. It's charging straight for Pieman, who tells the posh bitch get behind me as he curls his paws into fists.

It's like old times. Like he's back in the underground. Precision. Profound reflexes. Laying jabs. Side-stepping. Snapping fingers, seizing skulls and meeting faces with his kneecap. Driving a knuckle into a lonesome eye to pop it. The brutality comes easy, like slipping on a glove and returning to glory he'd left behind.

When Tess screams he looks up. There's more of them. Nasties with bigger horns and weapons and testes, and that's fine because he can take them. The Pieman is getting up off a whimpering cyclops, panting but exalted. People are running to him, he sees. They need him. They need someone to protect them, and that's fine because he can take them.

Get behind me, he tells them all.

And they do so as the demons swarm.

THIRTY-EIGHT.

WASHINGTON, D.C. – 12:03 EST

"My fellow Americans…

"Today I must address a crisis facing our brothers across the Atlantic. I'm sure news of it, in one form or another, has reached many of you already… The time has come that I must address this enemy in our midst. They are strangers from… somewhere else. Strangers that are not of our world… Many of you probably… won't take this news well. Many will find this impossible to believe.

"I myself find this impossible to believe…

"This is not a hoax. This is not some ruse or flimflam and wherever you stand now, whether you watch me on television or hear me on the radio or the web – whatever you do, please *listen* to me. Please *believe me*… This is what I have to tell you…

"For hundreds of years now, we as a species have come to understand the ways of our planet and our universe and we have mapped the bounds of possibility as we know it… but in the last few days it's become apparent that we've been wrong. There are still possibilities that go against ration and go against everything we know. These strangers invading the United Kingdom and the Republic of Ireland… They are not human. You've heard rumours and have read and have seen things on television and online, and I'm sorry to admit that the claims are true…

"These strangers – these scourges invading our world – are hostile in the most extreme fashion. Their intentions are not clear. Their ultimate goal is not yet known to us. But we do know that they are killers. They are… torturers… and arsonists and rapists… and it would appear as though they're set to destroy us… But I vow to you: they will fail so help us God.

"Right outside the fences, right this very moment – pause the teleprompter please, I'd like to say something… Right outside the fences right now are about five hundred Americans hollerin their heads off at the White House here… They demand I step down in light of this and the future that'll follow. Ain't no motherloving sense in having a pacifist fight our battles – the chump should hand off to a more capable man. And for hours now I've been dang keen to agree with em. It's no secret at all, I never liked feudin and I never wanted war… but I ain't never been a fan of evil neither…

"My friends, America does not *abide* evil. America has *not* abided it. Not when they pick on us or when they pick on the weak and innocent abroad and not when they drive a couple airliners into our hearts do we *ever* abide evil in this world. Not for – turn the *prompter* off, Lou; I'm *done* with it.

"My fellow Americans, today and for every day that comes to pass I make you this promise… These *demons* will know the lash of humankind. I am going after them with everything we've got and come the dawn we will send their broken survivors back to Hell. This invasion will be *stopped*. This nightmare will end, my friends…

"There will be the peace we dream of, I swear it."

HEMSEDAL – 19:11 CET

Drake's *Energy* is blaring out of Dustin Tomson's iPhone speakers in the living-room while the actor is in the washroom flexing in his briefs. Kary sits on the sofa and listens against her will. Currently streaming on her cellphone is the Presidential address given just minutes ago by Duncan Clark in the Oval Office. Their normally blithe commander-in-chief appears to be wounded. Angry. He's confident even if his voice falters. It's hard to hear for her boyfriend's music, but it sounds as if Clark's ready to kill. Kary glances through the comments below the video

(no way this is true)

(Im sitting down to breakfast with the fam when this interrupts the kids cartoons. This is not happenng. Somebody tell me this is fake.)

(Seriously is this all fur real??)

(Jon Rambo for President!)

(Even an avowed Clark hater like me can appreciate this.)

(Im Joining! Im killing those f&#!ing THINGS!)

(WTF IS HAPPENNIG???)

(Earth will burn #TheFirstIsFirst)

(he's still a pussy btw)

(HOAX)

and she can't take the heartbeat pulsing in her head. It's the room and the lights and the heavy beat of the music and I got enemies got a lotta enemies and Dustin grunting and shouting bursts of adrenalin at himself in the bathroom mirror and she has to escape. She's set her pink phone down on the couch and she heads for the doors leading out onto the balcony. She's opened them to feel the chill again and see the restful white glow of the mountains in the moonlight. She nearly stumbles like she's drunk as she hurries out onto the stone overlook and she grasps its railing and breathes heavy lungfuls of the raw air in the hope that her chest and insides will freeze.

"…Everything alright?"

Kary gasps and spins. She sees her bodyguard Franklin Grier standing against the wall and finishing a cheap cigarillo. She figures he's been out here enjoying it for a while now. It and the peace of loneliness. She's swallowing the lump in her throat while gathering thoughts she'd rather burn.

"…You… you wouldn't believe…"

"…I know. I been reading it… Want a *puff*, Miss Benz?"

Kary looks to the cigarillo the bodyguard holds out to her. Tells him thank you but no. It'd probably make me gag. She's holding her brow tightly ruffled and she can't stand the pressure in her chest and maybe the mountains will calm her so she turns to them. The singer watches them sit quiet and still and she envies them.

"Did you know I'm… I'm not really very outgoing…"

"Your lyrics sometimes suggest otherwise, Miss Benz."

"…Nobody wants a pop song about the truth. Not when I'm… not very wild. Or if I prefer Netflix and instead of clubbing or… or fucking all the time."

"I know. I've seen that over the past couple months working for you. I've never seen so many films with subtitles." Grier smirks and notes: "Pretty funny though, huh? Being *famous.*"

"…I used to pray to be famous."

"I did that. For a time."

"And why'd you stop?"

"Well, I was thirteen and found something better to do before falling asleep. I didn't want to call God's attention to it so I stopped talkin to Him every night."

Kary smiles, contemplating prayers she's held onto as a wind comes and chills her, but she only gently shivers. Her forearms cross below her breasts and hold tight against her body but she can take the freeze. She's taken a lot worse.

"…I've wanted to be famous ever since I was a little kid." The popstar's soft hands take the stone railing again and she adores the snow lit up by the moon. The peaks of the mountains stabbing into the sky. Regaling as she remembers: "…I lived in this shitty house in backwoods Iowa. My bedroom was the nursery because I was the youngest accident and my parents were too piss-poor to get a bigger place. Wasn't any room on either side of my bed – I had to climb onto it over the footboard. But every night before I did I got down on my knees. I prayed to God. I prayed that one day I'd be a famous singer… and I could buy a house somewhere beautiful… Have a proper bedroom and millions of people to love me, without… without it being so hard."

"…What made you stop praying?"

"…I signed a record deal."

The door behind them opens suddenly. Grier looks to Dustin but Kary doesn't turn around, doesn't take her eyes off the glowing slopes. The actor is still shirtless and is slick from his impromptu workout. From his iPhone speakers in the suite they can still hear Drake. He looks to the bodyguard and then to the singer standing in a light sweater and jeans in this freeze.

"Sup, babe." It isn't a question. "I'm almost ready to go."

Kary keeps staring at the mountains to avoid the sight of her boyfriend. The actor is clenching up for the cold but he refuses to shiver. Just sort of grimaces like a shit. Then he tells the bodyguard we're heading out soon – why don't you warm up the car?

Grier eyes the singer before he wets his fingers and pinches out the cigarillo, mumbling: …Yes, sir.

The bodyguard examines Kary once more and decides he can do nothing to help her except leave her alone. He hopes the actor will see that too. Dustin looks to Kary and says c'mon. She asks him where he's going and he tells her we're meeting up with my cousin. We're gonna go bar-hopping. It'll be fun. Kary turns and sees the bodyguard is gone, and she's alone with her beloved.

"…I think I'm gonna stay in."

"…*What?* …We're goin out, Kary. C'mon."

"I don't want to go out tonight."

"…The fuck are you *talking* about? Come on, ho. Y'aint staying here alone to grate your fuckin leg off again. Let's *roll*, babe."

"Have you not… *followed* what's going on in the UK?"

"I'm not in the UK, Kary. I'm on vacation in… fucking winter wonderland. Whatever it's called."

"Dustin… It's not safe out there."

The actor blinks. Twitter notifications ring out on his phone.

The singer turns her back on him and it hurts.

"…I've been cheatin on you."

"…I had a hunch, Dustin."

"So?"

"So what?"

"So you gonna fight for me, babe? C'mon."

"…Not right now."

Dustin doesn't understand and it's a bother. It hurts.

"Stay on your balcony then. *Fuck*. Don't catch cold."

Kary is glad to hear him relent. He's pissed but he'll forget it by the second or third bar on the hop. Dustin leaves her and it feels good. Feels like drying off on a cold summer day. She hears him close the doors but due to the wind she doesn't hear him set the lock.

Dustin shakes his head irritably as he returns to the bedroom to choose a shirt and a Moschino hoodie. On the dresser he's set his toiletry bag and a bottle of Valentino cologne, which he applies liberally above and lets it rain down in a cool way. Before he leaves the suite he spots Kary's pink cellphone on the sofa.

Dustin snatches the phone and pockets it.

Let her freeze. Bitch is crazy.

Heading down the hall to the elevator, he steps inside and presses for the ground floor. As he descends he hears Vivaldi and smells the perfume in here leftover from a previous occupant.

Ducking by tourists that seem to double-take and recognize him, Dustin hastens to avoid them, here passing the concierge booth. The doorman opens the heavy door and the star exits into cold. He sees the limo idling directly in front of him.

For Kary Benz, in the aftermath, there's numbing bliss. Still on the balcony, relishing cold and wind and altitude and the darkening view of the range. Alone. Alone, she thinks. She did it.

This is what she wants. Needs. The isolation is what gives her courage. It's a chance that tomorrow might be a day when people out beyond her shell could make sense to her.

…You know what I see…

The words in a free-forming tune escape without her intending much to sing. Tears have turned to glass at the corners of her eyes. She grips the marble railing with hands she barely feels anymore. Somebody else's hands, numb in euphoria.

…beneath the black cloud looming in the sky…

Her fair brow beneath highlighted bangs ruffles and remains petrified in such biting air. The freeze is burying down into her bones. It's all she wants, she needs, to stand and envy mountains.

For a moment there's no brutes around. No one here but me...

All around me, I see... I think I'm finally free.

Her stomach aches. She hasn't eaten since brunch with Grier. Now she could use something like hot soup in her belly. She'll dine alone and watch a movie or continue to feel and produce music and it might truly be a pleasure. So she's finally giving up the vista and stepping toward the door into the suite.

It's locked, and when the realization hits Kary just snaps. She begins to shiver as her eyes puff and redden. She hammers on the door with raw frozen fists. She shouts to other balconies below her but no one is out on any of them.

No one can hear her.

After a little while Kary doesn't know what time it is.

Having searched her pocket for her phone, she's remembered she left it on the couch inside. She doesn't know how long she's been out here now, entirely underdressed. The numbing winds are no longer friends. They beat against her without break and she has to curl up beneath the stone railing to shield herself. But even down here she shivers for the cold. Even here she's going to freeze to death. Everything in her vision is turning baby-blue.

The windows. For five or ten minutes she's been looking at them. Looking through a veil or film of blue. She might break them. She could charge and tuck in and take to them like a skinny cannonball. They'd break, maybe. Maybe she'd be cut by glass but it's better than dying out here. It'll cost for the repairs. I'll have to tell the hotel manager I locked myself out. I'm always doing stupid things. I'll just admit I was dumb, and that's probably what her beloved wanted. Kary takes a deep breath and she forces herself to stand. Her veins sting and her muscles are stiff. Again she looks over the railing to the balconies below her. She shouts and cries out but nobody hears. She doubts that anyone can hear.

As she weeps, as she freezes, as she goes blank, she sees the rock cliff twelve floors beneath her. The drop from here has got to be eighty feet or more and she could take it. When she lands she'll find solitude. Rest. Mountains. Just one jump over the footboard and she'll find her comfy bed.

So, before bedtime, she decides to pray to God like old times.

But when her eyes lift and look to things in the sky she can't believe what life has brought her now. The cold means nothing.

When she smashes herself through the window she's slit herself in places. Bleeding out. She lands on the floor of their suite and she's gasping and shaking and glass shards stick into her shoulder and kneecaps but she's hurriedly scrambling to her feet, but she isn't quick enough. She screams when a monster like a Kodiak bear lands on top of her and brings her back down onto the glass.

And there's silence.

Silence, until there's this sharp *whistle*. And the star lifts her head trembling, wincing, glass shards in her skin and the beast on top of her drools and dry-humps. The star, when she looks up and sees the horned inhuman in the parka, only whines shrill and ruined.

Rosier the Vanisher likes Kary Benz immediately.

Smiling, looking upon the star, asking her: "…Down to fuck?"

FORTY.

The Pieman, so bruised, is still on his feet.

They can't get a cab so they've walked four or five blocks – it's hard to tell exactly how far. There's too much going on and every few feet they pass more people fleeing. People avoiding the grills of speeding cars. People looting shops. People holding bibles. A platoon of soldiers hustles down the street followed by a Land Rover. Seeing uniformed men with machineguns, Curtis urges Tess and Pieman to keep low and keep moving. Now, he says. Royal Army'll keep the freaks busy. We can slip through under the radar.

"Now where'd you learn to be such a strategist, Mr. Merchant?"

"I was big into Warhammer when I was young."

"What's Warhammer?"

"A game with little... Does it *matter*?" Curtis directs them down the alleyway they come upon. "It's as clear a path as any."

Pieman leads into the alley and Curtis and the little Rottweiler follow. The socialite is closely behind, though the giant could take or leave her. Finding their way onto Moseley Street. More of the same unreality and they attempt to find passage through it. When the giant hears a scream he turns and sees Tess is holding her posh bag back from a snatcher with long hair and too many earrings. The Rotty barks at the assailant but only so much as it can do at his age. At least the giant is scary enough. He's at Tess's side in moments and he grabs the sorry shit by the back of the neck. Squeezes just enough the prick sees spots and finally lets go of the handbag. Tess backs away and Pieman drives his wrecking fist.

"That'd be my money's worth right there."

"This itty git's worth five large, is he? Why isn't I a millionaire then?" The Pieman drops the winded scally against the asphalt. "If he's worth it, pay up."

"All I was attempting to say, Mr. Pupsy, is I *like* this bag."

"Pieman."

"I'm sorry?"

"*Jesus*..." Pieman shakes his head. They hurry onwards down the sidewalk, staying close to the buildings. The giant leads with Tess behind him and Curtis at the back. "Don't call me Pupsy. Never call me Simon. My name's fuckin Pieman."

"Well perhaps if I saw you bake and sell a pie..."

"You don't have to question it. Just do it."

"Why the tenor? Weren't taught any decency on skid row?"

"You ain't payin me for nothin yet, woman, least of all decency. And I haven't got none to donate."

Squealing brakes, so the trio looks to the street. A very short man screams when a Dodge Avenger loses control and runs him down. The car loses traction, careens sideways, flips. It takes out a stop-sign before obliterating the corner windows of a bank. Others bolt in hysteria. Curtis hurriedly picks up the Rottweiler puppy to save it being trampled. Tess and the two strongmen turn to gaze down the street at the wall of grey smoke that billows in from the north that's vanishing the city one foot at a time.

Speeding cars and trucks have formed a pileup in their panic and smash themselves into a wedge between a dump-truck and oncoming traffic. Engines are bursting into flame. Injured drivers crawl out of their vehicles but can't move fast enough before the smoke swallows them. Sirens are muffled. Guns fire.

From out of the grey wisps and cinders come pale figures. On the land and in the air. Some small and some very large. Some very quick. Pieman tells them to run. Head for the alley. But everyone has the same idea. People are stampeding away from beasts that swoop down on them. One that's flapping wings of rancid feathers lands like a raptor on an older man's shoulders and it rolls to bring him down. Talons slit his carotid artery and free a pressurized quart from his throat. The Rotty is crying in Curtis's arms.

A demon looks to Tess when her fear draws its attention. Curtis sees it lift off the hood of a Beamer and sail towards her as quick and swift as a falcon and when it seizes her defensive arms and pins her against the concrete she screams in its face. It's leaning in to kiss or gnaw her when it's suddenly cracked by the stop-sign that the Dodge tore out of the sidewalk moments ago. The sheer force of the blow knocks the freak a good four feet before it smashes against the jagged window-frame of the bank. It shrieks brutally, sounding primeval. Livid. Its flight is awkward as it flies a dumb indirect route to a rooftop above.

The Pieman clutches his stop-sign. He holds out his free arm to his floored employer, asking her: Y'alright, woman?

"No I'm fucking *not*!"

Tess takes his huge hand and he pulls her up like he's lifting stacks and she thinks her arm is going to be ripped from its socket. On her feet now, she grasps her throbbing shoulders and they all look up to see the beast that attacked them.

Its wings slow and reposition to ease in and onto the edge of a building across the street. It perches like a gargoyle and glares down at them over fleshy caruncles and dewlaps enveloping its curved beak. Ashen-grey feathers knocked loose from its wings fall gently to the sidewalk as a donkey's tail flicks agitated from side to side. Blood trickles from the perfectly clean slash across the side of its enlarged bald head.

Eyes like a hawk narrow at the giant.

"…I think you might've made an enemy, Mr. Pupsy."

"That's twice, woman. Say it one more time and I leave you here. I'll leave you behind and march on, woman."

"I'll follow you."

"I'll cripple you."

The vulture is suddenly diving, attempting to hook talon razors into the Pieman, but it's greeted with another punishing slice of the metal stop-sign. Slit across the belly, it screeches and beats heavy wings against the giant. Nearly gives him a concussion. Nearly knocks him down. It ascends to avoid the sign and dives down again before the heavyweight can react.

The vulture manages to get close enough and its claws tear off most of Pieman's left ear. The giant howls, unfocused, unprepared, and the vulture dives for him. Smashing him down onto asphalt.

Down, bleeding, ringing in his ears. There's a demon screaming on top of him, sinking claws into his pecks, but the Pieman can't hear the stupid bird. He hears no one counting down from ten.

Nine.

Eight.

The fight, he sees. Back in the glory days. People all around him shouting for the thrill. Tess harrowing her cheeks. Curtis rushing in to help his mate and the vulture bashes him away with one swipe of a heavy wing.

Six.

Five.

Charlene, he sees. Beyond the ropes of the ring, disgusted and walking away, he sees, with a vicious thug named Gareth Bates. I coulda fought that prick today. I coulda protected my sister.

Three.

Two.

One.

And the vulture widens a fleshy beak for the final strike, and the Pieman pulls his stop-sign and bashes it against the beast's chin. It tries to flee but the giant seizes its donkey tail and he's up and he's tugging and he's angry and the vulture produces this escalating howl as the giant rips its backside apart. It takes to the air.

Tess is grasping the Pieman, who hunches over and bleeds out his marred head. Bleeding from his chest. Panting. Holding the tail.

"We gotta go!"

"What for?" Holding the tail. "I'm *winnin.*"

"That thing'll *kill* you, you twit! *Run!*"

The daemon lands atop a lamppost and seethes, hating the giant and his friends – focusing on only them amid the flock.

Pieman slings its tail over his shoulder, it sees. Snapping his wrist and flicking the blood from his hand when he stands and glares up at the monster that glares back at him. He'll take it on. He grips the stop-sign to do so. Spits onto the street. But there are beasts approaching. More fly above their heads and charge down the streets on the backs of unnatural black horses. It takes both Tess and Curtis to pull the giant away – pull him into a corner shop. In a confined space the vulture won't be so fast, so flighty, and maybe the giant can kill it there. If not, then at least they'll breathe freely from the smoke.

Stock rattles off the shelves around them. Curtis lunges out and covers Tess with his arms to shield her from bottles of Ginger-Ale toppling off a rack. Tess covers her eyes. The Rotty barks.

Panting, listening to fires and anarchy and barking, Curtis looks to his hulking gym-mate and sees he's on his mobile. Pieman holds his iPhone to his bloodied mutilated ear. Curtis asks him who the hell he's calling and Pieman tells him he's calling Charlene.

Gotta reach her.

Gotta know.

That's what he says, panting, bleeding, pumped. But Charlene never answers. Pieman waits for her voice but she never answers him. It's just ring ring ring as Birmingham burns outside.

FORTY-ONE.

Reagan and the handyman named Durst carried the body into the streets so drowned in smoke. Abigail joined them because she had to say goodbye, leaving her son safe with her sister and the old woman in the pharmacy. They made haste and with scarves tied over their faces to breathe not the cindery smog.

Durst set Mike down. Abigail wept. Reagan held the gun.

Durst told them we gotta get back inside. But Abigail wept and knelt down in front of Mike in the street to ask how. You got me. You got Brent goddammit. How.

…How can you gowan leave us… in this hell?

Abby weeps and Durst eyes the smoke surrounding them.

It's Reagan Brodie who crouches down beside the widow, the hairdresser, her neighbour back home in Darrows. With her arm around her shoulder she tries to tell Abby she's wrong. You're not alone. It's okay… We're going to survive together.

Grabbing food and toiletries. Grabbing insulin for old Lora. They horded supplies before leaving the pharmacy for Durst's hardware-shop next door. First job on the handyman's list was boarding up the front window so he screws plywood in place now as the group sits in hiding, trapped.

Abigail is inconsolable, sat on a lawn-chair from the only set Durst had in stock. Reagan, beside the young widow, comforts her as best she can despite having nothing to say.

Another widow – Abby's sister Alicia – is watching.

Further away, across the shop next to the window shielded by layers of plywood, the barmaid grieves her own husband and it's what keeps her frigid. But as she stands here and listens to Cillian Durst's power-drill, Alicia strangely doesn't much think of Fred.

Instead she watches Reagan Brodie hug her weeping sister. Fred didn't like her, minute he saw her when they all came to the pub.

Durst looks over at Alicia.

Something just off about her, Alicia says.

The handyman nods and glances back at Reagan and Abigail. Lora Malik sits on a stack of extension-cords, unhearing anything, holding Brent who wonders in grief. Alicia watches it all and she listens as Durst drills one final woodscrew to protect them.

Out there in the smoke, they hear and they feel a tremendous crash. Something landing, maybe. Something gargantuan setting down. It's enough to topple them, and Lora falls over on the coils and only just manages to keep her hold of Brent, who wails. The old woman shouts to the rest struggling to keep their balance.

"What the rumbling shite was *that*?"

The group blinks, terrified, ignorant and it's terrifying. No one answer. It's the handyman though who finally looks to Lora and confirms: You *heard* that, Lora?

"Give us some credit, dear. I'm hard-a-fuckin-hearin, but dear cripes I can hear a bloody mountain when it falls down."

And here the old woman stands holding the infant in shaking crinkly arms. Abigail watches through tears, scared for her son. Standing up to take him, to keep him safe with her. That's what she'll do – that's the only thing she'll do now. Lora doesn't notice she's lost the boy. God, she says and her hand reaches to the gold cross on her neck. Looking up. God. tell us what's happened. Where's these cuntfreaks come from?

No one answers. They all look at Lora. No one answers.

Who's done this to us?

LONDON – 16:14 GMT

A daycare-centre called The Garden Path outside Slough. Most of the children weren't brought in today. Sundays are usually a slow day but today, in the wake of the plane crash in Hyde Park, there's

242

only a third of the expected lot here.

Eve Grimly is left with six children today. At six, Eve's the youngest and the others call her weird. Pure cream hair cut short, silvery-blue eyes, the fairest white skin, always in longsleeves and pants and she wears a hat in the summertime to protect her from the sun. The other kids came up with the name Pasteface and by now they use it exclusively when addressing her.

Today Eve's collected the *Snakes and Ladders* game from the shelf, wanting to play it but none of the children regard her at all. They don't speak to her when she comes around. So Eve's gone to Natalie, who's playing dolls with a couple other girls.

"Wanna play with me?"

"I'm playin with Sam and Liz right now." The other girls stare uncomfortably at their younger white peer. Teenaged Natalie – the caretaker's daughter – doesn't look at all like she wants to play with anyone. Proposing: "What about one of the boys?"

"They don't like me."

"Eve, you're all kids. You don't know what you like." Natalie's scared. Telling the outcast: "Go try. Just... ask them."

Eve lowers the game. Stepping away from the girls. Glancing over at the four boys in the far corner. They're fighting, it looks like. Or wrestling or something. Two of them are doing most of the job while one watches and one sort of lays in a kick or two without bias as to his target. Eve's walking over to them when they all suddenly feel a shudder run through the building. The lights flicker. Natalie leaves the room. Eve carries on toward the boys still in battle with themselves on the padded interlocking mats in the shape of jigsaws.

"...What are you doing?"

Tim, the one not participating in the row answers: "They're dukin over who's gonna marry Kary Benz." He looks over at her and her board-game. "Whaddaya want, Pasteface?"

"Nothin."

"...Nobody's gonna play that wichoo."

"Why?"

"Because you suck." Looking to the little girl. "You gonna suck the colours outtavem. Ugly pasteface."

Here again, a quake. Lights flickering and the children glance up to the fixtures in the ceiling. The girls are worried. The boys have stopped their horseplay. Eve too is aware that things are awry but she isn't sure what's the trouble, retaining her grip on *Snakes and Ladders*. When the lights go out and stay out she hugs the box and takes a seat on the floor while the girls start crying and the boys shout. Out there in the world is a riot that's getting loud.

Waves of galloping horses, they hear.

Natalie is returning to the playroom and she's followed by her mother, Emily. Old and very thin, mascara running from her eyes. They both aim flashlights and they shine them on the kids they're charged with and they try to calm them down. Stop screaming. The small albino girl shies her sensitive eyes when the flashlight beam is shot at her. Eve looks around at the hubbub in the darkness and doesn't know enough to be so scared.

"*Everyone* – everyone, *please! Hush* now! *Hush up please!*"

But they won't. Natalie looks to her mother.

"Should I check the breakers?"

"Worth a stab."

"You'll be alright with this lot?"

Emily frets but pushes her daughter along, guidiing her to the hallway that leads to the basement stairwell. Emily stays to manage the wildings. Nags them, raising her voice, flicking the flashlight on and off. Liz and Sam stand close to their caretaker but the boys won't settle. Running around, crashing, hurting themselves which only revitalizes their cries. The eldest of the bunch, Tim, is thirteen and he's tripped on and onto the craft-table and his knee throbs and he yells curses his daddy taught him. The youngest boy is Paul at eight and he's come to the windowsill and he's looking out at the yard where they play football. The swingset and fence and front gates. Smoke rolls in, rising into the atmosphere from streets away. The floor rattles. A stampede's approaching. Miss Conners shouts for Paul to get away from the window. The other boys lose themselves and huddle around their guardian and weep. Aiming her flashlight at all corners of the playroom, Emily lands it on the small white-haired girl.

Eve still holds *Snakes and Ladders*, sitting alone.

"*Eve*! Come *here*, sweetheart!"

The little albino girl looks up at the caretaker.

There's a *crack* and they scream and they realize it came from the front door just down the hall. There's another starting *crack* like a battering ram is bashing it to splinters and the girls are bawling and holding onto Miss Conners' skirt and the boys are whimpering and another *crack* and Emily gasps and looks to Eve and tells her to come here. So Eve does. She's getting up slowly. She's crossing the spacious playroom to the group and the only source of light.

There's another *crack* that's cut off by the crashing of the door as it breaks apart. The girls scream and so does Paul. Emily stands in front with the kids at her back. They face the arched doorway into the playroom when one last *crack* smashes the door open and orange flittering light shines in from outside. They hear cheer like rugby hoodlums and then charging footsteps and they listen as a horde barrels into the daycare. Miss Conners holds her breath when Samantha shrieks and gives them away.

The first to reach the archway is old but brawny. The children cower when it appears in the beam of Miss Conners' flashlight. It has a white beard like Father Christmas that hangs down a wide torso armoured in chainmail. Its arms are like those of a lifelong ore-miner and it's got the slouched back to go with them. A bald head and small horns. A tail like an ox snaps back and forth behind it. In its left hand it carries a tall iron trident.

Emily listens to the kids whimper as they look upon the aged daemon. Frightened beyond anything. Horrified to witness an extant monster like they've seen on the telly. It's right here.

There are more of them but they're wild and storm throughout the house like ruffians at a kegger. But the aged knight remains here and stares upon the guardian and her children. He tilts back his head. When he raps his trident against the floor, Emily finally faints and collapses to the rug.

That's when the kids see the obese one.

Waddling pathetically on stump hooves like a hog's, supported by a ragged walking-stick of calcified wood. He has to weigh four hundred pounds at least. Incredibly pale except for his hair, which is raven-black and stringy. His beard is beaded in three strands that fall from his many chins. Ears long, pointed, limp – they droop beneath two horns that extend horizontally from his temples. A huge lionskin cloak is draped over his back. Atop a nest of matted sweaty hair rests a crown of bare fingerbones trussed with wire.

The fat thing of regality steps at a pace into the playroom. The children watch, trembling almost silently. Samantha weeps. Paul whines. None except Eve can stand the sight of him. Maybe it's the colour of his skin. So Eve's stepping forward, carrying *Snakes and Ladders* and she approaches the crowned morbidity, who in turn studies the little white-haired girl. Curious when she holds up the game, he looks upon it and the faded pictures on the decades-old box. Eve looks to him with hope and then asks him if he's ever played before. The fat daemon shakes his head, amazed, smiling at faded illustrations and the little girl who wants to play with him.

FORTY-TWO.

Prime Minister Patricia Halton leads Marlene Jacobs-Moore and two of her security agents out of Élysée Palace and into the great courtyard outside. There's a helicopter from the Armée de l'Air that's arrived and waiting for her, as requested by Président Yves Lemieux on her behalf. The Prime Minister strides in haste and in sorrow when Defence Secretary William Kagan finally catches up to her. Shouting to her. Stop. Panting, demanding to know what the hell she thinks she's doing.

Halton tells him I'm going home.

"Madam, you can't!"

"Clive can't be moved here. So I am going to him."

"Are you off your bleedin trolley?"

"My husband is dying, William!"

"So grieve then. Suffer it."

"Oh, fuck yourself."

"*Think* about this!" Kagan grabs her wrist. "Be sensible!"

"Don't touch me! There's one thing I can do right in this world and that's to bloody-well be by my husband's side! I will have my goodbye, Will!"

"What about the beasts, mum?"

"The beasts aren't yet swarming London. I can make it."

"I'm getting calls that beg to differ. The masses are as far south as Birmingham. By now they're probably right outside London. If you go in there to hold Clive's hand you'll die with him. Patricia, think it through."

"I have."

"Prime Minister, just-"

"There's no debate here, Will! This is it!"

Halton has to shout to be heard over the roar of the helicopter blades she now strides underneath. A secret-serviceman helps her to climb aboard and before Marlene joins her Kagan steps up to the door and reminds Patricia that first you are a leader. She shouts back, telling him no actually. I married Clive six years before I took office, Will. When he hangs his face she assures him I'll be back. Promising: I'll be a leader then.

Lemieux holds a glass of ice-water and stands at the window of the Salon doré and looks down upon the courtyard at the British PM now lifting into the air. Behind him stands Édouard Allander, whom he glances to after the helicopter has begun to fly northeast toward The Channel. Toward the United Kingdom of the damned.

Allander is stonefaced. Blank and hard and without a word to speak. He's holding a manila folder under his arm. Lemieux runs a hand across a sweaty upper lip and then sips the water his secretary brought for him. And here he turns and looks over at Stephen Fowley, who's still seated in the same light fauteuil that looks like it can't bear his weight.

"Monsieur Fowley... May I ask you something?"

"Of course. Uh, oui. And call me Stephen."

"Stephen, excusez-moi. In a... event like this... in a *crisis* like this... to who do we owe ourselves?"

"How do you mean, Yves? Owe ourselves?"

"Our conviction. Does this go out to our voters, or to the books of history? To future generations to look back on what we each of us did for the sake of humanity?"

"Well I'd suppose the second one, wouldn't I? Obviously."

"Absolument." Lemieux looks over to his defence minister, who's stepping forward and handing the Président the file-folder. Allander steps back after the French leader breathes out, gazing at Fowley. "...A freight ship from Scotland was found this morning in Norway. Sometime last night, the ship was attacked by this *things*... The men and women on board were... killed. Before that, one of my naval ships which patrolled near England was sunk into The Channel eleven kilometers from my shore."

Fowley frowns. Chews his gum a little less.

"...What's it mean?"

"This means, monsieur, that they are not mindless beasts we are dealing with. This means, Stephen, that before any more of them get out into Europe we need to contain the islands."

"How would that be?"

"Airports, to start with. One thing proved he could hitch a plane to London. All boats and ferries. The Eurostar and the tunnel, we need to seal them off."

"Cave the tunnel in." Allander adds: "Sunk under the water."

"Are you *mad*?" Fowley frowns. "I can't trap my entire country over there! Patricia just flew over! You expect me to just-"

"I expect you to be thoughtful where Patricia never could be. She is stubborn and I have not minded to tolerate this... but not when she threatens the safety of my people. *All* people. Monsieur, *we are*..." Lemieux sets down his glass of water but he still looks sweaty and sounds of a parched tongue. "*Pardon*..." He clears his throat and wipes his forehead. He takes a seat in the wingchair beside the Deputy Prime Minister. "...You understand what is going on here, yes?"

"I'd like to think so."

"And you know that this is not limited to Great Britain alone. You know what is at stake here, yes?"

"...Yes... Oui, Yves."

"Bien. Then I think we agree... Do we not?"

"...I..."

"We cut the isles off. Cut off anything that tries to cross the waters until we understand better." Lemieux leans forwards in his seat. His eyes do nothing but beg. Sweating. "...You are *with us*, are you not? For the sake of our lives, Stephen, please... tell me you understand what has to be done."

LONDON – 18:38 GMT

Heathrow Airport far exceeds capacity. Father and daughter waited in line for over an hour to check in. Getting through security was another hour. They've meandered through scores, scared but easing now that they've almost fled. They're close. But flights all day have been delayed time and again. People watch the board steadily push departures and they grow wary, knowing what haunts outside this airport.

Clara Towns, amateur film star, five months pregnant, sits on the floor because there are no unclaimed seats. There's barely any unclaimed floor-space. The terrified arrive every minute to catch flights. The young mother-to-be keeps to herself, keeps hunched over beside her suitcase, crowded by thousands as she writes in a wirebound Hilroy notebook belief that she's going to survive this story and see her delivery day. See her wedding day. Saying I do. Saying I love you too. Clara pens her hope to see it, at least.

Hearing trumpets blare, Clara glances up from the notebook. Looks around at a sea of passengers waiting to escape. She knows she heard a trumpet again but there is none. It's inexplicable. It's all in her head. So she chalks it up to nerves and stress – maybe a brain tumour. Maybe she's going insane.

Most people in here now are fixed on flatscreens suspended in odd corners. News broadcasts following the crisis which the BBC have deemed Judgement of the British Isles. The beginning of the end. Many of them watch in silence, unable to deny circumstances. Clara, like most of them, believes only what she can. And still she writes wedding vows which will probably never be spoken because there isn't much else to do.

Uwe Marrs meanwhile roves through the surmounting sea of passengers. Bottles of water cradled in his arms. Passing a terminal bar and a bowl of fresh fruit that people steal from now and then. Hearing riot, people surge with panic and point at the windows.

There's something in the sky above London.

Uwe finally returns to his daughter and their bags on the floor.

"How can this happen?"

"…I don't think I can answer that, Uwe."

Passersby glance at the pregnant young pornstar. They look to the man and the goatee and they murmur. Uwe doesn't hear them, hearing only the TV over the rabble of those by the windows and a BBC newswoman reporting from in London. Is this an act of man or an act of God – we don't know. We've closed the front gates. Barricaded the doors. We will hold this studio and stay on the air for as long as we possibly can. The camera turns to show clusters of employees huddled together in the soundstage. Security stands around with pistols. Crewmen are brandishing mic poles and light-stands. Screeches of things somewhere in the building. We will survive to bring you the news.

When Clara speaks, Uwe doesn't hear her for all the noise.

"Did you say something?"

"I said… I said I'm mental."

"…Why?"

"I'm sitting here writing this. Believing in a shred of possibility that… I'll… But the fact is I'm trapped." Clara tells her father. Her pen frozen on the paper atop a half-finished L. "It's hopeless."

"Don't."

"I'm trapped, alone with a baby. And you."

"Don't. Please."

"I never wanted to see you again."

Uwe frowns, nodding for spite.

"You called me, Clara. Not the other way around."

"…I thought you might've had money saved up after all these years." She looks down to her distended stomach that peeks out of her sweater. "Leave it to me to crawl begging to a poor man."

"Add that to the list of bad habits you got from me, honey."

"What, man?" Clara asks: "Delusion?"

"I was gonna say the fact that you don't know what you need. Possibilities is a fine enough example." Her father sighs. "Today, on that note, I look at you… and I wonder about my grandchild in you, knowing there's a golden chance." Clara doesn't listen. She doesn't want to. "...And what I need, what I... need... is the possibility that you'll let me see that child when we get out of here. You'll let me see that child and know him and know that he's yours, and that you are mine... After a life of scorn and shitty choices, I need today. Today I need the possibilities."

"You could always sell your soul to Satan, man."

"Just peek out the window and shout to him then?" Uwe smiles sad. He drops the bottles of water atop his carryon. Saying: "No... Clara really. What if your kid doesn't even know me? And he doesn't know I existed and never knew what my thoughts about him were... What I thought about anything?"

"He'd survive with or without your opinion. Even in Hell." Clara closes her notebook. Selects a water and unscrews the cap. Looking and seeing past the priest. "Thanks for getting us tickets."

"We're going to get out, honey."

"Uwe, man, I told you... Just face it-" Clara miserably nods in the direction of the digital board of departures. Uwe looks to see the word *cancelled* now flashing beside every flight. "-we're not getting out. No one's going anywhere."

Uwe is frozen, aghast. Other people in the sea call or text or rabble and pray. Outside, smoke gathers. There're horns in a grey and orange sky. So Uwe turns to his daughter, freaking, seeing everyone freaking, telling his daughter we need to find you space to lie down. Quick. Spread out the luggage, honey. But Clara can't hear her father or anyone else in the terminal. All she hears is a trumpet blaring in her head all over again. So loud it hurts and she crumples over on the floor. Seizing her ears and screaming.

Uwe shouts but Clara hears trumpets and screams.

The baby inside her, she thinks. It's kicking.

252

FORTY-THREE.

Sixteen-year-old Natalie Conners heard the door smashed upstairs. Heavy feet charging, children running, she knew what it meant. She took to the furnace room in the back of the basement and she closed the door and she's been hiding ever since, listening to the break-in upstairs beneath the steady *whirring* of the furnace. She turned the flashlight off to preserve its battery. She's tried her cellphone dialling 999 but she can't get through and it just rings endlessly. Half an hour ago she called her mother but Emily didn't answer. It went to the outgoing message. This is Emily Conners of The Garden Path daycare. I'm sorry I missed you. Please leave your name and number and I will get back to you as soon as I can. Natalie is scared for her mother and the children.

It's been an hour now and she can't stay in this black *whirring* cell anymore. Natalie's turned on the flashlight. Reaching her hand out, grasping the knob which she turns over the course of a solid minute. At first she aims the light at the floor but then slowly tilts it upwards as she bravely leaves the furnace room and steps out into the basement and she shines her light around slowly to survey her surroundings. Things are mostly as she knows them – nothing is down here. She's alone.

The beam lands on a grinning face and Natalie gasps.

Dropping the flashlight, which clatters.

It stood in the corner beside a pantry of cans and jars. It was staring up at her with pleasance held in a massive mouth. Trying not to whimper, Natalie lowers herself to find the flashlight on the floor, now pointed at triply-segmented legs like some malformed arthropod. Staying low like a mantis with wriggling toes. It isn't moving, even when Natalie finally picks up the flashlight.

It grins. Its stunted torso rests atop a nude pelvis and groin and erection. On top of its shoulders lobs a bean-shaped head moulded to house its aberrantly wide mouth of grit-like teeth. It really grins like one real cheery son of a bitch.

All Natalie can do is tread slowly toward the stairwell.

The second her foot touches down on the first step, the happy thing moves. It's a modest stride in her direction. It's not rushing. It hasn't lost its smile. Its eyes dart down to her feet then back to her face. Smiling and standing still again. So Natalie takes another step. And so does he. Disturbed. Beyond disturbed. Natalie would run but she doesn't have the nerve to take her flashlight off the freak. It's something that contests everything she's ever known so she can't look away despite the nausea and the ache in her brain. She can't put her back to the little monster. She watches it closely when she takes another step. It does the same.

Its eyes so fascinated. Down to her feet. Back to her face.

Natalie runs. She bolts up to the landing and then turns and shines the light to see the thing and it's at the base of the stairwell and smiling and she's screaming and stumbling up the final climb and throwing herself through the door out into the hallway. She falls at the dirt-covered feet of a tall and strong and bearded knight with an iron trident in his hand. He looks down at Natalie, and she up at him. There's no air enough to scream anymore.

The daycare – her mother's home and lifelong dream – is still without power but they've lit torches and stabbed them into the drywall. The linoleum is riddled with scratch-marks made by hooks and hooves. She sees blood here and there and she hears unrest thumping through the bedrooms upstairs. Through rooms and hallways around her. Hell is all around her.

Natalie's brought here into the cafeteria. This is where children are sat along the long table to eat nutritious lunches most days, but today there are no children present.

Seated at the middle of the table is the obese crowned one. He sits upon a lesser minion that's bent over on the tarsus claws of an arthropod. Another daemon stands behind him and holds him as a backrest. A third one stands nearby holding a silver pitcher of wine. The fat royal's removed his lionskin cloak and wears only his crown and a vest stitched of brown cloth. His garments are clean save for a few dining stains. Through a slot in the back of the vest hang plucked wings that are horribly shrivelled as if atrophied and begging to rot off his body.

At current, the prince plays *Snakes and Ladder* with a little albino girl named Eve Grimly sat on a demon beside him, appearing ill but moving her blue game piece. Landing on a ladder. Up one row.

Hammered into the table are four iron stakes in a rectangle five feet long. Shackles chained to each of them. Beside the obese one playing games and panting for mild exertion, there are bones and skulls glistening in the fire light. Natalie sees. Little Eve hands the die to the prince. And Natalie can't move. She just gapes.

"…I can smell it on you." The obese one wipes his mouth and rolls the die. Speaking English well. Moving his red game piece along the board, he glimpses Natalie, bored, noting: "Ignorance. Fear and… purity. You have never been spoiled before." Landing on a snake. Two rows down. Smacking lips. "…I find abstinence keeps the flesh delicate… You'd be divine with wild rice."

"…*Who*… Who the hell *are you*?"

"…Belphegor… Belphegor is my name."

"*What*… *are* you?"

"Do you not know of me, stinky?"

"…Where is my mother?"

"Your mother…"

"Where *is* she?"

"…I do not know… She was too scrawny for me. You would have to ask the legion what they have done with her." Belphegor glances over at the bearded knight standing behind the teenager. "Furcas, tell us what became of the woman here."

"They had her, the legion." The knight answers. "Afterwards they burned her."

"There you have it, stinky. Will it please you to see the bones?"

Breaking down. Natalie is unknowing how to cry for this. She's silently shivering as she crumples over and presses her face into the floor. And she smells it and it smells like nothing or maybe it's just dust. And a bit of faint lemon from the last cleaning. Flashes of her mother in her head. Flashes of monsters. She only smells the floor again and shakes and cries and she smells the floor.

Eve should cry for nice Natalie, her friend, she knows.

Belphegor hands her the die, so the little albino girl rolls.

The crowned daemon holds out a bronze goblet and his imp is refilling it with dark wine. Another has flown in from the shadows beyond the torches' reach and it's landed on the table and it's grabbing for the wet bones left lodged in the shackles to add them to the pile. Belphegor is leaning back against the struggling arms of his imp who kisses his plucked shrivelled wings. The prince looks across the table at the teenager who can't stop smelling the floor. Her mother can't be burned. The children are alive somewhere.

Eve lands on a safe square and gives the die to Belphegor.

The old silver-bearded knight steps forward then.

Are you filled, my prince?

Funny joke, Furcas. It's been funny for millennia. Belphegor looks to the knight, asking him: Who remains?

Chef Vifröus still prepares your main dish.

Who remains of the samples then?

Only one, sire. Male.

Let me have it then. Belphegor rolls the die. I am starved.

Natalie hears their unintelligible banter, demonstrating ruin as she does. But when she pleads the monster prince to show mercy the other demons hanging from the ceiling drop down and swarm. The obese one orders the girl be gagged.

Winged hogs have flown in carrying a boy named Tim. The eldest at thirteen. And the white white girl whom the other kids call Pasteface watches him as he's lugged to the table. Natalie sees through claws that gag her and she watches as Tim thrashes and yells curses his daddy taught him. Laid down on his back in front of a prince and Eve. Five of them grasp the boy and they fasten him in the shackles. Tim, struggling, is hoarse, shrieking, looking to

Eve who watches. Screaming help me. Please. Screaming.

It's Natalie though who's heard.

"*Stop!* Stop, damn it!" Horns hold Natalie down. "Leave him alone!" Horns try to quiet her. "What's he done? He's *innocent!*"

"I judge dishes for their satisfaction. I do not eat to punish." Belphegor is leaning forwards again, looking across the cursing boy and the little albino girl. Asking: "But if he is innocent in your eyes, why do you believe guiltlessness exempts him from the menu?"

"It's decency."

"It seems like imposition."

"...*Don't*... Just leave them alone."

"Trust me. You're going to like this part."

Impish aberrations hold Natalie. They've silenced her and their prince lets eyes fall onto Tim who whimpers, tugging shackles on the dining-room table, wordlessly begging Eve, who rolls the die expressionless and lands on another safe square. Tim pouts, and he looks to the crowned obese one who salivates.

"Hi, little boy." Reclaiming his knife and fork, Belphegor looks to Tim to assure him: "I'm going to indulge and so are you."

And the legion at the table and others in the room and others holding Natalie all chant in their tongue. Praise the Third and feast.

Praise the Third and feast.

Tim thrashes. The first taste taken by the prince is the one to collapse a mind. Natalie bucks but monsters pin her, tearing her shirt and jeans. One of them slices olives and tosses them onto the teen. Others salt her. Belphegor watches and carves a spastic white thigh and it's his turn so little Eve hands him the die and, on the orange-bathed walls, the torches burning around them cast flitting silhouettes in which nasties gambol about a banquet.

Their celebration has only just begun.

TYGERS & LAMBS

(December, After the First Snowfall, Smoke Over Ireland, Isles Are Quarantined, Airports and Ferry Services Terminated, Channel Tunnel Sealed, Weak Cellphone Reception, Rolling Blackouts, Harvey Nest Was Right, Most Watched YouTube Vid Is of Jogger Killed By An Outworlder In Hyde Park, No One Answers)

FORTY-FOUR.

What had happened was a dawning.

A boom spread across the British Isles in the form of a wall of pent-up smoke burped from the other side. Things came within the smoke, shrouded by it, spreading as far as their numbers could before the eruption dissipated at the ends of England. The advance halted at the water. The conquest spanned less than ninety-six hours, which the world has since titled Judgement.

Ten days have passed. The smoke by now has lessened to smog that wafts across Britain southeast from across the Irish Sea. Over Ireland and western Scotland hangs black sediment and sulfur swirling with permanency through which no satellite signal can penetrate – all of it coming from a town called Darrows Glen.

The northern coasts of France and Norway are evacuated. Towns and cities including Bruges are emptied of the locals, whose homes are leased to the government at cost. They are ushered by the hundreds of thousands into camps established in fields outside Nantes and Brussels. So too are Britons and Irish vacationing abroad at the time of Judgement who no longer have homes to return to. Many have posted pictures and tweeted about the inhumanely small tents and the sheer suffocating volume of people all shoved like cattle into these so-called *Camps d'Honneur*, but who can do anything besides piss and moan.

Since the Judgement Days, four of the outworlders have been shot down by forces along the coast. Each endowed with magnificent birdlike wings, the smallest of which had a span of approximately eleven feet. That was the first and it came just days after the takeover of London. It came in the morning when a fog was laying thick on the Strait of Dover. The ships, copters and satellites couldn't see it but it was spotted by men on shore who in later interviews said it looked spent and frozen.

Artillery men fired M242 chainguns, remotely controlled and

with laser sighting, landing almost half of the sixty-four rounds fired. Amazingly the beast was not brought down, but it did retreat into the fog and was lost by radar soon after. Its fate is unknown but it's presumed it didn't make it back to England.

On the first of December, another came. Or it tried. It ventured about halfway across before it was spotted by helicopter patrol. Pilots reported in their transmissions that the thing looked like some huge gruesome falcon. They fought it, chasing it back toward Britain. But they and another copter got too close to enemy shores. Swarms overtook them before they could retreat. Before they could react. Both were brought down. All said, it lasted about a minute and forty-six seconds.

Two other demons came just last night. Both larger. They came at just about midnight and were picked up by radar while still halfway across the sea. A target-seeking anti-air missile was launched via naval ship three kilometers from the shores of Calais. Ships were deployed early this morning to search for any remains of the creatures in the icy water. It is not known to the public yet if anything was found.

On Top of World and its hypnotic clapping and bouncy optimism just brightens the otherwise shitty hardware store in Ferris that's kept minimally lit with candles. Alicia Pederson grinds her teeth upon hearing the song play on the crackling old boombox that Cillian kept behind the checkout counter. She turns and gazes miserably at the radio covered in sawdust and just hates it, wondering how can they play that? ...Where'd you get the swollen plums to play that yoke?

"...It's pirate radio at this point." Her sister Abigail has her eyes closed and she's holding onto her toddler Brent. She's seated on a stack of mulch sacks and resting her head against a set of drillbits, saying: "They can play whatever they please for as long as they survive hi... and have access to a transmitter."

"But why mock us?"

"Ah they don't mean to mock… We all need to escape."

Alicia shakes her head indignantly and turns away. Looks to the windows boarded up with Durst's lumber and nails. The man knows his woodwork. He fortified the front entry and the back by screwing sheets of two-inch plywood overtop the doors. Planted beams into the floor to support the window barricades. But despite survival, or maybe because of it, Alicia has been inconsolable. She's made sure all around her are aware.

"We shouldna stayed here… Inna *hardware shop*…"

"Where would we gone then, Ally?"

"Coulda driven more… Found a right gaff. We cudda boarded up somewhere *better* than this iffy dust-bucket…"

"How much tools and lumber could we fit in the Dacia? With all us? And *food*?"

"I'm just sayin… didn't have to be *here*."

Imagine Dragon is suddenly silenced and Alicia's spooked. Then she's almost happy about it. She's looking over at the dirty boombox in the light of the candles and beholds it like a broken mirror. She breathes out and doesn't see a point in breathing in.

Power's out again.

"Aye. Could be for a lot longer this time… Means it's gonna be a grand night for snowmen in here."

There are slow footsteps coming from the back of the shop. Three of them, each different. Lora Malik is approaching down an aisle of lightbulbs and dimmer-switches. Shuffling atop a leg and a prosthetic and a walking-stick. She says the wankin lights in the back just died.

"Power's out, Lora."

"Say again, dear?" The old woman dourly crumples her face when Abby repeats herself. "Shit then. Just… Chrissake." Leans against her cane. Shakes her head weakly. "I'm getting just a bit tired of this…Never thought I would die in bloody candlelight."

"Other places got better hydro then this ringpiece fuckin shop."

Alicia points this comment at her sister, who's still holding her son and has still got her eyes shut. She doesn't want to see this world. She doesn't want to hear the bitterness or bother responding. So Ally asks her sister or implores her why not check your Twitter shit. You got a *following* now, doncha?

"…Only because I started hashtag-whatishappening."

"Well why doncha ask *them*? You charge your mobile there?"

"I did."

"You get a signal then?"

"Sometimes."

"Well so why doncha *ask them*?"

"I have." Abby tells her. "There's nowhere to go, Alicia."

There's a distinctive round of five modest knocks at the front door and though it's muffled by all the extra plywood Alicia hears it and she's petrified. Gaping at the door. Starting to sweat. Lora shuffles over and unlatches the deadbolt the handyman added. A bit of snow and ash blows in with the December winds while the door is opened, and Reagan Brodie is entering in haste followed by the shopkeeper, Cillian Durst. They carry bags marked with the Lloyd's logo – they've been scrounging around for supplies in the pharmacy next-door.

After they hurry into the shop Lora refastens the deadbolt and Durst tiredly drops the heavily loaded bags to the floor along with the rubber-mallet he brought for protection. Reagan is struggling on and bringing her load back towards the checkout counter to set it all down. She says she found more candles over there but the few preservatives are just running out now. Even the rubbish foods are dwindling.

"I think maybe other raiders found the bastard. Took lotta the scran. Lot less there than when we went last week." She looks around for a moment. Asks: "Power killed again?"

"Seems it." Ally's on her knees and rooting through Cillian's bags almost desperate, asking: "Find me a new *toothbrush*?"

"Brush, aye, and polish. None of them cakes you like though.

All gone this time."

"Aren't we fucked then? Aren't we fucked here?"

"Please stop yer grousing, Alicia. Damn ye."

"Can *you* take this, Abby? Can *you*, Lora? Y'like sleepin on bags of horseshit? Heatin canned meals in a microwave in an employee break-room? Nothin to do except sit around waitin for the power to go out again so we can *freak the fuck out*?"

Cillian, who's heard enough of Alicia's bitching for the past month, is taking up a few bags of canned and boxed food in one hand and a case of bottled water with the other and he's marching on to the back of the store. His shirt is ripped at the sleeve – a memento gained while barricading the shop. His thumbnail is black from where he misdirected his hammer building a crib for Brent. Lora shuffles agedly to join him and maybe have a decent conversation. Reagan opens a bottle of orange-soda she found next-door and she takes a seat in one of the lawn chairs they brought up here when they decided someone should guard each of the doors at all times. She drinks back the tepid beverage and listens to the sisters bicker yet again. Watches them, pondering.

"Is this *it*? Is this all we're livin for now? "

"It's all we got, goddamn it."

"We should be *out there*, not settlin in to raise a fuckin *family*!"

"Only thing we can do, Alicia, is to wait for soldiers to rescue us. We ain't gonna survive more than a few days out there by ourselves!"

"S'far as I'm concerned, you should've left me back in *Dublin*!"

"You would've *died* right there with Fred!"

"*Don't fuckin say his name*!"

All so quickly the wrath peaks and bursts and Alicia breaks down next to the bags of toothpolish and deodorant and chocolate-bars. Her shoulders rise and fall as she cries out insuppressibly. Quaking for long horrendous howls and short despairing shrieks. Brent wakes up and is whining. Reagan worries they're making too much noise. Someone or something out in the dead town may hear them and find them. What will happen will happen.

Abby is holding tight her son and hushing him with gentle lulling and Alicia is finding herself. She's vented and coming down. Wiping wetted eyes but staring at the floor, still hopeless. We... we haven't seen the sun in a week now... Suppose it means we're gonna lose all the grass and plants and shite if the smoke remains... This really will start lookin like Hell soon... Sinking further. Curling up on the sawdust covered floor. Whispering to nobody. Or thinking maybe, she isn't sure. I might... Might have to join Fred... Just stroll on down the lane a while till something comes out of the ash and finds me.

FORTY-FIVE.

WASHINGTON, D.C.

In his study on the eastern side of the House. Pine-green walls, tan drapes, oil paintings of a battle between blue and grey, the signing of the Declaration of Independence, Washington on the Delaware. In a glass curio cabinet is a crystal ashtray owned by Niels Bohr, received as a novelty from Samuel Seale after the last elections. On a shelf beneath the ashtray is an original copy of *The Incredible Hulk No. 2* – first-ever appearance of the monster with his trademark green skin. Clark's got a Bluetooth attachment in his iPod. Wireless speakers play Warren Zevon *Don't Let Us Get Sick*.

On the laptop opened in front of him are images of the crisis in what's now classified as the Restricted Zone posted on a blog entitled *Help! God Is Trying to Kill Me!* but Clark doesn't look at it. He's seated in the armchair next to the bay window and gazing at a sunrise on the horizon. That guitar being sadly plucked. Transfixed in a line of thought he grasps like a club.

"...Sir?"

Clark turns and looks to the man standing in the doorway. Ever calm, but resistant to him and the ruckus toward which he's called. Hell he's charged with vanquishing. Asking Chief of Staff Henry Falwell if he believes this is the end. Are they right to call this Judgement. Falwell has difficulty answering. Clark holds a hand up to rescind the question. For the most fleeting instant he glances at carnage on his laptop before he hastily closes the browser.

Falwell clears his throat and takes half a step into the office, telling Clark that our reconnaissance boys stationed in Iceland have launched the drones. They'll fly into the smokelands where the satellites can't see through the smoke.

"The Germans sent others out from Belgium." Falwell frowns at the expression on his leader's face. Paused a moment before:

"Hopefully they can paint back the dark spots on the map."

"…Thank you, Henry."

"Three are programmed to head straight for the origin-point in the north. This town of Darrows Glen… meaning we may finally see where those rotten freaks are coming from. Once we know that, it's just a matter of time." He says: "The end is in sight."

Clark blinks. Then he starts smiling and sniggering at nothing like he's drunk or delirious, unsure of what humour he's struck. When his phone starts to ring he removes it slowly from his jacket and sees it's his wife calling. Taking the phone to his ear, asking Faye what's up darling. His eyes widen and he's getting to his feet when Faye tells him their son stabbed himself.

Four minutes later and it's the breed of chaos that repels him. Clark listens to Randy shrieking unintelligibly. The boy's caretaker, Dr. Audra Heard, assists secret service who carefully restrain Randy as the doctor examines the fork-inflicted wound in the side of the young man's stomach. Paramedics have been called by Faye, though Audra believes he's well enough to be driven by themselves. And the President, standing back and watching and saying nothing, can't stand the load suddenly swelling in his brain. He's sweating. Ruckus and glimpses of red. He's looking at the expression on his son's face and the confusion of unexplainable pain he wants to go away, and Clark has to turn and leave. Headed west, walking through the wide corridors of his White House.

Secret Service opens the door for him as he approaches, and Clark steps into the Oval Office. Shutting the doors. Shutting out the rest of them and breathing hectically. Wiping the sweat from his forehead, he turns and looks into the room and he narrows his eyes tiredly when he sees his Vice President seated at one of the Kennedy sofas on the peace rug. Samuel Seale looks up at Clark and can't help but notice his calamity.

"I could swear you have your own office, Sam."

Seale smirks but somberly, gesturing to the white sofa opposite him. Clark sighs as he falls back onto the couch and looks over his friend's face bearing the same desolation. Looking to the Kitari Labs coffee-table between them when Seale asks if a date has been set yet for a meeting of the world leaders.

"It's set." Clark breathes out, straightening his lucky necktie. "Two weeks from now. Just before the holidays."

"They figured out *where?*"

"In Paris, so they're saying."

"Paris?"

"The frontlines. To see for ourselves the edge of our world." Clark's leaning forwards and rubbing his face with his hands and groaning, saying: "I still can't wrap my head around this, Sam."

"You're not really trying... *Are* you, Duncan?" Seale narrows his eyes at his President. "Watched any of the videos? Seen the pictures? ...You see it, you might start believing with the rest of us." Clark doesn't remove his face from his hands. Seale crimples his lips dissatisfied. "Personally, I don't figure you're supposed to wrap your head around this, my friend..." Memory jogged, he lifts an eyebrow to mention: "You know, funnily enough, I was thinkin about us again. As younger men still looking forward."

"Is that to say we're looking backward now?"

"I think now, given the circumstances, we're lookin every which way." Seale blinks and shakes his head, tallying his musings, asking: "Do you suppose that, back then on in our prime, we would've handled the idea of... the *supernatural* any better?"

Clark wonders. And he soon answers: "No. But I might've had acted better before God." He removes his face from his hands. "It's like that discussion we had, flying in from New York last month. That idea that people can... *believe* in things that they don't actually believe. Faith that a loved one can survive cancer or win the Super Bowl. Committing to magic then pissing ourselves for a wizard. World peace, I figure, ain't no different from hellspawn, ol dog. We're a species that's got the capacity to fathom the impossible, but to see the impossible will make us shit our damn britches. We aren't perfect things." Taking a deep breath, Clark claps his knee as he comes finally to a conclusion. "That meeting in Paris, Sam... I'd like you to go on my behalf."

"...Why's that, Duncan?"

"Sam, I uh... It's just, I don't think-"

The President is interrupted by a jingle played by both the phone in his jacket and his coffee-table in front of him, which here lights up and displays an incoming call. Clark looks over to read the caller ID. The number's blocked but the name reads BT Bob Merran. Seale just smirks when he sees it.

"I'll be damned. I wondered how long it'd be before he shoved his nose into this mess."

"How did Bob get my number, Sam?"

"I, uh..." Sam's tilting his head, scratching his lower lip with his teeth. "I have no idea." And he notices that Clark is still staring at the table, not moving, not answering. "...Ain't you pickin up?"

"I should go... Randy... stabbed himself with a fork."

"He *what?*"

"He... has these bad spells."

"...And so... how come you're settin here with me then?"

Clark taps his teeth, frowning wide-eyed at the ringing coffee-table, and again he buries his face in his hands to hide, saying I need to spend more time with my son. I have a duty to my son.

"And what about your duty to Americans?"

"...He's one of them."

Clark stands. As he leaves, Seale grimaces and asks him what happened to the man who addressed the nation ten days ago. That was a man of action, Duncan. So who's gonna be our hero?

Clark doesn't turn to answer before he's fled.

GAINESVILLE

Big-Time stands amid what he's amassed.

This is his glass solarium, which he converted into his own private aviary to support his affinity for all things ornithological.

Gutted the majority of the center of the floor – had to bust down windows just to transplant trees in here, which are now kept vigilantly trimmed to keep from growing through replacement panes. Both Sasha and Erin are in here on a weekly basis to refill feeders and mop the birdshit from the floors surrounding the gardens and the single winding marble pathway that cuts through them. Bob stands on this bridge now between a eucalyptus and a palm. He holds onto the marble railing and gazes up at a pair of zebra finches he bought from a dealer out of Australia. He's dressed in an overcheck cashmere jacket and tan trousers. His hair is slicked back but it's not be intentional or achieved with any product. His face is blank and concentrating on the birds. There's a Model 500 cannon in a holster beneath his coat.

Even though she stands just six feet away, Bob still can't hear his wife calling to him. He's listening to his diamond-encrusted Vertu cellphone. Ringing out. His call going unanswered – going to voicemail and a recording that directs him to enter his passcode to access this mailbox. Bob scowls and removes the phone from his ear. His wife speaks his name again and he finally turns to look at her.

"Who're you calling, Bob?"

"...Someone who thinks they can ignore me." Bob slips his Vertu into his jacket pocket, eyeing his wife, considering her like an uncharacteristic remark. Soon noting: "...I don't see you in here often, bunny."

"I'm not crazy about the stench." Estelle presents him the magazine that she holds folded open to the page with the headline *Big-Time: Badder Than Any Wolf*. Holds it so her husband can see. She tells him: "I thought you should see this."

Bob's got his head tilted upward, gazing at his birds. Not looking at the magazine, he asks her what it says without really giving a damn.

"It's an article on your takeover of Kitari Laboratories. There're also some questions regarding the incarceration of your former partner at Ellis Communications, now that groups are starting to take his claims of innocence seriously... This'll *hurt you*, Bob. The FBI could reopen the case. Though... at least with the invasion they might be preoccupied."

Big-Time barely hears his wife. His eyes fix on the birds that jet through the eucalyptus branches above him. He's lost up there with them. Estelle waits, accustomed to disregard she's known since the honeymoon. It's a moment or two before she finally speaks his name to ensure he's still with her.

"Can you hear me?"

"...Mostly." Bob blinks. "...What magazine is that?"

"Forbes."

"Forbes... They've forsaken me. Duncan Clark has forsaken me. My investors look to forsake me. I'm surrounded by people who aim to carve and eat me, bunny." Big-Time finally turns away, letting his fingers drag over the top of the sculpted marble railing onto which he held. Looking at his wife. Considering her with a smile and asking her in some covert whisper: "You're not gonna let me down too, are you?"

Estelle blinks. She doesn't let her gaze drop to the bulge of the Smith & Wesson on his hip. She steps forward and stands at his back, slipping her hands around his waist and kissing his neck, elegantly changing the subject.

"...This crisis overseas has me... scared, Bob."

"Consensus of the world, bunny. But don't you worry your pretty perfect self." Vigour holds in Big-Time shoulders and spite floats in Big-Time irises. "My eye's been on em for some time now."

"You? ...Because they're fucking your baby?"

"Since they took down the very first Ellis site, and every one of my offices and every one of my customers, bunny. And my prospective customers. My good fellow man... Baby, I have every reason to keep my eye on em."

"...What the hell are you gonna do, Bob?"

"I started some wheels turnin, bunny, but one thing is damn certain about these so-called demons, if that's what they are… Merciless monsters from another dimension." Bob's tense with that focus remaining on the finches on the branches above him, their colours striking amid the green. "They never seen monsters like we got here."

Sasha Stokes prepared turkey club-sandwiches for lunch but only Bob and Estelle ate. The children do their own thing for meals and Sasha mostly ends up taking their dishes home with her. As she walks into her charming shack she hears her roommate is in and has got the television tuned to the same bullshit she's been watching for the past month. Johnny Cardell. Word of the Lord, or at least one of the loudest.

Sasha rolls her eyes and brings the club into the little kitchen. Listens to the Louisianan televangelist even though it saps her of her appetite. She's unwrapped the saran off the plate and she's removing a wooden skewer from the tiered sandwich and she's preparing to take a bite. Listening.

"-and everything we know is happening in Great Britain across the ocean is just making us *sick* to our stomachs. Making us doubt in everything we know. Making us question the Lord. And what do we do then, my friends? Let me hear it – shout it out!"

"*Look to the Book!*"

"That's absolutely *right*. Just look to the Bible, friends. *Look* to the *Book*! Revelations 14:15 – 'another angel came out of the temple and called in a loud voice to him who was sitting on the cloud, "Take your sickle and reap, because the time to reap has come, for the harvest of earth is ripe".' And maybe it's just me, but I think this big ol wicked world has been ripe for *some time now*." An audience cheers and applauds with fearful rage. Johnny Cardell is shaking his head, wagging his hand, assuring the flock: "We knew this was coming, people. The crisis in the deserts. Them towers comin down. Gays infesting. Bombers in Boston. Bombers in France. Planes vanishing into thin air. Hurricanes and earthquakes and floods enough to bury us all. This internet. Infinite knowledge in the palm of our hands, eating the apple from the tree of life like the serpent said so – my friends, Judgement was coming all along. We chose to ignore the signs."

Sasha listens and she has to grimace with disgust, asking the maid in the next room: "You have twenty minutes for a lunch-break, Erin – you gonna watch *that* claptrap the whole go?"

"Doesn't matter what I watch on this dang box, you still gonna ride me for it."

"Only because I can't wrap my head around it."

"You ain't Christian, Sasha?"

"Doesn't take a Jew to call that horse-shit."

"I was right to watch Harvey Nest, *wassun* I?"

Sasha rolls her eyes. Keeps eating but only due to habit and when she's finished she'll promptly find herself on the front porch for a Camel before returning to clean the Merran mansion. Serve the Merran clan. In the meantime she forces another mouthful down her throat. Erin is going on in the next room – saying Johnny Cardell only wants to help mankind. Help make sense of what's going on over there.

"-and this will *not* be solved by building a wall, brothers and sisters. By shootin those guns. Launching those missiles. This is the Almighty's battlefield, friends... We can't even imagine-"

When the head maid hears the thumping of boots coming down the laminate floor of the hallway she knows her son is currently home. He's normally out in the daytime finding work or searching for a place to live. So that's the first flag raised, alarming Sasha just beneath her focus on lunch. She's got a mouthful of half-chewed turkey club when she turns and sees Aiden Stokes appear in the kitchen doorway. Carrying his army-green duffel-bag. All at once, she knows. She hates it. She can't swallow quickly enough and she gags.

"*...You're not.*"

"*Ma-*" But he's silenced. He's met with mom's slap across his face. Aiden bites his lip, setting a hand to his reddening cheek, letting his eyes return to the mother whose scowl weakly trembles as she breaks down. He asks her: "What about *Jacob*?"

"*You're damn right!* I already got *one* over there set to die!"

"Jake ain't scared, ma."

"Jake's *always* scared, dammit. You know how he gets. You know how he is." Feeling her limbs start to shake. Her chest start to constrict. "He wants so bad to be his dumbspit daddy and it's gonna get him killed..." Sasha looks to her firstborn. "...and now you're so goddamn cruel to me, you'll go off to join him."

"I called last week... I'm meeting up with my unit in El Paso tomorrow."

"*No.* No, Aiden, no! *Goddamn it!* Put this bag down! You're *not!*"

"I have to."

"You know what's gonna happen over there!"

"Ma, *Jake's* over there."

"I *know!*" Sasha is falling backwards. Falling against the counter. "Goddamn it, Aiden... Not *both.* Not... I just got you home." Sinking down on weakened knees, she has to hold onto the counter to stay upright. Looking up at the ceiling. "Not both, you asshole."

"Ma..." Aiden's put his hand on her shoulder. Looking down at her. She's small and she's disassembled by him but he takes the guilt of it. He endures despite the sting. He has to and he knows it, telling her why. "The world is being... attacked. They *need* soldiers over there. Every single man they can get. Fuckin pussyfoot *Clark* won't order us in but at least he left it open to men of honor."

Trying to smile but unable in her misery, Sasha shakes her head. Men of honor, she says. Haven't I known my share of honorable men. She's almost indignant, her face almost unkind as she turns away and looks to the ceramic plate and the half-eaten turkey club, listening to the evangelist on the TV in the next room.

"You're your father's sons, both of you." Sasha tries to smile but the pain is too much. She breathes and slowly reclaims the lunch she no longer considers food. Remembering her husband. "Oh how he wanted to die with a gun in his hand."

"Dad believed in this country, ma."

"Your daddy believed in the battlefield, Aiden. War was better than football to him."

"Dad was a decorated lieutenant."

"Your daddy killed fourteen men in Kuwait, and when he came home he only ever talked about killin before he shipped off again. The two of you were army dogs the second you came outta me – that's the blood he gave you." She says. Hating it. "Goddamn brothers in arms." The maid observes her firstborn, settled now but no less destroyed. She'll save the club and hopefully keep it down at dinner. She'll take it wine and some Camels. "…Aiden, you want to go try and save your little brother then I ain't gonna stop you. I respect it – I respect *you*, hon… I just…" She looks into his eyes. She sees them as they were when they first met twenty-seven years ago. "…I just can't stand you leaving me."

I'm not. He tells her. The tall soldier bends down to hug his mother with firm strong arms. Telling her it ain't goodbye, ma. Have a little faith in me.

I do, pumpkin.

Aiden leaves. Sasha watches him through the window, sees him descend the porch-steps and head out through the trees toward the back gate by the river, heading out into the world to fight for it. Like his father. Like his brother. Like all the men in her life.

"I didn't mean to overhear." Erin murmurs cautiously, tiptoeing in from the living-room. She's quiet, approaching and setting her hand on Sasha's shoulder. "…You okay, m'dear?"

…No.

Sasha watches Aiden turn and wave upon reaching the gate, and she holds up her hand though she knows he can't see her. As Aiden leaves the great Merran estate, his mother watches. Weeping calmly. She wipes her eyes. And she blinks when a red and yellow conure lands on the cast-iron tea-table on the porch outside.

Along with Erin, they quietly awe at the bird.

"...Pretty... Don't see many like it, huh?"

Low and listless, Sasha agrees.

"What'd he be, you think? A parrot or something?"

"Or something."

"Is that... I mean, that's not Bob's bird, is it? Him who got loose. Remember?" Erin, excited, asks: "Should we... catch him?"

"...His name's Will Halloway. And I wouldn't worry it none." Sasha mopes, watching it, telling Erin: "Probably it's better off."

The conure ruffles its feathers, hopping to and fro on the table outside, and then it takes flight. The maids watch it sail away, and as they stand halted and alone they listen to Johnny Cardell who's preaching in the next room as Sasha hides her doomed eyes and Erin does her best to see the bird that disappears in the blue.

Look to the good gracious Book, friends. Do not be afraid of what you are about to suffer. I tell you, the Devil will put some of you in prison to test you. Cardell quiets down. Looks to the flock. Be faithful, even to the point of death, and I will give you life as your victor's crown.

FORTY-SIX.

HEMSEDAL

The pilots are young men but not rookies. Considered proficient fliers by fleet commander. Their copter, marked with the insignia of the Royal Norwegian Air Force, is one of four Bell 412 crafts currently on a strict patrol around Frossunslott Skisenter and the mountains upon which it stands. They keep within a designated radius and stay between six hundred and four thousand feet above the barren range. Their shift will end soon at last and they'll be replaced by another pair of pilots in another 412 until a plan of attack is decided and enacted on the hotel fortress.

Base calls up at one o'clock. Asks them for their final report, which the co-pilot provides. No change, no sighting of the enemy forces outside the lodge. Requesting permission to return to base. Request granted. Replacements to meet you directly – hold position until their arrival. The pilots nod and sit tight. Won't be long now.

When lips whistle it's almost unheard over the four thunderous spinning blades holding the craft two-thousand feet high in the icy air. The pilot doesn't hear anything but the co-pilot believes he heard it. He frowns and after a moment he turns in his seat to glance into the cabin behind them.

Did you hear that?

Pilot asks: What?

Co-pilot tells him: I heard something.

Unbuckling his seatbelt and getting up, he's going to check the cabin out – telling the pilot, who nods before gazing back himself and seeing nothing. He listens to other 412 pilots radioing base. No sightings. He listens to the thunderous propellers. He's keeping his eyes on the snow-covered hotel that houses the freaks and, when the time comes, he hopes he gets to fire the first missile at it.

Still staring at Frossunslott, he notices in his peripherals as his co-pilot returns after a while and reclaims his seat. Almost sounds like he's panting, out of breath. The pilot looks over to ask him what he found, and instead he realizes it's someone else. Dressed in a Hello Kitty shirt that appears much too big for him. A tail like that of a donkey falls from the right leg of dirty white Fruit of the Loom underpants. His skin is pale but not inhumanly so and his blonde hair is cropped around two modest black horns protruding from the corners of his forehead. His face is short but thin and his irises are black. In both hands are stiletto daggers, ten inches long and made of wrought iron. Thin as a pencil at their widest ends and with flat I-shaped grips. The weapons drip onto the floor of the copter. The demon, still panting, turns to look at the pilot.

"You would not believe how many times I had to stab him."

The pilot is reaching for the pistol on his belt, switching to automatic controls in order to hold their altitude, shouting mayday into his helmet radio. We're being attacked. Enemies have taken the aircraft. A stiletto buries into his chest, his heart, and over and again. He goes limp, shivering slowly and then stopping, dropping his pistol with a *clang*.

The whistler is observing his corpse as he slides his daggers into the tattered woven belt around his waist. He's reaching forwards and taking the aviator sunglasses off the pilot. He tries them on and looks around through their lenses and smirks for the novelty. He lifts a naked foot and kicks the throttle forwards. The Bell 412 nosedives into the valley. The whistler disappears before the crash and resulting explosion.

A one-bedroom suite on the third floor is Kary Benz's prison. Chained around the neck as other hotel employees and guests who've been interned along with her. They've been relieved of clothing and personal possessions so as to be ready. A tattoo of Cantonese characters and fading scratches on a supple starved hip, the star breathes and waits for sense or conclusion either way.

About fifteen minutes ago the door opened and daemons brought in one of the prisoners that they'd entertained last night. She's thirty or so. Nice face. The body of a young mother. When they took her she was kicking and thrashing, but when they brought her back she was left in a trance. Staring vacant, leaking fluids from where they had her. She was chanting in a whisper of ruin she's been enlightened of and she's proceeded to chant every so often when the images and smells and pleasures return to her, getting weaker as she dries up.

No... Stop it... Please

Kary hears her but from a distance. She only recognizes any of this through denying eyes and for ten long days she's been building up her rose-coloured wall to block it all out. She refuses to see the horde of dirty nudes shackled in the dark. The footprints and handprints and assprints of blood soaked into the carpet underneath her. She won't listen to the moaning and the rattling of chains. She won't accept the concerto of licentious brutality. Won't hear the woman's chant. The singer doesn't weep for herself and she hasn't bothered for quite some time. It's nothing new.

Please no... Please... Stop... Don't

All in all, the horror isn't horrifying anymore.

A little boy no older than twelve is tugging helplessly on the chain locked around his neck. Whimpering, begging in Serbian. Chained so closely to the ground he remains lying on his side. In the gloom his face can't be seen. His father nearby has been dead for hours now. He was taken and was gone for days before they brought him back in a coma. His lower-jaw disjointed. He succumbed to his injuries, they assume, and the reek is beginning to accumulate and they catch whiffs with every breath. The pop-princess won't smell it though. Won't see the little boy.

No... Stop...

None of it is there. Nothing can ever touch her.

Please just stop

A startling *crash* and people stir and they look to the door that leads onto a modest balcony. Out there somewhere in the valley, another copter must have come down. The captives have no strength to moan for it. The ones chained closest to the window just shiver for the freeze. Kary's almost as cold as them, beyond the numbness she used to adore, but she doesn't hug herself or chatter her teeth. She doesn't think twice about the helicopter. She, like others here – like the chanting mother or the Serbian boy – have barely any reason to live.

…Hey…

Somewhere among them.

Hey… Miss Benz…?

Kary doesn't move but her eyes roll upward. There's the shadowy face of a teenager she knows was working here as a bellhop the night the hotel was taken. A fan. Along with the rest of them, he stinks of body-odour. The sweat of horror that's dried onto his skin and matted down his hair. He's only a few meters away, stripped and chained around the neck like all of them. The boy looks to her with sad wonder.

"I'm… I'm a big fan… You're a genius."

Kary doesn't want to respond. Doesn't want to speak. So she feigns confusion. She doesn't acknowledge the teen and looks away. He calls to her again and she points to herself coldly and asks if he's talking to her. She tells him he's mistaken. But he tells her she has that tattoo on her hip. The one she got for Dustin Tomson last year. He says I'm a big fan of your music. Kary turns away and leans against the wall. Leave me alone. I just want to be alone.

"…You actually shine like an angel…"

Those were Grier's words, verbatim. But she knows the bodyguard isn't here, so Kary has to close her eyes. In that moment she figures it's her teenage fan again, but this voice is not his. It's not weak from malnutrition for one thing. It's a matchless voice in fact. Gruff and older, seeming to be at perfect ease. So she opens her eyes and she has to roll over as much as the chains will allow. She sees the freak sitting atop the corpse of the Serbian. He's got pallid skin like the others. Aviator sunglasses and dressed in a Hello Kitty tee sprayed with the blood of pilots that were young but not rookies. Pleasantly he smokes a Belmont cigarette but holds it unusually as if he isn't quite used to it yet.

"You made your life in music. Didn't you?" Kary only stares at the freak. So do other hostages chained along the walls and floor around her. The daemon that's appeared from nowhere ignores the rest and remains fixed only on the star, saying: "I have that feeling or... I've seen you before, or heard that voice. I feel like I've known you somewhere in the world."

"...You..." Astonishment, daunted by fear. "...speak *English*?"

"I speak any language. I ought to. I've heard enough of them."

"...You *aren't real.*"

The monster raises his thin eyebrows. Looking down at the smouldering Belmont, he again smiles. And he's retrieving one of the stiletto daggers from the band of his underpants and he's slicing the hand that holds his cigarette. Dilute blood is freed. Kary gapes at the wound he self-inflicts and is neither unsettled nor gratified to see him harmed. The daemon wipes his blade off in the Serbian boy's hair and tells her reality is a funny little thing when you think about it. Then he awkwardly sucks back another drag and, though he might enjoy the taste, he still appears a novice.

Someone across the room is speaking up. A broken man. His face and light hair are stained in blood that's five days old. He reaches a cowering hand out to the daemon and cries to him. In Norwegian, he begs for freedom. Have mercy. Others see a window and join in the grovelling and the freak listens and shakes his head.

Kary frowns. Weak and hungry, she's still angry. Demanding: "Who *are* you?" Her eyes want to look away but she refuses them. Lips curled and loathsome, demanding: "Who the fuck are you?"

To which her visitor chortles conservatively as if at the joke in a best man's wedding toast. He has to take a moment in pensive silence just to think about it. He has to remember his name.

"...There are those who call me the vanisher. Though..." The blonde monster, as he continues to recollect existence, titters and then flicks the ashes from the end of his Belmont. "...some would think of me as Rosier. I'm afforded one as much as the other." Rosier is taking one last drag and, as he crushes out his smoke against the drywall, he looks the singer over fondly. "I'm pleased to meet you... What is your name?"

Immediately they hear: "Don't you *know*?" And both Kary and Rosier turn their heads to see the tall teenage boy chained up a few feet away from the singer. Her fan who's up and eavesdropping, asserting: "That's *Kary Benz*, asshole."

"...Kary Benz." Rosier repeats, asking the fan of the star: "Tell me some things about Kary Benz."

"She's an artist. And she's brilliant." The boy scowls, clenched with hostility. "All she ever did was make music."

"I knew it."

"And if you try and touch her-"

"If I touch her, what would you do?"

"...I'll kill you."

"That's all?"

"God help me, I'll kill y-"

But as he threatens Rosier, he realizes the monster's gone. The vanisher no longer sits atop the Serbian. No puff of smoke. No flames. He's gone. And a *clinking* tug of chains is heard before the teenager yelps and falls back against the floor. The yanked leash nearly collapses his windpipe.

"Kill me yourself, boy. Learn some independence."

Gasping, clutching the chain locked around his neck, the teen looks up at Rosier who now stands behind him. Kary sobs in the meanwhile, unwilling to see her fan fight to breathe. Lips curling, she spits at the vanisher.

"How can he?"

"How can he what?"

"How can he learn anything when you've chained him down?"

"I didn't chain him down. Imprisonment is flesh in time and space. You wouldn't know what we're all missing out on." Rosier watches the singer turn away. He's frowning, but not at her. "...But I remember life out there, what it was once... I hold on to the scraps I have left."

Rosier takes the time to glance around at the many faces and voices of the chained feeble who cry and beg to him. But they're just minds in bodies. He's chosen the pairing he prefers and is humoured to see her disgust. Her inability to receive him. So he presses his lips together.

He whistles to get her attention.

"It's interesting you're a singer, Kary Benz..." Rosier steps back toward the popstar. Ignoring hands and faces that condemn and plead. He tells the star: "He's wanted entertainment down there."

"*Why?*"

"...Why?"

"*Why are you doing this?*"

"...Catharsis. You haven't listened to me at all." Rosier is frowning. Considering. "I enjoy, Kary Benz. There *is* nothing left." He ditches the frown as the moment passes. He's holding up a white finger. "We are all left to damnation by design."

"You want to wipe us out... Wipe out mankind."

"Mankind is kindling." Rosier observes his slit hand. Clenches it in a lazy fist. "Earth will burn, I have no doubt... My part in it, I assure you, will be inconsequential."

The fan is struggling to push himself off the floor. Grumbling through a bloody mouth and clouded eyes. His heart races. His throat aches. The first sight he looks to is the singer. He listens to the gravelly unreal voice of the monster – taunting the girl in some ways and yet bracing her in others. Warning her. Wiping the gore from his mouth and nose, the fan remains quiet as commanded but he watches the daemon shrug, still amused and still only beholding the girl.

Kary breathes feverishly. Glaring at the floor. Hating.

"*Why?* Why do you need us?"

"We don't need anything, Kary."

"...Then let us go."

"*Oh,* he won't permit that."

"You keep saying *he. He. He.* Who is *he?*"

Here the vanisher smiles.

"He is Prince of the Fourth." Rosier recites this like scripture. "I'd suppose..." This thing again titters but only for a moment, presuming in some mirth: "I have never died... but I would suppose he is someone you'll remember as you leave this world. He'll be inside you when you go." Before he disappears, he hears hissing. He looks back at the Serbian corpse, and a double-ended headed adder slithering out of the cold rectum, slithering in opposite directions on the floor and not going anywhere. Kary whimpers. Rosier tells her: "He'll be seeing you soon, Kary Benz."

And then the vanisher's gone.

FORTY-SEVEN.

Sat on the toilet with his pants around his ankles, Stephen Fowley tries to get a grip on himself. He's been trying for ten cataclysmic days that never end. He's staying in a suite granted to him by Président Yves Lemieux and right now he's flushing the toilet and zipping up his fly. Splashing water on his face. Observing himself in the mirror and he's deciding he's lost a bit of weight. He has more silver in the chin-hairs of his goatee. More laugh-lines than memorable laughs. It kind of looks like life's given up on him.

Fowley is reaching a hand into the inner pocket of his brown jacket. Producing a small plastic vial. And he holds it up to squint upon it through reading glasses and abhor how little white dust remains inside. When there's *knocking* it startles him and he nearly drops the vial. Looking to the door, wondering if he should speak at all, he's afraid when he asks who's out there.

"It's Will Kagan, sir."

"Oh... I won't be a moment."

"May I ask what you're doing in there?"

"...Why?"

"I've been waiting twenty-three minutes."

"How... How did you get in my suite?"

"You left the door unlocked. Again."

"...I, uh... I won't be a moment."

Fowley is unscrewing the vial cap with chubby fingers. Taking his reading-glasses from his eyes. He's tapping out a paltry line atop the left lens. Blocking one nostril and snorting with the other. He stomps his foot and breathes deep. He folds up and pockets the glasses along with the capped vial. He doesn't look at himself again in the mirror before he turns off the lights and steps out into his suite in Élysée Palace.

287

Out here is the British Secretary of State for Defence. William Kagan's been waiting for the leader of a nation to which they can't go home. And he sees the puffiness in his alert eyes and the ugly verve causing his stout body to tremble. Causing his nose to sniff so obscenely. Fowley is too tired to deny anything, he just bends down to pull up his pants and button them.

"…I hope your mum's proud of what she raised, sir."

"You go right on and hate me, Bill."

"I shall. And I've always preferred Will or William." Kagan steps forwards another foot or so, observably detesting the fat wreck before him. "I've been told you're meeting with the world leaders in two weeks… You have the honour of representing my country."

"*Our* country, Will."

"And you'll do it wonders sniffing like a basset hound."

"Yeah well, where the hell's *Patty* then? Where the hell's she to man this ship? She scuttled off to be with her poor husband. Skipped fearlessly back into Hell because, above everything else, she was so *brave*, wasn't she? Wasn't she just *brilliant?*"

"Aren't you, Fowley? Aren't you a brilliant sod?"

"I'm *nothing* next to her." Fowley looks to Kagan before looking down at the blue carpet floor. Frowning but mildly. Dejected more than anything. "…I was always just a footnote beneath her… I was always 'and'. And Stephen Fowley. And the deputy prime minister. And even still the little hag hated me."

"You leave little to like, sir."

"…I guess I thought different. Unfortunately. What was it that made *you* hate me?"

"I didn't always hate you. But I made a point to start when they condemned Patricia Halton to die over there."

"That's not what happened…"

"You condemned everyone."

"Without that *quarantine-*"

"*You* just stuffed your fat face while they damned your country.

Damned *millions* of the people that believed you would lead them. Instead you sold them out to die or probably worse."

With his lips so curled, Kagan bares his teeth, but he relents and forces himself to cool. In pain nonetheless. Clutching a fist now and then.

"Did you know my wife never got on that plane to Bruges like I told her? Like I begged? She and the kids stayed behind. Refused to leave without me…" Kagan is staring at Fowley. "Did you know that, sir? Did you know I'm here, and they're there? And that's because of fat useless you." He stares but Fowley won't meet him. He says: "You degrade Halton for her nerve… but goddamn me if she didn't tower over you."

"Exactly, Will." Fowley nods, slighted but unable to rebut. Except to remark: "That's why they're going to name The Tract after her instead of me. Even though *I'm* the one who supports it. *I* saved *billions* where Patricia Bleeding Halton would've let the world burn if it meant fighting for her own. *That* is the toll of nerve." He's rubbing his sniffing nose. "And my *mum*, for your information, always dreamed that I'd be Right Honourable Prime Minister of the Kingdom."

"Well God save you both, sir… He certainly couldn't be bothered with the Kingdom."

Kagan glares at Fowley a moment longer before his image begins to burn his pupils and he has to look away. Breathes out. The two men turn in silence to watch the news playing out on the flatscreen on the vivid red wall.

"-has stated there's a chance they can cross the English Channel, so eyes continue to watch the Strait of Dover as the closest point between France and Britain. French Minister of Defence, Édouard Allander, has been overseeing preparations to transform the stretch of the northern shoreline into a militarized *tract* that will act as a safeguard against invasion. President Lemieux has been quoted as saying that establishing this tract is their first priority, and that he intends to name it after British Prime Minister

Patricia Halton, who reportedly was the first to propose the quarantine."

Fowley has to close his eyes, feeling Kagan's glower on the back of his head. He steps over to and takes a seat in the fauteuil that faces an impressionist painting of the Seine beneath Notre Dame on a winter's night. His gaze hangs on the cathedral lights done in oil on the canvas and the way it's painted almost casts the lights out of the painting and into his suite, he believes. Or it could be the drugs.

"So why'd you come tonight, Bill? ...Are you here to kill me?"

"I've considered it at length, sir."

"And?"

"...Not tonight, no."

Fowley nods and Kagan sighs. They both allow themselves to hang on that final note, contemplating in the suite of such intense red. Parisian furnishings. A stench of lavender. Enraged winds howling against the window. Again they just watch the TV together while grieving their loss. All of it.

"-saying that the quarantine is firmly extended to civilians as well as the invaders, due to overwhelming reports of a neurological virus inflicting the people. Given everything else that these invaders are capable of, there is a very real possibility that mind-control or some sort of demonic possession could become an epidemic if spread to the outside world. With no way of knowing if humans are now controlled by the enemy, NATO is currently not budging on their current ruling.

"In other news, still no word on the whereabouts of British Prime Minister Patricia Halton. It's been reported that Halton returned to London by helicopter after learning that her husband, Clive Halton, was injured in a hit-and-run in the hysteria of the Judgement Days. Halton has not been seen nor heard from since. In her absence, Deputy Prime Minister Stephen Fowley has assumed responsibility of Great Britain and will address all issues in governing the quarantined nation during-"

The door slams. Fowley blinks and glances over the wing of his fauteuil and realizes Kagan has stormed out, unable to tolerate it. And maybe Fowley can relate. His hand feeling for and finding the remote, turning off the TV, he's standing up and sniffing and blinking erratically, wandering without knowing what else to do. Staring out the windows and overlooking Paris' first snowfall of the season, which covers the streets lit by a million lights. Looking down on all the people, Stephen Fowley is alone.

It's the drugs, he's pretty sure. And the stress. But mostly it's the loneliness. He's sure it's isolation that makes him see shadows out there among the snow-covered rooftops. Surreal almost suitably, moving across the prominent renowned architecture of Paris. Some small and some larger, grander in the scope of the steeples of churches they effortlessly swallow. Like watching the shadows cast on mountains by clouds in an irate atmosphere. Looking up to the night sky, Fowley can't see anything to cause them because there's only infinite white flakes up there. So the shadowmen, he's sure, are purely in his head.

FORTY-EIGHT.

Prying off the plastic cover under the base of the lantern. Fitting in a couple fresh double-A batteries. Lora Malik hits the little switch and the bulb illuminates and she gawks at it with eyes magnified behind spotty bifocals. The old woman sets the camper's lantern down atop an unloaded crate of Christmas-light sets in the storeroom of Durst's hardware shop. She sits back in a dusty swivel-chair circa 1983 that's seen more usage these past ten days than it saw in three decades in the corner of Durst's office. She stares at the light and mindlessly caresses the gold cross on her necklace.

Outside these walls – outside the shop – it sounds like a car is driving by. They don't hear that very often. Once a day at most. Lora can barely hear it with her poor ears. She's holding a finger to her hearing-aid and adjusting it and listening as best she can to the muffled distant motor beyond the silence. Then it's gone and she blinks and shakes her head. When the door opens in front of her and she sees Reagan in the dim yellow she thinks she's looking at an angel come to claim her. She smiles to after a moment and she looks to the gun in her hand.

"So now... not that I'm second-guessing, dear, but... why were *you* left in charge of that thing?"

"I was the one holding it when the vote was tallied." Reagan observes the Beretta. Always inspecting the safety switch. Always admiring the weight of it. "You want it back, Lora? S'yours."

"Ah, keep it. That fuck'll snap me in half if I pop it off again. I'm..." Smiling sad. "I'm old, dear. We're both better off."

"...Aye sure then." Soon breathing out and taking a seat on a foldout chair set up near the lantern. She's looking to the old woman in the dim yellow and asking: "...How come y'never told me about your man there?"

"Say again?"

"I said... Ye never told me your husband was in G2."

"Me husband?" Lora leans in to hear better. She sort of shrugs. She's soon offering: "Well... You're not a keen one for drudging about the past. I wasn't about to come down for tea and start singing that song one Sunday." As she takes the opportunity to remember her husband, Lora smiles a little bit. Taken to a better time. "But ah, he was a wonderful fuckin man, he was. Really... God blessed me."

"God likes to bless us with things we'll love."

"...Reagan... y'don't believe in God."

"I don't know if I do. But I know I don't have faith in Him."

"Now's not the time to lose faith."

"S'that what y'think?"

"What I *think* is that God will be the one to save us from the hellfire. If not Him, who?"

"Lora..." Reagan's face is crimpling with sorrowful hate as her head lobs to the side – exhausted or overwhelmed. She assures her former landlady: "I haven't trusted in God since He took my son from me..."

Lora's solemn again.

"Ye never told me what happened."

"I don't like drudging about the past."

An unanticipated tear runs down Reagan's cheek and she wipes it away, still attempting to remain detached, looking like she's been hollowed out. She returns the hand to the gun in her lap and rests her fingers on the barrel. Runs her thumb over the front sight. She looks to the battery-lantern set on the crate of Christmas-light packages and stares at the low-wattage bulb inside the plastic orb. Dimly yellow.

"Six years ago, well before I moved to your basement... I was in the city then."

"How did it happen?"

"…Bolted out in the street."

"Say again?"

"He… He ran out into the street, and a… *truck*… I don't know why the hell he did it."

"How old was he?"

"Nine."

"*Five*, dear?"

"*Nine*, I said to ye."

"Nine? …Old enough he shoulda fuckin known better."

"That's what I kept telling myself, aye… but in the end that was the proper torture." Reagan is taking up the handgun and trying to tuck it away in the pocket of her flannel jacket. "I was a right holy different person before that day."

Lora gets it – why Reagan never looks behind her.

Said ye, um… ye were a schoolteacher, aye?

"I was. But I… I couldn't stand to look at their little goddamn faces after that." Reagan hangs her head in the dim yellow at the edge of the darkness, weakened, hating. "I lost every-" She stares and soon blinks. Swallowing spit through a clamped throat. "If there's a God then He took everything… Y'said God is the one to ask if I want answers, not a child of His. Lambs know fuck all. But the fact is I asked Him a lot when Justin died. I kept asking… I kept asking." She glimmers. Shuts her eyes to hide. "He never answered then so why bother now? Isn't this the end of the world? …Seems pretty clear He made His choice already."

And there's quiet, then Reagan and Lora both listen to a sudden *thud* as a heavy thing lands on the roof of Durst's shop. Dust rains from the rafters. The old woman scrambles – sits forward and bats at the lantern to shut it off. The yellow is black. They don't move and keep very quiet. It sounds as if the other four are doing the same wherever they are. Lord help us if little Brent starts crying.

Reagan hears the footsteps above them. Then, outside in the distance, a crash like a bad collision. The steady roll of a car horn cutting through the hush. The thing on the roof sounds as if he's excitedly running. Suddenly the footsteps are gone. Maybe the thing jumped up into the sky. Other feet and hooves and wings are heard in the streets. Screeches and laughter and cheers. Rumbling through the ground. There's got to be hundreds of them out there, so the women keep still until there's quiet. Reagan switches on the lantern again and sees the old woman is fingering her golden cross and some bitterness inside her is tempered.

Out there in the smokelands there's a haggard BMW that's been knocked off the road, collided into a petrol tanker left abandoned on the shoulder on the Ferris town limits. The woman in the passenger's seat was killed instantly, exiting through the windshield and landing on the crumpled smoking hood onto which the tanker leaks its haul. The driver and the man in the backseat are aching, armed with submachine-guns. Russian shouting in a heavyweight tongue. Their extensive telltale ink speak of the organized-crime they once excelled in, as does the accuracy of their barrage when they unload upon the monsters swarming through the smoke in the dry night. In cold air and warm winds. The horns take the bullets and frenzy. The Bratva criminals bellow curses as they hold down their triggers and are met by the enemy and their firearms are taken and their arms are taken and their legs are taken and huge pale freaks tease stumps as more and more join in and some roll on the road and laugh and some enjoy masturbation and some watch at peace. Hundreds crowd and wait for their turn.

When the tanker finally explodes, those in close enough proximity take the brunt of the force. A couple are blown away, detonated, but the majority love the fire. They dance.

FORTY-NINE.

BIRMINGHAM

The edge of a metal stop-sign is scraped against the concrete floor and a Rottweiler pup whines. Chester, they named him. He's running back and forth, raising and lowering his head, barking at the sharpened sign and the grating screech it conjures. The dog whines and looks up at the built giant seated on a crate of bottles. The Pieman ignores the dog, continuing to develop his weapon as he watches his mobile charged by an unsteady current.

Day ten and the two gym-mates and the posh bitch and the stolen dog are trapped in a corner-shop somewhere in the middle of Birmingham. They stay mainly in the basement where stock was stored, which by now is getting meagre. They've locked the door that leads upstairs, and on occasions when footsteps are heard sometimes the doorknob is jiggled. By humans, they hope. Whoever they were, none ever busted the door down.

They sit here. Waiting for no salvation in particular.

Tess Breighton still is shouldering the thin strap of her Saffiano handbag. Still in her cashmere sweater taken from the selection at one of her three Klementine Boutiques. She's just gotten out her right earring and that's it. That's the last of her jewelry. She holds it all in her palm. Necklace, rings, bracelet, watch, the lot. The glinting gold she would die before removing. It leaves her bear. It leaves her strange. But the handful at least occupies her wanting fascination.

"I know a man..." Eventually she thinks aloud. "He owns a... a sky-diving operation just south of London – he has his own plane. I mean, he... can fly one. I believe he's got one. Good guy. Good uh... Helluva golfer." Tess jangles the jewellery lightly. Then she shuts her fingers and hides it all. "If he's still alive, he might be able to fly us out of here." She's telling herself as well as Pieman, if he's listening. Broken. Frowning upon realization. "Except, we step outside this bloody shop and that sodding vulture is gonna tear us apart... We can't get out, can we?"

Pieman's scraping the stop-sign.

"...We're laying low for the moment."

So Tess indignantly nods.

"Staying put, I'm *sure*, has nothing to do with the fact that you've sparked a mutual vendetta with that prick... Now it waits day and night for us to show ourselves."

"I didn't spark shit, woman. I answered a call."

"You ripped its tail out of its ass."

"I did." Pieman glimpses the long and malformed tail like that of a donkey which is now knotted around his vast waist, saying: "...Champions get a belt. I always got a belt before."

"You're not in the ring anymore."

"Sure we are."

Scraping. The dog cries out again, so Curtis Merchant appears from the employee washroom pulling up his dirty pants and hurrying toward the pup. Holding and settling it. Shh. Shh, pup. Pieman keeps scraping, his gaze remaining fixed on the cracked screen of his iPhone. When it flashes and tells him the power's back on, he lifts the phone and dials for his sister. Charlene. He holds the mobile to his ear. He doesn't scrape.

But there's no signal.

Power's out again and the iPhone dies.

The Pieman lets his eyes wander, looking to the struts of a beam holding up the ceiling. Asking either of his companions: "How long's it gonna be before the world fights back, dammit?"

"Don't kid yourself, smiley." Tess scoffs, rolling her eyes with her mouth cocked in cynicism. "This is the unknown. That's the scariest savage of them all. People have one thing and one thing only to look out for when they're at their most terrified..." Tess smiles bitterly, sorrowfully, stashing her gold in her Saffiano and watching the floor with glimmering eyes. "We will be alone in this, Mr. Pupsy. Some of us... more alone than others."

The giant grimaces at the mention of his name, but he's too predisposed to lash out at all. Tess meanwhile keeps her eyes on the floor. She blinks, a tear releasing when she does. Pieman looks her over, but only with the corners of his eyes, but however little attention he gives her he still sees the ruin. The woman's heart drops every time she hears a scream out there.

"...Your kids." He asks: "...How old is they?"

Tess is wiping her eye. Clearing the ache from her throat.

"...Fourteen and, uh... and nine."

"...How *far?*"

"Just north of Brum. West Midland."

The giant nods. He hears *crinkling* and he gazes to Curtis and sees he's unwrapping one of the few remaining packages of beef-jerky. Chester's sitting in front of him and looking up with its mouth shut but drooling. whining, starving. They hear screaming somewhere in the streets aboveground, but it isn't interesting.

The iPhone flashes again. Power's back. He calls for Charlene.

Pick up. *Pick up*, stringbean. *Pick up.*

"Simon?"

That name. Pieman clenches his teeth and he looks to Tess, still listening to his call ring out. He sees the woman he's trapped with and her tears are what cut him down like a redwood.

"I'm going out there."

"You're gonna die."

"Regardless... I have to get home."

Pieman hears her, staring at her. The call ends with Charlene's voicemail and he hears it too. The signal's lost and his sister's voice is silenced mid-sentence. Pieman remains on Tess. Then he pockets his phone and he scrapes once again.

"...If I get you to your kids..." He continues scraping, but less now – caught up in his calculations, looking at struts. Tess considers him, reading him but only seeing muscle. Nonetheless, there's contemplation in his voice. "...When the time comes, you get *three* of us on a plane to leave this shithole. If you really got a way to a plane, then you get me three seats on it."

"I'm sure that won't be an issue."

"It won't. It's gettin the last passenger that's the fucked part."

"…Who will you be saving, Mr. Pupsy?"

"The only person I'm worth saving at all."

"A *she*, I suppose?"

"But not how you fuckin suppose it."

Tess smirks, breathing. Thinking herself.

"…Where is she?"

"Liverpool, with a demented juicer who'll… who'll definitely put up a fight for her when we get there."

"…A battle through Hell to spar for a maiden. Quite the Arthurian legend you aim to make for us." Tess studies the giant who stares at struts holding up the ceiling. Reciting: "To Liverpool, then down the Yellow Brick Road to London… to freedom."

"Nothin like a cheery jog in England."

"I'm sure…" The posh woman breathes deep as she considers the giant's proposal. But she can't think on it worth a damn. All she thinks about is getting out. Getting home in time. "You know what kind of road you're setting us down on. Don't you?"

No I don't. Pieman stops scraping the stop-sign and raises it, gazing upon the fine edge he's developed and nurtured now for over a week. He glimpses the posh woman, then his mate and the starving dog, then the struts holding up the ceiling, scowling amused, saying we'll know what kind when it's behind us.

Outside, atop an icicle-adorned awning of a sushi restaurant is perched a birdlike atrocity who boasts a scar across its skull drawn by a stop-sign. A gouged rear-end where a tail used to wriggle. The thing has stayed here now ten days. Never blinking, never taking black eyes off the corner-shop that hides the champion.

FIFTY.

About fifteen kilometers north of the London city limits. An area known as Gidmeadow. Frost covers the crop fields dotted here and there by cars and trucks that sped across the mud in flight and got stuck. Farms have been burned to the ground and some still simmer and leak smoke into a starless sky.

In the barn and house and pens of a poultry farm a few miles from the motorway is a rollicking throng of things feeding on raw eggs and hens. Chasing the farmer's daughter around and setting fire to the straight-trucks and sheds. Most of them are portly but some very gaunt and skeletal, some short and some impressively tall, all bent on devouring as that is their pleasure of choice.

In the small private stables is where their prince is eating, joined by a little albino girl named Eve who sits in manure and hums softly. Tonight they're hosting a new guest for dinner.

Belphegor is seated atop the backs of imps in his legion who hold him up in agony, drinking sherry from bottles found in the root-cellar. He uses a pair of brass knives to cut pieces from the dead horse laid out in front of him. He's eaten almost a quarter of it and left bones and entrails and he's cutting another piece out of the chest-cavity. From out of the feed-storage at the east end of the stable come the feeble wailings of a woman in peril.

Across from him and Eve, sat upon a similar throne of freaks, is a warhawk. Patricia Halton is tattered, squalid and bitter. Lips press together in hatred, petrified this way. She was brought here by the beasts who downed her helicopter when she returned to see her husband before he died. None of the outworlders spoke when they modified her and they took away her chance of escaping here and now, and time since then has been a blur amid horrible things to know in the world. The warhawk looks down at her lap, seething, hating, and she's staring at the stumps made of her lower thighs. It kills her when the obese one speaks.

"I don't often invite others to dine with me."

"...I must be *special* then."

"Forgottens named you ruler here, Ms. Halton." The morbid host swallows horsemeat he's chewed. Overseeing his guest with the welcome he's afforded her. "I find the prospect of subjects choosing masters to be intriguing." Wrinkling his brow, which hardens for dissatisfaction, he prods her: "Meat is most prime at the temperature set by life. Do not let it die all the way through."

So Patricia looks to the horse. She prefers to starve.

The little albino girl, she notices, just sits in shit and hums.

When the bearded knight returns, the prince welcomes him. Belphegor greets Furcas with tired merriment. He asks him to join in the feast, but the knight shakes his head and leans upon the iron trident. He tells his lord that this banquet must soon end. We have consumed, sire, but do not let the feast consume you.

Belphegor titters through horse in his molars.

Nothing will ever consume me, Furcas.

In the Void you keep, perhaps... But no longer are we in the shelter of our home. This is the realm of the chosen.

And you will see me feed on it, mile by mile.

You have no intention of conquest... All you do is sit and deny the proposals of fate. And *fatten* yourself more and more... And one day you will burst, sire. Not because of the feast, but because you never let yourself *out*.

"What are you ugly buggers *saying*?" Halton's butting into an alien discussion she can't decipher, scowling and shaking with the rage and unrest that's kept her heart pumping throughout this. "What the bloody hell *is this*? *Who* are you? *Who are you*? *Who*-"

A heavy hand is visited against the prime minister's jaw. A backhand. A smiting. For a moment Halton sees stars and despite the pain that goes with it she prefers seeing the harsh dazzle to seeing the freaks. Belphegor, however, is waving a knife listlessly in calm opposition.

"Furcas, I remind you: she is our guest. And she is right... She should know." The crowned obscenity holds out his arms, a knife in either greasy hand, introducing at last: "My name is Belphegor, Prime Minister... I am Third of the Seven."

"...Seven *what?*"

"Seven princes chosen to rule seven rims of perdition."

"...Where are the other six?"

"You do not ask questions."

"But I did."

The prince sits back, contemplating his response and whether or not he'll offer it. Eventually, cutting into the horse, he grants: "While I do have spies to keep tabs, I am not entirely aware of my fellow seven or their exact machinations. Though I am aware of some rumours..."

"What rumours?"

"You do not ask questions."

"But I did." Halton scowls. "*I did.*"

Belphegor smirks and drinks wine, belching whimsically before tossing the bottle over his shoulder. They all listen to it shatter.

"...I know of *two* that escaped into this world when the door opened. One was Prince of the Fourth. As I understand it, he managed to flee these islands with a select few of his legion. He commandeered a ship with the aid of a talented nomad, a *menace* among the rims known as Rosier the Vanisher. They now hold a fortress in your cold mountains in... in Norway." The prince smiles. "Lust is the Fourth's pleasure. I imagine he and his legion are enjoying human flesh a little differently than me and mine."

A wailing moan. Sounding aged and agonized and delirious, coming from behind the door into the feed-storage. The old woman in peril. Halton hears but forces herself to ignore – to keep from vomiting or snipping the threads of her sanity. To endure, she utilizes the only emotion she suits best.

"And..." Clenching teeth. Hating. "What about the *other?*"

"The other..." Belphegor raises his brow, three beaded strands of his goatee sheening in the light of the lanterns. Another of his imps is flying in through the door of the stables, having fetched a fresh bottle of sherry. "The other is the one who overthrew your lands. The other is the one who devastated your armies. He is the one who rules the largest legion of all – the Seventh." Reclaiming his knives, returning his gaze to the gutted horse, he tells her: "And wrath is his boundless desire. You know of wrath, don't you Ms. Halton? When I look at you, I… I think of terrible… bloodshed."

Halton doesn't refute. Rather, her expression confirms him.

"It was you then. You seven… bastards. You did this to us."

"I assure you, I in no way propagated our coming here."

"…You lie."

"It would not be my first sin, Ms. Halton. But the fact remains that, for the first time ever, my hands in the matter really are clean. Frankly, I do not know who connected our worlds, nor do I know why… but I enjoy what I can. I do enjoy this." Shaking a knife at her. Chastising a fussy eater. "*Please*, Ms. Halton. I really hate to see food wasted."

Patricia looks down to the mass of dead horse that's slumped between her and her host. She's been given no knives to use, and it's clear how she's intended to dine. Furcas watches as she gags at the stench, the indignity and revulsion, and all the while the fat supreme returns his focus to his knives and continues to saw pieces from the horse.

The door to the feed-storage is opened and a monster exits. It's tall and broad-shouldered and it wears a floral kitchen apron. It's got a rag tied over its face to hide its mouth and chin. Wingless but with the tail of a salamander. It's walking backwards, pulling a wheelbarrow in which the farmer's wife lies groggy and agonized. Her blouse and bra cut free. Her blemished sagging torso rubbed with mustard, slit down the middle from between her breasts to her naval and then sewn together with cooking-twine. There's spinach garnishing the barrow.

Vifröus, dear artist… what have you prepared?

Both Belphegor and Halton oversee the woman as Vifröus sets

the wheelbarrow down next to the dead horse. The woman yelps lowly in an ailing daze, nearing unconsciousness as her stitched stomach distends violently against her own intention. She listens to the horrified squawking. She feels the flapping of wings and bobbing of necks and the scratching of feet that claw bowels. Vifröus is proud. Belphegor is pleased. Furcas stands tall. Halton holds a hand over her mouth as her gaping eyes glimmer.

"I won't have you snubbing the main course, Ms. Halton."

"...Please... You need to kill me."

Belphegor's swallowing his latest mouthful, shaking his head as if at the ignorant declarations of a stubborn child. Listening to the woman in the wheelbarrow stop whining and fade. The muffled cluckings and flappings continue within her and the prince grunts and looks to his chef, smiling his compliments, listening to a little albino girl hum, and then he gazes back to his special guest.

"Ms. Halton, you *must* try it. Vifröus has as renowned an eye for presentation as he has a tongue for the exquisite." The stomach wriggles. Bruising spreads across her sewn-up abdomen. There's squawking, clucking. "I'm a big fan of dinner and a show..."

"...You bloody savages."

"Ms. Halton, I have shown you every courtesy as my guest-"

"*Courtesy?*"

"-and you are still an ill-tempered boor every step of the way."

"...Why won't you kill me?" Patricia seethes through lips pulled taut at the corners, over teeth she keeps barred. "What purpose could there be in keeping me alive now?"

"That'd be the human question to ask."

"Reason is exclusive to humankind, is it?"

"In any form it takes it's always selfish."

"So what does *immortality* do for your reason then?

"Immortality is not granted to universes, never mind the things within them. In truth, I can be undone, Ms. Halton, same as you. But no, I'll never expire naturally. As for what design has done to my *reason*... Reason only came about when faith was born." The little imp is tugging on the corkscrew, spinning in mid-air when the cork finally pops out, spilling the sherry a tad before handing the prince his new bottle. Belphegor drinks and he swallows, chugging. He hands the bottle back to the dizzy imp before returning black and amber eyes to the warhawk. "…What I think you mistake of us most is that we've spent eternity fixed in an endless loop down there. Thinking we do not know how long it's been and every moment is freshly seen… I know all too well how long it's been. Time marches on for all of us, Ms. Halton, but especially for the undying." Knives in hand again. Looking to the hind legs. "You say I come from Hell but you do not know what Hell is, Prime Minister. Did you know there is no faith in Hell?"

"I don't care."

"…No. You don't."

"You really believe you bastards are gonna win here?"

"Against forgotten things as brittle as your kind?"

"We'll *undo* you. That's what we do. That's the human way." Looking over the prince, Halton reads his ugly face. And the slightest of smirks finds its way inching into her cheek. Cruelty, like the prince presumed. Tailored to her and striking, she wears her cruelty well, promising him: "It will be humans who finally undo you, I promise on the life I have left. We will find a way."

"Why do you think?"

"…Must be our God-given reason."

"Yes. I know."

Here Furcas strikes Halton, but to silence more than smite. Lashing out his staff and catching her across the side of her skull. The former Prime Minister collapses off the imps that hold her up. Chewing his horse meat, Belphegor looks over Halton and decides she's unconscious.

That was not a nice thing to do, Furcas. She was fun, I thought.

I cannot *stand* your lethargy, sire, and I will have my say *now*.

You forget your place.

You have no desire for all you could master. All you could *rule*.

I do what I do best. I feast on the fish I can catch when the river is… When the river is so so deep.

My lord, you deny yourself. You must act. We must *fight*.

What will we fight for, Furcas? Belphegor cuts off a hunk of forearm from the chicken surprise and he's asking his knight and advisor: Do we not have everything we could ever relish? Right here, right now – *this* is a banquet amidst eternity and I finally have something fresh on my plate. Is this not enough?

For now… But what will become of this pity when the legion of the *Seventh* comes to collect his territories…? What dominion will you have to defend for us? What of the Third legion?

My legion is nothing compared to that which *he* commands. Yet you believe I would stand a chance in holding these lands against the Seventh?

Not all of this land, sire. Furcas gestures a daunting arm to the window of the pen that's screened with chicken-wire dirtied with feathers and gossamer. Gestures at farmlands in the night. Saying: *His* armies have so much to rule out there. He has borders on all sides to now defend. He will spread himself thin, as that is his blood. You, my prince, can focus your force and hold rule over humbler territory. But we must act now and not sit *feasting* in defeat.

Eve, hungry, leans forward and bites into the horse.

Humming a Kary Benz song.

Belphegor shows no sign of considering his knight. Instead he watches as a few imps are tending to Patricia Halton. Carrying her away, floating with little grey wings. They'll tend to her injury. They'll keep her alive. Belphegor calls to her, saying I hope you're well enough in time for breakfast. Halton tries so hard to extend her middle finger as she's carried away. Chickens then burst out of the farmer's wife and cluck madly and gasp for air and shake the gore from their feathers. The prince observes the chickens in the body, and then looks to the bearded knight with the trident.

So what do you propose?

Let us rule again, sire. I beg…

What will I rule, Furcas?

This London, sire. Their great city where they ruled. Take their capitol and eat it, sire. We must. You must. Let us claim this London in the name of the Third.

Furcas begs him, and Belphegor deliberates and burps and glances over at the chickens that shake blood from their feathers and tumble out of the farmer's wife. Eve, he sees, is eating a horse. The prince deliberates his legion and what he owes them. Raising his glass to toast.

Praise the Third and feast, the prince says.

Furcas raises the iron trident.

Praise the Third and feast, he says.

Praise the Third and feast, they all chant. Feeding.

Praise the Third and feast.

FIFTY-ONE.

"I promised her! You don't understand! *Stop!*"

"Sir!"

"I can't leave now! Stop! I promised her, dammit!"

Franklin Grier, bodyguard to the stars, pleads with the soldiers ushering him out of the motel just outside Hemsedal. Despite his protests, they're evacuating the town by order of NATO and Norwegian Prime Minister Norma Samburg.

Dustin Tomson, whom a few of the soldiers seem to recognize, is shown a tad more gentility. One trooper is even carrying his suitcase for him as he adjusts the iPhone earbuds in his ear. Ingrid, the Swedish blonde he left Frossunslott Hotell to fuck, keeps up behind them with her bags in tow and soldiers tailing with rifles held ready. They ask the actor if he'd please hurry up.

Ease out y'dutch bitch, I'm dipping already. Jesus.

Dustin and Ingrid continue to the sedan, where the bodyguard still pleads no. You can't do this.

"You don't understand! I have to stay! I have to find Kary-"

"Sir, get in the car. You are to vacate this town."

"But Kary Benz! Kary Benz, the *singer*, is in that hotel-"

"I cannot help you. If you have not evacuated within the hour I will place you under arrest, sir." He doesn't want to. He's charged with it. Ordered. "I'm sorry." Gesturing to the car again, he's prompting: "Please... Let us find her, sir."

So Grier lowers himself, crouches and slides into the driver's seat of the sedan. The soldier shuts the door for him and the bodyguard sulks in desolation as his hands take the wheel. And as Dustin reaches the car, he looks over the rim of his Ray Bans at the soldier who's opened the door for him. He appears tongue-tied, but nonetheless offers his condolences.

"I'm sorry for your loss, Mr. Tomson."

Dustin holds his head back a tad as if shoved. He swallows and nods, creasing his brow almost invisibly. He says thank you.

"Kary Benz was... sublime." Clarifying: "Her music, I mean."

Dustin doesn't respond to this, but his hand slips into the pocket of his Gucci jacket and he feels what's inside. He finds the phone he stashed there. The soldier holds out his hand to guide him and Dustin holds out his hand to observe the pink iPhone. He ponders it, crimpling his brow now so it shows, achingly, and he clears his throat and tells the soldier I found this lying around. Someone lost it. So the soldier reaches out and takes the phone and Dustin walks onward. He looks up over rooftops above at Frossunslott Hotell on the mountainside.

Sitting in the backseat next to Ingrid. The soldier shuts the door for him. Grier's eyes in the rearview disturb him and he's cross and he doesn't approve when Ingrid asks where they're headed. The bodyguard up front, changing gears into drive, just tells her it's the actor's call. They're off as commanded, but Dustin doesn't direct the bodyguard and doesn't acknowledge the beauty. His mind is elsewhere, his attention fuzzy for the most part, and his eyes stare out the tinted windows and fix upon the snow-capped range that surrounds them.

The soldiers, rallying up the last of the inhabitants of Hemsedal, are cracking on and moving out. The man who watches the sedan pull away from the curb now looks down at the bright pink iPhone. Some random lost phone. When his unit continues their route to the next building on the street, he follows as ordered, tossing the phone in a trashcan when he departs.

It's actually beautiful, this Cavalier Ebony vertical that's set to the side of the stage in Frossunslott's jazz-bar. She plays now. She plays no tune in particular, just makes music to serenade horns that dragged her here. Kary Benz is back in the spotlight she remembers, nude and with a new chain locked around her neck. Lit by torches, she caresses the ivory keys, commanding them feebly and making structureless melodies to drown out the cries and screams behind the wall she surmounts minute by minute.

A pale hand smacks her upside the head and she stops playing and her fingers freeze forming a C-chord. It's a female voice that's dominating, sultry. Kary refuses to look over at her assailant but she listens when the buxom freak talks to her in pure English.

"Rosier said you could sing."

The superstar hangs her head over the ivory.

"...I can't sing..."

Kary breathes out and waits for the female to leave her. Let her play the music like she's supposed to. Just let her suffer the notes before at last she's killed. But that isn't how this goes. That isn't Hell. The pinkish-white smooth hand of the freak seizes her jaw. Forces her head to turn. Forces Kary to observe her, close enough their lips almost meet and the star so nearly breaks to witness her.

Coffee-coloured hair, straight and long. Coveted frame of a Prada-model and rich violet-brown irises around unflinching pupils. A set of men's swimtrunks over hips and ass. A wooden scabbard attached to her waist by a leather belt. Cherry-red nipples in the center of plump breasts. Compared to the other monsters, this female is somehow more human, like that... that vanisher.

The female observes Kary. And she licks the tip of the singer's nose before letting go, telling her to continue and to sing. So the star is playing the keys, lachrymose, holding back sobs. She listens as the female in the swim-trunks steps away to join the fun that transpires. Kary hides away in melodious notes, safe behind her wall.

"Miss me?"

Empty eyes glance over. Her hands play the ivory in the key of G and the singer looks to the left of her vertical at the demon who introduced himself as Rosier the Vanisher, who's once again appeared from nothingness.

"You don't have to, you know."

Tears on the ivory.

"…I don't have to what?"

"Miss me." The daemon smirks at the star before glimpsing the fun. Sighs as if gazing at a still cottage lake, watching an old woman as she's fitted with an iron heretic's fork before she's dragged away by his kind. Assuring the singer: "…You will never have to forget me, Kary Benz. I am never too far away."

Again Kary has to stop. Her hands hold steady, motionless, hovering above the keys. She's unwilling to play any longer – keeping the music locked in her head. She listens to the steady rhythm of a different diddy. Desolate whimpers and throaty cries that regularly exceed beyond the acceptance that's overtaken the victims. Too many victims. When Kary turns – and when she looks back at the vicious daemons raping a throng of men and women – she feels the vomit begin to build in her stomach, shoot up her throat.

Purging, it occurs to her she hasn't eaten in days.

Sing!

Tears reach the bottom of her face and when they do they leak down onto her breasts. Onto her forearms and the backs of her hands and onto the ivory. She knows it's useless but there's no stopping and none of the monsters notice her blubbering or the filthy puddle she's made. They relish their pleasure of choice.

These are just a few of the hellspawn that rule Frossunslott. Many of them tall. Most over six feet but many over eight and with ample bulk to match. Arms and chests built for conquest. Daunting black crow wings and most with the huge horns of alphas. One with a repulsive frown of jagged fangs. One with the arms and torso of a Kodiak bear. A number of them with the cloven hooves of mules and mares. Here in the lounge of the hotell they harvest pleasures without bias to age or girth or gender. They lunge with genitalia of obscene shape and breadth, some akin to human parts and some more like cattle or wild dogs. Beside

Kary's vertical is the vanisher, who very suddenly lives up to his title. Then he returns a few moments later and he has a lit cigarette in his lips. His hands newly spattered with blood. Same position as before. Same untroubled expression. Seemingly, he never moved a muscle.

"You know..." Rosier exhales a plume of smoke and then looks back at the ugly puddle spewed by the superstar. "He's been listening all morning. I think he likes you, which... has the good and the bad to go with it."

"...Your... prince?"

"Of course."

"...Who?" Kary plays. It's pretty and forlorn, slower with confusion. And as she plays she glances over at the talented one. "Who is he?"

"A being of adoration." Rosier, always holding the cigarette uncomfortably in pasty fingers, smirks at the girl commanding the ivory. "I thought I knew pleasure. Millennia went by, and... and then I met him and I joined the Fourth legion... Even still I sit and study day by day. I'm a student and he..." A pause as he breathes the stuffy malodorous air, shaking his head and contemplating the words he's after. "...is truly an exceptional teacher." A thought appears to catch him off-guard and the vanisher creases his pale brow. He asks, recollecting beauty: "Do you know how wondrous are the colours of the sky? The, uh... Uh..." He's gone. Returns in a moment with a pamphlet from the hotel lobby, reading it with the cigarette hanging from his pallid lips, saying: "The Northern Lights... You know of them, Kary Benz?" He waits for Kary's response but she doesn't have one or won't give one. "...The prince was out observing them the past few nights. Them and the great white moon. And I thought about how, back home, he always had musicians to feed him lullabies... Music is a pleasure we share, your kind and mine. I think it's the greatest gift God gave us."

The singer opens her mouth to speak, and instead she suddenly faints. Hunger and misery disabling her whole, nerve by nerve, and she's numb. And she's suddenly faint. Toppling off of her bench, Rosier catches the star. He holds the girl in his arms, and weak and dazed she looks up into his face. He gazes back into her eyes, admiring her. Kary hates him in return.

"The... there is no God..."

"Don't be so vain, Kary Benz. Earth is the center of life no more than perdition." Lowering on one knee, he grasps Kary's shoulders and then hoists her back onto the bench. "...Master on High didn't stop creating when he created us, and it's ignorant to think He did. He makes so many universes in so many dimensions. He's made infinitesimal amounts of beings in all sorts of variations of what you or I think of as life, and He creates a billion more every instant." The vanisher's now frowning – Kary can't tell if it's with ire or pain. Gently Rosier places the star's deadened hands upon the ivory. "...There's a Great One out there. But He forgot all of us a long long time ago."

A bronze sword sticks into the side of the Cavalier. Kary looks over at the female who hurled it. The one with purple eyes and perfect proportions. She's yelling to the vanisher – chewing him out, it seems. Speaking in something like bastardized Latin and telling him: Be gone. The girl does not need to be spoken to. She needs to sing, Rosier.

Rosier shines his grinning white teeth at the succubus standing among the horns and the humans. There's a young and overweight man bleeding on the floor, left foot mashed after he just kept kicking and running away. He's seized by Lilith and he bawls as she forces his face onto her breasts. Lips onto a red nipple. Kary looks away and Rosier takes another drag, informing her: "Lilith, you'll find, is desperate to please her prince. She yearns for his..." Exhaling another cloud, smiling: "...his adoration."

Kary doesn't want to hear anymore, and she startles herself when her fingers press the ivory keys again. Screamed at – told to sing. She listens to her music as her throat tightens, and with her vocal chords and windpipe clenched this way she can only sing softly but it's effortless euphony. Though it's choppy for the pain, her voice is always at home in song.

"No texts, and no calls, don't hear from you at all. But maybe I already knew." Tears on her hands. "Yeah I probably knew, cos it's nothing new." Carnal moaning. Grunting. Beasts at play. Rosier watches her and listens and smokes without grace. "You warned me, baby, I recall... I should have never loved at all..."

The scourge with Kodiak arms swipes claws across a woman into whom he finishes. The bear rises. On humanlike feet and lumbers across the parquet that's polished with streaks and pools. It approaches Lilith and the fatman whose face is trapped between her thighs. Bear paws seize an ass to mount and shove inside and the man screams into Lilith's warm pallid lips.

So now... all alone... So... so...

Sing!

"S-so sick I'll smash my phone-" More tears land and dry on the ivory. "-if I keep longing for your name... And it's pretty lame... And I hate this game." The bear bucks into a flabby ass. Claws bury into the rolls of a pimpled back. Pinkish-white thighs and fingers hold his head in place as the fatman wilts. Kary shuts it out. She sings louder, almost beautifully. "But you're so big and I'm so small... I should have never loved at all."

Resolute fingers beat down the keys. She forgets the hunger of her emptied stomach. Forgets the weight of the chain around her throat. Forgets the chill on her naked skin and the smell of the vanisher's cigarette. She doesn't hear revelry occurring throughout the darkened lounge and she plays the tune. When footsteps shake the floor beneath them, the vanisher smirks.

"The siren calls out her adorer." Rosier crushes the cigarette against the Cavalier. Kary frowns, plays, hitting the notes harder. Making the music demonstrate her loathing. Another footstep unsettles the ground and the vanisher bows, telling the star: "I wish you luck, Kary Benz."

"Why bother?"

"Catharsis. I told you." He smiles. "…I hope we meet again."

And here, like that, Rosier is disappeared again. The severe footsteps get closer. Kary plays on, doubling the length of a bridge, and she glances up at the tall black curtain along the back of the stage. It shudders when another incredible step resounds. And again now, more disturbed. Some of the daemons behind her shout out in frenzy. Orgasm. Lilith pulls the fatman's head so his tongue reaches deep before dying. Lilith howls as she comes. Kary clears her throat and approaches the next verse as a large salmon-grey hand slips in between the black partitions.

Don't cry, and don't pout, one more lay and it goes south. The hand is pulling back the curtain and massive black horns and the oily loose feathers of a diseased bird are first revealed from the shadows. What's with all the shame, this was preordained. You warned me… Huge shoulders reveal. Bestially muscled, five-hundred pounds over eleven feet tall. A wingspan of four meters folded now and held close to a sinewy body. The stringy tail of a steed and alabaster genitalia swinging between gorilla legs. You warned me I was just a doll… The great prince bends down and leans in and tries to catch Kary's gaze, but the star clenches her eyelids. But you aren't tough, no. And I stood tall.

I stand tall.

Lilith leaves the fatman while the bear finishes with the other end. Yells in their tongue: Lord Prince. Accept this music girl. Just for you, Master of Will. Asmodeus, Fourth of the Seven. The great prince remains bent low, blank eyes a foot from the little singer, and Kary feels hot breath run across her skin. Eyes pressed shut, unseeing the prince that sees her, singing a world-famous voice.

"…I should have never loved at all…"

FIFTY-TWO.

Here's a cheap Hilroy notebook full of empty vows, and he's got it opened in the damned world. Uwe Marrs sits along the terminal bar in Heathrow Airport, where he and his daughter and a total of six thousand survivors have been trapped for ten days. They were on their way out. They were all so close. But then the planes were stopped and flights were cancelled and they're not going anywhere. Now they're citizens of Hell. Here, they endure it in the usual ways.

Your drink, sir.

The bartender sets a highball glass in front of a former priest. Uwe nods, mouthing thank you, and he stares at his drink. A deep breath escapes him and he gazes at the wedding vows his daughter wrote and he's fixed on a line or two here and there. One in particular, one about unity. Her soul right there in blue ballpoint ink. As his eyes cloud he reaches for the glass of whiskey that's been coming for a long long while.

"I knew you'd never really quit."

Wrapping his fingers loosely around the glass, Uwe glances over his shoulder to see his daughter stepping up behind him. Clara Towns, five and a half months pregnant, looks upon her father with the same alienation and tedium she's shown him since he flew in from Vienna almost two weeks ago. Uwe wasn't expecting anything more. He just watches the booze swirl around his glass.

"...Seems a little pointless to feign innocence when we're already damned."

Clara scoffs but has no better response. She tosses an unopened package of pretzels on the bar and they land next to the drink that Uwe limply grasps and the ex-priest observes them, frowning, hating to see so many like these the past few days.

317

"…You skipped lunch again?"

"I'm not hungry."

"And you're never hungry, but the *baby* needs food."

"Only if I intend to bring it into this world."

"What does that mean?"

"Means… maybe I'm not so cruel, man. Not everyone believes in sacrificing babies to the devil."

"I've told you before that's not what Satanism is, Clara."

"My bad." Clara clenches up. She looks at her father almost indifferent or ghostly, she asks: "Why'd you steal my notebook?"

"In all honesty? I was hoping to find some indication, some… clue as to the identity of your baby's father."

"You could've just asked me."

"I did, honey. Three or four times now."

"Oh. Right."

"…Who's the father, Clara? If not Kodi, then who?"

"I don't know."

"How? How can you not know?"

"Because."

"Because why?"

"…Because it was an orgy, man." Clara tells him stark and with vacant eyes, fighting disgrace. Staring at her notebook in front of her father. Remembering a night five months ago, and it kills her. Shame loosens the flesh on tired bones. "…It was this big special the director had planned and they… paid well. Fifteen men, three girls, all bareback. I was on Molly for most of it and I don't remember. I don't… I don't remember how many came in me."

Uwe is again eyeing his daughter beside him, unable to provide any response either of them would easily accept. Looking at her and then down at the baby-bump. Beyond that he's only barely fathoming her rich history or the plainest workings of her mind. That's the way it has always been with her, and he tells her as much. Sad and shamed as she is. I've never been able to meet you halfway, Clara. When you were a little girl and I danced with you to the radio I could never tell if you were laughing or crying. I never knew if I was coming or going.

"Is that why you left?"

"...Sure, sweetheart... I didn't know what else to do."

"It's fine, man."

"That tidy word again. Perfect for the lifeless."

"No... I lived without you, Uwe. Just look at me now, for Christ's sake." Clara watches her father close the notebook she's clung to like the high rungs on a ladder. "And now, you and me... we're going to die here."

"Please don't say that." Uwe, hurt, frowns again and glances over at other survivors around them. "You can't talk like that."

"You think any different?"

"You can't talk like that, Clara. The security goons hear you tweak and they'll throw you out of here like the others. You think you'll fare well out there in those streets?"

"Those gomers can't hear me."

"But the children sitting to my left can." Uwe clears his throat, keeps his voice hushed but sure, advising: "There's not a man alive that needs to hear that kind of rubbish." He eyes the drink he doesn't drink. "First and foremost, you maintain order."

"Even in Hell?"

"If you can. Step one is fighting your fear."

"S'that easy, is it? Overcome your fears?"

"You'll never overcome. But fight it, honey."

Uwe takes up his glass finally but doesn't bring it to his lips. Just cherishes it, and his daughter looks over at the children to Uwe's left. Looks around at cowards behind them. She slides over her notebook and watches her father as he leers into the amber.

"You aren't wrong to believe in life and... the blessings you hope for in those pages." Uwe breathes out, still staring at the liquor he's craved for too long. "...It's all I've ever wanted for you, despite what my actions suggested."

Clara sighs. Uwe figures she's bored with him as ever.

"You as a drunk and a deserter didn't faze me. I knew my dad. I knew you were a man who despised a greater power and anyone dumb enough to subscribe to it. And I knew you left me and mum and you let us rot without you…" Uwe assumes she's finished. It sounds that way. But after a pause she offers: "I know that… we would've rotted a lot faster with you around."

"My hope is you never know the misery of leaving happiness behind."

Clara scoffs. She has no better response, seeing him as he is now: older and fruitless but, above all, collapsed. She sees him.

"I'll never love you, Uwe. I can't ever… *begin* to even like you. That's fact."

"Facts are all I've ever believed in."

"I won't ever love you, man, but I do at times… respect you."

Uwe narrows his eyes as the words sink in, and before long he has the understanding enough to smile. Knowing pride, he thinks.

…If I need just one excuse to drink. Raising the glass, the priest drinks but just a swallow. Then he sets it down as he enjoys that old familiar friend linger and that dear sweeping coolness that cushions aches and worry. It's not so exhausting for a moment.

Behind and beside and all around them are another five thousand stranded passengers. They sleep upright along the walls in the various gates and they sit at tables or the bar to eat pretzel-packets and they crowd around washrooms waiting to clean their hair and faces in the sinks and they stand and form trepid clusters at the tall windows to watch the smoke rise from different corners of London. To watch for horns in the grey skies.

Airport security has gotten a handle on the survivors here. It took the better portion of two weeks before the madness had finally gotten out of their systems and doom took its place. The officials patrol the five occupied terminals armed with the minimal firepower kept on site in lockup. They'll maintain this haven and hope that soon rescue will come from the mainland.

My feet… Holy shit, they're killing me.

Clara glances down at her legs. Frowning at her feet and the ache. Telling her father they're so fuckin *swollen*. Uwe looks to his daughter and he can see the nausea overtaking her body and brain.

"*Eat*, Clara... Eat the peanuts and then we'll find some out-of-the-way inch of the floor. We'll prop your legs up – lay out some clothes for you to lie down on. You need to keep your feet elevated." And he frowns when he realizes her eyes have welled up and her cheeks have gotten so red. "*Clara?*"

Clara bites down. Holds a hand to her mouth to keep it in. But she can't. And her eyes are brightly red, glimmering in the lights of the terminal bar. They hate her tears, she knows. The eyes, mommy. Her hand leaves her mouth to hide her eyes.

"*Clara...*" But she breaks. It leaks out behind her hand. "Oh, dammit, Clara..." Uwe has got his arm around his daughter's shoulders. "*Look.* Look here-" He opens her notebook for her to see. "*-look. Open your eyes.*" He's turning pages for her but she won't look at them. He holds his daughter. "Clara, remember why you wrote these down." Uwe can't hear his own words, only the struggle and the ache his daughter can't withstand and the sobs that burst through the levees. Uwe clenches his lips. He takes up the peanuts and sets them before her. "Eat something, honey... *Please*. Please, *eat* something. You can't *let go*, h-"

Alarms drowns out his final word. Radios holstered on security-officers are crackling to life and frantic voices come through amid bullets ripping out of pistols. Men stationed in Terminal One are calling out for backing. We're being hit over here. Three just smashed through the windows and they're coming at us.

Repeat. They're inside Terminal One. We are under attack.

And the screeches are heard and gunfire swells and the walls shake and someone yells run for your life. Clara is among the first to panic, her notebook knocking over Uwe's unfinished drink as she rushes to her feet. Clara, wait. No. But she doesn't listen to him. They can't hear anything. Everyone's deaf when the window shatters and a pigman flies into their terminal.

φ φ φ

No energy left to scream. His gut is collapsing in on itself from hunger. He barely has the strength to lift his head or arms or fingers. Every breath he takes brings with it the stench of his putrefying cellmate and the swarms of maggots that savour the rot. Kodi Becker, skinny and useless prat, has been locked in a jail-cell for ten days now. He's curled against the concrete wall in the police-station basement, forever awaiting an arraignment that will never occur. Trembling. Dazed numb but still weeping dehydrated tears, breathing hoarsely, blinking once every twenty minutes or so. He's not even mindful of the gore dripping from his lips and chin onto a skinny chest as he soundlessly utters Clara... Clara...

He removed his Adidas jacket. He needed it to strangle his cellmate in his sleep, which wasn't an easy task since the bruiser woke up halfway through dying. After that, Kodi never put it back on. He uses it as a blanket when it gets murderously cold down here, which has been far too often the past couple nights. He shouted out until he was too starved and then he began to eat and then he shouted again. He shouted for the longest time but now his throat is raw and he doesn't want to eat anymore and his hope is pretty much depleted. What the fuck's the point.

In the meantime Kodi watches the mesmerising shadows that are cast against the walls and ceiling. They watch him. They've been hanging around. Occasionally, when Kodi is most delirious for the thirst and hunger, he hears the shadowmen speak to him with voices that come from nowhere. Tell him good for you. Good for you. He wonders how Clara is doing and if she's still with that piece of shite father of hers. Given the odds, he figures at least one of them must be dead.

A week ago he stopped eating his cellmate. Began stomping maggots. He's bit calluses from his own fingers and toes. Morsels are what've kept him alive for this long, but the feasts are getting too difficult to consume. He can't eat the bruiser or the maggots or himself anymore. He feels sick like worms are growing in his stomach. He feels lightheaded and he can't see straight. But still he sees the shadowmen.

They've been with him since the plane crash. They're gone for hours sometimes but they always return. They flow across the ceiling and walls like sentient oil spills. He hears their voices in his head, with accents both outdated and out of place. American. Sounding as if from Alabama or Georgia or Mississippi. Saying Kodi. Son, you gotta eat. Supper's on, sugar.

"…I shoulda j-just died."

Kodi

"The big cunt…" Kodi tiredly casts his eyes at the rotten half-corpse. "He… He coulda just… just beat me dead. I… I didn't want to kill him… Sure as hell didn't think I could ever… Big big git, innit he…?"

It was him or you, son

Trying to push himself off the floor.

"…You…"

You made us proud, boy

"…What did you do to me?"

Kodi

"You… got in my brain…"

Him or you, sugar

"…You made…"

The skinny chav slumps over again, gasping for breaths he's exhausted. He hasn't got anything in him to hold him up. He can't suck in enough air down a raw throat and it feels like he might suffocate and he can't die fast enough.

One of the shadows is running across the floor and up the wall again. Morphing into the profile of a face. Kodi hears its voice coming from nowhere or everywhere and it tells him you're disgraceful. After all we've done for you. Sugar.

"You… you're just shadows…"

Kodi… Your daddy and I ain't yet givin up on you

"Not... not my father. Not my mum."

Donchu mouth at your momma

"...Please..."

Y'better listen to your daddy

"...Please stop."

The dying degenerate pants feebly as the second shadow appears on the ceiling above the first. Shrinking while wedges cut into itself, looking like a hand and fingers. The voices scold him. Threaten. It's been a long long time since we had a youngun but I can still beat a switch you won't ever forget.

There are footsteps upstairs creaking the frozen floorboards of the police-station. Muffled voices, so quiet they're barely heard. Sounds like a group of four or so moving quickly, probably headed to the weapons locker where they'll find it's already been raided. Kodi's heard others like them, and when he had more voice in him he would scream out. He would kick and pound the door of his cell. But he can't do more today except lie here and whisper please... let me out. His eyes grow wide as the shadows near him and there's no crawling away even if he had the strength to crawl. He listens to them in his head, and he tries to scream out to whoever's upstairs but he can't. The shadow is coming, slipping into his mouth and eyes and nostrils.

What are you doing

He wants out, y'durn fool

You coddlin him

I ain't. Just is, he needs to be fed

The boy just needs to fetch me a switch

Upsie-daisy, sugar

Kodi's got life in him again, it just isn't his own. He watches himself lift off the ground, reaching out his arms, walking toward the bars of his cell. He's screaming but not through his vocal chords – screaming only in the furthest recess of his mind and he isn't heard. On the wall and ceiling creeps the remaining shadowman who's just a shapeless horror again. Kodi's weeping, he's sure, but not through his eyes. He watches hands when they seize the bars of his cell. Pleading no. No. The bars bend a little by the pull of his skinny arms and his dawning freedom is dread.

Escaping, trying to stop himself from marching down the hallways of a station filled with uniformed corpses. Frozen, stuck to the floors in unlit icy rooms. Kodi sees. He wants to return to his cell and his cellmate.

The city outside, when he finally finds it. Kodi Becker stands on the steps of the West End Central Police Station, looking out on London. Commandeered eyes gape to take it in wistfully though unafraid. His irises, new prison bars. Behind them, he screams out from the back of a lowly submitted mind. But someone returns, coming from his own lips to his own ears in some aged woman's voice, telling him to hush up. Momma'll keep you safe.

What are you doing to me? …What are you going to do?

"Momma's gonna look after you, sugar."

My… my mum lives in Manchester.

"Aw, she dead by now, Kodi. I'm your momma."

Together, they stare out at the city and the monsters that soar among ruined buildings and the burned gardens and trees. Bodies stacked into firepiles that smoulder around them. There's thunder in the clouds.

There are a few survivors. They're chased by pudgy imps who hunt with crossbows. There are black warthogs ridden by skeletal lancers. A bearded knight with a trident leads a crowned obese prince who's carried on a throne held up by struggling subjects. Beside him is a little albino girl in a floral dress. And there's a legless woman who looks very much like Britain's Prime Minister in an iron cage.

There's distant and extravagant shattering glass and something immense has just smashed through the western dial of Elizabeth Tower and it's taken on the wind toward the London Eye.

Kodi's hand lifts up to feel the air. Feel his cheek.

What's happening? Kodi asks.

The woman's voice comes from his lips, saying I can feel again. I can feel. Staring at his hand. Saying I can see a hand. I have a skinny white boy's hand.

What's happening? Kodi asks.

And daddy, formless around the chav's ankles, answers him as leaves blow across the shadow: ...*We don't know a durn thing more than you do.* And he continues undulating, reshaping darkness over the ashes and leaves. *I sure as shoot don't remember this world.*

Together they stand on the steps of West End Central station. As a family they look out at the city and together they watch the hands of the great clock dislodge and plummet onto the Palace of Westminster. They watch the massive winged thing swoop upon the great Ferris-wheel and it raises its head and bellows at lightning and thunder.

FIFTY-THREE.

Holding tight the Hilroy notebook, Clara runs with the crowd. Runs on swollen feet. Runs from pig freaks soaring through the terminal. Uwe chases his daughter but can't keep up and can't cut through thousands of hysterical others. Clara. But she doesn't look back. He loses sight of her for a moment. He hears screaming and turns to see a hog that's seized a young ginger-haired woman and is sailing off with her. Another one races behind the masses, armed with an iron gladius, sparring with security-men as they pump futile ammunition into its torso.

The notebook is knocked from Clara's grasp. It skids across the floor, stepped on by a dozen different shoes. Uwe sees it. Watches his daughter who pleads to everyone who won't listen. Desperate, she tries to navigate them but she trips and falls on swollen feet that can't stand anymore. Shoved by the horrified, she falls into the path of chaos where her arm is trampled. Her shin. Clara cries out, watching Dune boots tear pages from the journal.

Uwe!

She cries his name. And Uwe is coming. The wings of a hog flap above their heads. An obese fellow in a parka cranes his neck as he runs and in doing so he's losing balance. He's tumbling. He's falling. Uwe watches aghast. Three hundred pounds of the man slamming hard onto Clara's stomach. Uwe screams no.

The pain that's erupted in her abdominals shoots through her core, instantaneously ruptured. She's flattened and the pressure spurts into her brain and it feels like her head will pop. Blood pumping hectic under the man, she feels ruin in place of the baby.

Uwe pushes people out of his way. Grabbing hold of the man and heaving him off his daughter. He lunges and grabs hold of her, trying to shield her from mindless feet that stomp on them both. She cries out as Uwe pulls her legs under him then shoves bodies of the crowd away. Get away. Get *away*. The howling damned give them just enough room. The priest pulls them to their feet. Pulls her arm over his shoulders. They make their way across the outskirts, by the windows lit by lightning.

"*Uwe.*"

"Clara, *breathe!*"

"*My stomach! My-!*"

Clara's shrivelling. Uwe crouches to keep holding her. Tell her ignore it. Ignore pain. Ignore the guns. Listen, honey, listen to me. Hear me. She hears thunder. Grunting hogs. The priest glances around at a pity of mice and holds onto his daughter.

The demons go after the masses, chasing them toward the exits of the terminal and, funnelling through the doors, they're picked off by the pigs. Uwe watches and helps Clara walk, leading them toward the women's lavatory as everyone flees. Ignore it, he says.

Locking the door. Muffling horror. Listen to me. Standing in the dim light of candles lit in the lavatory, Uwe tells Clara I was haunted but she just weeps and holds onto her stomach.

"When I was a kid-" Clutching her and hoping her eyes are shut. Saying: "-I was… haunted by something. I never told you."

Gunshots rattle off again like firecrackers. Men fight pigs. Pigs take men. Clara shakes in Uwe's arms.

"Listen! *Ignore them!* I want you to know, Clara."

Warmth leaving her. Coldness overtaking her body.

The baby's crushed, she knows.

"I believed in Heaven." Uwe says. "I believed in eternal bliss after death. I saw existence as this bright image of a film strip. At the… the bottom left, the film strip has a very distinct beginning. And it runs perfectly straight due right, and that's life on Earth."

There's a *crash* against the lavatory door.

Uwe guides his daughter into a stall. Shuts the door. He tells her to lock it. To hide. She protests and he tells her: Just listen to me.

Screeches of things coming for them. People are caught. People are eaten. Bashing against the lavatory door, they're coming.

"That *strip*, Clara – it wound around and went back and forth.

I'd see it head further away into the light, and it keeps going and keeps going, back and forth, fading into the light not because it's ending... because you can't see how far it goes. Heaven. *Eternity*."

The priest outside the stall keeps talking amid the onslaught. Hearing the bashing, the door about to break. And Clara, hidden in the stall, sits upon the toilet and feels warmth trickling into her thigh. Feeling nauseous. Feeling pain. Pressing her fingers to the crotch of her sweatpants as Uwe continues.

"It *never* ends. Existence never ends and I found the prospect... I found it appalling. I was born, and now I'm sentenced to eternity. It will never end. I'll wake up every morning forever. It won't end. Forever..." Clara, staring at the blood on her fingers, listens as the lavatory door is battered as if by a log. Staring at the red gushing out of her and running a hand over her baby bump. Uwe clenches up and tells her: "I was haunted by eternal existence."

Speaking loudly over the screams. Over the gunfire.

Bashing on the lavatory door.

They're coming.

"It's funny for a child..." Uwe produces a smile, staring at the door that's breaking down. His voice trying its best, telling his daughter: "I didn't fear death, Clara... I feared Heaven, but I never feared death." Closing his eyes, hoping his daughter can hear him. "I don't fear eternity anymore... I'm open to possibilities."

Clara hears the bathroom door smash. She cowers on the toilet, hiding her legs, refusing breaths. A snarl, she hears. She can't hear Uwe but she can see his shoes under the stall door. He backs up a step, just one. He won't make a sound. She listens for her father but only hears the thing with hooves that ambles slowly.

Its breathing is loud. She sees glimpses of a hulk through the cracks of the stall. Sees it approach Uwe, who doesn't retreat. His shoes stay planted even when the hooves stop right in front of him. Clara hears her misery faintly dripping onto the tile floor. She has to bury her eyes in her arm.

Uwe tells it or tells his daughter or tells himself, almost unheard but nonetheless unfaltering. Don't fear eternity.

The sounds of a thrashing and Clara crumples upon the toilet, lowering her legs, unable to hide anymore from what's coming. Listening to evil unfold. When the beating ends she sees Uwe land on his back on the floor just outside the stall. Eyes bloody, gaping at the ceiling before they roll upward. Before they look to her. She can barely see him through the shimmering hell in her vision.

Here the pig abruptly howls. Stepping frenetic, stumbling. It sounds like it crashes into the sinks. Clara hears the door. Hears it's leaving the lavatory in a hurry. When it's gone, she exits.

She's kneeling down beside her father.

Huh... Hide, honey.

There's no hiding. Stay with me, Uwe. Taking his hand to hold. Are you okay, man? ...Please. Speak to me....Are you okay?

Trying to smirk, crying, Uwe tells her: I'm fine.

Clara listens to a stampede. Rushes of air as things take flight. Shattering glass as windows break. Gunfire lessen. Screams turned to wonder. Uwe, gasping for air, beholds Clara leaning over him. She straightens the silver pentagram over his panting chest and he sees her looking at him. He sees her smiling her best at last.

Through windows looking out onto the taxiway and curtain, the survivors watch beasts flap rotten wings, cutting through lightning skies, fleeing as if frightened. People watch them disappear into storm clouds. Someone stands on a mutilated Hilroy notebook. And Clara, huddled before the priest, wails and slips from his slackening grasp. She lies on the floor beside him, hugging the throbbing bump in her belly and she suddenly feels a kick.

The baby, still alive. It kicks for the first time. It's gentle. It feels as if it's growing awfully warm inside her and, beyond that, she's sure she hears the fanfare of trumpets, as if someone special was arriving to the ball.

FIFTY-FOUR.

Lora Malik shakes the radio but there's no sound because there's no power. It was off most of the night and all morning and there's still nothing and they don't know if it's gone for good this time. Reagan Brodie, seated in a lawn-chair near the front display of wheelbarrows, watches the old widow. Then looks to the young widow. Alicia Pederson, who's been stacking gallon-cans of primer into a house or castle on the floor. Wired beyond belief, flinching every time the walls creak. Reagan, in contrast, is dead-eyed as if this is an unending acid-trip and none of it matters. Assured that none of it matters.

Lora's tapping the hearing-aid in her ear.

"I think the battery in this piece a'shite finally croaked."

"So there *were* batteries innem?" Reagan smirks at her landlady. "You're sure there?"

"Say again, dear?"

"Nothin, Lora. Bitta jest."

Lora smiles and nods and Reagan figures the poor buzzard heard her. She rests back into the lawn-chair. Alicia continues to build her paint-can palace.

Cillian Durst, coming up from the back of the shop, is pulling on a jacket while holding a carving-axe he's kept dear. There's a utility-knife sticking out of his pant-pocket. In a handcrafted sling made of coveralls he stores a wrecking-bar. The handyman asks Lora what kind of batteries are they. Says he'll see if they got any next-door.

"Wassat?"

"Them *batteries*, I said. Give us a look."

The old bird jimmies open her hearing-aid with a brittle yellow nail. Cillian takes the batteries and stuffs them in a coat pocket.

Reagan rubs her arms and asks him how's the woodstove coming.

"Quick as ever."

"How much longer?" Alicia's asking, shivering half-deliberately to demonstrate her opinion. Demanding: "By *tonight*, y'think?"

"Should be. Had to finish that crib for the dote."

"Y'been *busy*, Durst."

"Just a yoke for me. Gotta keep busy." Cillian shrugs. "I'm goin stir-crazy back there, need to get out a minute or the next nail I drive'll be into me head."

And Abagail, who's approaching quietly from the backroom, apparently agrees. She's telling the shopkeeper wait up and she's yawning and appearing in the aisle of snow-shovels. Says she's gonna tag along. There's nothing she needs and she doubts she'll even grab anything over at Lloyd's, but she's got to get out.

Alicia, bug-eyed on the filthy floor, asks what about Brent.

"Sleepin." Abigail observes her sister. Her ratty hair and ragged shirt collar and chewed fingernails. Ally's setting another paint-can on her rickety castle but her jittery hand knocks the whole thing down. Abby waits for some response and then tightens her lip at the silence. Instead she looks to Reagan. "…Don't suppose you'd mind watchin him a minute?"

So Reagan tiredly nods and she hoists herself out of the lawn-chair. Alicia watches, then snaps her head left at the sound of the wind. And Abigail is claiming one of the wrecking-bars from a shelf near her and telling the handyman to lead the way.

Unlocking and opening the front door, they face the hell out there. And although it's familiar it's immediately striking them as a miserable stab to memories they'll never revisit . They step out and observe. They grieve, but it's all old news. It's exactly as they expected and Abigail clenches her teeth before speaking.

"Mother a'jaysis… It really is Hell froze over."

Cillian shakes his head. Tells the young widow don't run until you hafta. Abby nods, blinking away any unsung reply.

The handyman leads and she follows and they listen to the soft crunching of their boots in the wet gritty snow. Lora has gotten up and she waits by the door and watches them and clasps her mouth shut with an aching tingling hand. The stagnant air is brutal but when the wind blows there's some hint of summer in it. Benevolent warmth dirtied by cinders that brush against their cheeks and foreheads. There's another gust of tender wind brushing back Abby's clumped bangs.

Cillian whispers. Keep movin.

They've made it about twelve feet from the shop. They take their time – as much of it as fear will allot. They creep like cats to remain unheard. Fifteen feet and it seems like the coast is clear. All might be good.

"My sister… She's a header, aye?"

"She's tight puckered, oh aye. Figure it stands to reason." The handyman answers. "Hard for anyone to remain calm in somethin like this, especially after watching your man… burn." He looks around. Watches the shadows on the grey snow. "Still, I keep my distance from her."

"…Alicia say somethin to ye, Cillian? About *me*?"

"Actually, no… Said about that *Reagan*. Not to say I was pryin – was askin about her husband before he… Well… *Anyhow*, she told me bout how that boy didn't think much a'Reagan."

"My fiancée didn't trust Reagan either. He was *sure* she knows something she ain't tellin us." Abby shrugs. "But then, Mike was always sorta paranoid. He'd suspect a Jew of stealing his hotdog."

"What do *ye* think?"

"I think… I'd be dead if it wasn't for Reagan Brodie."

The young widow looks ahead, marching, smelling the fires in the distance all around her. She breathes out a cold cloud and then suddenly there's this sound and she stops. It's coming from above. She whispers to ask: Oye… *Hear that?*

It's approaching by air and it's coming up on them fast. Lora is close enough – she can dash back inside the shop – except she can't hear what's coming. She doesn't have a clue and that's why she's still standing there. Abby and Durst are too far. Too far from home and too far from Lloyds Pharmacy. They're out in the open and there's nowhere to hide. So they freeze and they tilt their heads to watch for the daemons, ready for them either way.

The thing just *zooms*. It appears over the roofs of buildings in front of them and sails over their heads and it's gone. A beige airplane, but it looked too thin to house a pilot. Looked notably modern, so Durst supposes it was one of those drones he's heard about. Remote piloted, so I guess that spares a precious life the risk. Agreeing, Abigail just lowers her head, and she gazes around at the deserted street of ice. At cars and debris and bodies hidden under frost and soot. Her throat clenches but only for a moment.

"…I… just thought of something."

"Important?"

"…Nay. Nay, just… Today…"

"What?"

Abigail blinks. Wonders. Stares at what was once the town of Ferris and which now is an apocalyptic headstone among the smokelands. And as they continue quietly toward the pharmacy she tells the shopkeeper today would've been Mike's birthday. In two weeks it'll be Christmas.

The first rock falls from heaven and it dents the hood of an abandoned Hyundai. All the rest soon follow and the riot swells into a thunderous rhythm. The experience is a hideous wonder.

Some are pebbles but some are as big as cherries and they rain down on Ferris like a hailstorm. Alicia and Cillian flee for their lives – headed for the pharmacy. The handyman takes one to his shoulder and it's small as a pellet but, fallen from the clouds, it rips into him and causes him to yowl and stagger. Abigail catches him and tries to hold him up but he's so heavy. They're almost at the door. They can make it, she's sure. They can make it. She tells herself as much before another black little rock catches her ankle and cripples her. She falls and so does Cillian and they both land beneath the aluminum awning over the Lloyds entrance. They pant and bleed and listen to the igneous rock raining down from the smokeclouds.

The storm drowns out the *whir* of the unmanned plane getting away from them.

"I had a boy just like ye..." Whispering, Reagan doesn't want to wake the child. "He got to be a bit older, but I remember him at about your age... I was complete then. I... found myself. S'not a feeling I can... just... allow... Not when I have options."

They're alone back here in the handyman's old office. Reagan leans against the crib that Cillian built for the toddler. Little Brent. Lit by the camper's lantern, Reagan found the boy asleep and serene here, even when the roof is suddenly barraged by heavy solid hail or meteors. Reagan is startled at first and nervous for a while, but before long it barely even registers. It keeps on but she doesn't care. She feels strong, almost. She hasn't been strong in years.

Throughout it all, the boy stirs but doesn't wake.

"...I'm sorry about your daddy and... everyone." Stabbing in her throat. Cinching her vocal chords. "It's taken me too long to say it, but..." The words almost lost amid the raining rocks above their heads. "I know what I've done. I *know* what I deserve. I'm so, so..." Tears that coat her cheekbones shimmer. Her mouth is tightly shamed and her eyes only see the fires that are trapped in them. The boy finally wakes from the noise. "I can nay give back to ye or anyone else all that's lost. And I'm *sorry*, but I..." Heaving in a lungful and breaking in her mind. Piercing in her eyes. Dropping her gaze onto the fretful toddler who looks up at her, confessing: "I'm not giving up yet... I'm gonna have my son again. Whatever it takes." Brushing his fine fair hair, gentle and soothing, the mother tells him: "...You'll see."

φ φ φ

Above burnt frozen fields of grass and waste and bodies and clovers. The drone sails over the Restricted Zone, passing over Ferris as an eye mounted to its undercarriage snaps two-hundred frames a minute. It chronicles the smokelands en route to its programmed destination, journeying deeper into black that veils the island. There's a digital screen in its guidance system in the bow of the plane and it reads thirty kilometers from target coordinates.

Twenty-nine.

Twenty-eight.

The closer it gets to Darrows Glen, thicker lies the smoke. Brighter burn the fires that decimate. Wreckage rules and less and less do the structures of human design stand. They're all heaps of white and grey flakes slowly blown down by heatwaves coming from the north. Pummelling showers bash it and nearly bring it down.

Twenty-five.

Almost. They tell themselves, watching. Almost.

Men and women hang agog on every frame being broadcasted by the Unmanned Aerial Vehicle. Sitting at the controls and standing and spectating in a US command-center established outside Höfn, Iceland. Watching curious and disturbed as an RQ-4 "Hawk" travels at supersonic speeds and shows them the landscape of the lost world that's pelted by stones from heaven. In seven minutes, it will reach Darrows and the origin point of the outworlders. It will find the door there, of which theories have been traded worldwide.

There's damage to the right wing and alerts blare. Something's ruptured its fuselage. They watch the monitors and the big board and deal with hell as it comes. Searching the footage where winter is no longer present. There's no snow or ice. Volcanic ash and pebbles drop from abhorrent skies. Burnt forests smoulder. Dead fields and hills and rivers of molten rock. Twenty-three kilometers. The UAV is in a dark fog and the ground is no longer in sight of its electric eye. So people squint, searching the footage for some sign of the doorway.

They need to know.

The feed falters a moment. As it flickers, they see the Hawk is knocked off its course. Its right wing broken and dangling by wires and the drone is veering downwards and sinking through the smoke. Rocks continue to pelt and reshape it and the plane shakes the barren heath when it crashes twenty-two kilometers short if its target. Sparks and fire and smoke billowing. It all amassing in an atmosphere that sees no sun. People watch. It's all black save for untamed orange. They listen and they hear drums played in the igneous rain. Guitars and fiddles and oboes, jaunty and rhythmic, even catchy. They gape at the glow wherein outworlders dance on air, rejoicing conquest, cheering and hooting their celebration only just warming up.

No one knows what to say after the feed cuts out and it's all gone. They stand still, mute, contemplative and baffled, shrinking back from the monitors and what they've observed. Still with the tune in their heads. Shunning each other for shameful unknowing, all are left alone and astounded by the reaches of horror for themselves and the world and they hear their phones are all alive playing unharmonious rings and ringtones and it's ugly and getting louder but no one picks up a phone. So the riot doesn't stop and it won't because that's not what happens here. People call but no one answers. That's what happens here.

MARK SANT

Mark Sant lives in Vaughan, Ontario.
Family and friends are his world. He writes for them.
All other fans are a bonus.